"CIVILIAN SHIP, THE *VERITY*, REPORTED LOST ON STARDATE 43021.5. A SATURDAY."

"We're sure it's a displacement? Not a time dilation event?"

"Long-range scans show a temporal anomaly near its coordinates."

"Active?"

"Nearly closed. Starship on the scene scanned it—looks like a cosmic-string Kerr loop, probably triggered by the fighting near Regulus."

"Twenty-two days after the battle?"

"Twenty-two light-days out. Didn't open until the radiation surge hit it."

A chill ran through Dulmur. "If the disruption originated in the present, it could've caused an alteration downtime."

Lucsly shook his head, holding up his temporal tricorder. "I checked the shielded records," he said. Those records were protected from quantum alteration by multiply-redundant phase discriminators, a technology adopted nearly thirteen years ago. In the event of an alteration, records of the original history would be preserved in the DTI database. "No identifiable divergences. The *Verity*'s displacement is a self-consistent event."

Dulmur sighed in relief. "So all we have to worry about is thirty-eight people who have to adjust to being fifteen years out of date."

"And two months and four days," Lucsly inevitably added.

Dulmur let out a low whistle. "Twenty-three sixty-six. One of the most peaceful years in recent history. After the Cardassian treaty, before Wolf 359, before the Dominion. To come out now, in the middle of the wor~~st~~ ~~~~~~ Federation's ever known

Lucsly nodded. "T~~D~~

"You said it." He si

one."

STAR TREK®

DEPARTMENT OF
TEMPORAL INVESTIGATIONS

WATCHING
THE
CLOCK

CHRISTOPHER L. BENNETT

Based on *Star Trek* and *Star Trek: The Next Generation*®
created by Gene Roddenberry
and
Star Trek: Deep Space Nine®
created by Rick Berman & Michael Piller
and
Star Trek: Voyager®
created by Rick Berman & Michael Piller & Jeri Taylor
and
Star Trek: Enterprise®
created by Rick Berman & Brannon Braga

POCKET BOOKS
New York   London   Toronto   Sydney

Pocket Books
A Division of Simon & Schuster, Inc.
1230 Avenue of the Americas
New York, NY 10020

This book is a work of fiction. Names, characters, places, and incidents either are products of the author's imagination or are used fictitiously. Any resemblance to actual events or locales or persons, living or dead, is entirely coincidental.

First Pocket Books paperback edition May 2011

POCKET and colophon are registered trademarks of Simon & Schuster, Inc.

For information about special discounts for bulk purchases, please contact Simon & Schuster Special Sales at 1-866-506-1949 or business@simonandschuster.com.

The Simon & Schuster Speakers Bureau can bring authors to your live event. For more information or to book an event, contact the Simon & Schuster Speakers Bureau at 1-866-248-3049 or visit our website at www.simonspeakers.com.

Designed by Esther Paradelo
Cover design by Alan Dingman; cover art by Cliff Nielsen

Manufactured in the United States of America

10 9 8 7 6 5 4 3 2 1

ISBN 978-1-4516-0625-6
ISBN 978-1-4516-0629-4 (ebook)

To my father
(1933–2010 CE)

*"Time is a companion who goes with us
on the journey and reminds us to cherish
every moment, because they'll never come again."*

People like us, who believe in physics, know that the distinction between past, present, and future is only a stubbornly persistent illusion.
—Albert Einstein (1955 CE)

People assume that time is a strict progression of cause to effect, but actually, from a non-linear, non-subjective viewpoint, it's more like a big ball of wibbly-wobbly . . . timey-wimey . . . stuff.
—Steven Moffat (2007 CE)

PRESENT TIME
STARDATE 58188.4 TO 58193.8

I

March 10, 2381 Common Era, Gregorian Calendar
A Tuesday

Department of Temporal Investigations Branch Office
San Francisco, North Am, Earth
18:32 UTC

"Stay back, all of you!" cried Special Agent George Faunt. "Or her time is up!"

Great, thought Marion Dulmur. *Just great.* A veteran DTI agent had suffered a breakdown after a particularly stressful mission, taken a researcher hostage at phaser-point, and turned the San Francisco office into a siege zone . . . yet he couldn't resist making a lame time-related pun. *I hate those.*

Outwardly, Dulmur kept his cool. Poor Rani Mohindra's life hung by a thread right now. George Faunt was a good agent, a man Dulmur had worked alongside for years. But he wasn't the first to be overwhelmed by the existential crises this job forced a person to confront day in and day out. "Just take it easy, George," Dulmur said as gently as his gravelly voice would allow. "Just relax, take a deep breath, and think about this for a minute." He winced, but it was too late to call it back.

"A minute?" Faunt barked a hysterical laugh, and Mohindra jerked and whimpered in his grip. "How many minutes of my life have I given to this job? Six million, five hundred and thirty—no, twenty-seven thousand, seven hundred and, what?"

Thirty-two, Dulmur filled in despite himself, and Faunt caught him doing the calculation. "You know, don't you? Down to the millisecond! This job, this job—they train you to pretend time is this rigid, exacting thing, to break it all down into precise durations and dates . . . but it's just a distraction, Dulmur! The truth is that time is chaos, it's meaningless. All we are is random quantum fluctuations that can collapse into the cosmic foam just like *that!*" He punctuated it by jamming the phaser harder into Mohindra's cheek. She closed her eyes and her lips moved in prayer.

Faunt's careless cruelty made Dulmur angry, but he couldn't hate the man for it, not after what he'd been through. It had only been three weeks and a day since the final blitzkrieg of the Borg invasion. Dozens of worlds had been razed before the collective effort of several Starfleet crews had persuaded the powerful Caeliar race to take responsibility for their role in the Borg's creation and eliminate them as a threat once and for all. The truth that those crews had uncovered about the Borg's origins had been the DTI's worst nightmare brought to life, a time travel accident that had led to devastation across half the galaxy.

And yet the Department had more immediate concerns than that ancient anachronism. In the wake of a disaster like this, there were always going to be those who tried to go back in time and undo it, whether through cosmic anomalies, ancient relics, or untested warp modifications—which were more likely to destroy the aspiring travelers than anything else, but still posed unpredictable

risks to the continuum. Even some in the UFP government had wished to suspend the Temporal Prime Directive, delve into the DTI's top-secret vault on Eris, and
use some confiscated alien artifact to go back and "fix"
things. Director Andos had her work cut out for her trying to convince them that they might do more harm than
good—a difficult position for her to take considering
that her homeworld of Rhaandarel had been one of the
casualties.

   And then there were the visitors from the future who
tended to congregate around major historical events. The
historians could generally be relied on to minimize their
intervention (though there were some infamous blunders
such as the Rasmussen affair), but you never knew when
someone might come back with a more sinister agenda.
The number of identifiable anachronistic incidents during the Borg invasion had actually been much lower than
expected, and the DTI's top analysts were still assessing
why. But Faunt and his partner Ranjea, one of the Department's most reliable teams until now, had been assigned
to the most serious incident so far, a temporal rift which
had opened up on the ruined surface of Coridan. Faunt
and Ranjea had concluded that a timeship from the thirty-
sixth century, probably a historical observation craft, had
gotten too close during the Borg attack and been crippled.
Prochronistic travelers often underestimated past technology to their peril. For whatever reason, no one had come
back to retrieve the crashed vessel or prevent the temporal
core implosion which had opened a subspace fissure reaching centuries into Coridan's past.

   On the mission, so Ranjea had dutifully if reluctantly reported, Faunt had been almost overcome by

the temptation to send a warning through the rift. He couldn't save anyone directly, but he suggested leaving a message that would reveal itself shortly before the invasion. Ranjea had insisted that tampering in Coridan's past could disrupt key events leading to the creation of the Federation, but Faunt had argued that it was worth the risk. The debate had been rendered moot when observations through the rift had revealed a massive orbital space station whose transmissions identified it as an outpost of the Vulcan-Andorian Empire. The fissure wasn't just intertemporal but interphasic, opening onto an alternate quantum history of the universe. A message sent into the past of a spontaneously divergent timeline would have no impact on the events of this one.

Faunt had been devastated to have his hopes dashed so completely. He had been ordered to take a recuperative leave, but then this breakdown had happened. Maybe if Ranjea were here, he could get through to Faunt and talk him down. But the Deltan agent was still in Greenwich, helping Director Andos finalize tomorrow's monthly report to President Bacco. Dulmur would simply have to make do. "Listen, George, we all know how you feel. This has been hell on everyone. Including that young lady you've got there. It's been hard on her too. Do you really think making things even harder for her is going to accomplish anything?"

Faunt scoffed. "Accomplish? Nothing we do 'accomplishes' anything! We pretend we're protecting the timeline, keeping reality safe, but the truth is we can't do anything. Space and time are just too big. At any moment, everything we know could be wiped from existence by Temporal Cold Warriors from the future, or by Starfleet idiots stumbling through yet another space warp or ancient portal, or by a Q playing a practical joke! And all we can do about it is file reports after the fact and pretend it makes a difference! We're deluding ourselves if we think this job actually means anything!"

"It means we try, George," said Dulmur. "It means we do what we can, the best we can. Just like you've been doing for a dozen years." He was careful to dial down his long-practiced precision just this once. "You're a good man, George. You don't want to do anything you'll regret."

"You just don't get it," Faunt moaned, shaking his prematurely grizzled head. "Kill her, don't kill her, none of it makes a difference to the multiverse. If I blow her brains out now, there'll be another me who doesn't. I could kill everyone in this room and you'd all be fine in a million other timelines! So why not pull the trigger?! Why not do whatever the hell I feel like?!" he snarled.

"Bull!"

Every head in the room spun toward the source of the contemptuous exclamation. There stood Special Agent Gariff Lucsly, Dulmur's partner for the past fifteen years, eight months, and fifteen days, on and off. The way the lanky, gray-haired agent strode forward into the line of fire made Dulmur fearful that he might not make it to their sixteenth anniversary.

"You know better than that," Lucsly went on, lecturing Faunt as if he were a trainee who'd fumbled an exam question. "Neurons are classical objects. Any alternate quantum solutions to the universal wave equation won't affect the decision-making process in your brain. If you have a reason to kill in this quantum history, you'll have the same reason in any other history that branches off from this moment."

The others in the office were staring at Lucsly in shock as he confronted the gunman. Was he crazy? Was he so hidebound, so obsessed with accuracy, that he'd risk his life, and possibly others', just to correct a misunderstanding of temporal theory?

Hell, yes, Dulmur thought. But there was more to it than that. Gariff Lucsly knew how to use his obsessions to his advantage, and he knew he could trust his partner. "That's basic Many-Worlds theory," Lucsly went on, striding closer to Faunt, drawing his gaze away from Dulmur. "It doesn't mean every imaginable reality happens, only those that have a reason to happen. You know that, Special Agent Faunt." By now, Faunt's phaser hand was wavering, swinging between Mohindra and Lucsly. But Lucsly didn't flinch. He was on a roll. "So stop abusing temporal physics as an excuse to dodge responsibility for your own choices!"

Dulmur, having eased behind Faunt while Lucsly lectured, now moved in, forced his arm skyward, and wrested the phaser from his grip in one smooth motion. Faunt didn't even resist as Dulmur tossed the phaser aside and pulled the other agent's arms behind him; he just broke down crying. Mohindra, also crying, ran into Lucsly's arms. Lucsly stiffened, more uneasy with this than he'd been with a phaser pointed in his face, and showed relief when the security personnel moved in to take charge of her. Dulmur was just as glad to hand Faunt over to them, but for different reasons. It was always tough when one of their own broke down. *That could be me someday,* he always thought.

But then he looked at Lucsly, and it heartened him. His brief brush with human contact now behind him, Lucsly was solid as a rock again, a constant in a chaotic reality. Lucsly was the one human being that Dulmur was certain would never be overwhelmed by the existential angst of facing a mutable reality. He simply didn't have the imagination for it. He had his job, his purpose, and he pursued it with unfailing clockwork precision. He was an anchor that Dulmur was grateful to have.

"Thanks, partner," Dulmur said, giving him a quick, professional smile. "Good job." Lucsly just offered a small nod in reply. It was all they needed.

"Got a new assignment," Lucsly told him as if it were just another day at the office. "Unplanned displacement, arrival detected three hours, twenty-seven minutes ago. In the dead zone, Regulus sector."

"Uptime or down?"

"Up. Civilian ship, the *Verity*, reported lost on Stardate 43021.5. A Saturday."

"We're sure it's a displacement? Not a time dilation event?"

"Long-range scans show a temporal anomaly near its coordinates."

"Active?"

"Nearly closed. Starship on the scene scanned it— looks like a cosmic-string Kerr loop, probably triggered by the fighting near Regulus."

"Twenty-two days after the battle?"

"Twenty-two light-days out. Didn't open until the radiation surge hit it."

A chill ran through Dulmur. "If the disruption

originated in the present, it could've caused an alteration downtime."

Lucsly shook his head, holding up his temporal tricorder. "I checked the shielded records," he said. Those records were protected from quantum alteration by multiply-redundant phase discriminators, a technology adopted nearly thirteen years ago. In the event of an alteration, records of the original history would be preserved in the DTI database. "No identifiable divergences. The *Verity*'s displacement is a self-consistent event."

Dulmur sighed in relief. "So all we have to worry about is thirty-eight people who have to adjust to being fifteen years out of date.'"

"And two months and four days," Lucsly inevitably added.

Dulmur let out a low whistle. "Twenty-three sixty-six. One of the most peaceful years in recent history. Before Wolf 359, before the Dominion, right around the Cardassian truce talks. To come out now, in the middle of the worst devastation the Federation's ever known . . ."

Lucsly nodded. "TDD'll have its work cut out."

"You said it." He sighed. "This is going to be a rough one."

U.S.S. Everett NCC-72392
March 12, 2381 CE (A Thursday)
03:14 UTC

It took thirty hours, eleven minutes for *Everett*, the *Nova*-class Starfleet scout attached to the DTI, to reach the Regulus system at high warp. The *Verity* and its occupants were being held there for now to minimize their exposure to the society of their future, a standard policy to mini-mize culture shock. Dulmur had suggested that policy was redundant here, but as Lucsly had reminded him, rules were rules.

Now, the *Verity*'s captain, a Bolian named Falvin Dor, sat in briefing room one, across the table from Lucsly. "When did you first detect the anomaly?" the agent asked.

Dor gave an unamused laugh. "Detect? Thing opened up practically in front of us. Before we could veer away, we were caught in its gravity well. Damn near tore my ship apart." The hairless, blue-skinned captain wore a jumpsuit bearing the Regulan flag, a stylized representation of the unique shape of the system's star, a flattened blue oval brighter at the poles than the equator.

"Mm-hmm. And what was the exact time of the event?"

Dor glared. "Why does it matter?"

"Just getting the facts, sir."

"I don't know, four-three-oh-two-oh point, some-thing. Check the logs if you have to. I had more important things to worry about."

Lucsly made a mental note of the captain's defensive-ness. "So your attention was on the anomaly."

"My attention was on keeping my ship together. I didn't know what had grabbed us, I just knew I needed to get out of it. We're not built for that kind of stress."

Lucsly nodded. One of the universe's best defenses against accidental temporal alteration was that most natural time warps involved intense gravity fields and energies. In most cases, only a ship with an active warp drive, its engines already generating the necessary exotic particles to avert a stress-energy tensor runaway, could survive passage at all, and even then, the added gravitic stresses and energy surges could overwhelm all but the most robust of starships— which was why most such displacement events happened to Starfleet and other military vessels. The *Verity*'s crew and passengers were lucky to be alive. They survived only because the Kerr loop had been so atypically large that the tidal stresses at its center had been reduced.

"So what happened next?"

03:21 UTC

"Once things settled down, we sized up the damage," said the *Verity*'s pilot. M'grash was a young Caitian female with a dark gray mane and gray-and-white striped fur. "Klega said he could get us to port under our own power, but not on schedule."

"Klega is the chief engineer?" Dulmur asked.

"Yes." She hesitated. "So the captain had me call ahead to Regulus Control, tell them we'd be late. And—and there was nothing. No answer. I tried other frequencies, but . . . nothing. In the whole system." Her claws dug into the table of briefing room two, but her voice remained flat, almost numb. A native of the Caitian colony on the largest moon of Regulus VI, M'grash was taking the loss of her home system quite hard, but sheer fatigue had set in by now.

"So I scanned ahead for Reg III, and it . . . it wasn't there. None of the planets were where they were supposed to be. I widened the scan, and we found them, but they were in the wrong places in their orbits."

"And that's when you figured out you'd traveled through time?" The pilot nodded. Dulmur reflected that such an anomaly would stand out in this system more than

most. Regulus A had grown giant and bloated by swallow-
ing the cast-off atmosphere of its dying companion, now a
white dwarf. The ancient cataclysm had destroyed the system's innermost planets, but several outer worlds had been
warmed and rendered habitable. Those worlds had long
orbital periods, ranging from 21.65 years for Regulus III
to 46.8 for Reg VI, so a displacement of fifteen years and
change would have put them well out of position.

Dulmur went on gently. "So . . . you found the planets, and you saw . . ."

A low rumble sounded in her throat. "Death. Ruin.
Nothing left."

"I'm very sorry for your loss, ma'am."

"Thank you."

"What did Captain Dor do then?"

"He told me to check the FNS bands." A natural
enough reaction for any UFP citizen, to tune in the Federation News Service for more information. "But they were
dead too. I scanned the whole subspace spectrum, but
there was nothing. Nothing close enough to make out."
She was quiet for several moments. "That's when we knew
it wasn't just Regulus. The whole sector, more. For all we
knew, the whole Federation was gone. We thought . . .
maybe we'd come forward hundreds of years. Thousands."

"What did you do next?"

"The captain . . . we had a passenger who was a
physicist. He remembered that."

Dulmur checked his padd. "Doctor . . . Wataru
Takizawa?"

"Yes. The captain called him to the bridge. He helped
us figure out what had happened."

"The navigation logs show that you made a series of

short warp hops until you settled on a distance of just over three light-weeks from Regulus, a few AUs past the anomaly. Was that Takizawa's idea?"

M'grash closed her large gray eyes. "Yes. He scanned the planets . . . figured out whatever happened was less than a month ago. Had us look using lightspeed sensors, find the spot where we could meet the light and see what happened. Like it was happening in front of us, right then."

From an Einsteinian perspective, it was, Dulmur thought. Lucsly might have said it aloud. But it was the last thing the distraught pilot wanted to hear right now.

She shook her head. "What we saw . . . what we learned after the rescue ship answered our distress call . . . we'd never even heard of these Borg." Dulmur nodded. Jean-Luc Picard's first contact with the Borg had taken place some five months, two weeks before the *Verity* was lost, and they had been a folk legend in the coreward Beta Quadrant for at least fifteen years before that; but it was a vast galaxy and not every contact or legend became common knowledge. "Borg" hadn't become a household name until Wolf 359. "And now we come out and find they'd destroyed everything as far as we could see. We couldn't believe it. Couldn't understand how this could come out of nowhere."

"Why was it so important to find the exact moment and cause of the destruction?" Dulmur asked.

05:47 UTC

"Wouldn't you want to know? To get any answers you could?" Doctor Wataru Takizawa shook his head. He was a big, burly man, far from the stereotype of a physicist.

"There was no FNS, no other surviving planets or ships in comm range, no one we could ask for answers. I realized there was a way we could find out ourselves. We get so used to subspace radio and sensors that we forget there's a simple way to look back in time, just by using light."

"Interesting choice of words," Lucsly said. "Did the possibility of going back in time enter your mind?"

"I didn't think we could," Takizawa said with a shrug.

"You'd just come through a temporal displacement vortex."

"I didn't know that. I thought it was just an intense gravity well. I assumed we'd been subjected to extreme time dilation."

"You're an astrophysicist, Doctor," Lucsly said. "You mean to tell me you don't know what a Kerr loop is?"

"Of course I know about Kerr singularities in theory. But they're not my specialty. I have a passing familiarity with the equations, but that doesn't mean I could recognize the actual sensor readings."

Lucsly studied the doctor. "So you had no thought of returning through the vortex, taking back the data you'd gathered, and warning people of the disaster."

Takizawa considered. "No thought? I wouldn't say that. I've read H. G. Wells and sh'Lesinas, run the same time-fic holos as anyone. It's a natural enough thing to fantasize about at a time like this. But I never thought we actually had a chance of doing it. I know there have been cases of time travel—why else would there be a department to investigate it? But it can't be very common, can it?"

Lucsly didn't answer. One of the unacknowledged parts of the DTI's job was to keep knowledge of temporal incidents from being any more widely disseminated than it had to be. The more rare and unlikely the public believed temporal displacement to be, the less chance there was of idiots trying to slingshot around their local suns to undo a bad relationship or win the Lissepian Lottery. Of course, normally they would just get their vaporized atoms scattered across decades, but you could never be too careful.

"So why did the ship subsequently head back toward the anomaly before its engines failed?"

"We didn't. Captain Dor headed us back to Regulus to search for survivors." Takizawa gave a sharp laugh. "Look, the ship barely made it through the anomaly the first time. Even if we had known there was a way back, we couldn't have risked it in the shape we were in. And after the warp drive failed, there would've been no point in trying anyway."

"So there was no hope of repairing the engines?"

06:11 UTC

"None," said Vorlis Klega, the *Verity*'s engineer. "They suffered irreversible damage as a result of the passage."

"Irreversible?" Dulmur echoed, examining the diminutive, gold-skinned Ithenite male.

"Well, certainly within the time we—the time before Starfleet found us. The main plasma injectors were fused. We were going nowhere."

"But not until two hours, thirty-seven minutes after the passage, during which you made several successful warp jumps."

"Against my recommendation," Klega said. "I could tell the injectors were on the edge. The captain risked it anyway, and that last jump blew them completely."

Dulmur frowned. "The plasma injectors are highly

shielded, well inside the ship. That's not the sort of damage you'd expect from gravitic turbulence or Hawking radiation."

"There were power surges. Some effect of the weird energy fields interacting with our EPS grid . . . ask Takizawa, or some other physicist. All I know is, the injector manifold needed a complete rebuild before we could go to warp again." He pursed his lips in sympathy. "The passengers got pretty banged up too, in the passage. That poor girl, Teresa . . . something . . . might've died if you'd taken longer to find us."

"Teresa Garcia. Any idea why she took such severe injuries in the passage?"

"She was wandering where she wasn't supposed to be," Klega said. "Down in my engine section, there are exposed structural members, hot conduits . . . someone who doesn't belong there can get themselves in trouble."

"Forgive me, Mister Klega," Dulmur said, "but you sound almost satisfied that Ms. Garcia was injured."

"Do I? I apologize," he said with little sign of sincerity. "I get . . . very protective of my engines. Of course I'm glad she's recovering." His golden face grimaced. "Although with all the death we've come out in the middle of, what difference would one more really have made?"

08:27 UTC

"Yeah, that's what happened," Teresa Garcia said. She was a young woman with shoulder-length black hair and large, dark eyes, one of which was still partly swollen from her injuries, though the swelling was diminishing under the ministrations of the *Everett*'s head nurse. Those eyes remained downcast, rarely focusing on Lucsly or Dulmur.

The two agents exchanged a look, then turned back to face the young graduate student in her sickbay bed. "Would you like to elaborate?" Dulmur asked. "What were you doing in the engine section?"

Garcia was slow to answer. It was a challenge getting her to open up. "I was . . . curious. I've always been that way. Wanting to see what's under every rock. It's why I went into archaeology."

"Warp engines are an odd subject of interest for an archaeologist," Lucsly observed.

"On Earth or Vulcan, maybe," she said, showing some animation for the first time. "But there have been warp-capable civilizations in the galaxy for over half a billion years. I . . ." Suddenly she became subdued again. "I wanted to learn more about modern warp systems for comparison."

"Was that going to be your field of study at the Regulus III Science Academy?" Dulmur asked.

Garcia winced. "'Was.' I guess . . . I guess they wrote me off for dead fifteen years ago anyway. Now . . . it's the other way around. Shows what they knew, huh?" She swallowed. "No, no, I hadn't really settled on a specialization yet. I was just . . . curious." Those great dark eyes darted around some more. "Look, can we do this later? I could really use my rest."

"Of course," Dulmur said. Lucsly looked disapproving, as usual, since he hated to waste time. But Dulmur knew that if they wanted any more information from Garcia, they'd have to wait until she was ready to tell them.

Dulmur led his partner into the office of *Everett*'s chief

medical officer, T'Manis. "Well, Doctor?" he asked her. "Do her injuries fit the story we're being told?"

"As I told you, it is difficult to be conclusive," the middle-aged Vulcan woman said. "Her injuries were rather hastily treated with a protoplaser and dermal regenerator, obscuring much of the evidence. Yet what evidence remains is difficult to reconcile with the witnesses' accounts. The pattern of coup and contrecoup injuries is more consistent with a stationary body being struck by blunt instruments than by a moving body colliding with hard surfaces, though if there were failures in the artificial gravity system, the distinction could be blurred. And certain of the subdermal contusions and skeletal fractures are more consistent with being struck by fists than with the kind of mishap described. But the regeneration work performed aboard the *Verity* makes it difficult to be certain."

"Perhaps intentionally?" Lucsly asked. "To hide evidence that she was beaten?"

"That determination is beyond my purview," the doctor said.

"We need her to tell us what really happened," Lucsly said, heading back toward the ward.

"When the time is right," Dulmur said, his tone bringing his partner to a halt. "Let her be for now. We have other places to look."

Regulus Passenger Lines Transport *Verity*
10:36 UTC
"It's all pretty banged up," reported *Everett*'s chief engineer, Ian Purvis, as he surveyed the cluttered engine section of the *Verity*. "Though in this kludge, it's hard to tell." Klega's assessment had been accurate, Dulmur

thought; it was a mess of exposed conduits, coolant pipes, and drive components, many with jury-rigged connections. Quite a few of those connections had been blown apart, and many components were covered in carbon scoring. The lingering stench made Lucsly's nose crinkle up.

"The passage did a right number on this thing, that's for sure," Purvis went on, running a hand through his wavy black hair. "Considering the damage, it's a wonder the warp drive held out as long as it did."

"So the plasma injectors could've been fused as a result of the passage?" Lucsly asked.

"Well, there are signs of EPS discharges like Klega said. They *could've* contributed to the burnout. On top of all the other abuse these systems took."

"Lucsly, Dulmur." The *Everett*'s science officer, Commander Heather Petersen, approached, holding up her tricorder—a conventional Starfleet science model, less specialized but more powerful than the agents' temporal tricorders. Petersen was a specialist in temporal and wormhole phenomena, a wunderkind who had made her name as a Starfleet Academy graduate student during the Bajoran wormhole disruption event of Stardate 48992, and she had a better relationship with the DTI than most Starfleet officers. "We've got DNA traces from Garcia and most of the crew and passengers in here. Some blood too, not all of it Garcia's. But a lot of them were injured, and some of the people who came back to help her would've been bleeding too."

"How many people does it take to deliver a medikit to one injured woman?" Dulmur mused.

Purvis frowned at them. "Hang on, Dulmur, are you saying you think that poor girl was attacked? Why?"

"Maybe for the same reason she was in the engine compartment," Lucsly said. "Was her DNA found on the plasma injectors themselves?"

Petersen shook her strawberry-blond head. "Inconclusive. Too much plasma damage."

"What, you think she sabotaged the engines?" Purvis asked. "Why?"

"That's for later," Lucsly said. "Right now, the question is whether."

"Well, some of this could be the result of sabotage, but with this system taking so many blows . . ."

"Timing is everything," said Lucsly. "What damage had to come *last?*"

Purvis turned to his diagnostic padd and ran some analyses. Meanwhile, Petersen turned to the older agent. "Lucsly, I know some things don't add up here, but sabotage? Assault? Why are you so sure there's some deep dark secret here?"

"Because things don't add up," he replied. "The events described in the witness accounts don't fill the necessary time."

Petersen smiled. "Most people don't have built-in quantum clocks like you, Lucsly."

The agent shook his head. "Even allowing for error, there just aren't enough things *happening* in their accounts."

"Here we are," Purvis put in. "The last damage would've been the EPS surges."

"Fits Klega's account," Dulmur said.

"Except, hang on," Purvis continued. "Mmm, no, the surges weren't the critical damage. If I were the doc, I'd say they were postmortem, not the proximate cause of death, as it were. No, that was here." He gestured to a point on his flow analysis. "A series of input malfunctions that, on top of the previous damage, fused the system. Could be a computer error, but the EPS surges wiped the logs so I can't be sure."

"Wiped the logs," Lucsly said.

"How convenient," Dulmur answered.

U.S.S. Everett
11:02 UTC

"We have a pretty good idea now what happened, Ms. Garcia," Dulmur said. "The crew tried to go back in time, didn't they?" Garcia didn't answer. Her dark eyes were fixed on the briefing room table, which still bore the scratches M'grash had left in it. "And you stopped them. Stopped them from doing something foolhardy, possibly suicidal, and potentially cataclysmic. So why won't you tell me about it now?"

Finally she met his eyes. "Don't you think those people have been through enough? Whatever they did . . . I can't blame them for it. Any of it," she said more quietly, looking away again.

"Maybe you're right. Maybe if anything counts as extenuating circumstances, this does. But that's not for you or me to decide, Teresa. The laws exist for a reason. You must know that, or you wouldn't have done what you did."

She took a shuddering breath. "I'm not even sure anymore why I did it. Or if I'd have done the same thing if I'd thought about it more. I just don't know."

"Then let's figure it out together," Dulmur said.

After a few more moments' silence, Garcia began to

speak. "It went like I told you before, at first. The vortex, seeing Regulus in ruins. The captain called Doctor Takizawa and a few others to the bridge after a while. I was one of them."

"Why did he ask for you?"

"Takizawa suggested it. Said he wasn't sure if we were forward or back in time, so an archaeology grad student might be helpful." She smirked. "He *said*. Fact was, he'd been coming on to me the whole trip. Hoped I'd be impressed watching him handle a crisis." She rolled her eyes. "Once we saw . . . what had happened . . . it wasn't long before the word got out to everyone. People started to ask if we could go back and change things. Takizawa took another look at the vortex and figured out there was a chance. But first we'd need to find out what happened and when so we could warn people."

"So you tracked down the edge of the light sphere so you could document the attack."

She nodded. "Then the captain . . . he gave us a vote about whether to risk another trip through. *Almost* everyone voted yes."

"Except you."

"The lone voice of dissent."

"Why did you argue against going back in time?"

Garcia shook her head. "It just didn't seem right. How did we know it would work? I mean, even aside from the danger of getting crushed in the vortex, just the idea of changing history—I mean, it's silly, isn't it? Change is something that *takes* time to happen. If something changes, that means there's a version before the change and a version after the change. How can a single moment in time come before or after itself? That's a contradiction in terms."

Dulmur was impressed. Garcia had hit on a key intuition about the nature of time that most laypeople overlooked. Of course, there were other key principles she was missing, hard evidence and quantum theory showing that a timeline could exist in multiple alternate states without paradox. But it wasn't as simple as erasing events that had already happened, despite how it might appear to amateurs. For a layperson with no training in temporal theory, Garcia showed surprising insight.

"So what did you think would happen if you survived going back?" he asked.

"Maybe we wouldn't survive. Maybe the laws of the universe wouldn't let us. I mean, yeah, there was that time-loop thing about a year . . ." She winced. "Sixteen years ago, but that was just a few seconds doubling back on themselves, like a fold in spacetime." Dulmur nodded. The Manheim Event was one temporal incident he would never forget. "It's not like one ship going back would make the whole universe fold back over and replay itself. If we did change things, we'd just create a parallel timeline, like in the adventure holos. A new history that's alongside the old. I mean, that follows, right? The only way there could be two versions of the same moment in time is if they happen at the same time. Side by side."

"Those are good arguments," Dulmur said without confirming or denying them. "But I take it you didn't convince anybody."

"Takizawa said it was possible, spun some theories."

"What theories?"

"I don't know. As far as I could tell, he was making it all up." She shrugged. "But it convinced the others."

"But not you."

Garcia shook her head. "They looked at me like I was a monster for not wanting to fix it."

"So why didn't you go along with them?"

"I just . . . Even if it could be done, I wasn't sure we should. It was a decision that should be made by someone more important than us."

"Did you tell them that?"

She nodded. "But Takizawa said the vortex was starting to close, that we wouldn't have time to call for help. And Dor said there might not be anybody left alive anywhere. It had to be us, and it had to be then."

"So they decided a vote of thirty-seven to one was good enough, and they set course for the vortex."

"But you weren't willing to accept that."

She shook her head again. "I knew it was a terrible mistake. If we could actually change history, how could we know we were making it better? What if . . . what if our warning made the Federation so afraid that it became a police state? What if taking preemptive action against an enemy nobody knew about yet spooked the Cardassians or the Romulans into starting another war? That might leave the Federation weaker when the invasion did come and make things even worse."

Again, Dulmur was impressed by Garcia's temporal intuition. "Did you suggest any of these things at the time?"

"No, I didn't have time to think it through yet. And they wouldn't have listened anyway. They didn't want to face this reality."

"But you could?"

"I didn't think we had a choice. So I . . . slipped out and went to the engine compartment. Like I said, I've read some stuff about ancient warp technology. I knew enough to know what systems I had to damage, though the best I could do was change settings at random and hope for the—well, the worst."

"But the others tried to stop you."

"They didn't know I was there at first." She shrugged. "Archaeologist, remember? I'm good at crawling through tight spaces, like maintenance crawlways." Her slight grin faded. "But once the engines started malfunctioning, they tracked me down pretty fast. And . . . well, you know what happened next."

"You need to say it on the record, Ms. Garcia."

She closed her eyes. "They pulled me away, screamed at me. I fought back, tried to keep doing damage. They piled on me, beat me." She shuddered. "It's all a blur after that. Except for Takizawa's face . . . he was right there at the front. He got his heavy mitts all over me after all, just not the way he wanted."

Garcia blinked away tears. "And then I woke up in your sickbay. And I saw the others . . . looking at me. And I knew . . . we were stuck in this future, with no chance of going back to save all those lives. I'd gotten my way," she said with sardonic pride, which then dissolved into a shuddering gasp. "I've never felt so ashamed."

11:37 UTC

"That . . . woman!" Wataru Takizawa cried. "I knew she wouldn't stay quiet!"

"In fact, she tried to protect you," Lucsly told him.

Dulmur, seated next to Lucsly at the table in briefing room one, added, "In spite of what you did to her."

"What about what *she* did? Damned sixty billion lives to annihilation!"

"Or saved trillions more in the long run," Lucsly said. "You don't know the whole story, Doctor. The Borg were the worst threat this galaxy's ever faced, and thanks to a whole sequence of events culminating twenty-four days ago, that threat has now been permanently ended. Go back to undo that sequence of events and you would restore a virtually unstoppable menace.

"Time doesn't let you pick and choose. Make a change for the better in one place and it can spawn a greater change for the worse somewhere else. It's entropy, Doctor. You must understand entropy. You travel into the past, it's an injection of higher entropy from the future just to start with. You do work to modify the course of events and you add even more entropy, more disorder." Lucsly shook his head. "The more we tamper with time, the more chaos we create. The best we can do is take the history we have and deal with it."

Dulmur smiled to himself. Normally, Lucsly was a man of few words, but get him going on temporal ethics and he became a revivalist preacher. Well, if revivalist preachers spoke in a no-nonsense deadpan. Still, at a time like this, Dulmur found his partner's passion for the cause—his sheer certainty that they were doing the right thing, no matter how painful—to be inspiring.

Takizawa wasn't impressed, though. "Just words, from a gray-suited bureaucrat looking for excuses to limit his imagination. Any work increases entropy. By your logic, we shouldn't ever try to build anything at all!"

"It depends on what you're tearing down in the process," Dulmur told him.

"We were trying to save billions of lives!"

"Oh, sure, and you showed your altruism by trying

to beat a fifty-six-kilo girl to death *after* it was too late to make a difference!"

Takizawa faltered. "So we got carried away. We were angry. Anyone would be. It's regrettable, but it was the heat of the moment."

"And it was against the law," Lucsly said. "So is attempted temporal alteration."

"The law. Like that matters at a time like this!"

Lucsly rose, and Dulmur followed suit. "Law is all that keeps us civilized at a time like this," Lucsly said. "And without the laws of time, none of the other laws mean anything at all."

18:02 UTC
Dulmur found Teresa Garcia in *Everett*'s observation lounge, looking out at the warp trails as the ship headed back to Earth with the *Verity* in tow. "You doing all right?"

She glared at him, but then she softened. "I was going to say that's a stupid question under the circumstances. But I guess after what all of you have been through . . . God, these past fifteen years . . . maybe 'all right' has to be a relative thing."

"It hasn't been that bad. Okay, we've had a lot of rough patches these past seven years in particular. But the Federation's a really big place. It can absorb a lot. Even after something as huge as this, or the Genesis Wave, or the Dominion War—you'll find out about those," he added at her puzzled look, "—there are still hundreds of worlds that are safe, secure, prosperous, and generous enough to help out the people who need it. So even when something really bad happens, it doesn't take too long to get us back on our feet again." He shook his head. "Maybe after all this, we won't bounce back quite as high for a while. But we still have plenty of what makes the Federation great—good people with good intentions and the means to do something about them."

Garcia smiled. "Nice sentiment. But how do you know there isn't some even worse disaster lurking around the corner?"

"Because I know a thing or two about the future," Dulmur said. "Nothing specific, naturally. There are laws about that too. But I know . . . and don't tell Lucsly I'm telling you this or he'll put me on report . . ." Garcia nodded. "I know that the Federation is still around in the future. In a lot of possible futures. And if there were something worse than the past couple of months heading our way, there'd be no future for us—*at all*. So I think we've weathered the worst of it now."

She looked out the window again. "At least you've had time to get used to it. It's still a shock for me." She shook her head. "I still can't blame any of them for what they did. Or for hating me for what I did."

After a moment, Dulmur patted her on the shoulder, very carefully. "You did the right thing, Ms. Garcia. More than that: you did the *hard* thing, because you knew it was right." He gazed at her until she turned to look at him. "I'd still like to know, though . . . you never really told me why you did it."

She looked within herself for a long moment. "I guess . . . it just seemed so childish."

"Childish?"

"To want to go back and make a bad thing not have happened anymore. That's not the way life works. Tragedy happens, and people just have to accept it and move on. Learn from it. Grow stronger from it. I . . ." She looked away. "I lost my dad when I was six."

"I'm sorry."

"Yeah. And I didn't get the chance to go back and 'fix' it. I had to live with it, deal with it. It hurt like hell, it tore me up for years . . . but it's part of who I am." She sighed. "We're the sum of our history. And there's always going to be pain in that history. I mean, God, look at what I do. I study cultures that have died. It's all about learning from tragedy.

"So I guess I just knew that . . . even with a tragedy like this . . . it happened, and you have to learn from it and keep going. If you can just cheat, if you can go back and make it unhappen, then you're stripping away the meaning. And that's not living. That's hiding from life.

"Oh, I don't even know if that makes sense."

Dulmur smiled. "I've rarely heard it said better."

Garcia smiled back, and he could see why Takizawa had flirted so hard with her. She was less than half his age, though, and he had other aims in mind for her. "So where do you go from here?"

"I've been trying to figure that out. There's no more Regulus III Science Academy, so my graduate career's shot. Not to mention that I've been legally dead for nearly two-thirds as long as I've been alive. Damn, I'm almost forty."

"I'm sure your mom would be glad to see you're alive."

"Yeah, there's that. I've already sent her a message. I was afraid she might've been one of the casualties, but she lives on Vega, and they've come through all the wars and things just fine."

"That's good."

"But . . . well, my mom is a strong-willed sort. Visiting is fine, but I couldn't just go home and live there. I'd feel too stifled. And . . . there'd be so much catching up to do. I'd always be out of synch."

"The DTI has specialists for this," Dulmur said, "people who can help you through the adjustment. You're not the first people to be displaced in time one way or another."

"I appreciate that."

He hesitated. "But I think the Department might be able to offer you something more."

Garcia furrowed her brow. "What do you mean?"

"You have a good instinct for time, Ms. Garcia. An intuition for how it works. More, you have a good instinct for protecting the timeline, and you've proven you're willing to do it at great personal risk. Even if it means being unpopular with people who don't understand why you're doing the right thing. Those are the qualities that can make for a fine DTI agent."

After a moment, her eyes widened and she laughed. "You—you're offering me a job?"

"I'm offering you a chance," he corrected. "DTI work isn't easy. There's an intensive three-month training program, and a lot of candidates wash out. And even if you make it . . ." He thought of George Faunt. "It wears on you in ways I can't explain. It's a thankless job, an unsung job. Most of it is classified, so you won't even be able to talk to your family or friends about it—if you can even hold on to them. People won't understand the strains you face, the responsibilities you hold. They'll look at you as a joke, a hidebound drudge, or a jackbooted thug. The job will dominate your life, make you question reality, cut you off from normal people and their normal concerns. And it can literally drive you crazy. I'm not doing you any favors by offering you this. The smart thing for you to do would be to say 'No, thank you' and go back to your studies." He gave her a sheepish look. "But we've had our losses too. We could use the help. At the very least, a student of galactic archaeology could be valuable as a researcher. But I think you have what it takes to be a field agent, Ms. Garcia. And that's not something that can be said about a lot of people."

"Wow," she said. "Really . . . wow." She was silent for fourteen seconds. "Okay. I'll do it."

Dulmur's eyes widened. "You, uh, you don't have to decide right away."

"You kidding? That's the best offer I've gotten all decade." Dulmur winced. "Oh. Sorry," Garcia went on. "I guess you've heard every time joke there is, haven't you?"

"Be prepared to get very sick of them very fast."

"Okay, seriously, then . . . it's a chance to do some good. What you do, it can't always be about making sure disasters happen, can it? It's about protecting people, preserving the good things as well as the bad?"

"We sure like to think so."

"Then maybe it'll give me an opportunity to balance the scales, do something positive. At least . . . if I learn about how time works, and why it has to be preserved, maybe I'll finally be able to know *why* what I did was right. So even if I wash out, at least it'll give me some perspective.

"As for the rest . . . I've never been one to go along with the crowd. If people can't accept me for who I am and what I believe, I don't need them anyway."

Dulmur had heard enough. He rose and extended his hand, and she responded in kind. "I'll be happy to sponsor your admission to the DTI Academy," he told her. "I have a feeling you'll make it."

"A premonition?" she asked.

"Oh, God, don't even go there."

"Sorry."

18:27 UTC

Lucsly wore a sour look as Dulmur composed his letter of recommendation for Garcia in *Everett*'s passenger lounge. "You think I'm making a mistake?" Dulmur asked.

"She lied about the attempted alteration," his partner replied.

"Out of altruistic motives."

"Those can be the most dangerous ones."

"She came through in the end."

"Only after we confronted her with the facts."

"She was scared. She'd been beaten half to death."

"So was it altruism or fear?"

"It can be both. People are complicated."

"Hm," Lucsly said. "That's the problem with them."

Dulmur chuckled. He knew Lucsly wouldn't be happy until he was back home, tinkering with his antique clocks, surrounded by their linearity and precision. But that was just Lucsly.

"You didn't think I'd be a good agent at first," Dulmur said.

"Yes, I did."

"Not that I noticed."

"I wasn't going to make it easy for you."

"No, you wouldn't have."

Lucsly examined him. "Is that why you're recommending her? Because she reminds you of you?"

"I guess I see a kindred spirit," Dulmur conceded. Thinking of Garcia's era of origin had reminded him of his own beginnings at the DTI, just a year and two months before the *Verity*'s displacement. His plight hadn't been on the same level as hers, but he too had felt cast adrift, torn from his intended path by a quirk of quantum physics . . . and strongly motivated to do something about it.

DOWNTIME
STARDATE 41697.9 TO 41906.7

II

Dulmur Residence
Motilal City, Nehru Colony
05:46 UTC

"Marion Frances Dulmur, do you have any idea what time it is?"

Dulmur winced at Megumi's use of his full name, not just for the name itself, but from the realization that he must have really irritated her to earn its use. "Sorry, honey," he told his wife as she gave off a massive yawn. "You know I lose track."

"Do I ever. Late to our wedding, but you can't be bothered to let me sleep till morning when one of your inspirations hits."

"Never gonna let me live that one down, are you?"

She stared. "And they call you a detective?"

"That's what I'm counting on."

Blinking the blear from her eyes, Megumi came into the study to look at the screen on his desk. "You got a lead?"

"Had a thought, had to track it down. Sorry, I thought I was being quiet."

"So you gonna tell me? Long as I'm up."

He smiled and put a hand on her waist. This was why he loved her. "I remembered something the client said about our guy. How he always served her Ongilin caviar when they ate at his place."

"Mmm," Meg said. "That guy knew how to treat a lady. No wonder she wants him back."

"That and the designs he seduced her in order to steal."

"Yeah, but *caviar*."

Dulmur suspected his client had lost her taste for Ongilin caviar lately. The man she'd known as Dennis Harmon had won her heart deftly, then broken it when it turned out he'd just been after her latest fashion innovation, a compact holo-emitter system that could project virtual images into midair for several centimeters around the wearer, letting one cloak oneself in intangible, dancing patterns of light and color. Dulmur found the whole idea quite frivolous, but this was the gig the Chandra Detective Agency had assigned him. And it seemed that fashion design was quite valuable to some people. Money may not have been an obsession within Federation society, but prestige and success were always valued, and whoever got credit for this fashion breakthrough would get more work, more parties, more suitors, you name it. Ms. Chandra considered this an important case, and she'd assigned it to Dulmur, giving her newest junior detective his first big chance to prove himself. His years of experience back on Centauri VII meant nothing to her; she was a true colonial, only judging people by what they achieved in their new home.

But Dulmur's brainstorm this morning gave him confidence that he was up to the challenge. "Anyway, I double-checked with her, and she confirmed it was genuine imported caviar, not replicated."

"Mm, and how did she feel about being woken up before sunrise?"

"Different city. It's a few hours later there."

"Lucky them. So what's important about it being imported?"

Dulmur smiled. "There's only one place on Nehru that handles the real thing."

"So you go there, show them the picture of the guy, and they can tell you his real name?"

"If he even used it. At least they can give me more to go on."

She kissed his cheek. "Good. Go find him."

"Now?"

"Like you said, it's already morning there. And you're not gonna be able to quiet down so long as you've got your hot lead." She bumped his chin with her fist. "So get the hell out of here so I can go back to sleep."

He chuckled, then kissed her firmly on the lips. It must've been some kiss, since he felt dizzy for a moment, like the universe was spinning around him.

She bumped his chin with her fist. "So get the hell out of here so I can go back to sleep."

He chuckled, then kissed her firmly on the lips. No dizzy this time. "You already said that."

"Did I? Must be sleepier than I thought."

Indira City
13:27 UTC

Dulmur ducked behind a public recycling station as a phaser bolt seared the air where he had stood. He waited tensely until he heard the shooter's footsteps receding; evidently Dennis Harmon would rather escape than finish him off.

Or rather, Daisen Hamor. His client's suitor had

turned out to be a Farian, disguised with cosmetic surgery to eliminate his frontal-nasal ridge. The staff at the import shop had identified him clearly as one of their regular customers. A little more legwork had led Dulmur to the one local cosmetic surgeon qualified and disreputable enough to do the work. He'd played tough guy and tried to intimidate the doctor with little success, but that was fine, since it had just been a distraction while the scanner in his pocket cloned the contents of the surgeon's computer and gave him an address. It had all been going smoothly until Hamor had opened fire. Dulmur had been taken by surprise. After all, why would anyone try to kill him over clothes?

Well, he didn't like to engage in species profiling, but if the culprit was Farian, the Orion Syndicate might be involved. Still, would even the Syndicate go to these lengths just to steal fashion designs? He suspected he was onto something bigger than he'd thought. He looked forward to the look of surprise and respect on Ms. Chandra's face when he brought this guy in.

But first he had to catch him. He'd studied a satellite map of Indira City on the way here, and he knew Hamor was most likely heading for the spaceport to make his getaway. Consulting the map on his padd as he ran, Dulmur formulated his strategy.

A shortcut brought Dulmur to a part of town dominated by single-story shops along the road. Nehru's gravity was about ten percent less than he was used to, so it didn't take too much effort to clamber onto the roof of one and wait. Soon, he saw Hamor emerge from an alley, glance furtively around, then dash across the street and into the next alley in his path—bringing him right toward Dulmur.

Even with the lower gravity, leaping off the roof and knocking Hamor to the ground hurt more than he expected. But that meant Hamor wouldn't be too happy about it either, which was fine, since he was the one with the phaser. Or he had been; the impact sent it flying, saving Dulmur the added trouble.

Regaining his footing, Dulmur hauled Hamor up into an armlock and slammed him against the wall. "Okay, pal, what's the big idea? Are next year's runway fashions really worth roasting a guy for?"

Hamor laughed. "You think this is about fashion?" He relaxed. "I thought you were a competitor, but you're just hired security, aren't you? Listen," he went on with a devious expression. "You have any idea of the espionage potential of this kind of holographic camouflage? You have any idea how rich we could both be if you let me go?"

Inwardly, Dulmur thrilled at the realization that this was an even bigger case than he'd anticipated. With this success under his belt, he'd have job security for sure, and then he and Meg could finally start a family. Next to that, no bribe could sway him. "Sorry, pal," he said, hauling Hamor around and starting to march him out of the alley. "I've already had a better offer. You're—"

He broke off as someone ran into the alley. Someone who looked exactly like Hamor.

The other Hamor gasped, pulled to a stop, and ran off into the street. Dulmur heard a curse from above, saw a movement on the roof, and looked up to see . . .

Himself.

On the ledge, ready to jump off.

Just where he'd been thirty seconds ago.

Dulmur stared at himself, who stared back at himself, and for a freakish moment it was like he was in both places at once.

And then he was in one place—the roof, looking down at himself holding Hamor. But Hamor had never entered the alley. He was running off . . . Dulmur turned his head to look for him, saw nothing. He turned back to the alley . . . and it was empty. No Dulmur, no Hamor, no phaser on the ground. And Dulmur's aches from the jump were gone. It was as if none of it had ever happened.

He shook himself. Hamor was running, and he was still armed. Dulmur had his priorities. He climbed off the roof, more carefully this time (or was it the first time?), and set off in pursuit.

But he was distracted as he ran, trying to figure out what had happened. Had he imagined the whole thing? As he ran, he saw people in the street, having animated conversations. He picked up snippets: ". . . and there I was back where I'd . . ." ". . . looking right at me, but it was me . . ." ". . . like time looped back, they're saying it happened all over . . ."

But that was a mystery for later. Right now he had to intercept Hamor before he got to the spaceport. Yet he was losing the trail, and all the people coming out into the streets to chatter impeded his progress.

Then he turned a corner and found a crashed ground transport blocking the road in front of him. From the way the driver was telling it, it had swerved to avoid an impact with *itself* and crashed into a building instead. The crowd of onlookers was too dense for Dulmur to get past, forcing him to find an alternate route. His odds of getting to the spaceport before Hamor got away were plummeting.

Although at this point, he was no longer sure what "before" meant.

Dulmur Residence
17:54 UTC

"She *fired* you?!" Megumi clapped her hand to her forehead, brushed back her lustrous black hair. "How could Chandra fire you?"

"He got away, Meg," Dulmur said. "Biggest case of my career, and he gets off-planet with the goods. I notified the authorities. Maybe Starfleet or somebody will get him. But *I* let him get away."

"But it wasn't your fault! You had him, but then that . . . time thing happened!"

Dulmur shrugged. "Chandra didn't believe me when I told her."

"How could she not believe you? It happened to everyone on the planet! FNS is saying it's been happening over half the quadrant!"

"Well, apparently Chandra missed it. Can't blame her—I think it happened to us this morning, just before I left, but I thought you were just repeating yourself."

"Yeah, but the next one was bigger, almost thirty seconds. And people seeing themselves . . . what was Chandra doing that she didn't notice that?"

"Probably asleep in her office. But she wouldn't admit it."

"And what about everyone else telling her it happened?"

"They tried. But the woman has no imagination. She thought the others were just trying to cover for me." He scoffed. "Like that creep Piccolo wasn't happy to see me fired."

Meg took a calming breath. "Well . . . maybe when she sees it on the news . . . realizes this really happened, and it wasn't your fault . . ."

Dulmur shook his head. "Not gonna happen, honey. That woman is legendary for her stubbornness. It's what made her a great detective in her day, but as an administrator . . ." He sighed. "Let's just say she's not going to lose face by admitting a mistake. She'll just tell herself she fired me for letting a target get away, and won't worry about the rest."

"Well, that's just not fair."

Dulmur rose and started to pace. "Maybe, maybe not. I had a shot to fix my mistake, and I blew it."

"Mare, I can't believe you're saying this! You're just gonna lie back and take it?" Meg rose and put her hands on her hips. "We were just getting settled, Mare. We were talking about starting a family. Dammit, I like it here!"

Dulmur winced, knowing there was nothing he could do to fix things. A colony like this wasn't as luxurious as Earth; people still needed to contribute materially in some way to earn their share of the resources. They couldn't stay here without a job, and there weren't that many openings here for a private investigator and a sculptor.

"Believe me, Meg, I'm as mad as you are."

"Then do something about it!"

"I intend to," he said. "But Chandra's not the one responsible here."

Megumi frowned. "Then who is?"

Dulmur looked at the holoscreen. "They're saying on the news that this . . . time thing wasn't natural. Somebody caused it. Somebody messed around with some kind of weird science and didn't care how many lives they screwed up in the process." He clenched his fists, seething. "They're the real criminals here."

"So what are you going to do about it?"

"I'm gonna do my job," Dulmur said. "I'm gonna find them and make them pay."

Vandor IV
Agrahayana 7, 2286 SE (A Friday)
20:43 UTC
It hadn't been easy for Dulmur to track down the source of the time distortions. According to the physicists he'd consulted, the quadrant-spanning event had rendered time and space so variable that it threw off their equations, making it impossible to narrow down the origin point beyond a volume about fifteen parsecs across. Dulmur had run a search for any time-related news pertaining to those sectors, and he'd found a tenuous link. Several temporal researchers, colleagues of a noted scientist (or crackpot, depending on whom you asked) named Dr. Paul Manheim, had recently been reported dead, and the transport returning their remains had originated in that sector. Dulmur had spoken to the transport crew and extracted a name: Vandor IV. He'd learned that Vandor was a remote, uninhabited binary system, but the Federation Science Council was reportedly opening a research annex in the system, under the purview of an obscure branch called the Department of Temporal Investigations. *Temporal Investigations?* Dulmur had wondered. Probably a bunch of bureaucrats responsible for maintaining a consistent Federation-wide time standard, resolving relativistic discrepancies and the like. But one way or another, they dealt with time, and they were going to Vandor IV.

Starfleet and its Corps of Engineers were handling the establishment of the research annex, but that wasn't as great an impediment to Dulmur as it might have been in another era. With peace prevailing in most of the Federation, aside from the occasional flare-up on the Cardassian border, Starfleet these days was as much a research institution as a defense force, and plenty of its vessels had civilian scientists, specialists, and family members on board. Dulmur's years working with security and surveillance systems gave him the skills and credentials to sign on as a sensor technician with the appropriate security clearance, once he called in a few favors and arranged for certain barter transactions benefitting certain members of Starfleet's personnel bureau.

So now, three weeks and change after Dr. Paul Manheim had ruined his life, Dulmur finally stood in the same room with the man. Manheim was an unimposing figure, bearded and middle-aged, looking a bit like Sigmund Freud. He had just come into the lab Dulmur was helping to bring online, speaking animatedly to a group of several people, including a Zakdorn male and a human male in conservative dark suits, an elderly Vulcan woman, and a younger dark-haired female from a species he couldn't place, human-looking save for a higher, narrower cranium.

"That's what I've been trying to explain to you," Manheim was insisting. "The event proves the nonlinearity of time. If the same event can occur two different ways within a single observer's measurement history, then the probabilities do add to more than one."

"Absurd," said the Vulcan. "Without unitarity, quantum theory becomes unviable."

"Exactly, Doctor T'Viss. Don't you see? We now have

experimental confirmation of a third dimension of time. That means the Bars gauge symmetry is no longer valid." Dulmur blinked. He hadn't even been aware there was a second dimension of time.

The high-browed younger female spoke up. "Meaning negative probability can exist after all!"

"Indeed. In fact, it must. It's the only way to conserve T'Viss's precious unitarity."

"By canceling out the excess positive probabilities! You're saying it's *locally* negative, like the Casimir Effect."

"A good analogy, Doctor, err . . . I'm sorry, what was your name again?"

"Naadri. Of the Paraagan Science Council."

"Of course."

"But how would negative probabilities manifest?" asked the Zakdorn male, an older fellow with pronounced jowls even by his species' standards. "What's the real-world meaning of a probability that is not between zero and one?"

"Well, you're getting ahead of the theory there, Agent Borvala," Manheim said.

But Naadri was still pondering. "Perhaps . . . some kind of retrocausal influence that acts to negate excess probabilities. A sort of 'anti-time,' as it were."

T'Viss scoffed. "That would entail negative entropy as well. How do you imagine such a thing would manifest physically?"

"In combination with positive entropy, I have no idea," Manheim replied, though Naadri retreated into thought at the question. "But if you'll consider, T'Viss, a force of negative entropy acting on a holistic level could explain the mystery of macrorealm convergence."

The Vulcan conceded reluctantly. "Hypothetically. If one accepts the convergence interpretation at all."

Manheim laughed. "Doctor, that is why I must continue my work! What we have achieved here is the first experimental confirmation of a principle that could resolve the greatest conundrums of quantum temporal physics. And that," he went on with a messianic gleam in his eye, "is only the beginning of the secrets it could expose!"

"And so that makes it worth it to you?" Dulmur was a bit surprised to realize the voice was his own. No, he wasn't in two places at once again, but he had impulsively spoken up, turning to confront the doctor and no longer caring about his cover. He had enough evidence by now to make a case anyway. "You think causing chaos across half the Federation is okay because you learned something about abstract physics?" He turned to the two DTI men in their dark suits. "And you! You're with the government. Why are you helping this guy instead of hauling him off to jail?"

"Excuse me, who is this man?" the bearded scientist inquired of the agents.

"That's what I'd like to know," said Agent Borvala, striding forward. The younger agent, a lanky, fortyish human with curly dark hair and a saturnine expression, followed close behind.

"I'll tell you who I am, Manheim! I'm one of the thousands of Federation citizens whose lives you ruined by playing reckless games with time and space!" He looked at the agents who now loomed over him on both sides. "And I'm here to ask my government why they aren't doing something to stop this guy from doing it again."

"The matter is under advisement," the human agent

said. Did Dulmur imagine it, or was that a warning glance he threw at Manheim? Could he have an ally here after all?

"Believe me, young man, the immediate threat is past. I underestimated the power, the multidimensional nature, of the energy source we discovered within this planetoid." Manheim shook his head. "And believe me, I paid dearly for that error. I am as dedicated as you to ensuring the accident does not repeat itself. Probably more so."

"Doctor," Borvala warned.

But Dulmur narrowed his eyes. "The people who died."

"Yes," Manheim said. "Colleagues and friends, all of them. A weight I will carry the rest of my life. But the work must continue to ensure they did not perish in vain!"

"Doctor, you've said enough," Borvala barked. "Agent Lucsly, please escort this technician to the security office. He's the one who should be answering questions."

20:52 UTC

"Name?" Lucsly asked.

"Dulmur."

"First name?"

The blond man fidgeted—a sign of a guilty conscience? Then he said "Marion" in a small voice. *Ah.*

Lucsly entered the name on his padd: DULMER. "No, with a U," the man said.

"There is a U."

"No, a second U."

Lucsly frowned. "Du-ulmer?"

He sighed. "Never mind. Look, Agent Locksley—"

"Lucsly."

The other man laughed. "I guess we have something in common, huh, pal?"

"That remains to be seen. Date of birth?"

"Stardate 15574.6."

Lucsly glanced up. "A Sunday."

The man blinked. "How'd you know that?"

The padd finally coughed up the security file for Dulmur, Marion F., civilian contractor. "How did you get here, Mister Dulmur?"

"By doing my job. I'm a *real* investigator. No offense."

Lucsly threw him a look. "Taken."

Dulmur winced. "Look, my clearance is in order . . . basically."

"But you came here with an agenda."

"Hell, yes. To find out who was messing around with time and not caring how many people's lives it screwed up."

Dulmur went on to explain how the negative-delay incident—the time loop, in the vernacular—had ruined his career prospects. Lucsly felt that Dulmur's sense of priorities was a little off; others had lost their lives, not merely their jobs. But there was something impressive about the man's outrage at the very idea of disruption to the flow of time, and about the lengths he'd gone to in order to do something about it. "I want to bring that man to justice," Dulmur concluded. "Nobody should have that kind of power over—over reality!"

Lucsly pondered his words and came to a decision. "Rest assured, Mister Dulmur, holding Doctor Manheim accountable for the results of his research is a high priority for the Federation. The matter has been investigated thoroughly, and the widespread effects have been found to be the result of an accident that could not have been anticipated. Manheim himself was almost killed."

"But you're letting him continue his work?"

"He's the only person who understands it well enough to help us make sure it causes no further disruptions." Personally, Lucsly thought Manheim had been insanely reckless to tamper with the mysterious dynamic energy source at Vandor IV's core—something that Doctors T'Viss and Naadri were theorizing was an interdimensional rift (natural, T'Viss said; perhaps artificial, Naadri said) around which the planetoid had accreted. But the Federation was largely populated and run by people who believed it was worth taking risks to expand pure knowledge, and so Manheim had been exonerated of criminal charges. At least the Science Council had had the good sense to place any further research under the direct supervision of the DTI, and to appoint his mentor Borvala, the best DTI agent Lucsly had ever known, to the task. "But you can be certain we'll be keeping his work under the strictest supervision from now on. Every possible precaution will be taken, and he won't be allowed to run a single experiment without clearing it with the finest temporal physicists in the Federation."

Dulmur looked him over. "So the DTI, you're not just about making sure everyone's clocks are in synch?"

"That's the Bureau of Standards. Our job is to keep *time* on course."

The blond man blinked. "Okay, you don't think small. So where do I sign up?"

Now Lucsly blinked. "I beg your pardon?"

"Well, if you're the ones responsible for keeping mad scientists like Manheim from resetting the universe's clock,

I want in. It's not like I have anything better to do, after he erased my future."

"This isn't a job you take on casually," Lucsly told him. "It's a grave responsibility, the gravest one I know. It demands total commitment and its stakes are higher than you can imagine."

"You think you can scare me off with a challenge, pal, you don't know how a Dulmur does things."

"You're right. I probably don't." Lucsly had never given the question any thought.

The door opened and Borvala came in. "Agent Lucsly, could I speak to you outside?"

He followed his mentor into the corridor. "Your assessment?" the Zakdorn asked.

Lucsly gave his report, then added, "I think he's harmless. Impulsive, but his heart's in the right place. He even wants to join the Department."

Borvala snorted. "He obviously doesn't know much about it, then."

"The more I learned, the more I wanted in," Lucsly said. "I think he might be the same way."

"You're serious?" Borvala asked. Lucsly just looked at him. "Of course, I forgot who I was talking to." The wizened DTI agent sighed. "Well, it's not as if the Department couldn't use a few more hands. I'd feel better about taking a desk job if I knew you had a partner you approved of."

"Hold on," Lucsly said. "I only said he might be serious about wanting to join. I never said anything about a new partner."

"Of course you didn't, Gariff. Change doesn't come easily to you."

"I don't want it to come at all."

"And perhaps I've indulged that too much and held you back. In any case, I've had about all I can stand of field work. Even a mind as formidable as mine can handle only so many paradoxes." Borvala narrowed his small, bright eyes. "You really think he'd be willing to apply?"

"He's dedicated," Lucsly granted with reluctance. "He came nearly a thousand light-years to confront a man for costing him his job."

"That's not dedication," Borvala said. "That's obsessiveness bordering on monomania." A sharp cackle shook his jowls. "You two *are* kindred spirits."

Lucsly remained skeptical. The man might be driven enough to apply, but his odds of surviving the rigors of training were slim. This was probably the last Lucsly would ever see of Marion Dulmur.

PRESENT TIME
STARDATE 58281.1 TO 58365.9

III

DTI Headquarters
Greenwich, European Alliance, Earth
14:11 UTC

"So how was the visit to your brother?" Clare Raymond asked.

Teresa Garcia bit her lip, considering her reply. Clare waited patiently, doing nothing to disrupt the sense of calm created by her office's decor.

"It was rough," Teresa finally admitted. "Last time I saw him, he was eight years younger than me, just starting to notice girls. He was a brat sometimes—of course—but he was . . . innocent. Not a care in the world. It annoyed me sometimes, him going about his games and models and daydreams while I was trying to study hard and get into the Regulus Academy. I told him he'd never amount to anything with an attitude like that. But sometimes I envied him that freedom, that lack of anything weighing him down."

She shook her head. "Now, suddenly, he's seven years older than me, and it's like he's lived lifetimes. Like he's a whole other person. Hell, it's hard enough to believe he ever got responsible enough to enlist when the Dominion invaded."

Clare shrugged. "Maybe thinking you were dead convinced him that life was shorter than he realized. Or maybe he'd been so carefree before because he had you around to be the responsible one."

"I don't know, maybe. I wouldn't have known how to ask . . . the man he is now. He's so . . . hard. So angry. The things he saw, fighting the Dominion and now the Borg . . . I just can't imagine. And it's like he resents me for getting to skip over all that. Like suddenly I'm the one without a care in the world." She looked down at her hands. "And I can't say I blame him."

Clare nodded. She'd heard similar stories from other *Verity* passengers and crewpersons she'd counseled over the past month. A temporal refugee herself, she'd gone to work for the DTI's Temporal Displacement Division in the hope that her experiences could benefit others displaced in time. She had been a middle-class homemaker in Secaucus, New Jersey, back in the late twentieth century, the mother of two young boys, when she'd died of an embolism during a business trip with her husband Donald. But Donald had invested in a company working with cryonics, the fashionable process of freezing the recently deceased in hopes that future medicine could revive them, and apparently she must have lingered long enough that he was able to make the arrangements to get her frozen promptly upon her death. She and nearly a dozen others had been launched in a solar-powered satellite as protection against power-grid brownouts, and that satellite had been thrown a vast distance across space through unknown means. Three hundred and seventy years later, the satellite had been found by the crew of the *Starship Enterprise,* who'd been too preoccupied with a mission involving the Romulan Star Empire to investigate that cosmic mystery. But they had found Clare and two others

still viably preserved, and the ship's medical staff had succeeded in reviving all three.

It had been tough for the temporal refugees to adjust
to a world so alien, a world that looked on their twentieth-
century materialism and insularity the way Clare would
have looked upon serfdom or foot-binding. A world filled
with aliens of all shapes, some of them terrifying, with
bizarre customs and attitudes of their own, yet living
side-by-side with the humans of this era and looking on
Clare and the other two as if *they* were the aliens. But in
time, they had all adjusted. Ralph Offenhouse, a businessman who knew how to come out on top, had gone on to
become the Federation's Secretary of Commerce. Sonny
Clemonds, a hard-living country musician, had become a
minor celebrity, performing his exotically ancient music all
over the known galaxy. Clare still collected all his albums,
or downloads or whatever they called them these days;
she'd never liked country music, but it was one of her few
remaining connections to the world she knew.

Like Teresa Garcia, Clare Raymond had turned to
family at first but had found it challenging to fit in. Certainly there was much about this time that was wonderful—no war, no poverty, transporters, holosuites, flying
cars, and medicine so miraculous that it not only brought
her back from the dead but let her be healthier now at
fifty-two (subjective) than she'd been before her demise
at thirty-five. But aside from remote lineage, she and her
descendants had turned out to have very little in common.
They had been unsure how to fit her into their lives, and
had often shown considerable embarrassment when she'd
inadvertently expressed an attitude that had been shocking
in this age. She'd always considered herself a tolerant sort,

but living in the twenty-fourth century had forced her to recognize how parochial, shallow, and prejudiced she had been in ways she hadn't ever imagined. (Her descendants had been mystified when she'd been more troubled by her great-great-great-grandson Jonathan marrying another man than by his sister marrying an alien.)

Still, what Teresa was going through was perhaps harder in some ways. Everyone Clare had known was gone, but that meant she had few expectations about the new people she met here. But to come back to a world so close to your own, still populated by the same people one had known, yet to find them so different from how you were used to thinking of them—that would be a whole different set of challenges.

"Do you really think your brother's right?" Clare asked. "That your situation is so carefree and easy? I mean, maybe you didn't have to live through it, but now you're getting it all dumped on you at once. And it's the reality you'll have to live with for the rest of your life."

Teresa smirked. "Oh, very comforting, Counselor."

"I'm just saying that maybe if you helped your brother . understand what you're going through, instead of just accepting that he's right to dismiss your point of view, it might help you relate to each other better. I mean, losing his ship and his crewmates—twice—must have felt very sudden and disorienting. You have that in common." Clare paused. "And maybe a touch of survivor's guilt too."

"I don't know," Teresa said. "You make a good point, but I'm not sure he'd be willing to listen. It's not like we were ever that close anyway." She smirked. "Does it make me a bad person that all the time I was visiting him,

I couldn't wait to get back here and get on with my DTI training?"

Clare thought about Lucsly, Dulmur, Ranjea, Yol, and the other DTI agents she'd come to know over the years. Most of them lived alone and had few ties, few commitments beyond their work. At first, Clare had found that sad and disturbing. It certainly wasn't the kind of life she would wish on a member of her own family. But those who did well at the Department's work were those who found meaning and purpose in it. Sometimes that meaning was a substitute for the rest of their lives, and sometimes it came at the expense of the rest of their lives. But sometimes it was a refuge for people who didn't quite fit anywhere else. People like Clare.

So she smiled at Teresa. "What I think . . . is that there's more than one kind of family."

Julian Days 2590812 to 2590823

The first thing Teresa Garcia learned was to be punctual. If there was one thing nobody at the Department seemed to tolerate, it was tardiness.

Everything about the DTI encouraged its recruits to concentrate on time. The organization's headquarters were located in Greenwich, home of the Royal Observatory, the globally accepted reference point for universal time on Earth for just shy of five centuries now. The HQ building itself, or at least its public section, was in a trio of large, semidetached Victorian houses situated half a kilometer north of the Observatory and almost precisely atop the Prime Meridian. The houses had managed to survive the Blitz in WWII, the aerial nuclear detonation and subsequent fires and riots in WWIII, the panic following First

Contact, and centuries of everyday use and entropy largely intact—with the occasional refurbishment and extension, befitting the headquarters of one of the Federation's most important agencies. But the bulk of the DTI's operation took place in the high-security underground levels stretching out beneath Park Vista and Feathers Place. As yet, Garcia had only the vaguest notion of what was down there. She had spent most of her time at the DTI training facility at the University of Greenwich, on the grounds of the Old Royal Naval College just northwest of HQ. It was a gorgeous place to study, the work of seventeenth-century architect Christopher Wren, and it was steeped in centuries of history and culture. Garcia could appreciate that as a student of archaeology; but moreover, the whole environment gave DTI recruits a sense of time and history as tangible, unshakeable things.

Which was comforting, since what she and her fellow recruits were quickly learning was that nothing could be further from the truth. History as they knew it was merely one eigenstate within a much larger quantum wave equation, a single facet of reality coexisting alongside many others. Reality was regularly splitting into new branches, and sometimes those branches could merge together again, eradicating whole timelines from existence.

Of course, the DTI's job was to keep that from happening to *this* timeline. But the Department's methods for doing so were more limited than the students had imagined. This came out in a lecture given by Agent Lucsly at the start of training. The gray-haired veteran agent and his partner Dulmur, legends in the Department, had both refused promotion to desk jobs, but apparently were entrusted with responsibility equivalent to a special agent-in-charge, and were often found at HQ reporting to Director Andos herself, participating in high-level decisions and the like. Yet they still made time to give orientations to new recruits.

When an Andorian *chan* named Sanioth let it be known that he was here for the adventure of traveling through time, Lucsly skewered him with a look and said, "Here's the first thing you need to know. The DTI isn't an adventure; it's a job. Adventure is what happens when things go wrong, and our responsibility is to make sure they *don't* go wrong. That means preventing time travel, not participating in it. If a temporal anomaly is discovered, we secure and patrol it. If an ancient time machine is unearthed, we confiscate it. If a scientist is researching temporal displacement, we monitor and regulate the research."

"But what if you're too late to prevent it?" Sanioth pressed. "What if you're on the scene and have to follow someone into the past to protect the timeline?"

"If you don't stop them *before* they go back," replied Lucsly, "then you haven't done your job right."

"That's easy to say in principle," Garcia put in. "But even the best agents aren't perfect. Is it ever allowed even as a last-ditch backup plan?"

Lucsly was slow to respond. "You're nowhere near ready to discuss that question. You need to learn the routine before you're qualified to deal with the unusual. The routine is what we're here to protect. Because when it comes to time, disruptions to the routine are just too dangerous. If you value *adventure,* then go join Starfleet and get yourself killed on some exotic planet. Adventure is the result of carelessness and poor planning. We have no use for that here."

Sanioth dropped out the next day.

Garcia didn't see his problem. As far as she was concerned, it was adventure enough just trying to follow the temporal physics lectures of Professor T'Viss. The elderly, white-haired Vulcan, one of the Federation's leading temporal physicists, had been with the Department since its founding a hundred and eleven years before. She grasped the nature of time in a way few others could, and she was disinclined to dumb her lectures down for her students. It was a struggle to keep up.

Even figuring out how to *talk* about travel through time was confounding, since tenses themselves were an issue. T'Viss grew stern and impatient whenever one of her students spoke of going back in time and creating a "new" timeline. "There is no 'new,'" T'Viss intoned. "No before, no after. In order to perceive the whole shape of time, one must step outside of time." She projected a hologram before the students: a simplified chart of the known timelines, ramifying out from left to right like a sideways tree. "From this perspective, the observer experiences no passage of time. Past and future are merely points on a curve. Change is merely the shape of that curve. All processes, all interactions, are to be treated as instantaneous."

Garcia struggled to grasp this. "So you're saying everything's predestined anyway? It's all happened already?"

"'*Pre*destined'? 'Happened already'? You must divorce your thinking from these illusory concepts of relative time! In physics, there is no preferred direction of time or causality. There is only the progression of cause and effect within the wave equation. As long as an interaction is logically consistent, the directionality of time is irrelevant."

"Okay, maybe I'm not saying it right. But what I mean is, if all timelines exist side by side, if you can't go back and unmake a history once it's happened, why do we need to worry about time travel? Wouldn't that just mean that any new timeline—"

"Retrocausally generated history," T'Viss corrected.

"—would coexist with the ol—the original—the seed timeline?" Just figuring out how to ask the question was enough to give her a headache.

T'Viss's answers were highly technical, but Garcia gradually managed to get the gist of them, largely with the help of a fellow recruit named Felbog Bu-Tsop-Vee. Felbog was a member of a species unknown in Garcia's time, the Choblik—small herbivores with deerlike heads and ostrich-shaped bodies, modified with cybernetic enhancements that gave them full sentience, arms and grasping appendages, and other advantages their native forms lacked. They struck Garcia as what the Borg might have been as cute woodland creatures, but she quickly learned that Choblik, generally a very levelheaded people, took umbrage at any comparison to the Borg.

Felbog was training to be a DTI researcher rather than a field agent, but he threw himself into it with great enthusiasm and dedication, and was glad to help Garcia translate T'Viss's lectures and equations into comprehensible language. "Of course it's a logical absurdity for a timeline to be erased," Felbog told her as they strolled through Greenwich Park on a lightly overcast afternoon. "Anything that's happened has happened. You can't change the shape of time as a whole."

"Because change is just part of the shape itself," Garcia interpreted.

"Exactly. So the only way one timeline could replace another is if they coexisted side by side from the moment of their divergence . . . but then merged together again once they both reached a later point in the timeline."

"Could that happen?" Garcia asked.

Felbog's cervine ears flicked in a shrug. "Quantum theory doesn't rule it out. Timelines diverge when they shift sufficiently out of phase to become non-interacting, but it's not impossible for them to interfere again at a later point in time. And if they did become entangled as a single system, then quantum information theory would demand that only one of the two conflicting sets of information survived."

"Since a given quantum history has to be self-consistent."

"Yes. It would be as if one timeline suddenly transformed into another. The previous events would still have occurred, but they would no longer be remembered. The information would have been destroyed."

By now, they'd reached the grounds of the Royal Observatory. As usual, there were a number of tourists congregated around the Shepherd Gate Clock, the large analog timepiece with its 24-hour face inscribed in Roman numerals, embedded in the brick column to one side of the wrought-iron gate outside the observatory. The "galvano-magnetic clock," as its inscription called it, had been the first timepiece to display and transmit Greenwich Mean Time to the world. It had long since been supplanted by more modern means, but it remained as a symbol of humanity's establishment of a single universal time standard.

Despite the tourists, Felbog continued his explanation. It was mostly theoretical, and few listeners could follow it anyway. "The catch is, for two timelines that have drifted apart to come back into phase would violate entropy. There'd need to be some kind of force acting to merge them back together."

"But there were documented cases where that kind of . . . merger did happen, weren't there?"

"The observers believed they did," Felbog agreed. Even this early in their studies, both students had heard the tales of Starfleet captains like Kirk, Picard, and Janeway, all infamous in the Department for their frequent temporal violations—including cases where, while in the protected field of a temporal displacement metric, they had witnessed the timeline seeming to change around them, as Kirk had in his first encounter with the legendary Guardian of Forever. "But because of the entropy question, many theorists believed they might simply have been jumping between two alternate histories, rather than seeing one overwritten by another. It's been a matter of controversy for over a century."

"Hm. Did they try asking the Guardian?" she asked, keeping her voice low.

"It never gave clear answers to much of anything," Felbog said. "Either it was operating on a cognitive level we're unable to comprehend or—"

"I know," Garcia said with a chuckle. T'Viss had gone on a lengthy rant about the Guardian when the subject had come up in class. *"'Let me be your gateway' indeed. What sort of 'Guardian' eagerly invites strangers to ransack the very thing it's guarding? Its behavior was not remotely rational or consistent. I daresay the device's artificial intelligence has been in an advanced state of deterioration for a considerable period of time. We're better off without it now."*

Some years back, the spacetime turbulence surrounding the Guardian planet had grown so intense that it was no longer safe to approach orbit or transport down. Perhaps the device had finally broken down completely, or perhaps it had come to its senses and was refusing to let anyone use it to tamper with reality anymore. Either way, nobody would be going anywhere near the Guardian of Forever for the foreseeable future.

But the Guardian hadn't been needed to resolve the mystery of shifting timelines. In subequent classes, Garcia struggled to understand the theory of a negative-entropy "anti-time" phenomenon that a Dr. Naadri of Paraagan had been developing for the past decade and a half. It seemed that T'Viss had a grudging tone in her voice as she spelled out Naadri's equations demonstrating how that force could act to facilitate the merger of two time-lines back into one, effectively resolving the long-standing theoretical debate.

Garcia wondered why they were getting their lectures from an old-guard physicist like T'Viss, who seemed to be well behind the state of the art, rather than the cutting-edge theorists like Naadri or Vard, whose break-throughs T'Viss explained grudgingly at best. But it seemed to be part of the general conservatism the agency stressed. Whatever sexy new temporal breakthroughs were being made, an agent still needed a solid ground-ing in the basics, the foundations on which the rest was built. Her job, Garcia was reminded daily, would not be to probe the frontiers, but to defend the established and the ordinary.

Although, from some of the tales she'd heard about the bizarre cases solved by Lucsly, Dulmur, and their fellow agents over the years, Garcia suspected that principle was more often an aspiration than a reality.

Julian Days 2590825 to 2590833

By this point, of the six other recruits Garcia had started with, three had dropped out, and Garcia was the only human remaining. She and Felbog shared their classes with a young Vulcan, Teyak, and a gold-skinned Selenean female named Borah. Humans like Lucsly and Dulmur were a distinct minority among the DTI staffers she met; the agency was dominated by species known for emotional stability or self-discipline: Vulcans, Rhaandarites, Zakdorn, Benzites. Felbog himself, though enthusiastic about learning, was not prone to passion or anxiety; Garcia doubted the work would stress him even if it weren't so easy for his cybernetically enhanced mind. She valued his calming influence and his knack for interpreting complex ideas. She doubted she would be able to make it as a DTI agent without his aid. Though she reminded herself that she still might not make it at all.

There was much more to the training than temporal physics, of course. Aspiring agents needed to learn techniques for investigation, enforcement, and if necessary, physical confrontation. Garcia took readily to the physical side of things, though she wished she could do without the firearms training. She didn't care for weapons, even nonlethal ones like phasers. "That's good," she was told by her weapons instructor, a joined Trill agent named Stijen Yol. "The people most reluctant to use weapons are the ones who can best be trusted with them." He held up his DTI-issue phaser. "This is a deterrent and a last resort. A DTI agent relies on her mind, her judgment, and her discipline. Wield those weapons successfully, and Time willing, you will never need to fire this one."

The courses on investigative techniques proved easy for Garcia to master as well, for the skills required were much like those of the archaeologist. Both involved careful, patient sifting through information, the ability to discern a tiny shard of useful information from the matrix that surrounded it, delicately extract it, and piece it together with other shards to reconstruct its meaning. Of course, not all temporal investigation was so difficult. The majority of temporal events in the Federation befell Starfleet vessels, for they were the ones most prone to investigate mysterious phenomena and most capable of surviving the stresses, and they were obligated to give thorough reports. Natural anomalies were not too difficult to detect, not with the array of gravimetric and chronitonic sensors the Department had at its disposal, and deciphering their mysteries was more a matter for physicists like T'Viss. And temporal researchers like Naadri and Vard usually had to do their work in the open, for the sake of peer review and access to resources, so the Department's job there was more along the lines of supervision than investigation.

Still, Garcia's own experience aboard the *Verity* showed that people involved in temporal incidents weren't always forthright about their actions. And there were researchers such as the now-retired Paul Manheim who conducted their temporal experiments in secret, either for fear of ridicule or because their ends were less than ethical. Not to mention the schemes that sufficiently reckless hostile powers might devise against the Federation from time to time. The "I" in "DTI" was there for a very good reason.

But the more the students learned about the various

forces arrayed against the Department, the more disturbing
it became. The basics were laid out for them by a young
DTI agent named Shelan, a female of the Suliban species.
She was a hairless humanoid with spongy gray-green skin,
but her features were pleasant and her eyes lively and smiling. She met with the remaining recruits in her office at
headquarters and spoke to them informally, insisting that
she'd been in their shoes only two years before and considered them kindred spirits. "By now you've heard of the
Temporal Cold War," she told them, "if you didn't know
about it already." Garcia was familiar with the concept, but
she'd always considered it a galactic legend until she joined
the Department. "It's a conflict being fought across the
ages by factions in many different centuries, even different timelines. And one of its fronts was in the middle of
the twenty-second century. A mysterious faction from six
centuries uptime, whose identity still remains unknown,
recruited a group of Suliban as its agents."

"Why not intervene directly?" asked Teyak.

"Because of the Temporal Accords," she said. "We
have an early version of the Accords today, a broad agreement among the major governments to avoid nonscientific
applications of temporal research, but in the future, when
time travel becomes a practical, reliable technology rather
than the result of lucky accidents or natural phenomena,
the Accords become much stronger, and there are uptime
agencies that enforce them: the Temporal Integrity Commission of twenty-ninth-century Starfleet, the civilian
Federation Temporal Agency of two centuries beyond
that, the Tholian Chronological Defense Corps which has
existed for centuries already, and others.

"That's why it's a cold war. The factions that want to

meddle with the past need to do so clandestinely, indirectly, to avoid exposing themselves to sanctions or counter-attacks." Shelan spoke in the present tense, the simplest one to use when speaking about time travel. As T'Viss taught, it was clearer to step outside of time and consider it all as a simultaneous whole. "The twenty-eighth-century faction chose the Suliban because we were an obscure people, a collection of small nomadic bands scattered across space, with no homeworld of our own. They gave genetic enhancements and anachronistic technology to one such band, which called itself the Cabal. Starting in 2144 and for a decade or so thereafter, the Cabal struck at various targets, mostly the Tandaran worlds, but also the Klingons, the Paraagans, the Tholians, and Jonathan Archer's *Starship Enterprise*. To this day, we have no idea what ultimate purpose their attacks were meant to serve." Shelan gave a heavy sigh. "Even though most of my people were uninvolved, they were blamed for the Cabal's attacks. The Tandarans imprisoned and persecuted us for decades, even after the Cabal's backers abandoned them. We learned to retreat more and more from galactic affairs, to keep to ourselves."

Shelan met the recruits' eyes one by one. "And after two hundred years, I think enough is enough. I didn't believe the Federation would still blame us for the actions of one group of our ancestors. So, over my family's protests, I came to Earth to become part of the Federation, to show my people and the rest of the galaxy that the Suliban don't have to be cut off anymore. That we can make a difference."

Garcia studied her. "And you ended up joining the DTI. The agency responsible for fighting things like the Cabal."

Shelan smiled back. "Exactly. I'll tell you something I don't like to advertise. I had an ancestor in the Cabal. Some vestiges of their Augment genes remain in me. I don't have their special powers—I can't alter my appearance or flatten my body and squeeze through a crack—but it's given me improved senses, good health, considerable flexibility and agility." She smirked. "Gifts from the Cabal's sponsors, which I hope I will someday get to use to bring them down."

Teyak frowned. "But . . . they won't exist until nearly four centuries in the future."

Shelan's bright, friendly eyes suddenly grew intense. "I'll outlast them if I have to," she said, and as Garcia looked into those eyes, she somehow had no doubt that the youthful agent could pull it off.

Still, knowing that so many other factions centuries out of the Department's reach were pursuing agendas that could erase reality as they knew it was disheartening to the trainees. True, there were other, more advanced groups upholding the Temporal Accords, such as the TIC, the Temporal Agents, and the mysterious, ancient organization known as the Aegis which had been safeguarding history for thousands of years. "But it's a vast galaxy," Shelan explained, "and even the Accordist factions can't police against every temporal intervention." Her vivid gaze took in the recruits. "That's why we're needed."

Julian Days 2590834 to 2590838

The next day, Federation President Nanietta Bacco held a press conference announcing that the Romulan Star Empire (the half of it that remained after the secession of the Imperial Romulan State) had joined with the Breen,

Tholian, Gorn, Tzenkethi, and Kinshaya civilizations in a new alliance called the Typhon Pact, creating in one fell swoop an astropolitical entity rivaling the size and power of the Federation and more or less surrounding it on three sides. The whole Federation was soon abuzz with speculation and concern; while the Pact's first action had been to *stop* Kinshaya aggression against the Klingons and its second had been to formally apologize for said aggression, the fact was that many of its members had a history of enmity toward the Federation. Among the DTI trainees, the speculations took on an added dimension. Had the Department known this was going to happen? If so, was it something they should have tried to prevent? Their instructors were quick to quash such speculations, reminding them that the Department's highest priority was to minimize any meddling in the natural flow of probability.

Indeed, as T'Viss's ongoing lectures spelled out, knowing *one* possible future wasn't the same as knowing *the* future. The Everett equations that had been the basis of quantum physics for centuries made it clear that time-lines diverged from each other spontaneously all the time, producing myriad parallel histories that could coexist indefinitely. It was only those histories created by time travel that could recombine with the branches they'd sprung from—and not always then. When a traveler went back in time and generated an alternative history, it remained quantum-entangled with the "original" history, retaining some of its state information so that the two timelines never went completely out of phase. "If the exchange of matter or information is only one-way," Felbog explained to Garcia, Teyak, and Borah that Saturday as they studied together in the gorgeous, mural-roofed Painted Hall on the university grounds, "then the entanglement is as well. The 'new' timeline"—it was hard even for him to avoid the misleading terminology, though Garcia could hear the quotes around it—"has a phase resonance with the 'old' one, so that some of its events might be influenced to occur in similar ways—the same people being born, meeting each other, and so forth. But other than that, it endures as a separate history."

"But if the exchange is two-way," Teyak replied, "then they are mutually in phase resonance and are drawn toward each other."

"Exactly," Felbog said. "And when the altered timeline catches up with the moment entangled with it in the original timeline—the moment when the time travel occurs—then the timelines come into synch and it's like opening a floodgate. The resonance draws them together, and the particles of one timeline quantum-tunnel to their positions in the other. The two timelines become one, and the original history is forgotten."

"Which is why Kirk and Picard saw the timeline change around them at the moment the time travel occurred," Borah concluded.

Garcia envied the others' ease with the physics. All of their species had an edge over her—Vulcans had their keenly trained intellects, Choblik their cybernetic enhancements, Seleneans their highly analytical five-lobed brains. All she had to keep her going was the *need* to understand time, the need to make sense of what her life had become. However much of a struggle it was, the physics was comfortingly abstract compared to the philosophical side of things.

"So if I did get thrown back in time and changed things," she asked, "my old history would be okay as long as I just stayed there, didn't try to go back?"

"*If* you could be certain the temporal passage was strictly one-way," Teyak replied sternly. "A black hole, for example. If any information flows the other way, that creates the mutual entanglement and the risk of terminating your home timeline, even if you do not go back." Garcia didn't appreciate his condescending tone. Teyak took it as a given that Vulcans made better DTI agents than humans, and he treated Garcia more as a rival than a partner.

Felbog swished his tail nervously at the tension, working the cybernetic digits attached to its end. "Besides," he added in a more friendly tone, "you can't be sure someone else won't make a round trip to try to retrieve you. There was a starship called *Defiant* where that happened, back on Stardate 48481—the crew saw the timeline change around them, so they went back after their displaced crewmates to try to retrieve them, and they made several round trips while searching."

Garcia's eyes widened. "So it was their search *after* the change that *caused* the change in the first place?"

Felbog nodded. "Or the last place, I suppose," he replied, taking too much pleasure in his own joke. "I guess that's why fixing temporal disruptions should be left to trained professionals."

Borah's cabochon eyes were always wide, but the way she shook her gold-tendriled head made it clear she was struggling with the causality of it. "But they couldn't have known. The change already happened before they made the decision to go back, so from their perspective, they couldn't have made any other choice. That means the change caused itself. A predestination paradox."

"Not a paradox, Borah. It's entirely self-consistent physically. It's only our expectations about causality that it contradicts."

Borah clutched her head in her hands. Garcia could sympathize. She took a moment to gaze up at the ceiling of the Painted Hall, losing herself in the lush golds, reds, and sky blues of Sir James Thornhill's elaborate mural. Finally her own headache subsided enough for her to ask, "So why is it always the altered timeline that wins out? What gives it the edge?"

"Entropy again," Felbog said. "When you come back from a future point in history, you inject a higher level of entropy into that past moment. So the timeline you create has slightly higher entropy than the original. It's water flowing downhill—a system always tends toward the highest-entropy state."

"Even when you've got negative entropy acting to merge the timelines?"

"That acts from outside the multiverse. Within the space-time shared by the two histories, higher entropy still wins."

Garcia shook her head. "And all this was just figured out in the past few years?"

"Well, the ideas have been around for a long time, but it's been unknown which model was correct. The recent work of Manheim, Naadri, and others has really cleared up a lot of uncertainty."

She whistled. "So for a century, the DTI's been operating on the assumption that time travel could erase this timeline, just in case, but they didn't really know. And now it turns out they were right all along."

"That's right," Felbog replied with his usual good cheer.

"And you don't find that a little scary?"

Felbog curved his neck into a Choblik shrug. "I'm an herbivore. Lots of things in life are scary. But we get the chance to do something about this one. Knowing the risk is real just reassures me that I'm in the right place."

Garcia smiled and clasped his bionic hand. "We both are, pal."

Julian Days 2590841 to 2590849

The existential realities of the job understandably took their toll on most of the trainees. Felbog treated it all as an entertaining intellectual exercise, of course. But Garcia had nightmares in which her reality changed around her and no one would believe it when she told them—or in which she herself was erased from reality, reduced to a negative probability ghost staring in at time from the outside, seeing it all as a frozen whole in which she had never existed and could not participate. Teyak admitted nothing, certainly not to Garcia, but he began to look increasingly haggard and haunted. Borah was more open about her anxieties, and Garcia wondered if she spoke for her Vulcan classmate as well. "I've been conditioned—no, *bred*—to think analytically," the gilt-complexioned Selenean said, her gemstone eyes showing nothing of the distress in her voice. "To assess the facts and calculate the single best option in any situation. But this is a fiction! No matter the situation, there are multiple outcomes. How can I judge one choice superior to another when I cannot anticipate a single specific outcome?"

"There is only one solution per measurement history," Teyak droned, seeming to take comfort in the litany. "Other histories are unobservable and thus not relevant."

"But we know that's not true!" Borah countered. "Nonlinear quantum processes allow information exchange between timelines. Other histories *are* knowable, even reachable, and thus are functionally real. With such a multiplicity of histories, how can any decision be meaningful?"

Borah grew increasingly paralyzed by her inability to make clear decisions, and the growing anxiety of the formerly unflappable Selenean put strain on the whole group. But the training process was designed to deal with the psychological stresses. They were guided through the process by Ranjea, a Deltan special agent that Garcia instantly fell in lust with. She tried to remind herself that Deltans had that effect on most humanoids thanks to their potent pheromones, but it was no use convincing her own hormones of that. Ranjea was gorgeous, tall and bronze-skinned with deep, soulful eyes and an elegantly shaped hairless cranium. It was hard to imagine an agent more different from the craggy-faced, avuncular Dulmur or the sour, aloof Lucsly. Ranjea projected the kind of secret-agent glamour that those two aggressively deconstructed.

"I know how hard it is to deal with this knowledge," Ranjea told the trainees in a warm, lilting baritone. "My own former partner ultimately had to resign because of it, despite my best efforts to help him through it. But there are ways of learning to cope. Techniques for meditation, new perspectives on the nature of choice and outcomes. I will guide you through these." Garcia hung on Ranjea's every word, though she had to remind herself to focus on what he was saying rather than just the mellow suppleness of his voice.

At first, she'd been surprised to see a Deltan DTI agent, given what she'd been told about the pitfalls of excess emotionalism in this job. But listening to Ranjea drove home that the Deltan people weren't just more emotional than most, but more emotionally mature and stable. They had their own path to mastery, one based on embracing and understanding their passions rather than repressing them as the Vulcans did. Ranjea's easy serenity was one of his most alluring features. He was just comfortable to be around—though by no means relaxing.

One of the first lessons he offered was to reject the belief that a person's decisions would directly cause the creation of new universes. "This is claiming a culpability that does not exist," Ranjea explained one day in the commissary at headquarters, a modern addition to the Victorian structure, with large picture windows affording a view of the Thames and Canary Wharf. "It's actually quantum variations that create possible histories. Billions of alternate states arise every second on the level of subatomic particles, engaging in a Darwinian competition until a stable few win out, spread into the larger universe, and live on as consistent timelines. But the competition usually resolves in nanoseconds, too quickly to have any effect on our thoughts and decisions. So in all those parallel possibilities, you'd still make the same choice. Most of the alternate versions of any given moment are effectively identical and quickly merge back into the mass."

"But not always," Borah said, her manner intense. "Say you're on a cusp of a decision that could go either way, the flip of a coin. If you're still in multiple quantum states at a key moment, you might decide differently in one."

"Yes," Ranjea said. "But if the decision has a minor enough impact on the universe, that branch will be out-competed, overwhelmed by the other streams that share a single redundant outcome. It will simply be a brief, quasi-stable fluctuation in the flow of time, quickly forgotten.

"So you needn't worry about every tiny decision, Borah. Most of those potential realities you're concerned about creating will never matter in this or any other time-line."

Garcia jumped on that. "But parallel timelines can last for centuries, not just vanish back into the foam."

Felbog chuckled. "Don't let T'Viss hear you call them that. Mathematically speaking, they're actually perpen-dicular."

Ranjea nodded. "True. Sometimes, an alternate prob-ability branch becomes stable enough to become a persis-tent reality of its own. But only if the variations are major enough." He gestured at the pastry Garcia was nibbling on. "You don't create a whole new reality just by, say, choosing an apple danish instead of strawberry. That varia-tion just gets lost in the flow. It's mostly the critical nexus points, the events where a specific change at a key moment can cause major, long-term consequences, that generate lasting alternate timelines. So it's not something you need to worry about when you're making ordinary, everyday decisions."

"How can you know what decisions are ordinary?" Borah challenged. "Say you crowd someone out of a lift instead of waiting for the next one. As a result, they fail to meet their future spouse, their children are never conceived, and an individual responsible for saving a planet is never born! There's no way to know which decision might be a critical nexus!"

Ranjea placed his hand atop hers, filling Garcia with envy and making her wonder if she should fake a panic attack of her own. "And that, Borah, is precisely why you are absolved of culpability for the decision. All that matters is what you choose based on what you *do* know."

"The man is right," came a new voice. Garcia looked up to see Agent Dulmur, who'd just strolled over from the replicators with a mug of coffee in his hand. He smiled at Garcia, and she returned it. Dulmur had sponsored her admission and took something of a paternal interest in her training, which she appreciated, having lacked a father figure for most of her life.

Dulmur turned a chair backward and sat on it, looking around at the trainees. "This is the bottom line. There's all sorts of psychological stuff Ranjea can teach you to help you cope with the heebie-jeebies and the nightmares. And that's valuable, if it works for you. I don't want to say a word against it," he said, trading a nod with Ranjea. "But lemme tell you the most important lesson I've learned in this job: Don't worry about the big cosmic stuff. Just don't worry about it. Focus on the job in front of you. Focus on what you can do in the here and now, and get it done. The bigger ramifications, the cosmic meaning of it all, that's for philosophers and physicists. We're cops. Our job isn't to think about it, it's to do something about it.

"Now, if meditation and Deltan philosophy helps you get past all this, that's great, I'm all for it. But once you get out there in the field, you don't need to worry about any of this stuff. We teach it because you need to know the nuts and bolts of the time machines and cosmic warps and whatnot that you run into out there, and so you'll know the right way to deal with a tricky situation, instead of just stumbling through it the way those Starfleet losers keep doing." Garcia chuckled.

"But it's just tools for the job. It's not something that should keep you up at nights wondering about the meaning of it all. I'll tell you what the meaning of it all is, boys and girls." Dulmur reached into his pocket and took out a holo of a chubby-faced, white-haired woman whose pale eyes and bulbous nose resembled his own. "This is my mother. This woman is a saint. End of story. And the concept of a reality without her in it is simply unacceptable to me. So I'll do whatever it takes to keep her around." He looked at each of the trainees in turn. "If the weirdness ever starts to get too much for you, to get in the way of doing your job, you just keep a picture like this in your pocket. A picture of someone whose existence in this universe gives it meaning to you. And you take it out and look at it and remember why it is you do this job." He studied the holo, smiling gently. "I tell ya, it really puts the big cosmic stuff in perspective."

At that point, Ranjea's comlink went off and he listened for a moment. "I'm sorry, I'm needed elsewhere. Thank you all, it's been a good session. And thank you, Marion." Dulmur winced.

Garcia lost herself in watching Ranjea walk away, and then was somewhere else for a few moments before a tap on the shoulder brought her back to reality. She and Dulmur were now alone at the table, and the special agent was grinning at her. "I know what you're thinking, kid. You know it'd ruin you for life, right?"

She winced. "I know, I know." Everyone knew the stories: Deltan sex was so intense that it was instantly, incurably addictive for a human. And that was the least exaggerated version. "Still, you have to wonder what it's like. It might be worth it."

Dulmur rolled his eyes. "Oh, boy. Well, I wouldn't know. Luckily he's not my type."

Garcia couldn't resist ribbing him back. "Well, I've heard some rumors about you and Lucsly. You two are kind of inseparable."

Dulmur glared, but took it in good humor. "Really, that's the best rumor you've heard about Lucsly so far? The grapevine is slipping."

"Oh, I've heard a bunch," Garcia said. "Let's see, that he's secretly a Vulcan . . ."

"Too obvious."

"Or that he's actually Abraham Lincoln, rescued from the Ford's Theatre and given a new identity."

"Lucsly hates theater."

"Or that he's a highly advanced hologram from the future, so perfect he even fools medical exams."

"No way. Holograms are far more three-dimensional."

Garcia laughed. "Ohh, you're awful! Whatever happened to partners sticking together?"

"Hey, Lucsly can take care of himself. He doesn't care how much ribbing he gets, as long as he gets the job done." Dulmur grew serious. "It's a great quality for a DTI agent, that kind of thick skin. A lot of people don't appreciate the kind of scrutiny we have to put them under. It's important to be okay with not being liked." He caught himself. "Not that we don't like Lucsly around here. Any ribbing, it's all in good fun. Everyone respects the hell out of him. This agency would fall apart without him."

"But he's not exactly easy to get close to, is he? What's your secret?"

Dulmur shrugged. "I figure it out, you'll be the first to know, kiddo."

Dulmur stood and glanced at his mother's holo one more time before pocketing it. "So that's your reason for doing this thankless job," Garcia said, nodding at the holo. "So why does Lucsly do it?"

Dulmur mulled it over for a minute, then looked at her and said, in all seriousness, "Because he's Lucsly."

DOWNTIME
STARDATE 42692.8 TO 42704.5

IV

Lucsly Residence
San Francisco
14:54 UTC

As usual, Gariff Lucsly awoke several minutes before his alarm went off, remaining in bed to ease himself into wakefulness, then rising as the alarm sounded at precisely 7 AM local time. He completed his morning ablutions at 7:15, was dressed by 7:18, and ordered his usual Saturday breakfast (two whole grain waffles topped with mixed fruit and plain yogurt, three sausage links, and 360 milliliters of orange juice) from the replicator. At 7:20, he commenced eating while listening to the morning news bulletin from FNS and checking his DTI padd for status updates. The empty dishes went back in the replicator at 7:35.

He was on call today, scheduled to report to the branch office at 9 AM. He preferred to walk, weather permitting; a field agent needed to stay in shape. The weather forecast today was for clear, hot weather, but the expected temperature at 9 AM was only 22 Celsius. Adjusting for likely pedestrian density at that time and in that weather, Lucsly would need to depart at 8:40 to arrive in a timely manner.

He was current on his paperwork, so that left him approximately one hour to devote to the antique Vulcan chronometer that was his latest project. It was a replica of a timepiece dating from circa eleven hundred standard years (fifteen hundred Vulcan years) before Surak, yet was remarkably intricate in its clockwork representations of the cycles of the Vulcan calendar. The intricacies and idiosyncrasies of Vulcan timekeeping had initially frustrated Lucsly. Though the planet's orbital radius of 0.56 AU around 40 Eridani A gave it a period of 177.6 standard days, Vulcans had long defined their "year," or *r'tas,* as exactly 1.5 times that, or 266.4 standard days (252 Vulcan rotations or *t'ved*), corresponding to the period of an orbital resonance between Vulcan and its sister world T'Khut. Vulcan's low axial tilt gave it little in the way of solar seasons, but the resonance with T'Khut had a significant effect on the tides of Vulcan's sparse seas, which in turn had an effect on the growing cycle in the arable lands proximate to those seas. Thus, both ancient and modern Vulcans had seen that cycle as a more useful basis for their calendar than the orbital period. Though Lucsly could see the logic of it, the idea of a calendrical cycle so diametrically out of synch with a planet's orbital cycle, its solstices and equinoxes, had always raised his hackles. That was why he had sought the challenge of reconstructing this intricate, ancient mechanical timepiece. Seeing the Vulcan chronological cycles distilled to the pure mathematical essence of interlocking gears, wheels, and levers, learning how to assemble those gears and re-create the cycles with his own hands, had given Lucsly a new appreciation for their unique symmetries. It reassured him that, even in the seeming chaos of nature, there were always comforting regularities to be found.

However, such regularities could be elusive. At 7:51,

only fourteen minutes into his session with the Vulcan chronometer, his padd signaled him with a text message ordering him to report to the branch office as soon as possible. The code was for a potential emergency situation. Lucsly sighed, affording precious seconds for a lingering caress of the delicate gears he had hoped to remain engrossed in for another forty-six minutes. But he quickly set that aside, donned his jacket, picked up his padd, and signaled the office's transporter station, requesting immediate beamover.

It took forty-two seconds before he felt the tingling begin. Lucsly made a note to chastise the transporter operator for such inefficiency. But five seconds later, at 7:52:53, Gariff Lucsly's apartment was empty.

DTI Branch Office
San Francisco
16:14 UTC
Junior Agent Dulmur grinned as he rushed toward Assistant Director Andos's office in response to her summons. His first case at last! It had taken long enough; he'd needed to deal with relocating, getting himself and Megumi settled in a new place on Earth, and going through all the Department's background checks and psychological evaluations before he'd even gotten to begin the three months of training. And in the weeks since then, he'd been assigned mostly to cleaning up the lingering paperwork on old cases, since new temporal events didn't crop up on a daily basis.

Now, finally, he had a chance to get some action and prove himself, and he was excited at the prospect. Until he entered Andos's office and saw who else was there already. "You're late," Special Agent Lucsly told him.

"Sorry," Dulmur replied, a bit breathless. "I had to—"

"Explaining will just waste more time."

Dulmur glared for a moment, then turned to the assistant director, craning his neck up to meet her eyes. Laarin Andos was a full-grown Rhaandarite, with about one centimeter of height for each of her two hundred forty-four years. Though somewhat androgynous to human eyes, she was marked as female by the silver-black spot on her high, bulging forehead, resembling an Indian *bindi* mark. "You wanted to see me, ma'am?" Dulmur asked.

"Yes," Andos replied in a deep alto voice. "I'm assigning you and Agent Lucsly to investigate a serious incident at the Warlock Station facility. Are you familiar with it?"

Lucsly? That sourpuss? Dulmur had been hoping for a partner with an actual sense of humor. But his superior had asked him a direct question, so he set that aside for now. "Yes, ma'am. The monitoring facility for the Type 3 singularity in Sector 006." The so-called "Black Star" of Sector 006 was infamous as the known or suspected source of multiple spacetime displacement events over the past few centuries. In the early twenty-first century, it had passed close enough to Sol system to swallow up the Voyager 6 space probe, which had come back much later as the V'Ger entity that almost destroyed the Earth. In 2267 it had sent James Kirk's infamous *Enterprise* on its first major journey through time, to the Earth of 1969. Not quite a conventional black hole, the singularity generated chroniton and other exotic particle fields that helped cushion the stress-energy effects of passage through its Cauchy horizon, increasing the likelihood of surviving a spacetime displacement even without warp drive and shielding. Its current location and trajectory placed it near

the major space lanes connecting Andor to Sol and Alpha
Centauri, and though "near" in interstellar terms was
generally nothing to worry about, the Black Star's exotic
properties and past history made it an unpredictable hazard. It was thus orbited by Warlock Station, a monitor-
ing/research facility jointly administered by Starfleet and
the DTI.

"Earlier today," Andos explained, "on Stardate
42691.62, the personnel of Warlock Station detected a
chroniton surge at a position approximately thirty-two
degrees ahead of them in their orbit."

"Where they would be in six-point-seven hours," Lucsly added. Dulmur rolled his eyes; the man was a walking
cuckoo clock.

"Upon investigating," Andos went on, "they discovered something disturbing: the wreckage of a station identical to their own, but slightly out of dimensional phase.
Scans revealed humanoid remains that matched the DNA
of the station's own personnel. It was a vision of their own
death, less than seven hours in their future.

"The station's crew remained to analyze the findings as long as they could, but as the critical moment
approached, the station's commander, Rif jav Balkar,
ordered an evacuation as a precaution. Balkar himself remained behind until the last possible moment, then left in
the final shuttlepod."

Andos closed her eyes. "At the critical moment, the
station continued through its orbit unharmed. But an
energy vortex materialized at the location of Commander
Balkar's shuttlepod and engulfed it. The vortex soon dis-
sipated, and the debris of the wrecked station vanished.
In its place, at the location where Balkar's pod had been

destroyed, they found particulate debris consistent with the explosion of just such a shuttlepod—if it had occurred nearly seven hours before the vortex engulfed Balkar."

"Wow." Dulmur tried to make sense of it, drawing on the physics lectures that were still fresh in his head. "So the wrecked station represented an alternative timeline that was averted . . . so the twinned timelines converged and the particles of the alternate station quantum-tunneled to merge with the originals?"

"Not exactly," Lucsly said. "You see   "

"But close enough," Andos said.

"Pardon me, ma'am, but is there really much to investigate?" Dulmur asked. "It's a shame what happened to Balkar and all, but we know the Black Star has all sorts of weird temporal effects going on around it."

"That was the first assumption of the station staff," Lucsly told him. "But that's because they didn't know about a very similar incident aboard a Starfleet vessel near the Endicor system on Stardate 42679.2." The agent watched Dulmur expectantly.

"Uhh, four and . . . a half days earlier," the junior agent interpreted.

Lucsly didn't look satisfied with the answer, but continued nonetheless. "The U.S.S. Enterprise encountered a duplicate of one of its own shuttlepods, carrying a duplicate of its captain, Jean-Luc Picard. Its log showed the destruction of the Enterprise approximately six-point-seven hours after the shuttle's detection. As that time neared, the ship was nearly engulfed in an identical energy vortex, and Captain Picard—both of him—was struck by some kind of energy discharge that effortlessly penetrated the shields and hull. The uptime copy of Picard, though his mental processes were phase-disrupted by the event, felt a compulsion to leave the ship in a shuttlepod and repeat the cycle. Instead, the downtime Picard prevented his departure and tried the opposite of his strategy, aiming the ship down the throat of the vortex rather than fighting its pull. The ship came out unscathed and the alternate Picard and shuttlepod underwent quantum convergence."

"You mean they disappeared," Dulmur said.

"I mean what I said. 'Disappeared' isn't a useful description."

Dulmur checked his padd. "Endicor . . . that's nowhere near Sector 006. So you don't think it's connected to the Black Star."

"At this point, we don't know the origin of these anomalies," Andos said. "Nor can we rule out further incidents. The *Enterprise* is too far away for us to interview its personnel directly, but our nearest branch office has debriefed their command staff via subspace. You and Lucsly will do the same in person at Warlock Station. Hopefully between you, you'll be able to find some common thread to help us predict and block these vortices."

Dulmur's excitement was returning. His first case was shaping up to be a big one. But the selection of his partner put a damper on his enthusiasm. When Andos dismissed them, Lucsly left promptly, but Dulmur lingered behind. "Why Lucsly, ma'am?"

"Excuse me?"

"The guy hasn't approved of a single thing I've said or done since we met. If I'm being evaluated for my performance here, I'm not sure you're giving me a fair chance."

Andos contemplated him. "Special Agent Lucsly's approach to interpersonal interaction is atypical for your species, which can lead to misunderstandings." He tried not to take Andos's words as condescension. It was a neurological fact that Rhaandarites' brains had more highly developed areas for processing social and emotional dynamics, so that the interpersonal problems that stymied humans seemed elementary and simple to a Rhaandarite. "For your benefit, I'll clarify that the fact that he agreed to partner with you at all is an indication that he's willing to give you a fair chance. To put it in human terms, Lucsly is not easy to get to know. But he prides himself on his precision, and would never willingly distort the facts. You will be assessed solely on your performance, nothing else."

"Okay, but . . . why pair me with him? I was hoping to work with Agent Sonaj."

"I felt you would benefit more from association with Lucsly. He is our most successful human agent, and thus might be better suited to guide you than a Vulcan would be."

"Species profiling? Is that what this is about?"

Andos's gaze softened fractionally. "Of course we always strive to be fair, but when different species genuinely do have different skills and psychologies, it would be unfair to deny it. There are few Vulcan comedians. Few two-armed humanoids can play a Terellian keyboard. And there are few successful human DTI agents. I don't say that to offend or exclude you, Agent Dulmur. I have every wish for your success. Which is why I'm giving you every possible advantage. Lucsly is not just our finest human agent, but one of our finest agents overall. I ask you to give him the same fair chance he will give you."

Dulmur sighed. "Yes, ma'am." *Just don't expect me to have any fun with it.*

Shuttlecraft *Deutsch*
Traversing Sector 006
21:16 UTC

"I've been thinking," Dulmur said. He paused to give Lucsly a chance to respond, but got only silence, as usual. Barely three hours into the trip, it was already one of the most boring journeys he'd ever been on. With an inward shrug, he continued. "Both vortex events involved a time loop. Like what happened in the Manheim Event." Again, Lucsly just looked at him, waiting for him to continue. "And one of them happened to the *Enterprise*. That was the same ship that was at the heart of the Manheim Event, the one that closed the rift inside Vandor IV."

"Mm-hm," Lucsly granted.

Progress! "So do you think these vortices could be connected to Manheim's work at Vandor?"

"We checked that already," Lucsly told him. "Manheim isn't running any active experiments, and the rift is still closed."

"Still, there's gotta be a connection."

"There have been temporal causality loops before," Lucsly said. "The Tholian incident of late November 2152. The Tigellan chronic hysteresis of Stardate 8009. The *Kyushu* incident of Stardate 40402."

"Don't you think it's too great a coincidence? The *Enterprise* involved in two time loops less than eight months apart?"

Lucsly frowned. "There's a hypothesis that being involved in a temporal displacement alters an individual's quantum probability matrix in a way that increases the probability of their involvement in subsequent temporal events."

Dulmur stared. "So go through time once and that attracts other temporal anomalies to you?"

The older agent shrugged. "It would explain a lot about James Kirk's career. Now another *Enterprise* may be following suit."

Dulmur shook his head. "No, I still say there's a connection. I read Picard's log of the vortex event—his Betazoid counselor sensed a kind of consciousness inside the vortex. Manheim also said he sensed some kind of extra-dimensional consciousness after the accident on Vandor."

"A vague impression from a man whose mental state was highly unreliable."

"I'm telling you, Lucsly, my gut tells me it all adds up to something!"

Lucsly's eyes fixed on him. "You need to understand something. Everything we deal with is counterintuitive. So don't trust your intuition. Focus on the facts."

Dulmur sighed. "I just gave you a bunch of facts!"

"Selected to fit your 'gut' feeling. They don't add up to anything yet. Wait until we have more information."

Dulmur gave up and seethed to himself for a while.

But half an hour or so later, once he'd calmed down, he realized that Lucsly had said "yet." As in, his evidence might add up to something later. It wasn't a glowing endorsement, but it was the biggest concession he'd gotten from Lucsly yet.

And it annoyed him that he felt so proud of that.

Warlock Station
19 et'Khior, YS 9051 (A Sunday)
19:59 UTC
Warlock Station had only suffered one casualty in the incident, but the staff was devastated by the loss. Rif jav

Balkar had been not only the head of the facility and a highly decorated Starfleet science officer, but practically an adoptive grandfather to the entire staff—save for Doctor Sagar bav Balkar, his chief subspace physicist and his wife, who was particularly devastated by the loss. Though Commander Balkar had argued as readily as any Tellarite, so the staff related, he had always done it with good humor and redoubtable wit. Being the butt of his latest clever insult had been a mark of pride to the staff. But Doctor Balkar was so broken up by her husband's loss that she couldn't even bring herself to say an unkind word about him.

Despite having some of the most advanced temporal monitoring equipment in the Federation, the station staffers could provide little more insight into the nature of the vortex phenomenon than the *Enterprise* had. They confirmed that it was extradimensional in origin, but that very fact made it difficult to analyze in terms of this dimension's physical laws. Beyond the appearance of time-looped debris or, in the *Enterprise*'s case, survivors, there was no prior indication of an imminent vortex event. And no one at Warlock could offer any theories for why the vortex had selected its targets. Picard's logs had suggested that the entity inside the vortex had fixated on him as the "brain" of the starship, and the targeting of Commander Balkar supported that. But there was no way of knowing who else the vortices might target. Some of the staffers were attempting to devise a detection strategy based on the conjecture that proximity to temporal anomalies might be the common factor.

Still, Dulmur wasn't convinced they were on the right track. Unfortunately, he had to question the grieving widow to pursue his hunch. "I'm very sorry to disturb you at a time like this, Doctor Balkar," he said as gently as he could. "But could you tell me if your husband was familiar with Doctor Paul Manheim?" He caught Lucsly staring at him, but declined to acknowledge it.

"Manheim?" the widow echoed after a moment.

"Of course," put in the station's second-in-command (now head), Lieutenant Commander Mara Kadray, a Cygnian woman with catlike green eyes and violet skin and hair. "Everyone knows that name after what happened last year."

"But did Commander Balkar know him before that?" Dulmur asked. "Did he ever visit Manheim's research facility in the Vandor system?"

"No," Doctor Balkar said after a moment. "No, we never met Doctor Manheim. We were distantly aware of his work. It sparked some minor controversy back . . . maybe fifteen, twenty years ago? But Rif afforded it little notice. It was hardly worth arguing with." She looked away. "Or so we thought at the time. Last year's events have forced a reassessment."

"Does this have anything to do with the vortex event?" Kadray asked impatiently, placing a protective hand on the widow's shoulder.

Lucsly gave Dulmur a look. *Satisfied?*

Dulmur sighed. "Just trying to clarify something, ma'am." He had to concede that the Manheim connection looked like a dead end.

But somehow he couldn't quite let go of the idea.

20 et'Khior, YS 9051 (A Monday)
07:06 UTC

"We have a defense," Mara Kadray told Lucsly the next morning. "At least it works in simulation. Comparing our

scans and the *Enterprise*'s scans of the vortex phenomenon, we've confirmed that it has the properties of a fairly
straightforward Tipler spacetime. The intense gravimetric
distortion creates a frame-dragging effect that produces
closed timelike geodesics."

Lucsly nodded. "I understand." It was elementary
temporal physics, dating back 391 years. Gravity warped
spacetime, and if it dragged the axes in the right direction,
then one of the spatial axes of the warped region could
align with the temporal axis of the broader universe, so that
movement back and forth through the space of the warp
would translate to movement back and forth through time.

"So it should be simple enough," Kadray went on,
"to generate an unpolarized chroniton field around the
area where a vortex will appear, then induce a polariza-
tion opposing that of the vortex as it begins to form. It
should cancel out the vortex and prevent its formation."
That made sense. Chronitons were exotic particles with
extreme mass and spin, akin to quantum black holes, and
they generated a microscopic frame-dragging effect of
their own. A polarized field of chronitons, all spinning in
alignment, could potentially generate a spacetime warp if
certain other conditions were met. So it followed that they
could cancel out an equivalent warp.

"Excellent," Lucsly said. "But it sounds like you'd
have to have it in place before the vortex formed."

"That's right."

"Can it be set up in less than six-point-seven hours?"

"Not from scratch. It requires specialized equipment
and expertise to operate. Chronitons are tricky to work
with. We'd have to construct the apparatus here and get it
to the site before the vortex formed."

"So we still need a way to predict where the next vortex will strike. Any luck there?"

"No," Kadray confessed. "We've alerted all the monitoring posts around known temporal anomalies, but there's no way of knowing which of them might be the next target. With only two data points, there are too many possible subspace simultaneity relations to narrow down a timeframe or propagation rate."

"Then maybe you're all looking in the wrong place," came a new voice. Lucsly turned to see Dulmur in the doorway. The junior agent's hair and suit looked rumpled, as though he'd been up all night and hadn't bothered to make himself presentable. Lucsly made a mental note to put a demerit in his evaluation.

"You're only focusing on the physics," Dulmur said. "But the *Enterprise* logs say there's a consciousness at work here. Something or someone targeted Jean-Luc Picard and Rif jav Balkar. So what's the common thread between the two of them?"

"They were the commanders of their respective facilities," Kadray said. "It targeted them as the 'brains' of the entities it attacked."

"That's what the alternate Picard said," the junior agent countered. "But we only have his word for that, and he wasn't exactly thinking straight. What if he guessed wrong? What if he and Balkar were the intended targets?"

"Why would an extradimensional entity target those two people?"

"Maybe because it had contact with someone in *this* dimension who had a grudge against them." He held up his padd. "I've been doing a little more digging into the logs of the Manheim Event."

Lucsly sighed. "Not this again." On some level, he respected Dulmur's bulldog tenacity. But the novice agent needed to learn how to focus it properly.

"Not quite. I was looking for a connection to the experiment on Vandor IV. But I should've been looking at the people. Listen." He worked his padd. "Captain Picard's interview with Manheim's wife Jenice. Starting two minutes in."

He hit the playback, and a female voice emerged. *"Jean-Luc, he would never knowingly do anything to hurt anyone."*

Then Picard's voice, familiar to Lucsly from his captain's logs pertaining to the Manheim event. *"Yes, I believe that."*

"But as he saw his goal getting closer, seeming possible, he became more and more obsessive. Maybe that clouded his judgment." A pause of approximately seven seconds, the sound of a person rising from a seat. *"This is not how I imagined seeing you again."*

"Nor I you."

"You've done well. A great starship in the far reaches of the galaxy. It's everything you'd hoped."

A diffident laugh, very atypical for Picard. *"Not exactly. Nothing works just as you hope."*

Dulmur shut off the playback. "You hear that? Picard wasn't just the captain of the ship that answered the distress call. He was Jenice Manheim's old flame! I did some digging—it seems they were pretty serious for a while, back in forty-two. What do you want to bet Manheim saw him as a rival?"

Lucsly stared. "You're saying he sent the vortex to kill Picard?"

"Not consciously. The *Enterprise* counselor said the thing in the vortex seemed to be acting on instinct. Maybe whatever extradimensional life force Manheim contacted during the accident picked up on his subconscious resentments. And now it's instinctively striking out at the people Manheim had a grudge against."

"But Commander Balkar never even met Manheim!" Kadray protested.

"You don't have to meet someone to be a professional rival." Dulmur worked his padd again and showed them a new file. "Look here. 'Unitarity Violations in a Nonlinear Spacetime and the Consequences for Alternative Gauge Symmetries.' Seventeen years ago, Balkar wrote this paper debunking Manheim's views on nonlinear time. It's a pretty harsh critique."

Kadray skimmed the paper. "Harsh? More like devastating. Ouch! I'm surprised I don't remember this paper."

"The guy wrote hundreds of papers," Dulmur said. "To him, Manheim was probably just one more upstart theorist to get his kicks arguing with. But Manheim was a fringe theorist with little respectability and Balkar was already one of the authorities in the field. After this paper, Manheim couldn't get grants for his research. He was practically laughed out of academia. It was a year later that he packed up and vanished for parts unknown. Manheim may have been insecure about Picard and his wife, but he must've positively hated Balkar."

"So does this help us?" Lucsly asked.

"Hell, yes! We need to talk to Manheim, find out everyone he has a grudge against, and get them under protection right away."

"But if you're wrong," Lucsly said, "we could be wasting our effort in the wrong places."

"I don't think I'm wrong. There was a co-author on that paper, a Doctor Yvette Michael. She was on a transport ship that disappeared in the Anchar Sector nine days ago. There was no distress call registered, no wreckage found, no way of pinpointing exactly where or how it happened. Just another ship swallowed up by the vastness of space. So nobody had any reason to connect it to the vortices."

Kadray had moved to her console. "We now know the subspace signature of the vortex events. The *U.S.S. Aquaria* was in the adjacent sector at the time . . . I'm requesting their sensor logs from the date in question." Since it was more than a week ago, the science vessel's logs would have been transmitted to Starfleet Command's mainframe by now, making them accessible to any Starfleet facility.

In minutes, Kadray had her answer. "There. A surge of chronitons and verterons consistent with the vortex signature, during the time window of the transport's disappearance. Agent Dulmur, I think we've just verified your prediction."

"Good work," Lucsly acknowledged.

"Turns out not everything we deal with is counter-intuitive after all," Dulmur said with an irritatingly smug expression. "Because sometimes we deal with people."

That presupposes one has an intuition for people, Lucsly thought. That was one area where Dulmur had an edge on Lucsly, but then, most people did. Still, the junior agent could stand to be less cocky about it. "Now what we need to do," Lucsly said, "is talk to Paul Manheim and hope he keeps careful track of all his grudges."

08:27 UTC

On the viewscreen, Paul Manheim was clearly devastated at his inadvertent role in the deaths of seven people, including the other occupants of Yvette Michael's transport. The sight mollified Dulmur's anger at the further destructive consequences of Manheim's reckless experiments. He found himself saying, "You couldn't have known this would happen, Doctor. Whatever's doing this, it seems to be acting on instinct. There's no intention behind it, yours or anything else's."

"That is little comfort, Mister Dulmur," Manheim said. *"I came out here seeking new understanding, and all I have achieved is the magnification of my own flaws."*

"We don't have time for self-flagellation," Lucsly said. "You need to tell us if there's anyone else you have a grudge against."

Manheim shook his head. *"I'm sorry, but I wasn't even aware I had such unresolved anger toward Balkar and Michael. And with Picard, I felt—that is, I thought I felt—"*

"Doctor!"

"Again, my apologies. I'm trying to think . . . it's been so long since I left civilization. Besides my wife, most of the people I've interacted with in that time are dead. Except for yourselves and your fellow agents and researchers."

Lucsly shook his head. "None of whom you met until after your interspatial encounter. The entity wouldn't have gotten any impressions from you about them."

"Then maybe there is no one else," Manheim suggested. *"Maybe there will be no more incidents."*

Dulmur had a thought. "What about your family,

Doctor? Nobody gets under your skin quite as much as family. Any unresolved issues there?"

"Well, as I say, it's been so long. My parents are long gone, and my brother and sister . . ." He froze. *"My elder brother. He teased me relentlessly. He had all the friends, all the athletic success . . . and Mother always liked him best, no matter what she claimed!"*

Bingo, Dulmur thought. "Where's your brother living now, Doctor?"

"I really have no idea. You could discover that better than I could. His name is Alan."

Lucsly was already working the computer console. Within moments, he'd tracked the information down. "Alan Manheim, brother of Paul and Erika. Currently resides in the Kaferian capital city."

Dulmur stared. "What would happen if one of these vortices opened up on top of a city of ten million people?"

Lucsly was already out of his chair. "Let's not find out."

Tau Ceti System
1 T'lakht, YS 9051 (A Wednesday)
19:36 UTC
Contacting Alan Manheim proved harder than anticipated. His listed address was no longer valid. Apparently he had been driven into seclusion by the infamy his family had gained as a result of the Manheim Event. And the Kaferians were fervent individualists whose government, such as it existed, was fiercely dedicated to the protection of individual privacy. Even declaring an imminent emergency couldn't help the agents get the elder Manheim's address. It seemed the information might not even exist in any government databank.

As Warlock Station's runabout *Brin*, piloted by Commander Kadray, neared Kaferia, Dulmur made several fruitless efforts to track down Manheim through the planet's public computer network, finding his queries met only with suspicion and disbelief. He was about to try claiming that Manheim had won the Lissepian Lottery when he heard Lucsly say, "Uh-oh."

"Uh-oh what?" Dulmur asked. To Lucsly's left, Kadray's oversized eyes turned to focus on him.

"We're now close enough to scan the area twenty-five arcminutes ahead of Tau Ceti III in its orbit."

After a second, Dulmur nodded. "Where the planet will be in six-point-seven hours."

"Mm hm. There's already a cloud of debris there. From the spread, it's been there for at least two hours already."

"It's not ordinary asteroidal debris?" Kadray asked. It was a fair question; Tau Ceti boasted an atypically dense cometary disk, mostly in the outer reaches of the system, but enough debris drifted inward to pose a perennial hazard to navigation. The Kaferians had survived the frequent bombardments by evolving the ability to hibernate in underground burrows for long stretches, though now their world was protected by one of the quadrant's most powerful planetary defense grids. Which would be useless against a transdimensional chroniton vortex materializing near the surface.

Lucsly shook his head. "I'm picking up considerable organic debris, dead vegetation . . . mineral composition consistent with Kaferia's soil and crust . . . signs of refined metals, polymers, crystalline composites."

"Anything to indicate what part of the planet it came from?" Dulmur asked urgently, aware that they now had less than five hours to locate Manheim and set up the chroniton field at his location. The prototype device they'd brought aboard the runabout wasn't remotely powerful enough to shield the whole planet, and it would take too long to replicate its components and install them in the defense grid.

Together, Lucsly and Kadray scanned the debris field. "No unique vegetation," the Cygnian officer reported. "There are remains . . . Kaferian, human, Andorian . . . not an unusual mix here."

"Damn," Dulmur said. "Wherever Manheim's secluding himself, he's not secluded enough. I was hoping if we didn't save him, at least we wouldn't lose anyone else."

"We would anyway," Kadray told him. "The seismic and atmospheric stresses created by the vortex would be disastrous."

"So how the hell do we find where it hits?"

But Lucsly was engrossed in working the console. "Well?" Dulmur asked after a moment longer. "What are you doing?"

"Consulting the Kaferian navigational database," Lucsly replied. "They track every piece of debris in the system. I'm trying to find the exact moment the debris appeared."

Dulmur rolled his eyes. "Does it matter at a time like this?"

"More now than ever. Kaferia moves through space at thirty-two kilometers per second. It takes three hundred seventy-nine seconds to traverse its own diameter. It has a rotational period of thirty-four hours, nineteen minutes, fifty-six seconds. If I can pinpoint the exact location in space and time where the debris materialized—"

"You can figure out what part of the planet's surface will be occupying that point in space in a few hours!"

"You're starting to catch on. In this job, precision is everything." Dulmur had to concede the point.

Soon Lucsly had his answer. "Uh-oh."

Dulmur threw him a look. "I wish you'd stop saying that."

"The debris field appeared four hours, fifty-three minutes ago. We have a hundred and nine minutes to find Alan Manheim and erect the chroniton field."

"Well, have you got a location?"

"Within a few hundred kilometers' radius," Lucsly confessed. "The unknown duration of the vortex and the . . ."

"Yeah, yeah, I get it. Let's get down there and start scanning."

It took more than half the remaining time to reach Kaferia, get clearance through the defense grid, and fly to the area in question, a densely forested swath of one of the two small continents in the western hemisphere. Though mostly undeveloped, the area sported several small communities and isolated outlying residences—a good place to go into seclusion. It took several minutes more to isolate the human biosignatures and send hails to their residences. None of those who responded knew Alan Manheim, and there were five that gave no answer, all too far apart to be shielded en masse. They would have to try each one in turn.

Dulmur was rather proud of his insights on this case, but in this last stage there were no epiphanies, no clever deductions—just the legwork that made up the bulk of a detective's job. After Dulmur had struck out with the two dwellings he visited—one housing a middle-aged poet seeking solitude to find her muse and ranting at Dulmur for forcing her to start over, the other housing an athletic couple who didn't appreciate having their honeymoon interrupted at the most inconvenient moment imaginable—he got a call from Kadray on his comlink. *"Lucsly has him. Stand by for beamup."*

By the time the runabout landed on Alan Manheim's property (with Dulmur back aboard), they had barely twenty minutes to get ready. "Can't we just take him up in the ship, away from the planet?" Dulmur asked.

"If you want to get swallowed whole when the vortex follows us," Kadray said. "We need the warp reactor to power the chroniton field. We can't have both."

"We could try steering through the center of the vortex like the *Enterprise* did."

"We still don't know why that worked," Kadray said.

"Eye of the storm," Dulmur suggested.

"Maybe, but I wouldn't want to stake my life on it. And the runabout's thrusters might not have enough power to overcome the turbulence."

Lucsly arrived with a confused Alan Manheim in tow. The elder Manheim resembled his brother but was older, lankier, and bald. "I'm still waiting for someone to explain what's going on here!" he groused. "What is this 'DIT' anyway?"

"DTI, sir. We'll explain in nineteen minutes," Lucsly said, "if we're still here." He turned to Dulmur. "There are other residents in the area. We need to bring them to the runabout while Kadray sets up the field. Even if we dissipate the vortex, there'll still be seismic turbulence."

"And likely some unpredictable effects from chroniton leakage," Kadray added as she worked her technological magic. "You'd best hurry."

"Fifteen minutes," Lucsly said, making it simultaneously a promise to her and an instruction to Dulmur. *The man's efficient,* Dulmur thought.

The two agents moved at a brisk pace to get to the nearby residences; transporter power was needed for the shield, so they had to hoof it. For once, Dulmur was grateful for the physical portion of his DTI training.

Over the next ten or so minutes, they corralled seven other people: four insectoid Kaferians, two Andorians, and a human, matching the bodies found in the debris. Dulmur tried not to think about how creepy that was as he persuaded them to come with him. He soon gave up trying to explain what the DTI was and started telling them he was with the Federation Science Council, here to warn them about an impending seismic event. It had the virtue of being technically true.

They collected the last local dweller and started making their way back with three minutes to spare. But as they ran toward the runabout, the ground started to rumble and the wind began to blow. Dulmur looked up to see a swirl of blue light beginning to form in the sky. "The field isn't working!" he cried.

"It takes time to polarize the chronitons to oppose the vortex!" Lucsly shouted back. "It could be a lot worse!"

They kept up their pace as best they could under the turbulent conditions. But soon, Dulmur began to stumble. It was as though the force of gravity was shifting beneath him. Perhaps it was being canceled out by the pull from the vortex. But as he tried to adjust, he found himself unable to control his body, and he fell forward, hitting the ground painfully. With difficulty, he wrenched his head around and saw the others stumbling as well. Only Lucsly retained his footing, though he was standing stock-still. "Wh-what's ha-ap-pening?" Dulmur said, finding it a struggle to get the words out.

"Tem-temporal narcosis," Lucsly said. "Chronitons . . . distort time . . . body's perceptions . . . motions . . . dependent on time sense."

Dulmur understood. If time around his feet was flowing at a slightly different rate than around his head, then his brain and his legs would be getting their signals crossed. Somehow, knowing that was the problem made it possible—though not easy—to adjust and regain some semblance of normal footing. Around him, the others were managing it too, with some difficulty. "Okay," he said, "n-now let's get . . . back to the ship."

But around him, the landscape seemed strange, unfamiliar. He could see the runabout ahead, but somehow he couldn't tell which direction it was in. He stumbled forward in what he thought was the right direction, but found himself no longer facing the ship. "Why . . . why can't I tell . . . ?"

"Time . . . space . . . motion . . . all parts of the same thing," Lucsly said. "Chronitons . . . shift axes of space . . . and time."

The cure was starting to seem worse than the disease. Though Dulmur reconsidered that when the ground convulsed beneath them and a nearby tree fell over, narrowly missing them. "How do we get back?" Dulmur cried.

Lucsly's face showed intense concentration. "I know the way."

"How?"

"Don't confuse me. Just . . . keep them calm. Follow me."

What followed was a confusing time of uncertain duration. With the ground, the sky, even his own body unstable, Dulmur followed the one thing around him that was constant: Agent Lucsly. Trusting him to handle space and time, Dulmur handled the people, speaking to them reassuringly, projecting confidence and authority to guide them forward even though he didn't know where they were going.

Finally they found themselves in the runabout, its shields protecting them from the chroniton field, and blessed normality returned. Lucsly looked around, confirming that Dulmur had gotten everyone inside. "Good job," he said.

Dulmur smiled. "You too. How the hell did you keep track in all that?"

He got a shrug in return. "I just do. Keep track of things."

Dulmur clapped him on the shoulder. "Good enough for me, partner."

Lucsly stiffened slightly, but gave him a nod of thanks before turning to Kadray. "The vortex?" he asked.

"It's dissipating," the commander replied. "It took a minute, but once I calibrated to its metric, I was able to counter it completely. If it comes after Mr. Manheim again, we can shield him more easily."

"I don't think it will," Lucsly said. "The *Enterprise* has reported no second vortex incident even though Picard got away."

"That's right," Dulmur said. "This force was acting on instinct, not malice. Probably didn't even understand why it was targeting these people. And maybe getting pushed back by the chroniton field will stop it from trying again."

Kadray shook her violet-maned head. "Still . . . it's a shame we couldn't have made contact with the entity. Studied it and its dimension of origin. There's so much we could've learned."

Dulmur rolled his eyes. That was Starfleet for you, always letting their curiosity get the better of them. All he cared about was that the danger was past, and all he wanted to do now was go home, file his report, and take a long weekend with his wife.

He met Lucsly's eyes, and he could tell that, aside from that last part, the older agent was thinking the same thing. *Maybe,* he thought, *this partnership will work out after all.*

PRESENT TIME
STARDATE 58699.8 TO 58738.9

V

DTI Headquarters, Greenwich
10:41 UTC

Director Laarin Andos sat at the desk in her underground office, her legs straddling Earth's Prime Meridian. Across from her sat two of her top agents, Dulmur in the Western Hemisphere, Ranjea in the Eastern. It was, of course, a completely arbitrary distinction, but it brought Andos some comfort. Her Rhaandarite people had a strong sense of spatial as well as social orientation, and in her position it was reassuring to feel herself physically anchored by the centrality of her location.

Although at times like this, it could drive home just how distant and unreachable the forces arrayed against the stability of the timeline could be. "The *U.S.S. Titan* has renewed contact with the Vomnin Confederacy, an interstellar coalition based in the Gum Nebula," she explained.

"I recall hearing about them," Ranjea said. "Isn't *Titan*'s current course somewhat beyond their territory?"

"As it was when the ship first encountered the Vomnin a year, six months, and four days ago, just in the other direction. Like us, the Vomnin explore far beyond their borders."

"Though as I recall," Ranjea said, "instead of seeking

abstract knowledge, they seek ancient technologies they can use to advance their own."

"I guess it's easier to scavenge other people's leftovers than invent anything themselves," Dulmur opined.

"Their own civilization was based on advanced ruins left behind on their homeworld by a colonizing race," Ranjea chided gently. "It's no wonder that they'd see value in recovering and developing such technologies rather than letting them decay into dust."

"But according to *Titan*," Andos said, "what the Vomnin have found now is more hazardous than an ancient ruin." She copied the data to their padds. *Titan*'s sensor scans showed a luminous sphere, not quite matter or energy, surrounded by gravity-lensed distortions of the background stars. "Its occupants call it the Axis of Time. It takes the inversion of spacelike and timelike axes to a rather literal extreme. Beyond that interspatial portal is a pocket dimension where movement forward or backward along its main axis takes the traveler forward or backward relative to our universe's time. It spans millions of years, allowing communication, commerce, and travel between widely separate eras."

"Holy shit," Dulmur muttered. "Sorry, ma'am. How is it that the timeline can even survive something like this?"

"That's what we need to investigate," Andos told them. "Reportedly, the occupants of the Axis have policies that they claim are adequate to protect history. President Bacco is not convinced of that, nor is she convinced that the Vomnin can be trusted to use the Axis responsibly, given their hunger for ancient technologies. At her request, Starfleet has authorized the use of a *Vesta*-class starship to deliver a DTI team to the Axis at slipstream velocity." The agents' eyes widened. Quantum slipstream was a new, experimental technology dependent on extremely rare benamite crystals, so Starfleet tended to limit its use to special circumstances.

Andos resisted the urge to rise and pace about her office. Her two-point-four-meter height could be intimidating to conventional-sized humanoids, and though Ranjea and Dulmur were veteran agents and colleagues, she still considered it a matter of courtesy to stay close to their altitude. If nothing else, it helped her resist the temptation to think of them as children. "Ranjea," she said, "we need our top diplomat to manage negotiations with both the Vomnin and the Axis occupants. That's you."

"I look forward to the challenge," Ranjea said, predictably enough. Deltans had a way of looking forward to every new experience. Even fear, pain, or death was simply a new sensation to discover. Andos hoped this situation would not be so extreme, though.

"I have another challenge to add to the experience, Ranjea," she went on. "Agent Garcia is due for her first field assignment. Are you up to handling her?"

Ranjea brightened. "I would certainly appreciate her company. I've been very impressed by her potential."

Andos had to agree. Of the newest batch of trainees, Garcia showed the most promise as an agent, though it was by default. I'stel Borah had dropped out of the training program after seven weeks, and Teyak had fallen short in the physical and psychological aspects of field training, grudgingly choosing to shift gears and become a researcher along with Felbog Bu-Tsop-Vee. Garcia had struggled as well, and for a time, Andos had feared they would get no new agents out of this group. But the young human had stuck with it, showing an admirable determination and self-discipline, and finally earned her badge as a provisional field agent eight weeks ago. She'd spent that time like many novice agents, making the circuit of DTI branch offices across the Federation to study their procedures and get up to speed on their open cases, but it was high time to test her out for real.

But Dulmur, here due to his role as Garcia's sponsor, had a less sanguine reaction. "Hold on," he said. "You're pairing Garcia with *him*? Sending them off *alone* on a mission? You really think that's the best idea?"

"Don't worry, Marion," Ranjea said. "I promise I'll have her home by midnight."

"Don't joke about that. Don't you even joke about it."

Ranjea grew more serious. "You know I would never take advantage of a human like that."

"Yeah, well, it wouldn't be for her lack of trying. The kid is madly in love with you, you know. And you know how cut off she feels, *and* how driven she is." Dulmur smirked. "Frankly, I'm as worried about your honor as hers."

"Dulmur," Andos said. "Garcia's infatuation with Ranjea is the one serious concern that remains about her capabilities as an agent. If she can't overcome it and learn to work with him in a healthy way, she'll have no future with this agency."

The human agent grimaced. "So you throw her in the deep end, is that it? Sink or swim?"

"We need to resolve this as soon as possible. And I have faith in Ranjea's ability to manage it."

"And what if it goes wrong? This Axis thing, it sounds pretty delicate. What if her infatuation makes her a liability?"

"I don't believe it will," Ranjea said. "This is an exercise in trust, Marion. And the only way to prove trust is to extend it."

"There's a more basic issue here, Agent Dulmur," Andos said. "We're shorthanded, and Garcia's our only new agent this quarter. I'm not going to bench her because of a personal issue, especially when it's an issue that's best confronted promptly."

Dulmur crossed his arms and sulked. "I still don't like it."

Yet Andos recognized from his body language and tone of voice that Dulmur was no longer arguing, merely making a final declaration of his feelings on the issue. She had anticipated exactly such an outcome before the meeting began. Human emotional and social dynamics were rather straightforward by Rhaandarite standards, tending to operate on only a few levels at a time. They were thus very easy to predict.

Deltans were a rather more socially mature species, their behavioral patterns more nuanced, but that was why Andos trusted that Ranjea would be able to manage Garcia's highly predictable responses. She would certainly attempt to seduce him during the journey, but Ranjea had abundant experience at letting humans down easily. Moreover, Andos was well aware of his deeply felt determination to live up to his responsibilities. He had failed to do so once, and though he managed the guilt in a healthy manner as one would expect of a Deltan, she could see that he never let himself forget it. Nor would he let himself fail in his obligations toward Garcia and the Department.

Once Andos dismissed the two agents, she stood to stretch her limbs at last, and again took the time to concentrate on her position in space, straddling the meridian that defined time for an entire civilization. Even though stardates were the official standard, twenty-four-hour universal time was still a convenient, linear way of marking the intervals of the day. There were those who questioned the use of the old British Empire's chronometric standard for the timekeeping of an interstellar civilization, feeling that a human standard was ethnocentric enough without it being one created to facilitate one nation-state's cultural, economic, and military domination over others.

But Andos found Greenwich Mean Time to be a more positive symbol. The time standard developed here had been in response to a fundamental problem of navigation on the high seas. Mariners had always navigated by the stars, but without knowing the exact time of day, it was impossible to know one's exact longitude based on stellar orientation. Thus, the British accomplishment of creating precision timepieces was not merely a tool of empire, but a tool of exploration, a vital step forward in the understanding of the universe. It was a triumph of precision over uncertainty. And it was the special conditions of this ocean girt planet, the need to navigate without landmarks, that had made it not only possible but vital, more important to progress than it had been on arid Vulcan or icy Andor, say. So continuing to use a Terran maritime observatory as the benchmark for a universal time standard struck Andos as entirely fitting.

There was a certain irony, though, to be standing here as she contemplated the hazards posed to the stability of the continuum by another sort of Axis of Time. That was just one of the many associations that raced through

Andos's pronounced frontal lobes as she pondered the problem. A pocket reality in which all times were effectively simultaneous, the Axis was reminiscent of the spacetime discontinuity known as the Nexus, but was far tamer and safer to access, making it far more dangerous in potential. As an easy passage to eras throughout history, built by unknown ancients, it also reminded her of the Guardian of Forever, which in turn reminded her of the very beginnings of the agency she now ran. She had been there from the start, a junior clerk for the Federation Science Council, though at the time she had not been privy to the classified events that had led to the Department's founding.

For centuries, the Vulcan Science Directorate had held the official policy that time travel was, if not a theoretical impossibility, then a practical one. They had concluded that it would require literally astronomical energies and that the divergent stress-energy tensor at a Cauchy horizon would vaporize any being or vessel that attempted passage. They had been proven wrong beginning in 2151 CE, when Jonathan Archer's *Enterprise* had become embroiled in the twenty-second-century front of the Temporal Cold War. The knowledge of time travel had been highly classified, though, and the mechanisms employed by the uptime factions had remained unknown. Thus matters had remained for a hundred and fifteen years, until Stardate 1704, when a warp drive accident aboard the subsequent starship named *Enterprise*—James Kirk's ship—had propelled it back in time three days, proving that negative time displacement was not only possible, but potentially achievable with contemporary technology.

In one of those mind-boggling coincidences that lent

credence to the theory that time travel rendered an individual susceptible to subsequent chronal displacements,
it was later that same year, on Stardate 3113, that a near
encounter with the Black Star had sent the *Enterprise* back
in time to 1969 CE. The same science officer responsible
for the warp formula that caused the earlier time displacement, Commander Spock, had been able to get the ship
back to its own time, but less than four months later, on
Stardate 3134, the *Enterprise* had been the ship to discover the Guardian—and the existential threat it posed to
all of history.

But Starfleet, being Starfleet, had been more focused
on the opportunity for discovery. In short order, they had
exploited both newly discovered methods of time displacement for research missions into the past—using the *Enterprise* again, of course, for at least they had the good sense
to keep the knowledge limited to those who already had it.
Moreover, only the *Enterprise*'s engines proved capable of
re-creating the temporal "slingshot" effect safely; whatever
Spock had done to them on Stardate 1704 had apparently
made a permanent change.

However, both research missions brought the timeline
to the brink of disaster. Kirk's well-intentioned meddling
in an Aegis operation in 1968 CE had almost thrown
Earth's history off course at a particularly turbulent moment, and use of the Guardian had temporarily disrupted
the timeline on at least two occasions, the Clan Ru incident and the historical expedition to the Empire of Orion.
(And possibly more occasions as well; it was difficult to
judge for sure where the Guardian was involved.)

Upon learning of the near-disasters resulting from
Starfleet's cavalier use of time travel, the outraged

Federation Council had passed new legislature severely restricting temporal research, and in 2270 CE had authorized the creation of the Department of Temporal Investigations to enforce those laws. The Department had been instituted within the bureaucracy of the Federation Science Council to give it a low profile as well as access to the necessary expertise. The 149-year-old Laarin Andos, barely out of adolescence, had happened to be cataloguing the FSC's past research into temporal physics at the time, and had thus found herself assigned to the new department's Greenwich headquarters despite lacking any real qualifications in the area. She had started out as its most junior clerk (despite being chronologically its oldest member), but her keen memory and problem-solving skills had served her and the DTI well, and her innate knack for social processing had helped her navigate the bureaucracy as the nascent organization competed for resources. There were times when, with the Guardian and the Black Star cordoned off and the slingshot effect determined to be a rare fluke, it had seemed there was little need for a whole department dedicated to temporal management. Indeed, when James Kirk and his crew had saved Earth by bringing a breeding pair of *Megaptera novaeangliae* uptime from 1986 CE to placate the mysterious alien probe/organism that had reacted vehemently to their extinction, while somehow managing to avoid timeline alteration despite numerous examples of reckless behavior (including the consensual removal from the era of Doctor Gillian Taylor, the Temporal Displacement Division's inaugural client), the whole underlying philosophy of the DTI that time travel was a hazard to be strictly regulated was called into question. But Andos's political savvy had helped the

Department survive until later temporal crises, such as the theft of an experimental protomatter weapon by renegade Aegis operatives on Stardate 8638 and the interspatial parasite infestation on Benecia on Stardate 9344, had proven its importance.

Gradually over the decades, Andos had risen through the ranks, not aggressively pursuing advancement but not rejecting it either. She had decided to become a field agent once she reached full growth at age 188, and twenty-two years later had earned promotion to assistant director of the San Francisco branch office—arguably the most important one, as it oversaw Starfleet's embroilments with temporal phenomena. It had been there that she had fostered the career of Gariff Lucsly, her finest agent, and later his partner Dulmur. Eleven years ago, though, she had accepted the post of Director, bringing her back to Greenwich where it had all begun—in more ways than one.

The symmetry of her career path brought Andos comfort, as did her proximity to the Prime Meridian. With her homeworld razed in the Borg invasion, these things were her only remaining anchors in reality. Of course, as a Rhaandarite she had a complete understanding of the psychological underpinnings of that illusion; indeed, it operated on a rather elementary, even juvenile level of cognitive processing. Yet she also understood perfectly why she allowed it to bring her comfort. In this profession, any such sense of anchorage was a valuable focal point, a reminder of her priorities and responsibilities. Seeing through the symbol didn't render it useless. After all, what was sentient interaction but the exchange and negotiation of symbols?

The Axis of Time, Andos thought. The name suggested

it held a similar symbolic value for its occupants. They might feel their culture, their identity, revolved around it. Did they have the same sense of it, though, as something to which a single consistent reality should be anchored? Or did they perceive it as something around which reality could rotate into many forms?

Privately, she admitted that Dulmur had been right. This was a sink-or-swim mission for Teresa Garcia. Andos had evaluated the potential social and psychological dynamics on levels that humans didn't even have vocabulary for, and was confident to eight degrees of freedom that the novice agent's sexual infatuation with Ranjea would not critically undermine the many assets she brought to the job. But there were many unknown variables on the mission ahead. And if Andos had overlooked some critical factor, the consequences could be profound.

But then, in this profession, when were they not?

U.S.S. Capitoline NCC-82617
13.18.14.1.17 15 Mac 1 Caban (A Monday)
21:58 UTC

Ranjea could sense Teresa Garcia's anticipation from the moment he passed along the order that she accompany him aboard the *Capitoline*. Even though he took care to keep his manner entirely professional, he knew that she saw this as a sexual opportunity. He could sense her hope that he intended the same, but could tell that even if he made no moves upon her (as of course he would not), she would inevitably come to him.

The *Vesta*-class starship could reach the Axis of Time in under an hour at slipstream speeds, but in order to save on precious benamite, it would use the drive only in short hops and travel at warp between them, for a total travel time of just under nine days. The first hours aboard were spent in briefings on the *Titan*'s recent encounter with the Vomnin Confederacy at the Axis site, as well as a broader review of that vessel's earlier encounters with them, first as an ally of the Pa'haquel in the effort to regulate the Gum Nebula's cosmozoan population, then intermittently over the remaining two months the vessel spent within that region of space. Ranjea looked forward to meeting them and experiencing their own particular forms of beauty, both of sensation and of thought.

Once they were shown to their adjacent quarters for the night, Ranjea chose not to disrobe for bed, for he knew he would be receiving a visitor shortly. Indeed, it was not long before Teresa Garcia came to his door, attired in a loose robe of Deltan design. Its complex red and gold hues brought out the rich brown of her eyes, and its cut revealed much of her athletic limbs as she moved. "May I come in?" she asked, her tone making the request an invitation in itself.

"Of course, Teresa. I've been expecting you."

She seemed surprised but heartened that he'd granted her access so readily. Clearly she'd expected to have to cajole him first. "You mean you . . . want me here?"

He escorted her in and let the door close behind them. "There is something we need to resolve between us, Teresa. I see no benefit in delaying it."

"Neither do I," she said, her skin flushing. She adjusted the folds of her robe, exposing more of her flesh with affected casualness. "Do you like it?" she asked. "I replicated it just for you."

"It's lovely," Ranjea said. "And it flatters you. I thank

you for the beauty of this sight. But you must know, Teresa, that this cannot lead where you wish it to."

"I know!" she cried with impatience. "I know the drill. I'd lose myself. I'd be addicted." She gazed up at him, her great dark eyes glistening with tears. "But I love you, Ranjea. That's already an addiction. It's the same kind of chemistry in the brain. The same craving, the same need," she said, stepping toward him and placing a hand on his chest. "The same pain of withdrawal. So what more harm could it do when I'm already hooked?"

"Teresa . . . please." He guided her to a chair, taking the couch just opposite her, close but not intimate. "Addiction is such a . . . crude metaphor for Deltan intimacy. It is nothing so vulgar as that. Our minds are predisposed to unitive experiences—to a sublimation of the sense of self, a perception of oneness with another being. When we make love, our sense of ourselves as individuals disappears. We join together wholly. We not only love each other, we become each other."

"Like a Vulcan mind meld."

"Somewhat, but more on a sensual, empathic level. For us, this . . . deferment of self is natural, commonplace. We can subsume and recover ourselves at will. But for a human . . ." He shook his head. "You could completely lose your sense of yourself as a distinct being. It is worse than addiction, Teresa. At least an addict can function if she receives her fix. If I made love to you . . . your very identity would be in jeopardy."

She rose again. "I don't buy that," she said. "I've heard stories about Klingons and Orions taking Deltan sex slaves. I know it's possible to survive the experience intact."

"For Klingons or Orions, perhaps, particularly in coercive contexts. For those with low empathy. But humans . . ." He smiled. "Look at what you have done in a few short centuries. You have overcome the differences among yourselves and become one world. You have seen past your differences with other species and shown them the path to greater unity. You have the potential for the same kind of empathy we have. It is not mature enough yet for you to handle our levels of intimacy. But it is enough to make you highly susceptible to the loss of self."

She studied him carefully, her eyes still brimming with passion, yet calculating at the same time. "Okay, granted. But who says you have to go all the way? Can't you . . . hold yourself back? Have sex on just a bodily level?"

Ranjea considered his reply carefully. Such low-level sex play was well within the Deltan repertoire, an appetizer before the genuine act or a quick, friendly flirtation between casual acquaintances. But what Teresa sought was a deeper bond of love, and if he entered into sex with her, he could not fail to respond to that need and draw her into unity. After so long away from his home and his loves, he had needs of his own. Yet if he confessed that what she sought were even theoretically possible, it would only make it harder to dissuade her. So he said, "Such restraint is not the Deltan way. For us, the meaning of the act is in the completeness of the bonding, separate beings becoming one in flesh, mind, and spirit. To join on only one level . . . it would be hollow, incomplete."

"But it wouldn't be to me!" she cried. "I don't want to sound selfish. But . . . you're so kind, Ranjea. So giving. I can't believe you won't even try, when I need this so badly."

"You desire it badly. That is not the same as need."

"And what about your desires?" she asked, stepping closer. "You said I was beautiful. Even if you can't experience it fully . . ." She let the robe drop. "Isn't half a loaf better than none?"

Ranjea did not look away from her nudity. She offered it to him as a gift, and he took it in that spirit, even if he could not embrace the full intent. She was indeed quite beautiful. Her vast dark eyes, full lips, and light brown skin were almost Deltan, yet her thick black hair, on her head and elsewhere, made for an exotic highlight. Her body's contours were compact and elegant, strong yet soft. He admired her beauty as a work of art.

Still, he could offer her only apology. "Teresa, again, I thank you for this gift. But . . . I don't wish to offend you, but although I appreciate your beauty, I'm simply not sexually stimulated by it alone. Deltans' main avenue of arousal is pheromonal, and you don't have a strong enough scent to entice me."

She blinked, taken aback. He hoped he'd finally convinced her, though he feared he had hurt her feelings in the process. Yet after a moment, she gathered her resolve and closed the distance between them. "Then maybe you just need to get a better whiff of me."

Her kisses were long, deep, and passionate. She administered them with appreciable skill as her hands roved deftly across his arms and back. Ranjea accepted the experience but did not respond in kind. "I'm sorry, Teresa," he said when she finally realized she was unable to evoke the desired reaction. "For me, arousal is not an involuntary process. It's completely under my control." He stroked her hair, offering comfort. "I wish I could give you the fulfillment you seek, but what you ask of me is simply . . . not healthy. Not for either of us. You need to let go of this desire."

She pulled away, flinging herself into the chair. Her nude body trembled as she fought off tears. "How? I've tried, Ranjea, I've tried, but you're just so beautiful. I love you. I need you so much."

"No, Teresa. What you need is a connection. You've been torn away from your own time, your lifelong goals. Your world, your very family, has become alien to you. Your introduction to this time was an act of persecution and rejection for the choice that stranded you here. And of all the friends you trained with, none managed to become field agents alongside you." He came over to her and put his fingers beneath her chin, tilting her head up. "You feel willing to risk losing yourself in me because you believe it would make you feel a part of something again."

She no longer held back the tears. Her eyes alone told him she knew he was right. "It hurts," she said. "Please. I need you."

Ranjea stroked her silky hair. "Yes. But not in the way you think."

He slid his hands down her bare shoulders and arms until they clasped hers. He concentrated, and after a moment, her anguish began to fade. She looked up at him with wonder. "Thank you," she whispered.

They simply held hands for a few minutes more. Finally, Teresa pulled away, frowned slightly, and asked, "What did you do? It's like . . . the pain was still there, but it . . . didn't matter so much."

"A taste of the unitive experience," he told her. "With the sense of self diminished, things like pain and sorrow don't seem as important. It's something we use as a therapeutic technique. It works on physical as well as emotional pain."

She blinked several times, tension starting to return, and she self-consciously retrieved the robe and covered herself. "But it doesn't last."

"No. It's an aid, not a cure."

"But if you could give me that much . . ."

"It's not the same. Trust me."

She winced, stifling a sob. "Okay, so tell me. How do I get over you?" She shook her head. "I feel like a fool, trying to seduce you like this. I'm . . . I'm a professional. I'm your partner, and . . . and that's what I need to be. So how do I stop . . . stop wanting you? Stop loving you?"

"You don't have to," he said. "You just have to stop craving me."

"But how do I do that?!"

"The same way I avoid craving you, even though I admire your beauty."

She scoffed. "Okay, that's not an answer."

Ranjea guided her to the couch, holding her hands. "Someday I'll tell you why I became a DTI agent. For now, let's just say . . . I inherited a mission. I was charged with an obligation, one that I felt a passionate need to fulfill, and I failed. So believe me, I know what it's like to have a passion frustrated. To be unable to remove that passion from your being even though you know it's unattainable.

"But the key is not to fight the craving . . . simply to accept it as an end in itself."

"I don't understand."

"Tell me. When you see a glorious sunset, or a magnificent ringed planet, do you desire to possess it?"

". . . No."

"But you do appreciate its beauty."

"Yeah. But . . . it's not something I can take home with me. I mean, I could take a picture, but that's not possessing the thing itself. That's just taking a longer look."

"Is that the only reason? If you could possess it, would you want to? Does it frustrate you that you can't?"

"No. I just . . . enjoy it for what it is."

"The beauty is its own reward. It enriches you even without being possessed."

"Right."

"So why not engage with other forms of beauty the same way? Instead of seeking to possess, to make them part of yourself, can't you simply celebrate them as they are? Let yourself become part of them?"

She nodded. "Subsume the ego. Don't think of the self."

"Exactly."

She looked him over. "So I can think you're utterly gorgeous, and love looking at you, but not go crazy wanting to have you."

"Exactly."

"So . . . can we practice?" She gave a wicked grin. "Maybe you could take off all your clothes and I could try to look but not touch?"

He chuckled. "I think that's rather too advanced a lesson for the first night. I think you should simply go to your quarters and sleep."

"Hey, I showed you mine! It's only fair!"

"Goodnight, Teresa."

She winked. "Well, it was worth a try."

He led her to the door. "If you need me, Teresa, I will

be here. I will give you the connection you need. But as your friend, as your confidant, and as your partner."

Teresa reached up and stroked his cheek. "I appreciate it. And, um . . . if you ever need someone to talk to about your . . . troubles . . . I'm here."

His hand rested upon hers. "I value that greatly, Teresa."

Despite her confident smile, he could tell she was shaking as she left. She would have a rough night. But he could tell he'd made the breakthrough. He looked forward to the more meaningful relationship they could now begin to build.

Vomnin Space Station Bezorek
13.18.14.2.5 3 Kankin 9 Chicchan (A Tuesday)
14:36 UTC
Titan was a fascinating ship. Teresa Garcia had never seen so many different species, particularly nonhumanoids, living and working together on a continuing basis. There had been nothing like it in her time. Indeed, the crew included members of multiple species that the Federation hadn't even met yet in her time, like Choblik and Pak'shree, not to mention ones that had been hostile in her day, like Ferengi and Cardassians. It was inspiring proof that the Federation's ideals of cooperation were achievable. For someone who'd been pulled from her own peaceful, prosperous time to find herself in the aftermath of the worst horrors in Federation history, seeing something like *Titan* was a great comfort that the future was still headed in the right direction.

Assuming the Axis of Time didn't end up derailing the entire past. Unluckily for the Federation, by the time

Titan's advanced sensor arrays had detected the temporal anomaly, the Vomnin Confederacy had already staked a claim and made contact with the inhabitants of the inverted spacetime (timespace?) within. They'd even built a station adjacent to it, where *Titan* and *Capitoline* were currently docked. *Titan*'s captain, William Riker, and his diplomatic officer and wife, Commander Deanna Troi, had raised concerns with the Vomnin about the risks posed by the Axis, but the Vomnin were more interested in the opportunities it presented. Bezorek Station was administered by the Vomnin Bureau for Historical Resource Development, the department that managed the exploitation of the advanced remnant technologies on which the Vomnin had built their civilization. The galaxy was littered with still-viable devices left behind by extinct ancients— from the ruins of Camus II to the Iconian gateways to the Guardian itself—but the Vomnin's home territory within the Gum Nebula had an unusual abundance of dead civilizations due to its turbulent conditions. The BHRD was the most powerful and important agency within the Confederacy, and they'd refused to recognize the authority of a starship's diplomatic officer to negotiate with them on an equal level, even though Troi was authorized to speak as an official Federation ambassador.

And so the DTI had been called in, though Garcia could tell from Riker's attitude that he wasn't thrilled about it. But to Garcia's surprise, Troi and Ranjea had greeted each other with more warmth, as well as familiarity. "I was the one who debriefed her about the Caeliar temporal loop following the Borg invasion," he told Garcia later as they headed for the meeting room aboard the Vomnin station, where Troi had arranged to meet them.

"As well as the Orishan tesseract incident of Stardate 57443. It was Agent Faunt," he added wistfully, "who spoke to Captain Riker."

"Looks like you and she hit it off well," Garcia said, then realized it had come out cattier than she'd hoped.

But Ranjea overlooked it. "She's an excellent diplomat. A strong empath, not a full telepath like most Betazoids. Highly intelligent, highly experienced. She's achieved some extremely difficult diplomatic feats in her time on *Titan,* and before that on *Enterprise.* I'll be glad to have her on our side for this. Particularly since she is, pretty much by default, our sole expert on the Confederacy."

"An empath, huh? Must make you feel right at home."

"I think it will make for a convivial partnership, yes."

"Just remember she's married."

He gave her a puzzled look. "Why would that—ahh." He laughed. "Don't worry; Betazoids are generally monogamous. As are human starship captains. And the Rikers are clearly a very devoted couple. I don't go where I'm not invited."

Or where you are *invited, alas,* Garcia thought.

When they reached the conference room, they found Commander Troi already waiting for them. It was surprising to see someone more punctual than a pair of DTI agents. Ranjea had to duck his head to get through the low door, though he made it look graceful and effortless. Garcia and Troi had to duck just a bit as well. Vomnin were of typical humanoid size, but they were facultative bipeds, knuckle-walkers like Trinni/ek or Terran apes, so they tended to build low to the ground. The wall consoles she saw around the station were mounted at or around floor level. The furniture inside the conference room was almost Japanese-style, a low oval table surrounded by a ring of cushions. A row of windows looked out upon the interspatial portal to the Axis of Time, a misty blue-white orb that seemed to balance on the edge of unreality. Around the perimeter of the room were a variety of sculptures and artworks, their condition pegging them to Garcia's trained eye as archaeological relics. They appeared to come from a variety of distinct civilizations and lacked any aesthetic or stylistic unity. Garcia had the impression that their purpose was less to serve aesthetic considerations than to show off the prizes the Vomnin had collected in their pursuit of useful antiquities. She wondered how the room appeared to Ranjea's heightened sense of aesthetics. His expression seemed intrigued and approving, but Garcia suspected he would wear that same expression if visiting a garbage dump, so long as it was one he'd never experienced before.

Or perhaps he showed approval for the benefit of their Vomnin hosts, who now approached them. Troi stepped forward to mediate. "Subdirector Vennor Sikran of the Bureau for Historical Resource Development, allow me to introduce Agents Meyo Ranjea and Teresa Garcia of the Federation Department of Temporal Investigations."

"Greetings," said Sikran in a rough baritone, rising to a more erect stance to greet his visitors. The Vomnin sub-director had orange-bronze skin, somewhat lighter than typical for his people, and wore a dark greenish suit that clashed badly with his complexion, making Garcia wonder if the Vomnin's wide, pale eyes saw in a different spectrum than she did. His hairless head was rather wide as well, as though a roughly humanoid face had been stretched out to twice its width and flattened somewhat top to bottom.

In conjunction with Sikran's well-fed stature, it gave him a Tweedledum quality. Or was it Tweedledee? "Welcome to Bezorek Station. May you benefit from the bounties of the Confederacy during your visit." Garcia stifled a grin at Sikran's blatant reminder that he considered them to be on his territory.

After introducing his aides, he gestured to the final occupant of the room. "And may I present the lady Lirahn, spokesperson for the Axis administration."

Lirahn had been holding back from the group, silhouetted against the glow of the Axis in the viewports. Now she glided forward and instantly commanded the room. She was quite humanoid in physique, though unusually tall, topping two meters. Her eyes were large and colored a silvery blue not unlike the Axis portal. Her features were strong yet elegantly feminine, her lips full and mobile. Her forehead was high, her cranium large and hairless. Her skin was a rich chocolate brown with diamond-shaped patches of forest green and gold adorning her skull, with more diffuse diamond patches running down her arms and possibly elsewhere. She wore a close-fitting, low-necked jumpsuit of shimmering black that called attention to her impressive curves. Even with Ranjea and the striking Commander Troi present, Lirahn was unquestionably the most captivating sight in the room.

"It is my great pleasure to meet you both," Lirahn told the agents in a dulcet alto. "It's fascinating how much changes across the ages . . . and how much remains the same." Her gaze fixed firmly on Ranjea's after roving up and down his body with an almost predatory hunger.

In turn, Ranjea clasped her hands warmly. "There are

wonders to discover in every age," he said. "May we ask what age is yours?"

"My dear man, in my time it was considered impolite to ask a lady her age," Lirahn teased.

"Ah, but age brings experience and wisdom," Ranjea said, "and is thus owed great reverence."

"To be specific," Subdirector Sikran put in, gesturing the guests toward the cushions, "Lirahn's people, the Selakar, occupy a time approximately eight thousand sun cycles before our own."

As per her training, Garcia had memorized the Vomnin calendar on the way here. A sun cycle was one orbit of the Vomnin home star's binary companion, which took some sixty-four years. That made Lirahn's time . . . "More than half a million years!" she said aloud, eyes widening.

"Remarkable," Ranjea breathed. "In all my time as a temporal investigator, I have never met anyone from such a distant temporal origin."

"The Axis spans a far greater interval than that," Lirahn said.

"We believe the Axis was built over sixty thousand sun cycles ago," Sikran said; Garcia silently translated that to nearly four million years. "However, the identity of the builders is unknown. For whatever reason, they seem to have abandoned it." His broad, froglike mouth turned up in a smile. "Or perhaps they deliberately left it for later civilizations to use."

"How far into the future does it reach?" Garcia asked.

"Less than half that interval," Lirahn said. "Some one million, four hundred thousand years from now, the Axis interface is destroyed in a supernova."

Garcia stared at her. "You catch on to our time units fast."

"No doubt one of the benefits of being a telepath," Commander Troi said. Her delivery was casual, but she met the agents' eyes pointedly as she called attention to the fact.

"And quite a formidable one, I sense," Ranjea added. The two empaths and Lirahn exchanged significant looks, and Garcia suddenly felt left out, wondering what sort of vibes were passing between them. At least Troi and Ranjea had made sure she was aware of the situation.

"Well," Lirahn demurred, "my species has been around for a very long time." She grew wistful. "Or it was. I fear we're long extinct by your time."

Garcia found herself wondering if Lirahn might have some notion of trying to change that. The Selakar woman's eyes locked on her. "Not to worry, Agent Garcia. Whatever my actions within the Axis, they should have no impact on your timeline."

Unhappy at having her thoughts so casually read, Garcia faced Lirahn down. "How can you be so sure of that? One small change at the right moment can rewrite all reality."

"At the right moment, yes," Sikran interposed. "But for how long? There are many factors and forces shaping the history of the galaxy. A given change may have a significant impact for several sun cycles on a particular world, in a particular territory of space. But in time, with so many other unrelated factors shaping events, those changes will be damped out. Even if a whole civilization rises where before it fell, and keeps another civilization from existing, what difference will it make to history thousands of cycles later when the species no longer exists?"

"That species would've interacted with others. Made changes that rippled outward."

"And those ripples are gradually damped, lost within the greater noise of cosmic events," Sikran said. He smiled. "Why do you suppose it is that you so rarely encounter time travelers from more than a few sun cycles away? It's because they can change little by traveling farther. It offends our sense of self-importance to admit it, but as worlds-shaking as the consequences of our actions may seem to us, they will ultimately leave little mark on the galaxy, except in profoundly rare cases. Over time, even highly divergent histories can realign."

Garcia remembered Ranjea's lecture back in Greenwich, about how the single reality she perceived was simply an average of multiple smaller realities that briefly branched off and were quickly forgotten. What Sikran described was the same principle writ large. Would all the different timelines that existed today eventually coalesce back into a single one, hundreds of thousands of years from now?

Trying not to lose control of the conversation, she said, "I know the theory. I also know that some changes are too great to ever be undone. What if a new timeline leads to the destruction of entire planets or stars? Isn't that kind of irreversible?"

"Which is exactly why there is no risk of such timelines eradicating our own," Sikran told her, grinning smugly. "Changing the mass distribution of the galaxy by destroying a star or planet will alter its spacetime curvature, rendering it impossible for the two timelines to become congruent. Particularly over the course of thousands of sun cycles or more, as the changes in galactic mass distribution propagate further."

"This," Lirahn said with a smile, "is the key to the safe usage of the Axis of Time. The interface," she said, gesturing to the eerily glowing warp outside, "only emerges into normal space at intervals of several millennia or longer, for only occasionally does its path through the complex curvature of subspace intersect with normal spacetime. As a rule, it's more than enough time for any temporal variations that occur to be damped down. Any changes made to one era along the Axis would have no serious impact on any subsequent era."

"Even granting that," Ranjea said, "what about the impact on the era itself? Introducing anachronistic knowledge and technology, or anachronistic species or diseases, could have far-ranging consequences."

"What is the difference," Sikran asked, "between that and normal space exploration? There is no single linear progression of technology in the galaxy. Within forty parsecs of here, there are worlds whose technology is more advanced than we can comprehend and worlds where they are only beginning to harness fire. Travel through space *is* travel through time in its own right."

"And history has shown that too great a technological divide can be disruptive if the contact is not managed very carefully," Deanna Troi put in. "This is why the Federation has embraced a policy of noninterference in the affairs of pre-warp civilizations."

"Believe me," Lirahn said, "the Axis Council has its own policies in place to manage contact. We have subjective centuries of experience mediating interactions across great divides of technological and . . . mental advancement." Did her gaze flick across Garcia? "All the concerns that you have faced only in the few weeks since your discovery of the Axis have been matters of primary concern to the Council for the duration of its existence." Lirahn reached across the table to stroke Ranjea's hand again. "The safeguards we have in place should satisfy all your doubts as to the safety of trade and cultural exchange across eras."

"That is heartening to hear," Ranjea replied, giving as good as he got in the flirtation department. Garcia hoped that he was just playing along rather than succumbing to her charms.

"But what about within an era?" she asked, as much to break their mutual attention as anything else. "What's to stop someone from entering the Axis, moving just a little bit downtime within it, then coming out weeks or months in the past and changing the, uh, local timeline?"

"Not possible," Lirahn said easily. "At those points along its length where the Axis emerges from subspace, the interface rotates its temporal axis into alignment with normal spacetime. The direction of time is the same for both, if not the duration."

Sikran made a throat-clearing noise. "I should add that passage into the Axis must be cleared through this station," he pointed out, apparently feeling the need to assert Vomnin authority. "We are more than capable of managing any temporal security issues without needing the Federation to dictate policy to us."

"No dictation was intended, Subdirector," Ranjea said, easily shifting his full attention to Sikran and reassuring Garcia that he wasn't in Lirahn's thrall. "We simply have reasonable concerns that we feel obligated to address."

"Perhaps," Sikran said. "But our past experience with *Titan* tells us that your Federation's well-intentioned impulses often fail to respect the jurisdiction of others. Just keep in mind that the Axis is a Vomnin discovery. You are welcome to negotiate for access, and we are certainly willing to hear and consider your concerns regarding temporal security. But ultimately, you are here at Vomnin indulgence. You have no territorial authority here."

Sikran's expression grew smug. "And if we should choose to develop this resource in a way you're not comfortable with . . . then there is simply nothing you can do about it."

VI

Kemrel Municipality
Tandar Prime (Rakon II)
15:41 UTC

Inspector Ranz gave the two human visitors' credentials a skeptical once-over. "What interest does the Department of Temporal Investigations have in a traffic mishap?" she asked.

"Professor Vard is a noted temporal physicist," said the taller, gray-haired one, Lucsly. "Our department has an ongoing interest in his research."

"Besides," said the shorter, blond one, Dulmur by name, "how often do you have a 'traffic mishap' where the occupants of the crashed vehicle find themselves suddenly standing in an alley without a scratch and with no idea how they got there?"

Ranz had to concede the point. As a rule, she was reluctant to defer to Federation authorities in what should be internal Tandaran matters. Humans had always taken a heavy-handed approach toward Tandar, going back to first contact, when they had forcibly liberated a group of Suliban from a Tandaran detention camp. Granted, the Suliban had been unjustly detained by the government of the time, but still, it had been the Tandarans' right to fix their own mistakes without Starfleet blasting in and resolving things by force. The bad blood had eventually subsided, and the Tandaran worlds had finally joined the Federation some sixty years back, but strove to maintain their independence as much as possible. The influx of refugees from Borg-devastated Federation worlds in recent months had brought some buried tensions to the surface, and while Ranz liked to think modern Tandarans were too civilized to act destructively on those tensions, she was uneasy with having Federation officials barge in and make imperious demands that might inflame them further.

Still, Ranz was admittedly out of her depth here. Her forensic teams had been unable to discover the cause of the hoverbus crash, let alone how the noted Professor Vard and his gaggle of graduate students had escaped unscathed. The thought that there might be some kind of temporal anomaly at work here made her hair stand on end. The Tandaran worlds may have boasted some of the most renowned theoretical physicists in the quadrant, with Vard and his forebears doing pioneering work in temporal theory, but national pride could only go so far. And Ranz had never done well in physics, which was why she'd gone into law enforcement.

"All right," she conceded, running a hand through her frosted black hair. "I'll let you see the evidence we've gathered and interview the survivors. But anything you find out gets shared with me."

"Anything we find out may be classified," Agent Lucsly told her.

"Now look here," Ranz said. "If there's something out there that poses a threat to Tandaran citizens—or something that can save lives otherwise doomed—I need to know about it, Federation secrets be damned."

"We appreciate your concerns," said Agent Dulmur. "I guarantee you, we won't do anything to jeopardize the safety of your citizens. But that doesn't mean we'll be able to tell you what we find out."

Ranz glared at them. "So I just have to trust you, is that it?"

"Yes, ma'am," Lucsly said, making it sound like a command. "You do."

Firstday/Vien 3/Bregat 8, YC 867 (A Sunday)
04:17 UTC

Lucsly and Dulmur found Professor Vard at the scene of his unlikely rescue, scanning the alleyway with a whirring, rod-shaped sensor device. Dulmur had met the man only once—arguably twice—but he was still much as Dulmur remembered him: a tall, flamboyantly attired, middle-aged Tandaran with a wavy shock of what appeared to be badly dyed black hair framing a heavily lined, square-jawed face. The V-shaped ridge between his bushy eyebrows was sharper-edged and narrower than most Tandarans'. His gray eyes brightened as the agents approached. "Ahh, the amaranthine Agent Lucsly. I knew it was only a matter of time before our worldlines would converge again."

"Professor."

"And this must be your partner, Agent Delmer."

"We've met," Dulmur said patiently, shaking his hand. "Eight years, three months, one week ago. And it's Dulmur."

Vard blinked. "Really? You're satisfied with a name beginning with 'dull'?" He shrugged. "Well, you are DTI."

Dulmur let it roll over him with practiced ease as Lucsly said, "Professor, we're here to investigate—"

"Of course you are. The greatest temporal researcher of our age almost assassinated? I daresay you'd better investigate! But not to worry, I've already made thorough scans of the area. With better equipment than yours, I might add." He flourished his scanning device.

"So you believe the hoverbus crash was an assassination attempt?" Dulmur asked.

"Surely you've spoken to the inspectors," Vard said, "and learned that the crash has no discernible cause. Sabotage by an anachronistically advanced technology is the only explanation. And look!" He showed them the readout on his device. "Look at the residual spin states in the indium nuclei in that display panel. A clear tachyon resonance signature. Based on the decay coefficient, the tachyon field strength at the moment of the crash must have been at least three-point-seven kilomalocs. Compelling evidence of a temporal displacement. The polarity and entropy readings are consistent with a prochronistic incursion."

"Do you know why someone from the future might target you, Professor?" Lucsly asked. "Are you working on any sensitive projects?"

"At the moment, I'm focused on teaching," Vard said. "Passing on my wisdom to the minds of tomorrow—surely there's no more important project than that."

"Then maybe you weren't the target," Dulmur suggested. "Maybe they were after one of your graduate students."

"Them? They're nobody!" Vard cried, incredulous. "Obviously they were after me for something I *will* do in the future. Something they hoped to prevent!"

"Leave the deductions to us, Professor," Lucsly said. "We still don't know for sure that the crash was a paracausal event."

"Well, can't you check your shielded files to determine if it occurred in the unaltered history?" He frowned. "No, wait. The shielded files would only retain information recorded before a merger of quantum realities, information that would normally have been erased in the quantum convergence. In this case, the attack would itself have caused a divergence of timelines, with the merger occurring in the future at the moment of the time travel. Any information in your files about the time of the crash would have been recorded in *this* temporal branching, so they'd be of no use to you."

Dulmur was surprised. "You know about our shielded files?"

Vard's expression was the worst simulation of modesty he'd ever seen. "I designed the phase discriminators they use, Agent Duller."

"Dulmur."

"Of course. Now, obviously, the next step is to figure out what it is I'm supposed to do in the future that they wanted to stop."

"Don't you think it's more important to protect yourself against further attacks?"

"No need," Vard said. "How do you suppose I survived the first one? One agency from the future tried to kill me, another acted to save me. Clearly keeping me alive is important to the future of the galaxy. I'm sure I'm in safe hands. Safer than DTI could provide, certainly."

Lucsly and Dulmur exchanged a look. The professor barely noticed as they moved to the rear of the alley, out of

Vard's earshot. "You know there's a possibility he's over-looking, right?" Dulmur asked.

Lucsly nodded. "That the crash was supposed to happen. That saving him and his students was the alteration."

Dulmur got a sinking feeling in his stomach. "What do we do if history says they were supposed to die?"

"Let's not go there yet," Lucsly said. "Let's focus on figuring out who came back. Maybe then we can find out what their purpose was."

Dulmur looked back at the professor, who was cheerily humming to himself as he fiddled with his sensor. Dulmur had never disliked someone so readily while so desperately hoping he was right.

16:55 UTC

With the chroniton scans proving inconclusive, Dulmur had proposed a more traditional approach to detective work: checking the area for DNA residue, reviewing security footage, questioning bystanders to find if they'd noticed anything unusual. Temporal operatives were skilled at making themselves nondescript, even invisible, but sometimes they were careless.

And sometimes they were familiar. A few of the witnesses described a woman leaving the alley shortly before Vard and his students were found there semi-conscious: a wiry, compactly built humanoid with black hair, brown or bronze skin, a temporal ridge that might be Tandaran or Bajoran, and perhaps some form of decoration or natural ridging on her ears. Luckily for the agents, Tandaran society still employed public surveillance more than most Federation worlds, and thus Dulmur was able to turn up one-point-eight precious seconds of security footage revealing a face he and Lucsly both recognized. "Jena Noi," Dulmur said.

"Jena Noi," Lucsly echoed, giving a solemn nod. He drew out his padd and began to enter text.

Dulmur saw that he was filing a report of Noi's presence with the Department. "Hoping to draw her out?"

"Mm-hm." Dulmur understood. Lucsly wanted this discovery, and its precise place and time, on the record . . . for posterity. It was the best way to send Noi a message.

"No need," came a new, clear voice. The agents whirled. There stood a familiar woman dressed in ordinary Tandaran garb: mahogany-skinned with just a hint of green, her face youthful with lambent gold eyes and fantastic cheekbones, her black hair pulled back into a shoulder-length braid exposing intricately scalloped, pointed ears resembling those of an Ocampa (a Delta Quadrant species Dulmur recognized from the logs of temporal incidents aboard the *Starship Voyager*, notably the biotemporal regression incident of Stardate 50812). If a time agent's goal was to be nondescript and blend in, Jena Noi's striking features made her a poor fit. No known species had her exact mix of traits; but then, she was most likely descended from multiple species, some not even contacted yet.

"Agent Noi," Lucsly said.

"Long time no see," Dulmur added.

"Longer for you than me, Dulmur," Federation Temporal Agent Noi said with a tiny smirk. "The lines give you character, in an old-fashioned sort of way. And Lucsly, I like the gray."

"Are you the one who rescued Vard and his students?" Lucsly asked. "Or the one who tried to kill them?"

"You know I can't answer your questions, Gariff."

"Who was the target? Who should we be protecting?"

"You should go home. Just report that everything is under control. You aren't needed here anymore."

Dulmur stepped forward, keeping a full head of bluster to fight the intimidation he felt at confronting a temporal operative from nearly seven centuries uptime. "This is our era, Noi. Our jurisdiction. We have a responsibility—"

"To uphold the Temporal Accords. You know the rules as well as I do, Agent Dulmur. You're asking me to pollute the timestream."

After that, there was nothing more to say. As much as it rankled him, Dulmur knew she was right. The flow of information from the future could alter the timeline. In cases like this, Dulmur had no choice but to turn off his need to find the answers, to let the mystery stand.

But that meant trusting the good intentions of a woman who, by her very nature, could never give him enough information to prove that trust was warranted.

Seeing that she'd gotten her point across, Noi turned to leave. But she paused and turned back, her expression softening. "Just know the threat is past. The timeline is as it should be."

"For now," Lucsly said. "What if the saboteurs strike again?"

"They won't. We got them."

She didn't hide her expressions as well as she should. "They won't strike here," Dulmur interpreted. "But there's something bigger going on, isn't there? Something that affects this time as well as yours."

"If there's anything the DTI can assist with," Noi said coldly, "you will be informed, insofar as temporal regs allow. For now, consider this an order from a temporally superior authority. Go home."

She strode briskly from the alley and turned the corner. Dulmur knew there was no point in pursuing her; even if they'd been right behind her, she would have vanished the moment she was out of their line of sight. And no one in the street would report having seen her at all. That was the nature of the quantum-tunneling time portals the Temporal Agency used. They affected reality on a subtle level, created an ambiguity the brain couldn't process, and so it was always impossible to perceive the moment of her arrival or departure. The brain just overlooked the discontinuity, as it would in a dream.

Sighing, Dulmur turned to his partner. "You know her better than I do. Can we trust her?"

Lucsly pondered. "To do what she thinks is right."

"Which isn't necessarily good for us."

Lucsly met his eyes. "She specifically brought up asking for our assistance."

Dulmur nodded, understanding. "You think she wouldn't have mentioned it if there weren't a chance it could happen."

"It's as much of a gesture of trust as we can expect."

"Maybe," Dulmur said. "But trust from Jena Noi has a way of leading us into trouble."

DOWNTIME
STARDATE 43731.5 TO 43738.6

VII

Day of Sharing, Week of Laughter, House of the Heart,
Year 467, Risian Calendar
A Friday

DTI Branch Office, San Francisco
16:38 UTC

"You're late," the transporter operator told Dulmur once he'd finished materializing. "Lucsly's gonna be ticked off."

Dulmur headed for the exit. "Yeah, when isn't he?"

"See what I did there? Ticked off? Like his clocks."

Dulmur ignored her. He had no patience for time jokes right now, especially since the order to report in had robbed him of the quality time he'd been planning to spend with Megumi today. It was the first chance he'd had in weeks to spend any real time with his wife, and he needed that now more than ever.

He stormed toward the assistant director's office, where he saw Lucsly and Andos meeting with an unfamiliar woman with long, braided black hair. He was ready to barge in and speak his mind about the sacrifice of his long-overdue vacation time, but some instinct caused him to slow. There was something in the way Lucsly and Andos held themselves in the presence of the woman, a mix of deference and extreme wariness, as if it were dangerous even to speak to her. The exotic-featured, dark-skinned woman, whose species Dulmur didn't recognize, looked way too young to command such deference. She wore an odd black uniform made of a shimmering, striated material, but it had no markings to identify her.

Her bright eyes fixed briefly on Dulmur and seemed to analyze and judge him in a split second. She turned to Lucsly and asked a question, her expression severe. Lucsly gave a cool reply, followed by a more emphatic one from Andos. The mystery woman appeared to relent, though not without reservations, and gave Lucsly a nod as she spoke again. Lucsly's eyes met Dulmur's through the window, and the younger agent took that as his cue to enter.

But instead, Lucsly moved quickly and intercepted Dulmur just outside the door. "Come on," he said. "We have a case."

"What? What case?"

"If you'd shown up on time, you'd know. I'll fill you in en route."

"Hey, wait a minute!" He dashed after Lucsly, who was heading back the way Dulmur had just come from. "For your information, I would've got here on time, but I got sidetracked by an argument with my wife."

"You seem to be having a lot of those lately," Lucsly observed. "I'd think you'd be able to adjust your time budget to accommodate them."

Had it been anyone but Lucsly, he would've taken it as snide. But Dulmur knew it was just his partner's perennial cluelessness about anything not chronological. "I *had* 'budgeted' the whole weekend to her. You know that. A nice long weekend to make up for having so little time for her lately." The past few months had been rough. He and Lucsly had been run ragged chasing down the Ky'rha Artifacts, a set of ancient time-displacement devices created by an ancient civilization that had been wiped out nine thousand years ago by the Shenchorig. Why the Ky'rha's mastery of time travel hadn't saved their civilization was a mystery; perhaps they'd simply fled into another time like the Sarpeidons had to escape the Beta Niobe supernova. Or perhaps the devices had been too few in number, too new a technology or too difficult to replicate. Only eighteen had been found in anywhere near an intact state. Mercifully, only two had been in working condition, and the Alpha Centaurian archaeological team that had discovered them, led by a Professor Miliani Langford, had used the second to repair the timeline after a member of their team had used the first to travel back to the prime of Ky'rha civilization and inadvertently created an altered history in which—according to Langford's debriefing— the Ky'rha had successfully repelled the Shenchorig from their territory, driving them instead to migrate toward the Alpha Quadrant and overrun the Federation core worlds in the sixth millennium BCE. Afterward, Langford had shown the good sense to contact the Department immediately and turn over the five devices her team had found, which were now secure in the Eridian Vault. Despite Lucsly's grumbling about civilians tramping around in the past without proper training, Langford had done the Federation a great service.

But thirteen of the devices had been taken off-planet by tomb raiders and sold to the highest bidders, and it had been a race for Lucsly, Dulmur, and their fellow agents to track them all down and confiscate or destroy them before they could be repaired. In some cases, they'd had to negotiate with their counterparts in foreign governments and trust in their good faith and judgment with respect to timeline integrity—not always a safe bet when dealing with the Romulan Temporal Assessment Group or the Cardassian Obsidian Order. Luckily, the Artifacts' technology was so advanced that no one had managed to figure them out yet.

Still, as long as the risk had existed, there had been no rest for the DTI agents. Even when Dulmur had gotten to spend time at home with Megumi, he'd been preoccupied with the hunt. At first, Meg had understood, thinking it was the same obsessiveness he'd always had. But she'd usually been able to get him to relax and step back from that. This time, with so much at stake for the galaxy, he hadn't been able to stop worrying for a minute. And he hadn't been able to explain why to his wife, since the specifics of the case were highly classified. The more time he'd spent away from home, or physically at home but mentally on the hunt, the more frustrated Meg had become. She'd even accused him of having an affair. He'd joked that he wished he had time for one, but that hadn't gone over as he'd intended.

Now that the Artifacts were all safely in the hands of either the Department or its more trustworthy foreign counterparts, the immediate crisis past and the timeline as secure as it ever got, Dulmur had been counting on this weekend to reconnect with Meg and make things right. So for this to happen now . . . "I gotta tell you, Lucsly, for once your timing is just atrocious."

"Not my decision. Threats to the timeline can crop up at any moment."

"Save me the recruiting speech. Couldn't you have gotten someone else to do it?"

Lucsly stared at him. "You're my partner."

"I know, but—"

"I'm the only agent Jena Noi trusts, and she approved you for this because of your connection to me."

Dulmur blinked. "Who's Jena Noi?"

"I'll tell you later. Right now, all you need to know is that we have to be at Risa within two days, eighteen hours."

"*Risa?!*" Dulmur grabbed Lucsly's arm. "Are you crazy? Meg already suspects me of cheating on her! How's it gonna look if I ditch our special weekend and go off to the hedonism capital of the galaxy?"

Lucsly pondered for a moment. "Bad."

"You think?"

"But we still have to be on Risa within two days, eighteen hours."

"Or what?"

"You really don't want to know."

Galartha Sector, Risa
Day of Release, Week of Laughter,
House of the Heart, 467 (A Monday)
02:39 UTC
Lucsly would tell Dulmur nothing on the transport to Risa, considering it insufficiently secure. It made for quiet company. Dulmur spent what time he could on the comm with Megumi, trying to appease her anger at him for putting his work above her again. But he couldn't get out of telling her where his transport was headed, so the call ended with two minutes, forty-eight seconds of shouting and profanities from Meg.

It was some small comfort that, upon arriving at the pleasure capital of the quadrant, Dulmur was given no opportunity to partake of the sybaritic indulgences that Meg had accused him of seeking out. No sooner did they arrive at the sunny Siraven Resort that Lucsly dragged Dulmur after him toward the rocky hills and cliffs beyond.

"Where are we going?" Dulmur asked.

"A series of subterranean caverns twenty-seven kilometers due east."

"Twe—twenty-seven kilometers? On foot? Couldn't we have beamed there? Or at least rented a hovercar?"

"Too conspicuous. We need to keep a low profile."

Despite being six years and two days Dulmur's senior, Lucsly handled the long hike much more easily. Before long, Dulmur understood why his partner insisted on walking to work, and realized he should make more of an effort to do the same. Though after about a dozen kilometers, Dulmur never wanted to walk anywhere ever again.

Once they reached a good resting spot protected from Epsilon Ceti's twin suns by a high rock face, Dulmur took time to catch his breath and drink a long draft from his canteen before saying, "So are you going to tell me what this is all about?" At Lucsly's hesitation, he went on. "That woman in the office, Jena Noi. She's from the future, isn't she?"

After a moment, Lucsly nodded. "Federation Temporal Agent, late thirty-first century."

Dulmur needed a moment to take it in. Even though he'd figured it out, getting confirmation had an impact. "And the Temporal Accords won't let her meddle directly in the past. So she recruits us?"

"Sometimes. A colleague or predecessor of hers, going by the name Daniels, sometimes recruited Jonathan Archer's aid back in the 2150s. These days, they rely on the Department. Keeping it within the classified loop."

"Not just the Department," Dulmur countered. "You said before, you're the only one she trusts. Why is that?"

"Long story." He rose. "Suffice to say, she knows I'll do whatever it takes to preserve the original timeline the way it's meant to be." Dulmur noted the fervent gleam in his partner's eye. Despite the proven existence of alternate histories, Lucsly devoutly believed that the timeline he inhabited was the true, original one. He considered it a matter of probability rather than faith; the "true" history of the universe was the most probable one, the one that would unfold most naturally in the absence of interference, and by definition, the timeline that any given individual, say, himself, was most likely to inhabit was the most probable one. Dulmur could quibble with Lucsly's reasoning, but he chose not to; for purely selfish reasons, he had no problem with putting this timeline first in his priorities.

"And that means," Dulmur said, "that she can trust you not to pry for information about the future, or reveal anything you do find out."

"Exactly. Come on, we only have two hours, eleven minutes."

Lucsly strode forward and Dulmur came after. "Until what? You still haven't told me where we're going."

This time, Lucsly didn't hesitate. "Nine days from now, a pair of Vorgon criminals from the twenty-seventh century will attempt to steal the Tox Uthat from the archaeologist who discovers its hiding place in the Galarthan caves."

Dulmur's eyes widened. "The Tox Uthat? You mean it's real?" Naturally he was familiar with the interstellar legend of a mysterious and powerful device hidden in the twenty-second century by a visitor from the future. An archaeologist named Samuel Estragon, recently deceased, had made the quest for the Uthat his life's work and had been periodically questioned about it by the Department. But despite that, no proof had ever been found that it was anything more than a cosmic myth.

"Mm-hm," Lucsly said. "And it's a very powerful weapon. Fortunately, the Vorgons will fail to recover the Uthat. Unfortunately, they will escape, having discovered its location."

"Oh, crap. You mean they go back to now so they can dig it up before that archaeologist does. Change history."

"That's what we have to prevent. Agent Noi tracked their timeship's course to two hours and nine minutes from now. Then she came back early enough to ensure we'd be there in time to intercept them."

"And do what?" Dulmur asked, suddenly very worried. "How can we compete with weapons from three hundred years in the future?"

"According to Noi, the Vorgons won't use lethal force against anyone from this era, for fear of disrupting history. They just want the Uthat."

"But they're disrupting history to get their hands on it."

"I said they were criminals."

"So do you trust this Jena Noi?"

A pause. "We have an understanding."

"What does that mean?"

"Wait." Upon cresting a hill, they saw they were no longer alone. A pond had formed in a natural depression, and on the edge of the pond were several very fit Risians of both sexes and several less fit tourists of several sexes, all of them in . . . well, not so much various states of undress as assorted variations on near-total nudity. They were all

too preoccupied in . . . what they were doing with one another . . . to notice the DTI agents. Well, almost all. One
particularly perky-looking Risian with tumbling black curls
and a wide smile waved at them without interrupting . . .
what she was doing.

Dulmur stared for a few moments. "What *are* they
doing?"

"*Jamaharon.*"

Dulmur shook himself and turned to look at his partner, who observed the scene with a clinical eye. "So that's
jamaharon?"

"The tag-team version." Lucsly met his eyes. "It's a
very sacred rite. We should leave them to it."

He started to move on, but Dulmur caught his arm.
"Wait. How do *you* know so much about it?"

A pause. "I'm not at liberty to say."

06:24 UTC

When they reached the right chamber within the underground cavern system, Lucsly and Dulmur heard movement within it. "We're late!" Lucsly hissed, making it a
curse. "Come on!"

Drawing their hand phasers, they flattened against
the sides of the chamber entrance. Dulmur peered inside. The chamber was roughly hemispherical, perhaps a
lava bubble whose roof had collapsed, creating a natural
skylight through which the waning light of Risa's suns
illuminated the chamber. Yet its lower portion was oddly
terraced, as though some ancient Risians had carved it
into a ritual site. In the far left corner stood two humanoids, a male and a female, using handheld devices to
project faint blue beams that disintegrated the centuries'

worth of accumulated dirt that made up the cavern floor. They wore dark, layered garments highlighted with silvery patches. Their skin was orange with purplish striations, their bald heads high and tapered, reminding Dulmur of terra cotta pots. Their lower faces and necks were covered in multiple breathing slits. He glanced at Lucsly, who nodded—these were indeed their targets.

It takes all the fun out of it when someone just tells you where to find the bad guys, Dulmur thought. But then he remembered he had a furious wife back home. *On second thought, the sooner we wrap this up, the better.*

After exchanging a look, the two agents barged inside, bringing their phasers to bear on the Vorgons. "Freeze! Department of Temporal Investigations!" Lucsly cried.

The aliens whirled, raising their disintegrators. "Drop the device, now!" Dulmur shouted, putting all his pent-up anger at the situation into the words. Apparently it worked; after trading a look, the female dropped the red crystalline device from her mittlike hand and the male followed her lead. "Keep your hands where I can see them," Dulmur ordered.

"And away from your heads," Lucsly added. Dulmur noted that each Vorgon had a small square device implanted roughly where a human's left ear would be. Was Lucsly just guessing or had Temporal Agent Noi tipped him off?

"Please, you must listen to us," the female said, her voice multitonal as it emerged from her complex respiratory apparatus. "If you are DTI, you must know we are from the future."

"Exactly," Lucsly said. "And we're arresting you for attempted historical alteration."

"No!" she cried. "I am Ajur and this is Boratus. We are temporal enforcers like yourselves, here to protect the timeline by recovering the Tox Uthat!"

"Not true," Dulmur said. "You're wanted criminals who've already made one try at the Uthat and have come further back to rewrite your own past."

The Vorgons traded a look. "You are well-informed," said the male, Boratus. "No doubt you have sources from the future. How are their actions any different from ours?"

"Because they're trying to keep time from changing," Lucsly said.

"So are we," said Ajur. "We intend to substitute a copy for the real Uthat, so that events will proceed unaltered."

"Don't you think people will figure out it's a fake?"

Ajur gave a wry tilt to her head. "The device will be destroyed shortly after its discovery—to keep it from falling into our hands. I saw it with my own eyes."

Dulmur's certainty wavering, he threw a look at Lucsly. The senior agent stood resolute, asking, "And what did you plan to do with the Uthat once you had it?" Clearly his trust in Agent Noi was real.

Boratus sneered. "A better question is, what would Kal Dano have done with it if we hadn't stopped him?"

"Kal Dano?" Dulmur asked.

"The inventor of the Tox Uthat," Ajur said. "The mysterious wanderer through time described in your legends. But he was no mere wanderer. His invention is a quantum phase inhibitor, a device that fits in one hand yet has the power to shut down all fusion in a star, triggering a core collapse and supernova-like explosion. Think about it," she told the agents, taking a step toward them. "Why would he invent such a horrible weapon and then take it into the past?"

"He was a Shirna, the great enemy of our people," Boratus said. "He intended to destroy our home system in the past before we even developed warp drive. Fortunately we intercepted him and forced him to hide it before he could use it. He was killed evading pursuit shortly thereafter."

"Requiring us to return home and peruse the historical record in order to track it down," Ajur finished.

"So if your motives are so benevolent," Dulmur demanded, "why not just let the thing be destroyed? You killed the guy for his doomsday weapon and now you want it for yourselves. Sorry, but that doesn't make me want to trust you."

"If the Uthat is destined to be destroyed," Lucsly said, "then let it be destroyed."

Sizing them up, Ajur made a decision. Her sincere expression gave way to a haughty sneer. "And who are you to enforce that decision? You're just DTI. Mere record-keepers and referees. You don't even travel in time. We'll simply go back and try again." Her hand began to move toward her head implant.

"Stop!" Dulmur shouted. "You do not want to test my reaction time, lady!"

Ajur looked bored. "Boratus?"

The male Vorgon charged them, forcing them to fire at him. His garment resisted the phaser beams, so Dulmur raised his aim to take Boratus in the head, stunning him. The distraction was enough to allow Ajur to touch her head implant.

And nothing happened. Looking skyward in bewilderment, she tapped it again and again, with no response.

"Computer!" she cried. "Emergency beam-out! Activate the temporal drive!" But still she remained in the cave.

"Something tells me your ship has been neutralized by someone who *does* travel in time," Lucsly told her.

"Yeah, you might want to surrender now," Dulmur said.

Ajur's nasal folds fluttered with furious breaths, but she lowered her arms in surrender. Lucsly kept her covered while Dulmur took a restraint band from his pocket and secured her wrists. He then proceeded to do the same with Boratus, who was already beginning to recover from the phaser stun.

With that done, he walked over to Lucsly. "So now what do we do with them? How do we try them when most of the evidence doesn't exist yet?"

"Leave that to me," came a new voice.

Dulmur whirled, lifting his phaser, but Lucsly pushed down on his arm and nodded reassuringly. Once he got a look at her, Dulmur recognized the speaker as the same exotic woman who had been in Andos's office. "Jena Noi, I presume."

"And you're Agent Dulmur. Pleased to meet you at last."

"Their timecraft's secure?" Lucsly asked.

"No problem."

"And what about them?"

"I'll take them back for trial in their own time," Noi replied.

"We would have done nothing to damage this segment of time," Ajur insisted to her.

"Shut up," the Temporal Agent barked. "Do you have any idea the risk you've taken, intervening now? Here?

With *him* of all people?" Ajur seemed chastened for reasons Dulmur couldn't grasp.

"Wait a minute," Dulmur groused. "If you were gonna intervene anyway, what did you need us for? Why not just do it all yourself?" *And let me have my weekend with Meg?*

Noi threw him an apologetic look that was irritatingly endearing. "The changes they want to make in history are very specific, so they're careful not to kill anyone in the past that isn't on their target list. But they'd have no compunction about killing someone from their future." She shrugged. "I could've defended myself, but at the risk of creating a disruptive battle where history says there was none."

Dulmur supposed that made sense. But he still wasn't convinced he could trust this woman. Who knew if the Federation of the thirty-first century still had the same positive goals it did today? "So who's really the good guys here? They said the Tox Uthat was invented to destroy their homeworld in the past. And it seems to me there's no good reason for bringing a doomsday weapon back in time."

Noi tilted her head and ran a finger along one scalloped ear. "Sometimes it's bad guys versus bad guys, Agent Dulmur. Both sides want to change the past for their own reasons. Our job as Temporal Accord signatories is to stop them all. And you two have done the timeline a great service today."

"Thanks," Dulmur grumbled. "Any chance you could send me back three days and let me have my weekend with my wife after all? Just kidding!" he added at Lucsly's scandalized stare.

"I'm sorry about your weekend," she said. "Even time travelers don't always have good timing. But things will work out the way they're supposed to." The wistful tone in her voice didn't reassure him.

Noi strode between the Vorgons and took hold of them, hauling Boratus's heavy frame upright with one dainty arm. Dulmur's eyes grew wide at the display of strength. "Thanks again, Lucsly, Dulmur. See you in the future." With a blue shimmer, they were gone.

"Can we get out of here now?" Dulmur said.

"Not yet," Lucsly said. He pointed at the large hole the Vorgons had left in the cave floor. "Nobody can know this happened. The Uthat needs to be there for its discoverer to find three days from now. We need some shovels and about, mmm, half a ton of dirt."

"Ohh, Lord," Dulmur moaned. "Now I really need a vacation."

PRESENT TIME
STARDATE 58746.7 TO 58806.9

VIII

U.S.S. Capitoline
13:47 UTC

After eleven days of increasingly circular debate, Ranjea, Garcia, and Troi had made no progress in persuading the Vomnin to restrict their visits to the Axis of Time, or in convincing Lirahn to impose restrictions on behalf of the Axis Council. And so Ranjea had come to a difficult decision. "I'm growing convinced," he told his fellow negotiators as they met in *Capitoline*'s conference room, "that Lirahn does not speak for all the groups that jointly manage the Axis."

Commander Troi nodded. "I feel the same way. She's difficult to get an empathic read on; her self-control is extraordinary. But I can't believe that so many disparate groups from so many vastly separated eras could be as completely in agreement as she claims."

"Exactly," Ranjea replied. "And I have gotten the clear impression from her that she's hiding something when she's pressed about differences of opinion within the Council." He took a breath. "I'm convinced we need to go into the Axis ourselves. We need to find what other voices there are within its leadership and whether we can cultivate them as allies."

"Whoa, wait a minute," Garcia said. "That would mean traveling through time. Isn't that against Department policy?"

Ranjea had been mulling that over for days, which was why he had waited so long to propose this. "Yes, technically. But if we remain within the Axis, if we don't return to our continuum except at the point of our entry, then we won't technically be visiting our own past or future. We'll merely be occupying points that allow *access* to our past or future, but lie within a continuum where our own time has no meaning or relevance. It's pushing the letter of regulations, I admit, but I don't believe we have a choice."

Teresa had relaxed as he spoke and was smiling now. "If you say so, boss. To tell the truth, I've been dying to get a look at the place. Not to mention the people. There might be living relics in there, representatives of dead cultures I've only known from their ruins. Imagine what we could learn!"

"Just be careful," he reminded her. "The exchange of information goes both ways."

She grew subdued. "Yeah, I know. Don't worry, I'll follow your lead."

He sensed the hint of bitterness in her words, knew she was upset with him, and he knew why. But he saw in Deanna Troi's eyes that she sensed it too and was ready to do something about it if asked. It wasn't Ranjea's way to retreat from dealing with a personal matter himself. But if Teresa saw him as the cause of her anger, perhaps she would be more receptive to another voice right now. And Deanna was an accomplished counselor; she'd had to be in order to maintain the stability of *Titan*'s remarkably diverse crew on a mission that kept them so far from home for so long. He could tell the Betazoid woman was brimming with compassion and the desire to help anyone in need; who was he to deprive her of the chance to fulfill that desire?

Once Ranjea had left the conference room to make arrangements with the starships' captains, Garcia started to head back to her quarters. But Commander Troi's voice stopped her. "You have doubts about his judgment."

She turned back to face the older woman, crossing her arms. "No, he's right. As long as we're careful, we're not breaking regs."

"All right. Then what is it about his recent choices that you *don't* agree with?"

Garcia sighed. *Counselors and their leading questions. I get enough of this from Clare.* "Okay. I admit it. I'm only human. I've accepted that there's no way he can be with me." There was no point in trying to hide her feelings for Ranjea from a Betazoid. "And I'm not jealous that he's hooked up with your Ensign Fell. I understand. She's Deltan, she can have what I can't."

Troi studied her a moment more. "Yet you're still angry at him."

"I'm not. It's his life, after all. If he wants to . . . go ahead and enjoy himself, it's up to him. Why should he care whether he does it practically right in front of me?" she finished through gritted teeth.

"So you think he's being insensitive. Flaunting his sexual freedom with his own people and failing to consider how it makes you feel."

Garcia blinked several times, clearing the moisture

from her eyes. "I don't know, maybe I shouldn't blame a Deltan for having casual sex. But he knows . . . he knows I'm lonely and I thought he was willing to help me through that, as far as he safely could." She'd been through so much counseling these past months that it didn't feel odd to open up like this to a near-stranger. "So to turn around and, and do this, and not seem to care how it makes me feel . . ." She broke off, shaking her head.

Troi's expression grew wistful, understanding. "Teresa, you need to know, there's nothing casual about it." She took a moment to formulate her words. "The Deltan oath of celibacy is difficult for them. They swear to it in order to protect others, but they're depriving themselves of something basic, something important to Deltan mental health. There are ways to compensate, meditative techniques and the like, but for a Deltan to go without intimacy with others . . . Imagine if you went to live on a planet where they didn't allow solid food. You could survive, you could compensate for the lack of what your body needed, but given the opportunity to devour a steak and salad, could you pass it up?"

Troi's words chastened Garcia. "I . . . I hadn't thought about that. How hard it must be for him."

"Harder for Ensign Fell, actually. Peya is young, inexperienced. And she's the only Deltan on a ship where visits home are few and far between. Moreover, she was injured last month, in *Titan*'s first encounter with the Sentry artificial intelligences. It was a frightening and traumatic experience for her, and she needed a unitive connection to help her heal. Frankly I'm grateful that Ranjea was there to help her. It would have been a longer, harder road for her if he hadn't arrived when he did.

"So ask yourself, Teresa: is that really a threat to your need for companionship? Or is it reassurance of his generosity toward anyone in need?"

Garcia was blushing now, abashed by her own insensitivity. On the surface, Deltans appeared so casual about their sexuality, so open and promiscuous that it seemed like a game to them. But Troi's words helped her begin to grasp that there was a far deeper intimacy to it on an emotional level—perhaps as deep as any bond between human lovers or spouses, but shared more easily with more than one person at a time. "I just . . . I guess I envy her getting to . . . know what it's like to be with him."

"Maybe what you need is a distraction," Troi said. "It's not the same level of companionship you're looking for, but there are lots of eligible males in *Titan*'s crew, and *Capitoline*'s too. I'm sure our men in particular would welcome a fresh . . . face. And I've seen the way they look at you. You should have no trouble finding companionship of your own."

Garcia stared at her, grinning. "So your professional recommendation as a therapist . . . is that I get laid?"

Troi chuckled. "I'd rather not put it that way for the record."

"Don't worry," Garcia told her. "I think you're suddenly my favorite therapist ever."

Shuttlecraft *Cincinnatus*
19:15 UTC

Ranjea's plan to enter the Axis had put Sikran in a bit of a bind. The Vomnin representative couldn't say no, since free access to the pocket dimension was what he and Lirahn were advocating. But if there were dissenting voices in the Council that might be persuaded to shut down that access, the Confederacy would be out one potentially very lucrative source of ancient—or future—technology.

So in the end, Sikran and Lirahn insisted on accompanying the DTI team as "guides." Ranjea accepted this calmly, telling Garcia that they would simply have to adjust to this reality as best they could.

Captain Riker insisted on sending along a couple of his people as well: *Titan*'s science officer Melora Pazlar, a low-gravity Elaysian clad in a formfitting antigrav suit, and Ellec Krotine, a Boslic security guard with golden skin and cherry-red hair. From the way they both stared at Ranjea, Garcia had to wonder if maybe Riker should have sent male personnel instead.

Once the *Capitoline*'s shuttlecraft was en route, Garcia shuddered a bit as it drew nearer to the diaphanous orb that was the portal to the Axis of Time. Next to her, Pazlar smiled at her. "Your first actual trip through time?"

Is it that obvious I'm a rookie? "Second, actually. First planned one."

"Oh. So you're nervous that something might go wrong again." Pazlar shook her head. "I can't blame you, after what we went through at Orisha."

"It's not that," Garcia told her. "I've just had it drilled into me for months that what we're about to do is a very bad idea. My first mission and already I'm dreading what the director will think of my report."

Krotine's green eyes widened in disbelief. "We're about to enter one of the wonders of the cosmos, and all you can think about is paperwork?"

Garcia didn't expect a Starfleet crewperson to understand. It was that mundane, procedural focus that kept a DTI agent grounded in the face of something like this.

Still, when the shuttle passed through the spherical portal, seeming to go into a spin in a direction Garcia couldn't directly perceive, and then emerged into the realm beyond, Garcia's sense of wonder emerged in full force. The shuttle seemed to be flying through a vast glass cylinder. All around it in a ring, superimposed on the still-visible background stars, she could see a distorted image of the shuttle's own lights. As the shuttle banked toward a course parallel with the cylindrical space, the reflected arcs of light moved with them and split into multiple rings, each one fainter than the previous.

But the light rings moved in the wrong direction to be reflections. As Garcia looked more closely, she saw that the rings of light before her, now drifting off to the side, were too dim to be a reflection of its window lights, and flared as the shuttle's aft thrusters fired to turn it. "The reflections are . . . backward," she said. "We're seeing what's behind us."

"Only one dimension of the Axis space is fully expanded," Lirahn explained. "In the other two dimensions, it is finite and closed, a loop of only a few kilometers. The light we emit loops around and hits us from the other direction. The multiple images are from the same light looping around repeatedly in a spiral path."

But as Garcia watched, the stars vanished, leaving only the shuttle's light. "What happened? The stars . . ."

Sikran answered this time. "We have moved from our initial position along the Axis, so we are now no longer in a place—or time—where the interface with normal space exists. So the stars beyond cannot be seen."

The Vomnin's words sank in. "Are we going forward or back in time?" she asked, hushed.

"Back," Lirahn said. "The Council is based near the midpoint of the Axis, over a million years downtime from your era."

"And how far is that to travel?" she wondered. The pocket universe of the Axis had no subspace in the conventional sense, and thus shortcuts like warp drive and transporters were useless.

"Not far. In your units, a bit over a kilometer per millennium."

As the shuttle moved downtime, they passed through more regions where the stars briefly became visible, at intervals Garcia estimated at several dozen millennia on average. "Pass through one of those and we'd be in the distant past," Garcia breathed, her heart racing at the prospect.

"Yes," Ranjea said. "Which is why we're not doing that."

At many of the interface zones were space stations, surrounded by brilliant rings of their own multicolored light; as the shuttle approached, the first harbinger of each station was a halo of progressively brightening rings and arcs of light, echoes generated as the light spiraled around the constricted universe over and over. It was hard to remember that the illusion of a closed cylinder was actually generated by an absence of boundaries, space physically looping back around on itself in two dimensions. Garcia imagined that what worked for light would work for objects too; if the shuttle flew in any direction perpendicular to the Axis, it would simply keep looping back around and around forever even while perceiving itself traveling in a straight line. That would be handy for any maintenance worker who lost a tool during an EVA, she thought; it would just drift until it hit the other side of the station.

Each station had its own distinct design, perhaps the work of those beings in a particular era who discovered and traded with the Axis. Before Garcia could ask the question aloud, Lirahn answered. "Each of the major powers administering the Axis brings in materials from outside to construct trade stations."

Garcia glared, not appreciating the telepath's intrusiveness. "How long has the Axis existed, internally?" she asked.

"No one is certain, but the first station was built several centuries ago."

Garcia pondered. From an internal point of view, every interface with the outer universe would've come into being at the very beginning of the Axis's existence. So people could've begun traveling out into her time very shortly after the Axis community came into being. "Why wait so long before making contact with our time?"

"Our scouts ventured out into your era at various times," Lirahn said. "But we found the region of space near the interface too hostile, due to a strange and dangerous spacetime anomaly nearby."

"The Null," Melora Pazlar said. "It drove everyone away from that part of space except the Sentry AIs who were created to fight it."

Garcia frowned. "But that was only defeated a couple of weeks before *Titan* found the Axis with a Vomnin station already there."

"Galactic drift carried the Axis portal beyond the Null region within the past year," Sikran explained.

"Ahh, here we are," Lirahn said. Ahead loomed an exceptionally massive and elaborate station, so large that it seemed to merge at some points with its own "reflections." "The structure takes advantage of the finite dimensions of the timespace," Lirahn said, again reading her thoughts. "At some points it actually extends far enough to touch its opposite end. One can travel through it endlessly in a single direction."

"A Möbius structure," Ranjea breathed, grinning hugely. "Magnificent."

Garcia realized there were no stars visible here, no interface with normal space. Of course, Lirahn was right there with the explanation. "The Council meets in a zone with no interface to avoid any perception of favoritism."

"Thanks, I could've figured that out on my own."

The shuttle flew into the open latticework of the station, and suddenly there was nothing but station visible in any direction, as if the entire universe around them consisted of a technological construct. In a sense, at least in two dimensions, it did.

Axis Hub Station
Middle Calabrian Age, Lower Pleistocene Epoch

Soon, the *Cincinnatus* docked in a vast hangar housing ships of dozens of unfamiliar types—although several had design elements that Garcia could swear she recognized from her studies of galactic archaeology. *If I can bring back answers to some of the great archaeological mysteries, can this kind of commerce through time really be all bad?* she wondered. In the corner of her eye, Lirahn smiled.

Once they debarked, Lirahn was promptly greeted by a quartet of crustacean aliens, wide-bodied creatures about a meter and a third tall with mottled blue-and-brown cara-paces, multiple stalked eyes, and six multiclawed limbs that seemed to function interchangeably as arms and legs. They addressed her in a fawning, obsequious manner; it was hard to be sure from their own alien body language, but Lirahn's air of superiority was crystal clear. One sidled be-hind her, crablike, and tilted its body, using its three right-side limbs to drape an ornate cloak around her shoulders while balancing on its other three limbs; its right-side eye-stalks rotated to observe the operation. Another extended a padd for her perusal; she glanced at it briefly, then gave the crustacean a look and sent it scurrying away on some telepathic command. The other two just fell in behind her, ready to serve if called upon. It was a display Garcia found distasteful. She glanced at Ranjea, but he was just taking the whole thing in with his normal, open curiosity—or at least that was what he was letting Lirahn think. Garcia tried to rein in her own reactions.

Close behind Lirahn's invertebrate retinue came a group of beings whom Lirahn introduced as fellow coun-cillors. Damyz was the elder statesman: a member of the Yeshel, one of the most ancient civilizations within the Axis community, dating from nearly three million years in the past. He was a stout, short-tailed biped with a blocky, short-snouted orange-brown head and dark eyes. He greeted the visitors with open arms and warm dignity, but seemed to follow Lirahn's cues.

Oydia was a smallish, silver-furred lemurlike female who introduced herself as a Caratu, a member of the Col-loquium of Progress, a peaceful multispecies community from some eighteen millennia in the past. Garcia had never heard of any such civilization from that era, which troubled her, since Oydia's description made it sound very expansive. How could it have been lost so completely? Still, she said nothing to Oydia about the possible extinction of her civilization, lest it prompt her to seek to prevent it. Over such a relatively short span of time, any changes to the timeline could easily affect the Federation. And Oydia seemed quite friendly with Lirahn.

The roles were reversed when Garcia met Temarel, a councillor from twenty-six thousand years in the future and the only member of the Council whose species Garcia found familiar. Her aspect contained both Vulcan and Romulan attributes, yet was subtly different from either. Yet the councillor, who called her race the Chenar, didn't recognize the names "Vulcan" and "Romulan" when Garcia asked—making her afraid to bring up the name "Federation" or "human." Temarel looked on Lirahn's ostentation with visible distaste, confirming that she didn't follow the ways of Surak.

Last but not least was Shiiem, a tall, slim humanoid whose bronze skin was covered in silvery filigrees that resembled ornate circuit diagrams, and whose eyes glowed with a soft red-orange light from within like a cat's. His people, the Zcham, came from over eight hundred millennia uptime, farther forward than any other councillor. While Damyz apparently functioned as a figurehead on the council, Garcia sensed real power from Shiiem. "We are always glad," the Zcham councillor said, "to hear the concerns of those charged with preserving the integrity of the timestream. All points of view on the question are welcome here." As he said that, his eyes locked with Lirahn's and seemed to flare briefly. The glamorous Selakar held his gaze without flinching. Garcia couldn't blame her, since

she seemed to have at least half the Council on her side—
whatever that side was.

It soon became clear that Lirahn and her cronies weren't
going to let Ranjea out of their sight. The Selakar was determined to control the agenda, and it would be difficult
to have any candid discussions with dissenters so long as
she was around.

Fortunately, Lirahn's attention was fixated on Ranjea—not just for the obvious reasons, but because she'd
apparently dismissed Garcia as a mere subordinate. She'd
been happy to lecture Garcia on the nature of the Axis,
but it had been like talking down to a small child. That
disregard gave them an opportunity. Just outside the
Council chamber, Ranjea stopped Garcia and said, "Listen, this will probably be very long and tedious. I can
handle it, and I know you're eager to get out and explore
the Axis. So why don't you go indulge yourself? See the
sights, learn whatever you can. Have fun."

She caught the subtext: dig for voices of dissent, find
the people or groups that could offer an alternative to
Lirahn's narrative. "How can I resist?" she said, winking at
him. He smiled and nodded. It thrilled her that she *knew*
with such certainty what he wanted. Was it some kind of
Deltan empathic projection, or were they just clicking that
well as a team?

Commander Pazlar ordered Krotine to accompany
Garcia for her protection. Garcia didn't like the Starfleet-
er's assumption that she needed to be nursemaided, but
she didn't mind having the lively Boslic guard along for
company. Krotine seemed as enthusiastic about exploring
the Axis as she was.

It put a damper on Garcia's plans, though, when Lirahn ordered one of her crablike servants—Siri, their species was called—to accompany the two women as a "guide." Or rather, Lirahn threw the order in the general direction of her retinue and let them hash out who would go. One Siri with more blue in its shell than the others volunteered to do the job, and the other two seemed happy to let it. "I am Vikei," the Siri introduced itself, the translator giving its voice a high but masculine timbre. "Anything you wish to know about the Axis, you may freely ask."

In the hours that followed, Garcia had to admit that Vikei made a pretty good tour guide, enthusiastically showing them all the sights of the Axis hub station. Krotine was particularly eager to ride the tram shuttle that traversed an entire lateral dimension of the Axis timespace, traveling constantly in one direction yet always ending up back where it started. The two women rode the shuttle through several cycles, unabashedly laughing and pointing like tourists as they experienced the novelty of going in a straight line that was also a closed loop.

Well, not entirely straight. There was a subtle bend to the tram's path, angling off to the left and then coming back to the right after a time. "I was hoping I'd be able to look ahead and see the back of our own tram," Krotine protested.

"Apologies," Vikei said, "but such an uninterrupted path could allow for dangerous feedback effects. A light shone down such a path, for instance, would continuously cycle through and reinforce itself, creating a runaway amplification that could be quite dangerous."

"Aww," Garcia said. "So you mean there isn't some pit

where you can drop something straight down and have it hit you on the head?" The women laughed.

"In fact, there are a few such enclosed conduits that function as generators, drawing electric power from a metal ball falling continuously at terminal velocity," Vikei said. "Although they have feedback safeguards in place as well. I would be happy to show you one."

"Just a generator?" Krotine sighed. "I was hoping for something more like indoor skydiving."

"Oh, we have that too," Vikei said, sounding disappointed. "I will take you to the recreation facility if you wish."

"Skydiving not your thing?" Garcia asked.

The Siri took a moment to parse her idiom, all six eyestalks focusing on her from several angles. "No, it's simply that the terminal-velocity generators are a Siri invention. My people were—are—rather accomplished engineers."

"So you're not just servants to the Selakar?"

The eyestalks looked around the car in all directions. "This is our stop," Vikei said.

"Which stop?" Krotine asked.

"Please, just come."

The young Boslic looked at Garcia, who gave her a small nod. "Oh, right," Krotine said, catching on that Vikei had a secret he wished to share. "Lead on."

Selakar-Era Axis Outpost
Early Ionian Age, Middle Pleistocene Epoch

"Thank you for coming," Lirahn said as she led Ranjea into the moderate-sized way station situated at the access point for her era. The council session was in recess for mealtime, and Lirahn had offered to show him this sample of her own era, clearly with an ulterior motive or two. Ranjea was playing along in hopes of gathering information, pretending to be responsive to her unsubtle sexual advances in order to get her off her guard, though he found it highly distasteful to use seduction to manipulate another.

"Not at all," he replied in his most charming voice, keeping his misgivings sequestered within his mind. "I'm fascinated to learn more of your era. You've been oddly reticent about it before," he said, his tone conveying merely regret rather than suspicion.

"Yes, I'm sorry, Ranjea. It's simply . . . it's difficult to speak of. Look around you," she said. The station they walked through was spacious yet largely vacant. Beyond the reasonably well-maintained docking area, the corridors appeared worn and neglected. What occupants the station had were mostly Selakar and their Siri servants. "Few from my time remain to take care of this facility," Lirahn went on. "And no one new has come for some time. Not until I discovered it."

"What happened?"

Lirahn bowed her head and wrapped her arms around herself as if chilled. "War. Centuries of horrible warfare, tearing across the galaxy." Ranjea responded to her cue, putting an arm around her back to warm her. The two-meter-plus Selakar glanced down at him in gratitude, holding the gaze for a smoldering moment, before continuing. "We thought ourselves to inhabit such an enlightened time. Over the millennia, the dominant races of the galaxy had developed our technology, our bodies, and most of all our minds to ever greater levels. We had banished disease and want. Our advanced telepathy brought mutual understanding, an anodyne to conflict. We had the means to fulfill our every desire."

She shook her head. "But such fulfillment only feeds ambition. It is the instinct of the animal to need, to crave, to lust," she said, her voice husky as her eyes held his again. "With every reasonable need fulfilled, ambition becomes unreasonable."

Lirahn stepped away, withdrawing the temptation in order to tantalize him. "Some of the great races came to think of themselves as gods, entitled to master the universe and remake it in their image. Dominant among them was the Arret Empire, a consortium of two great races, allies for so long they thought of themselves as a single nation." She looked him over. "One could have been the forebear of your own species, Ranjea, for the resemblance was great. The other may have been an ancestor of Councillor Temarel. For a hundred thousand years, they both spread across the galaxy, terraforming and settling worlds, gradually remaking it in their image. It was a benevolent conquest, though; where they found junior races, they mentored and cultivated them.

"But as the worlds ran out, their ambition remained. Both races craved dominion over the galaxy, and the longtime allies began to see one another as rivals. Countless generations of law and custom stayed them at first, but their minds were so powerful that subconscious desires could manifest and influence lesser, suggestible races. And so began a great war by proxy, as their junior allies turned on one another, finally drawing the master races into conflict as well. It was reluctant at first, but eventually their buried resentments erupted and became the driving force of the war. Now they openly used the other races as pawns in their great struggle, expending and disposing of them en masse. In their pursuit of godhood, they laid waste to their domain."

"Could no one stop them?" Ranjea asked. "Surely there were other races of comparable power."

"A few. But some had their own cravings for power. One race used their mastery of illusion to entice lesser breeds and draw them into their menagerie to be bred as pets and exhibits. Others erected temples on primitive worlds and presented themselves as literal gods, wielding their psionic gifts as proof of divinity. When the war spread to their territories, they fought back with all their means, but for their own power and rule, not for any others' defense. They only spread the devastation further."

Ranjea moved closer, reaching up to stroke her cheek in comfort that he wished could be more than superficial. "And what of your own people? Surely your mental powers rivaled the others'."

She shook her elegant head. "We strove to protect those we could. The Selakar had spent thousands of years bringing prosperity and enlightenment to the races of our region of the galaxy. We could not bear to see them fall prey to the insanity. But we were surrounded, outnumbered. Our worlds were devastated, our power broken. The survivors were scattered, left to wander in search of refuge from the enemies who hunted us."

She drew a trembling breath. "None found it . . . save us." She gestured around her at the station. "We stumbled upon the Axis after the fall of the local civilization that had traded with it. They had hoarded the knowledge of the Axis, so it was lost with them, unknown to our enemies. We found this station nearly vacant, for most of those who built and maintained it had returned home to defend their people—and die with them. But we had nothing left to fight for, and so the station became our refuge. The other races of the Axis took us in, helped us regain our footing. Their generosity saved us."

Her body language was strong, confident, despite the vulnerability in her words. But did that make it deception, he wondered, or simply an armor against despair? What if her tale were sincere?

She turned back to face him, her arms falling about his shoulders. "Now do you see why I value the trading potential of the Axis so deeply? My small remnant of a once-great race owes its continued existence to the goods shared with us freely across the millennia. And perhaps, if the council had not placed such strictures on trade before, the builders of this station might have been better able to defend themselves. I feel an obligation to them for giving us a new home. It's too late to save them, but if I can loosen the council's restrictions on trade, perhaps it can save another civilization in another era from a similar fate."

He clasped her shoulders. "And you brought me here to persuade me to loosen my stance."

"To show you why it is necessary, Ranjea. I could not make this case so effectively in the council chambers. There, the traditions of the Axis pervade the very walls. My voice could not be as strong."

"It seems you have a number of allies on the council already."

"Sympathizers, perhaps. But tradition still reigns, so long as a reactionary like Shiiem still holds sway. He obstructs all efforts to liberalize trade." Her hands now roved across his smooth scalp. "Should you continue to advocate against your era's use of the Axis, it would simply add another voice to the forces of tradition."

"Lirahn . . . you know my obligation is to protect the timeline."

"But what use is protecting the timeline if you do not protect the people within it? How is the transformation of a civilization's history worse than its eradication? How is forgetting an old life worse than having your life end in agony and fear?" Her hands roved down his body now, with considerable skill. "Of course there should be safe-guards, but they should not be so draconian as to render them hollow of purpose." Her face loomed closer over his. "You can understand that . . . can't you?"

Her kiss was aggressive, overwhelming, her embrace too strong to resist. Her mind probed into his just as avidly as her hands pulled off his suit. He went with it, responding in kind, meeting her power with skill, gaining the initiative by giving before she could take. He tasted her emotions, sought understanding of who and what she was. He found great conviction, anger, and need for control, but vulnerability and loss as well. He would have to meditate on them later to probe for their meaning. For now, there was only giving and sharing.

But only to a point. Once Lirahn was breathless with ecstasy, too overcome to dominate him anymore, he brought her back down gently and stepped away. "I believe the meal interval is ending," he told her, his tone apologetic. "We should dress and return."

Her displeasure at that suggestion was the most honest emotion he'd sensed from her. "I could call for a post-ponement."

Ranjea smiled. "My partner would worry."

"Be jealous, more like," Lirahn said with a chuckle. "Not that I blame her. Though I imagine even a taste of your passion would be too much for her little mind to take."

Suddenly Ranjea was very eager to bring the interaction to an end.

Axis Hub Station
Middle Calabrian Age, Lower Pleistocene

Vikei led the Federation women into a long conduit stretching out (back?) from the downtime end of the hub station. "For a long time," the Siri explained once he was confident they were alone, "we were unable to be anything but the Selakar's servants. Now—in my own time— the Siri are free, except here."

"Free?" Krotine asked, her green eyes widening in her pleasant gold-skinned face. "You mean you were slaves?"

"Yes, though most of us were unable to admit it. The Selakar held our minds in thrall, made us eager to serve them. In our own time, the Selakar's power was broken in the Great Psionic War, freeing our people—those who survived. But Lirahn and her allies discovered the Axis and fled into it before they could be captured. Most Siri here remain in her power, glad to debase themselves to her."

Great Psionic War? Half a million years ago? The archaeologist in Garcia was jumping up and down, eager to ask more. She knew of at least two powerful telepathic races, the Talosians and the Sargonians, whose starfaring civilizations had fallen in vast wars around that time. Was it possible they'd been participants in some even greater galactic conflict?

But this was not the time for that. Not when Lirahn

was keeping slaves. "But you're not under her control," Garcia said.

"Normally I submit to it, but I can break free when I need to."

"How?"

"With help and training from certain others. I am taking you to meet them. They will tell you more about Lirahn's plans."

Garcia smiled. "You're a great tour guide, Vikei. That's exactly what I was hoping to see."

Soon they reached a small chamber at the far downtime end of the conduit. It was nondescript save for its occupant, a Zcham female even leaner than Shiiem, though evidently in good health for her species. "Please sit," the Zcham said. Once the women had complied, the lanky, bronze-skinned humanoid stepped behind them and placed a silver-tattooed hand on each of their heads. After a moment, she released her grip. "Good," she said, then came around before them and lowered herself into a lotus position, closing her eyes.

"Um . . ." Garcia said after a moment.

The Zcham's eyes sprang open, glowing brighter than before. "Welcome," she said in a deeper, masculine voice which Garcia thought she recognized. "I am Shiiem."

Garcia blinked. "Uhh . . . are you related to Councillor Shiiem?"

"I am Councillor Shiiem."

"The same Shiiem who's meeting with my partner in the council chamber right now?"

"And is male?" Krotine added.

"I am using a proxy routine to operate my main body while I converse with you through the body of my colleague Hariin. This way we can speak without Lirahn being aware of it."

Krotine looked shaken, but DTI training helped inoculate one against the weird. "So you're some kind of telepath?" Garcia asked.

Shiiem—Hariin—whoever—shook his/her head. "In your terms, a cyborg. Mostly organic, but our integrated nanotechnology grants us many useful abilities," he/she went on, displaying the silver patterns adorning one hand. "Such as an immunity to Lirahn's telepathic manipulation."

"Ah," Garcia said. "I *thought* that was what you wanted to talk about. My partner and I can tell she's up to something, but we need to know just what it is."

"We are not entirely certain ourselves," Shiiem said, "but much is easy to surmise. Lirahn's race, the Selakar, were overthrown from their rule of a large portion of the galaxy, overlapping the current territory of the Vomnin Confederacy. Since coming here, Lirahn and her cronies have attempted to gain influence over the Axis. Her race has formidable psionic power, but my people's power has been able to match it and hold it in check. However, the Axis Council is democratically elected, and she was able to sway enough of the inhabitants to win a seat. Since then, she has been exerting pressure on the other councillors—subtly enough that we cannot prove telepathic manipulation, but there is no question in my mind that she is using it."

"So what is she trying to achieve, specifically?"

"She is advancing an agenda of freer, unrestricted trade among eras. She would strip away the safeguards we have always employed to preserve the safety of the timeline."

"Ah-hah," Garcia said, nodding. "Lirahn tried to

convince us there was no threat to the timeline over the long run. I knew that had to be a lie."

"Like the best lies, it has much truth to it," Shiiem replied. "In most cases, disruptions are damped down over the long term. That is why commerce through the Axis is generally safe. But a sufficiently great disruption, or one at a significant turning point, can have much farther-reaching effects. That is why Axis commerce must be closely regulated and monitored, its potential consequences assessed carefully." Shiiem tilted Hariin's head. "In the early days of the Axis, the fledgling Council often had to mount temporal rescue missions to repair major timeline alterations. In at least one case, they were unsuccessful." Garcia was afraid to ask if that case was in her future or her past. "Since then, we have developed safeguards that have kept the timeline free of long-term alterations. Now Lirahn seeks to erode those safeguards."

"But why?" Krotine asked. "What's in it for her?"

"We suspect her ultimate goal is to regain the power she formerly held," Shiiem told her. "How she will do that, and whether in her own time or someone else's, is unclear. In theory, undermining our commerce regulations might allow her to take powerful weapons or disruptive knowledge of the future back to her home era and use them to rebuild a power base. But the civilizations of her era were at an extremely high level of advancement, rivaling any other participant in the Axis, and far exceeding the Vomnin Confederacy with which she seems so eager to arrange free trade. What could they have to offer her?"

Krotine's brow furrowed, stretching the chicken-track indentation that adorned her high, smooth forehead. "The Vomnin scavenge ancient technology from all over.

Maybe they have access to something more advanced than their own level."

"But it would be old, worn out," Garcia countered. "Why not just pop down to the right era through the Axis and pick it up brand new?"

"Well, maybe they've unearthed some secret about Lirahn's future, something she could use to change it?"

"The same objection holds," Shiiem said. "There are fourteen interface zones between her era and yours. Any knowledge from her era would be far more likely to survive in a time less removed."

The Zcham's eyes closed for a moment. "I will have to return my full attention to the meeting soon. What matters is that, whatever her motives, Lirahn seeks power by undermining our safeguards and thus jeopardizing the timeline. It is in both our interests to resist this."

"Who else on the Council is on your side?" Krotine asked. Security thinking: size up one's allies and enemies.

"Only Temarel decisively stands with me. Her mental discipline lets her resist Lirahn's influence." So maybe she had some Vulcan heritage after all, Garcia thought. "Damyz is deep under Lirahn's sway. He is wise and experienced, but he laments that his people are forgotten by history. It is a weakness Lirahn exploits by offering him new power."

"And Oydia?" Garcia asked.

Shiiem sighed. "In theory, she is neutral. The Caratu are a highly social and empathic species. It has made them excellent mediators, the glue that binds the diverse races of the Axis, just as they did in their own Colloquium. But that same instinct to connect with others makes Oydia vulnerable to Lirahn's telepathic influence. I increasingly fear she is compromised."

A shudder went through Garcia. Deltans had much the same instinct for interpersonal bonding; closing themselves off didn't come naturally. And Ranjea had been spending an awful lot of time with Lirahn . . .

She rose. "I think we need to get back immediately."

"It is a valid concern," Ranjea said when the group met in guest quarters that subjective night. "Lirahn may indeed be trying to influence me on a subliminal level. She's certainly devoted a great deal of attention to me."

Garcia frowned. "What *kind* of attention?"

Ranjea shrugged. "Lirahn plays the seduction game as a reflex, using her allure to manipulate."

"And you let her?" she demanded, peering at him with suspicion.

"I played along to make her believe her seduction was working. But don't worry, Teresa. Her approach is rather . . . obvious. She has formidable mental and sexual power, but little finesse. I was able to manage the engagement, and I did not lose control of my mind or body."

He realized Garcia was staring. "You slept with her?"

"I didn't let it go *that* far," he reassured her. "I didn't want her to believe she'd conquered me completely. Besides, the idea of using sex as a tool of deception . . ." He gave a small shudder and shook his head. "I feel soiled enough taking it as far as I did."

Teresa seized on that. "Then maybe you didn't do it of your own free will. Could she have influenced you subliminally?"

"Naturally," he conceded, "I can't rule out the possibility. If empathic openness leaves one vulnerable as Shiiem claims, then I would be susceptible."

"Is that something you could resist?" Garcia asked, then tentatively added, "Will I have to take over the talks?"

Ranjea smiled. "There are elements of my celibacy training that I could adapt into a sort of mental shielding with a little effort. And to be honest, Teresa, without the disciplines of a telepath, you'd have no defense against her at all."

"Oh."

Melora Pazlar furrowed her angular brow. "So what does this mean for our mission? Is Lirahn's agenda a threat to the timeline? And if so, how do we stop her?"

"There is still much to learn," Ranjea said. "We must simply hope that the answers will reveal themselves."

IX

Rellon Ta, Pyrellia
09:32 UTC

"Agent Shelan, Department of Temporal Investigations."
The young Suliban agent showed her ID to the duty officer at the reception desk of the local Starfleet base. The
Tandaran petty officer stared at her for a moment before
summoning a superior to meet with her. Shelan tried not
to be self-conscious; the petty officer had probably seen
few Suliban in his life and was simply curious. But it was
difficult not to be a little paranoid in these surroundings.
Pyrellia was a Tandaran colony, a tidally locked world orbiting a dim red star less than three parsecs from Tandar
Prime. During the Troubles back in the twenty-second
century, it had been one of the worlds where Suliban had
been interned in concentration camps by the Tandaran
government. The camps had been in the barren, cold
wastes on the perpetually dark side of the planet, outside
the habitable band around the terminator. Pyrellia's atmosphere and hydrosphere circulated enough heat from
the sunlit side to keep the camps from freezing over, but
the perpetual darkness and chill had driven many of the
internees to madness and suicide. Of course, that had been
generations ago, and the modern Tandaran government

had formally apologized to the Suliban as a precondition for joining the Federation. Still, just standing here made Shelan feel as if she were walking on the graves of her ancestors.

But she had happened to be at the Aldebaran branch office when the call had come in the day before, making her the nearest agent available. She had a job to do. Shelan reminded herself that her whole purpose in joining the DTI was to move beyond the sad history of her people— and to start making new history.

Soon, Shelan was greeted by a tall Kreetassan male in a lieutenant's uniform. "Agent Shelan," he said in a deep voice, a formal smile on his heavily ridged brown face. "Welcome to Rellon Station. I am Emro Ganazeel, deputy station chief."

"Lieutenant," Shelan replied. She knew Kreetassans had elaborate rituals for greetings along with everything else, but had no idea what they might be. Fortunately, the lieutenant was cosmopolitan enough to settle for a simple handshake, a habit Shelan had picked up on Earth. "Forgive me if I forgo any pleasantries, but I'm eager to meet this mysterious arrival of yours."

"Of course. I'll take you to her." Shelan followed Ganazeel through the door and down a long corridor. "To be honest, I'll be delighted to let you take her off our hands. If she is from . . . where I suspect, she's not a problem I want to have to deal with."

"I know the basics, but could you tell me the full story from your perspective?" she asked.

Ganazeel paused his forward progress, considering his words. "There's not much more beyond what we reported. The lieutenant was found crawling out of the sunside wastes, dehydrated and barely conscious. It looked like she'd been there for days, all by herself. She had a communicator and a tricorder, she could've easily called for help, but she didn't. The people who found her brought her here. They asked her name, but either she didn't know or wouldn't tell them. When she got here, we tried to scan her combadge for an ID check, but she'd encrypted it somehow. Her tricorder too. We tried to take an image of her for facial identification, but she refused to let us. When we pressed the issue, she invoked a Starfleet emergency code, essentially declaring radio silence. The only other thing she would say was, 'Contact Temporal Investigations.'"

Shelan considered his words. "I see. Thank you."

"Agent, I can only think of one reason why a Starfleet officer would behave in that way, given that she summoned you."

"Lieutenant, I'd appreciate it if you wouldn't speculate. Clearly the . . . other lieutenant feels it's important to control information here. We can assume she has good reason."

"Of course. My apologies if I breached protocol."

Shelan smiled. "If you weren't curious, you wouldn't be in Starfleet."

They resumed walking, and Shelan pondered his words. There were possibilities besides the one Ganazeel probably had in mind. Pyrellia was in the Tandar Sector, and the Tandarans had a long history of temporal research. It was possible the lieutenant had discovered some secret that required her to remain anonymous until she could deliver it to the proper authorities at the DTI. For that matter, they were only three parsecs and three weeks removed from the retroassassination attempt on Professor Vard. Was it possible that this lieutenant had some information relating to that incident?

I can only hope it will be something that simple, she thought.

Soon they arrived at a private room and Ganazeel signaled for entry. "Lieutenant," he called. "Agent Shelan from the DTI is here to speak with you."

After a moment, the door slid open, revealing only darkness inside. "Send her in," a muffled female voice said. "Only her, please."

Ganazeel looked unhappy at the request, but Shelan smiled. "Thank you for your assistance, Lieutenant. I should let you know that we'll probably be beaming directly out from this room, if that's all right."

The Kreetassan shook off his frustrated curiosity. "Yes. Yes, of course. I suppose it's your problem now. Good luck with . . . whatever it is."

"Thank you."

Shelan entered the room and let the door close behind her. "Is it all right to turn up the lights?" she asked.

"Of course," the woman said in a diffident tone. "Lights."

The room illumination rose to reveal a striking human woman with light brown skin, shoulder-length brown hair, and large dark eyes over high cheekbones. Her lean frame was still attired in what was left of her uniform; she'd refused even to change or replace it. Although Starfleet uniforms were designed to regulate body temperature, she'd apparently found it necessary to abandon her uniform jacket and turtleneck. Though from what Shelan could see, her uniform was identical to current Starfleet issue. Her combadge was pinned to a teal blue tank top, identifying her as a science or medical officer. Her black trousers were of a self-cleaning material, but they were tattered around the knees as if from crawling. She looked tired, nervous, on edge.

"Shall we sit down?" Shelan suggested.

"Oh, of course. Please."

Once they were seated, Shelan asked, "So would you like to tell me your name?"

Those dark eyes sized her up. "With the understanding that anything I tell you is highly classified under the Temporal Prime Directive."

Oh, hell, here we go. "Understood."

The human took a deep breath. "My name is Lieutenant Dina Elfiki. I'm the chief science officer aboard the *U.S.S. Enterprise.*"

"The *Enterprise?*" She made a quick check of her padd. The Department always kept close watch on ships named *Enterprise.* "Right now, the *Enterprise* is assisting in re-settlement operations in the Sagittarius Reach."

"I know," Elfiki said. "And right now I'm aboard her. Let's see, I should've just filed a geological assay report about seven hours ago."

Shelan checked the Starfleet download logs, confirming that Elfiki had indeed filed that report from the *Enterprise* at the same moment that this Elfiki had been cooling her heels in this room. Shelan pulled out her temporal tricorder. "Do you mind if I scan you?"

"I guess you need to confirm I am who and what I say I am."

"And to confirm that you've traveled through time." Elfiki shrugged in acknowledgment, and Shelan activated her device. There was indeed a faint chroniton signature lingering on Elfiki, and her skin and clothing showed indications of exposure to exotic particles and Hawking radiation. It was consistent with temporal displacement, though Shelan couldn't identify the specific mechanism from these readings. In fact, there seemed to be a little of everything in the signature she was getting.

The chroniton residue was too decayed to let her narrow down Elfiki's point of origin, except that it had been in the future. She ran a quantum dating analysis on Elfiki's clothing, the only known means of determining an object's actual date of origin independent of its subjective age. Every object was imprinted at its creation with a faint echo of the wavefunction of its entire universe as it existed at the time, and while the technology to read that whole wavefunction did not exist, it was possible to read the interference patterns that arose between the individual and universal wavefunctions, an interference that grew stronger as the universe evolved over time. Moreover, the interference patterns were inverted when an object occupied a point before its creation, giving a negative reading to a quantum dating scan. But the technique had a margin of error of roughly one year, and the results of Shelan's scan were inconclusive. "So you're from less than a year in the future," Shelan said. "Could you tell me when, exactly?"

"I will," Elfiki said. "When the time is right."

"I see. I guess it'd be a waste of time to ask *how* you got back here."

Elfiki smiled. "It's never a waste of time to ask a question. But it's not a question I can answer."

"Because you don't want to reveal it, or because you don't know it?"

The lieutenant chuckled. "I don't know if it's even safe to tell you that much."

"Point taken." Shelan took a breath, let it out. "Okay. The Department has a protocol in place for something like this, though I don't know if it's been invoked before." Previous unplanned negative displacements had tended to cover a much greater span. In 2154, Jonathan Archer's *Enterprise* had encountered a version of itself flung back 117 years by a destabilized subspace corridor in the Delphic Expanse, and in 2373 the *Defiant* had undergone a strikingly similar experience on the planet Gaia in the Gamma Quadrant. In both cases, the crews' descendants had helped them avoid the original accidents, apparently terminating their own loop timelines. But neither event had occurred within the DTI's bailiwick, and Department policy, particularly for a displacement as small as this, was rather different. "And you seem to have intuitively worked it out already."

"Witness protection," Elfiki said.

"That's right. We keep you safely hidden until you catch up with your own worldline."

Elfiki met her eyes and smirked. "And watch me every moment to make sure I don't give in to the temptation to try to change something."

Shelan reached across the table and put a hand on her arm. "Dina, you practically let yourself die of thirst rather than risk contaminating the timeline. I don't think we have to worry about your sense of duty."

Elfiki closed her eyes. "I was sorely tempted, though. Another hour . . ." She sighed. "And I've got a long wait ahead of me. There are going to be . . . moments of temptation. Believe me, I'm grateful you'll be riding herd over me." She held Shelan's gaze again. "Just so long as you give me a chance to make a difference . . . after I catch up."

Shelan spread her arms. "Once that point is reached, you'll be free to do whatever you want. And until then . . . just consider yourself on a long vacation."

The human gave a small scoff. "Some vacation. I can't visit family, can't go out in public . . . you guys play poker?"

"Have you ever seen a DTI agent without a poker face?"

The women shared a laugh, but Shelan could tell Elfiki was nervous. Temporal displacement was always a stressful experience, and Elfiki's circumstances made it particularly difficult. Shelan clasped Elfiki's hands. "Don't worry. We have people in the Department who specialize in counseling displacees. We'll make sure you don't feel alone."

DTI Branch Office, San Francisco
2 Rabī al-Thāni 1814 AH (A Wednesday)
14:29 UTC

"My, you're looking old, Lucsly," Agent Revad of the Temporal Assessment Group said from the com screen in Lucsly's office. *"Time not agreeing with you?"*

"I can't complain," Lucsly told his Romulan counterpart. "I haven't heard from you since you switched sides. How does it feel working for the Typhon Pact?"

"Lucsly, don't make the mistake of thinking the Romulan Star Empire was ever on the Federation's side. We pooled our efforts against a few common enemies, but my priority has always been the best interests of the Romulan people. That's what the Pact offers us."

"Politics is fleeting, Revad," Lucsly said. "You know that, so you didn't call to make speeches. What do you want?"

"To offer you information. And see if you have any to offer in exchange."

Lucsly observed Revad's thin face and dirty-brown hair evenly. Whatever political rivalries they shared, the temporal agencies of the quadrant's various governments tended to cooperate, more or less grudgingly, where threats to their mutual history were concerned. "Do we have another common enemy?" he asked.

"Quite possibly. We recently discovered and averted a plot to cause a disaster on a planet in Romulan territory. The conspirators intended to blame the disaster on Federation sabotage, no doubt to precipitate a war."

"I take it the conspirators were anachronistic?"

"They're locals by origin, but chroniton readings from their base suggest they've been in communication with the future. Moreover, although Romulan, they possessed genetic enhancements considerably beyond the state of the art. They refused to reveal the origin of these enhancements before . . . losing their lives in an escape attempt."

Lucsly let the euphemism slide, for he was more concerned with the rest. Revad saw his reaction. *"Ah, I thought you would find that familiar. Didn't the Suliban Cabal have similar genetic enhancements from an unidentified future benefactor?"*

"You think the same being or faction is behind this sabotage attempt?"

"It's hard to be sure, but the evidence is suggestive. I was hoping your agency could provide more information."

"We've shared all our information with the other

Accord signatories," Lucsly told him. "You have everything we do. Probably more, given the Tholians' past involvement in the Temporal Cold War." While the Tholian Chronological Defense Corps had not been in direct conflict with the Suliban Cabal in the twenty-second-century front of the cold war, the two powers had clashed over the possession of a thirty-first-century Federation temporal displacement pod discovered by Jonathan Archer's *Enterprise* on November 16, 2152.

"Oh, come now, Lucsly. You think I'm not aware that the Department now has a Suliban member?"

"Agent Shelan has no association with the Cabal."

"That's not what our genealogists say."

"Ancestry doesn't prove association. Knowledge isn't genetic."

"Not in our species, but in the Cabal and its heirs, who knows? Come now, Lucsly. You wouldn't have recruited a Cabal-descended Suliban if you weren't getting something from her."

"What we're getting is her skilled and dedicated service. She volunteered."

"Oh, Lucsly, I'm hurt by your lack of trust. If you're concerned that my new allegiance makes me a potential threat to your precious timeline, don't be. The Pact has no interest in attacking the Federation in the past." Revad gave a smug smile. *"Why, without your sterling example to inspire us, we wouldn't exist. No, we'd rather compete with you for mastery of the future."*

"Then why hasn't the Pact signed the Temporal Accord?"

"It's a negotiation in progress," Revad insisted. *"These things take time. First we must unify the temporal policies*

of our own respective agencies. But you know that the TAG was and is still an Accord signatory—otherwise we would've wiped the Federation from history ages ago."

"It's not as if you never tried."

"Mmm, perhaps in some . . . other reality, now rendered irrelevant," Revad granted. *"And Accords or no, the Tholians have long since outgrown any desire to tamper with history."*

"But now that the Breen and Tzenkethi have access to the knowledge and artifacts in TAG and CDC possession—"

"They don't. Whatever the Pact's claims of unity, you can rest assured that the TAG won't let those creatures get anywhere near our proprietary . . . resources. And you know how territorial the Tholians are."

Lucsly pondered his words. "All right. It's not a matter of trust. If Agent Shelan had given us any new insights into the Cabal's benefactor, I would share them. If they tried to start a Federation–Typhon Pact war once, they may do it again, and target us this time. If so, it's in everyone's best interest to share everything they know."

Revad peered at him for a moment, then relented. *"You have a point, Lucsly. I believe you would share any information you had. You have no allegiance beyond the timeline."*

"If we don't keep the timeline safe, then—"

"Then nothing else matters, I know." The Romulan rolled his eyes, then sobered. *"If you do uncover any further evidence of a plot to start a war . . ."*

"We'll share the relevant information with the other signatories," Lucsly assured him. "But this will go easier if you can persuade the Pact as a whole to sign."

Revad nodded. *"I'll exert whatever pressure I can."*

"Good. We're all in this together, you know."

"I know, Lucsly. You taught me that."

After Revad signed off, Lucsly frowned, remembering something. He headed next door to Dulmur's office. "Let me see those DNA scans from Naadri's hotel."

Dulmur looked up. "You have something new?"

"Maybe." Despite Jena Noi's instructions, the two agents had continued to probe into the Vard attack insofar as they were able. They'd discovered that Doctor Naadri had been in Kemrel Municipality on the day of the bombing, and the Paraagan physicist had confirmed that she'd been intending to meet with Vard that day. It was too much of a coincidence that one prominent temporal physicist had been targeted for retroassassination on the very day he was meeting another, so they'd investigated further. "Call up that unidentified trace we found in the hallway."

Dulmur did so. "This one?"

"Mm-hm."

"Yeah, I remember. Probable Vulcanoid, but with unexplained anomalies." Dulmur looked at him. "You're thinking evolutionary drift? But there were no temporal signatures around Naadri's hotel."

"I'm thinking local talent." He filled Dulmur in on what he'd just learned from Revad.

When he was done, Dulmur whistled. "A modern version of the Cabal?"

"Stands to reason. If the tactic worked once, why not reuse it?"

"So the Cabal's Sponsor tries to kill Vard and Naadri. Noi comes back, saves Vard and his students, so we get a temporal signature there."

Lucsly nodded. "She said she caught them. Maybe she did it just before they got to Naadri. All contemporary, so no travel signature."

Dulmur took it in slowly. "So are we back in the Cold War? Another front opening up here?"

"Could be an isolated incident. Might not even be the Sponsor. Unrelated groups could use the same tactics."

"Still . . ."

"Mm-hm." Nothing more needed to be said. They would both be on their guard from now on.

Yeshel Outpost, Axis of Time
Late Piacenzian Age, Upper Pliocene Epoch

Tercsa Garcia walked alongside a being who was older than her own hominid genus. Councillor Damyz was showing her around his people's facility, one of the oldest in the Axis in both senses: positioned over two-point-eight million years BCE, it had been one of the first stations erected within the Axis, over three centuries ago by internal time. Damyz himself had lived for over half that span. It certainly put her own regrets at being fifteen years out of time into perspective.

"Indeed, ours is the earliest civilization currently participating in the Axis," the stout Yeshel told her in a kindly, quavering voice, turning his tortoise-like orange-brown face up to hers. "There are a few, ah, interface zones connecting to earlier times, you see, but for whatever reason . . . for whatever reason, either nobody lives nearby or they have no . . . or at least no *current* interest in our affairs."

"Maybe they decided it was safer not to risk tampering with time," Garcia suggested.

"Maybe, maybe. But it's their loss! We, we Yeshel

and our neighbors—or contemporaries, if you will—we
have benefited greatly. And . . . umm . . . ah, yes, this is
the important bit, my dear: we have done so without, oh,
what do you call it, eradicating anyone else from their later
existence! Hah!"

"But that's because you have policies in place to prevent that, right? And if those policies were weakened . . .
especially by someone with a self-serving agenda . . . then
somebody could end up being eradicated after all."

"Well, maybe, maybe. *If* the, ah, parties involved did
have such selfish motives." He made a hissing exhalation
that Garcia optimistically chose to interpret as a sigh rather
than an involuntary metabolic function. "I admit, as the
ones nearest the, ah, anchor end of things, my people are
the least affected by such concerns. There is a certain risk
of becoming . . . ohh . . . yes, complacent! Complacent
about the concerns of our, well, successors." He patted
her shoulder. "Which is why I always remind myself, my
dear, how important it is *not* to become that way. Ahh,
complacent, that is."

She smiled. Though his hesitant speech had raised
questions about his mental clarity at first, spending time
with him had left no doubt that his mind was still strong,
simply needing a little more time to get the job done than
in his youth.

"So what about the people who built the Axis?" she
asked. "Any idea what happened to them?"

"Only theories, young lady. Only theories. It seems to
me, though, that they must have been extremely advanced
to create such a thing. Perhaps they, ah, evolved to a, what
do they call it, an incorporeal level shortly afterward and
didn't need the thing after all! Heh-heh!"

"Well, can't you just go back to the beginning and find them?"

Damyz shrugged. "There's no way out through the endpoints. Too much energy, too much, ah, spatial disruption."

"That's strange," Garcia said. "To create a passage into the future and give themselves no way into it."

"Maybe there is a way in," Damyz suggested. "Just no way out. Perhaps they intended their journey to be one-way only. Oh, here, if you don't mind, I need to sit for a moment."

They rested on a bench opposite a portal and stared for a while at the ring of light surrounding them, showing them the station they occupied from every direction except their own. "It troubles you," Damyz said to Garcia. "Not knowing what happened to them."

"It does," she said. "I just think . . . it's important to remember the past. Not to lose its lessons. What happened anywhere in time, for better or worse . . . it shouldn't be lost."

"Ahh, but everything is lost, eventually. At best, only remnants survive." He gestured at the stars beyond the ring of light, the stars of his era. "Hm. Look at us. Out there, in the . . . well, what I consider the present, the Yeshel are a great civilization." He rumbled. "Well . . . perhaps not as much as we were. But our legacy is known throughout the quadrant." He raised his stubby arms into the air. "But you? You've never heard of us. Nobody here has ever heard of us . . . except through the Axis."

Damyz exhaled slowly. "All things are forgotten, my dear. Your civilization will one day share the same fate. So what . . . I ask you, what harm is there, really, in extending a bit of a lifeline from one age to another? Hm?"

Garcia found she had no answer.

Axis Hub Station
Middle Calabrian Age, Lower Pleistocene

"We're getting nowhere, boss," Garcia told Ranjea as they met once more with Pazlar and Krotine. "Damyz isn't budging, and I think he wouldn't even need Lirahn's influence to feel that way."

"I agree," the senior agent replied. "I've been able to make no headway with any of the other councillors, or with Sikran." He took a breath. "I think we have to concede that there's really not much we can do here. We were sent to negotiate with the Vomnin and the Axis Council, to make known our concerns about potential temporal disruption and attempt to find a mutually agreeable policy. Well, we now know that the Axis Council does currently have a set of reasonable safeguards in place."

"Safeguards that Lirahn is trying to undermine," Melora Pazlar put in.

"Evidently, but there is little we can do about it. It's a matter of internal politics."

Garcia frowned. "Boss, Shiiem and Vikei didn't go to all that trouble just to cry on our shoulders. They were asking for help."

"And so was Lirahn. While her methods are certainly questionable, it doesn't mean the essentials of her tale aren't true. Both sides are claiming to be the victims, and we can't know the real truth without more information."

"I don't think Vikei was lying to us."

"I'm sure he was sincere, by his own lights. Truth can

be multifaceted." Ranjea paused. "Either way, it isn't our job to swoop in and save the day. Our job is to uphold Federation law. And that includes the law that we don't impose our will on foreign governments."

"But—"

"Teresa." She fell silent, waiting. "We can't take sides here. We have done what we could to persuade the councillors not to revoke the trade limits. We have informed Sikran of our concerns that Lirahn may be trying to use the Vomnin for some end. But ultimately it isn't our place to decide what happens here. It's theirs."

"But what about the threat to the timeline?" Krotine asked. "That's basically your whole thing, isn't it?"

"We're here to assess that potential threat, yes. But there are limits to what we can accomplish if foreign governments are determined to follow different policies.

"Besides . . . given the vast time spans involved, it is possible that any changes Lirahn might make in the past, for better or worse, would damp down to nothing by our time. And any truly lasting changes would be more likely to affect Vomnin history than our own. The Confederacy is aware of that risk, but they're determined to proceed with this relationship anyway."

"Captain Riker won't like the idea of just laying the problem in the Vomnin's lap and flying away," Pazlar said.

"Yes, the captain's reputation precedes him," Ranjea replied. "And believe me, the prospect of leaving a threat to the timeline unresolved troubles me more profoundly than you can know. But we are here at the Vomnin's indulgence. By their law, they have a territorial claim here. And if they insist that we leave . . . well, they have a lot more ships close at hand than we do." He shrugged. "We may have to settle for doing the best we can and moving on to more tractable problems."

"Well, you do that if you think it's best," Pazlar said with a look of distaste. "But if it's all the same to you, I suspect we'll want to keep *Titan* around here for a while. You know, to explore the Axis and its cultures."

"You are more than welcome to remain," Ranjea told her graciously, "and achieve whatever good you may. Just so long as you don't leave the Axis in any past or future era," he added, "or reveal too much about the future to anyone from the past."

"We know the Temporal Prime Directive," she riposted. "Time travel's caused us more than enough trouble already."

"Yeah," Garcia said. "It has a way of doing that."

DTI Headquarters, Greenwich
3 Rabī al-Thāni 1814 AH (A Thursday)
13:09 UTC
"I feel like an impostor," Dina Elfiki said. "The real me is out there living her—my life, and I'm stuck here watching from the outside."

Clare Raymond nodded understandingly. "For me, it was like I was a ghost," she said, repeating the story she'd told fellow displacees many times. "Just a relic who'd lingered beyond my time, having no place in the world. Feelings of dissociation and alienation are common for displacees."

"But this is different. I *really* don't belong. I can't even leave this . . . gilded cage without risking a time paradox." The Egyptian lieutenant glanced furtively at the entrance to her "guest suite" on the deepest, most secure level of the underground HQ complex—an entrance that both women knew had guards outside it at all times. "Not that they'd let me anyway."

"But look on the bright side," Clare said. "In your case, it's a temporary condition. In a few months, or whenever, you'll be able to go back to your life again, and this will all just have been a strange interlude." She felt a twinge of uncharitable, twentieth-century envy. Not only was Elfiki unfairly gorgeous and successful, but her temporal displacement was a walk in the park compared to Clare's and many others'. But Clare quashed that sentiment; it was a relic of the smaller, shallower person she'd been in her old life.

"Yeah, I hope so." Elfiki fidgeted for a few moments. "In the meantime, do you know how frustrating it is to know, every day, what's going to be on the news feed, and not be able to tell anyone about it?"

"I can imagine how tempting it must be," Clare said. She smiled. "I used to have dreams all the time about waking up back in the nineteen-nineties and telling people what the future would hold. Not to warn them about World War III or something like that, but just to show off. There's something about having that edge, knowing something other people don't, that makes you feel special. But it's no fun if you can't tell anyone."

"It's more than that," Dina told her. "Damn it, I'm a science officer! It's my job, my instinct, to share information with people!"

Clare tilted her blond head, divining that this wasn't about fun. "Especially if it's important, right?" Dina didn't reply. "You're upset that you can't tell people about the event that sent you back here. Was it . . . something bad? Something dangerous? Something you think you should be allowed to prevent?"

The lieutenant gave a heavy sigh, then rose to pace for a moment. "I wish that were it," she confessed. "It's not just that I'm not allowed to say what happened. I don't really know exactly what happened myself. I came in on the middle of things." She turned to face Clare again. "That's one reason I came to the DTI. I'm hoping maybe I can learn something about what happened—what's going to happen. Maybe if I watch events unfold, knowing where they end up, I'll be able to piece something together. And this is the best place to be for finding out about anything temporal."

"But it must be hard to do research when you're not allowed to reveal what it is you're looking into."

"That's the tricky part." She shook her head. "Maybe I should tell someone. Maybe it's something that should be changed, that needs to be changed. Maybe if I just confided in you, you could tell me how to proceed."

Clare held out her hands palms first. "Whoa there. I don't know if that's such a great idea."

"It would be in the strictest confidence, right?"

"So is everything else you've told us. But this goes beyond confidence. You could tell us something that might cause someone to act subconsciously in a different way. There's already a risk just for those of us who know you're here at all."

Dina sank into her seat again and sighed. "Of course. I'm sorry, I shouldn't even have brought it up."

"It's perfectly understandable. Don't worry about it."

In truth, Clare thought, she was probably the one who

should apologize. The prospect of being given knowledge of the future, actionable knowledge that could potentially alter events for better or worse, had frightened her when Dina had offered it. She didn't want to be saddled with that kind of responsibility, that kind of choice. She left the big-picture stuff to the agents. She was just a homemaker who'd found a new career holding the hands of fellow refugees in time.

DOWNTIME
STARDATE 45703.8 TO 46008.2

X

Indianapolis, North Am, Earth
14:49 UTC

Clare Raymond was sobbing to herself in the sonic shower
when her great-great-great-great-great-granddaughter-in-
law found her. Louise Cara Raymond was a big, spirited
Latina with a generous heart, and she readily climbed into
the cubicle and took her husband's distant ancestor in her
well-cushioned arms. "*Bisabuela* Clare, what's wrong?"

"This shower," Clare sobbed. "I hate this stupid
shower. I want a real shower, with water!" She knew how
pathetic she must sound, but after struggling for nearly
four years to get used to this life, she no longer cared.
She'd hoped to at least get her crying done in private, as
usual, but this stupid so-called "sonic" shower didn't even
make enough noise to mask her sobs.

"Well, why didn't you just say so, sweetie? We can get
you a water shower. It's easy enough."

"No!" Clare pushed her away and climbed out of
the cubicle. She put her hands in the sink to activate the
faucet—at least that still had water, though no knobs
or levers—and splashed her face to wash away the tears.
"No, you don't understand. I don't want an indulgence.
I want . . . I want a shower. A good old-fashioned shower

that gets lime on the showerhead and mildew in the cracks between the tiles if you don't clean it every day. God, how I hate mildew!"

Louise stared at her, not understanding. Clare knew how shallow she must sound. Despite her matronly looks, Louise was a professor of exobiology at Indiana State, just like her husband, Clare's direct descendant Thomas, who looked so uncannily like her dear, departed Donald. Their eleven-year-old, Mary, was already starting to study quantum gravity in school, and Darrell, who would be eight in December, already displayed computer programming skills that Clare would never comprehend. People in this century just made so much more of themselves than she ever could.

Clare gathered herself while Louise wrapped a robe around her. Her body was bone-dry, but she appreciated the concession to her dignity. "The point is . . . at least back home I had something to do. Something that made me useful. It wasn't much, but it was something."

"Don't say that, *bisabuela*. You took care of your family. That's everything."

"But now . . . the showers clean themselves, the floors clean themselves, the replicators handle food and clothes and garbage . . . what's left for me?"

"I know, I know." It wasn't the first time they'd had this conversation, though it was the first time she'd embarrassed herself quite so much. "Clare, you know the kids love learning history from you."

"No. They indulge me. Half the time, they correct me. Tell me things I didn't know about my own time." At first, she'd thought Mary and Darrell were just confused because her era was so far in the past. But when she'd checked the databases, even when she'd studied news and historical accounts written in her own time, she'd been abashed to discover how narrow and insular her view of the late twentieth century had been. She'd never even heard of Khan Singh or Vasily Hunyadi, she'd been totally wrong about the motives behind the Tiananmen Square protests, and she'd thought the Shah of Iran was a benevolent leader rather than the brutal dictator he had been. And that wasn't even mentioning all the earlier history she'd never learned, the history of Asia and Africa and the American Indians that had been totally ignored in her schooling, the great civilizations that had thrived in regions she'd assumed were primitive and wild. Sometimes it felt like Mary and Darrell only looked forward to her lectures so they could laugh at how quaint and ignorant her notions were. She knew they loved her, but love could be condescending.

"You could always go back to school," Louise said. "You're never too old to learn."

"But there's just so much. Not just this world, but so many others. By the time I got caught up, I *would* be too old."

"To spend the rest of your life learning?" Louise asked, shaking her head in wonderment. "What could be better than that?"

Such a twenty-fourth-century attitude, Clare thought. Thomas and Louise and their kids were the closest family she had, yet they were alien to her in so many ways. So she put it in the only terms she knew they had in common. "I just want to be able to take care of somebody. And not just babysitting." *Sitting "babies" who are more informed and comfortable and secure in this world than I am, whose houses take care of them better than I can.* "I want to make some kind of difference. But I don't know how."

Louise led her into her bedroom so she could get dressed. "Have you talked to Sonny or Mister Offenhouse about this?" she asked as Clare slipped on the old-fashioned bra and panties that made her feel comfortable despite being worse for her circulation than the modern equivalents.

"They can't understand. They've both found new careers, new ways to be useful." She knew from experience that Ralph Offenhouse would just give her a pep talk about his own achievements and barely even notice she was in the room, while Sonny Clemonds would just invite her to a party and try to get her drunk enough to agree to spend the night with him. Once had been enough, thank you very much. She didn't feel he'd taken advantage of her; it had been just as much her taking advantage, seeking respite from her loneliness. But it had felt hollow and desperate in the morning. All she told Louise, though, was, "Aside from when we came from, we don't have anything in common."

After that, the conversation drifted off into awkward trivialities as it always did. Louise took her downstairs and made one more stab at teaching her to play Roladan Wild Draw, which was like a strange cross between California lowball poker and Truth or Dare. Louise had the FNS newsfeed on in the background as they played, something Clare was convinced she did on purpose to distract her poor old *bisabuela*. She was just about to give up and suggest they switch to gin rummy when she heard something on the newsfeed that caught her attention.

"*. . . reported lost nearly ninety standard years ago. The*

vessel was reportedly trapped in a form of suspended anima-
tion within the Typhon Expanse, where it was discovered
and freed by the U.S.S. Enterprise *under the command of*
Captain Jean-Luc Picard. The Bozeman *and her crew are*
expected to arrive at station Deep Space 4 in two days, and
already, surviving family members and descendants have
been notified. There are sure to be some tearful reunions in
the days to come. The Bozeman*'s rescue should also be a boon*
to historians . . ."

"The *Enterprise*?" Louise asked. "Weren't they the
ship that rescued you? *Dios*, they sure get around."

"Ninety years," Clare breathed, barely hearing her.
"That's going to be rough. To adjust, I mean."

"Oh, yes. Who'd know that better than you?"

"Right. Who would?" Suddenly Clare felt something
bubbling up inside that she'd been missing for four years.
At long last, she realized, there was a way she could be
useful.

Deep Space 4
Setting Orange, Bureaucracy 41, 3534 YOLD
(A Tuesday)
03:08 UTC

"I'm sorry, Mare, but by the time you see this message, I'll be
gone."

Megumi's Dear John letter kept replaying in Dulmur's
head hours after he'd received it. Even though he'd had
every reason to know this was coming, the reality of it had
left him in shock. *"I know what you'll say. 'Be patient, we'll*
talk this through.' But when, Mare? We never talk anymore!
You're never here! Even when you're here, all you think about
is your work, and you can't tell me about it. So we have

nothing to say to each other anymore. You say it's important, but how can it be more important than us?"

He'd never been able to make her understand. He loved her so much, wanted to spend every possible moment with her. But there were so many threats to the timeline, more than anyone would ever expect. Something new was always coming up. Like spending two fruitless weeks interrogating Berlinghoff Rasmussen—a glib, shifty twenty-second-century inventor who'd stolen the time pod of an uptime historian and attempted to pirate modern technology so he could "invent" it in his own time, endangering history for personal profit—who had cheerfully evaded all their questions about whether he'd pilfered from other eras of history or where and when the errant time pod might have arrived in the past. Or spending the next month trying to dissuade the Klingon High Council from approving the proposal of Korath, an up-and-coming young physicist/inventor from the Cambra system, to develop a battlecruiser engine capable of reliably surviving a Tipler slingshot maneuver, enabling Klingon warriors to travel into the past and participate in the great wars of history. (Lucsly had ultimately persuaded them it would be a dishonorable breach of the Temporal Accord, no matter how much Korath had tried to spin it as permissible "historical research.") Or spending another three weeks helping the First Federation investigate an anachronism in their historical records before finally determining that it was simply a historiographic error rather than evidence of a timeline disruption. The Firsts were known for their excess of caution, but like firefighters, the DTI had to respond to every alarm just in case it was real.

Whatever the source of the trouble, however far it

took Dulmur from home, it added up to the same thing. If he didn't fight to keep the timeline intact, Megumi's very existence could be erased, reduced to a vacuum fluctuation in some other history. He couldn't let that happen if there was anything he could do to protect her.

But now that she was gone, Dulmur felt like a fool. Why hadn't he seized every precious moment with her that he could, knowing that it could all vanish at any moment? *One way or another,* he added grimly.

"You can't go back," Lucsly said. "You know that."

Dulmur started, taking a moment to realize his partner wasn't talking to him. Across the briefing room table sat the command crew of the *U.S.S. Bozeman,* now in their fifth day in the twenty-fourth century after spending eighty-nine years, eight months, and twenty-three days of objective time caught in a temporal causality loop, reliving the same few hours over and over. Right now, Dulmur knew just how they felt. *"I'm sorry, Mare, but by the time you see this message, I'll be gone."*

"You don't understand." The *Bozeman*'s acting first officer, Lieutenant Parvana Whitcomb, leaned forward urgently. She was a young human with blocky mid-Eurasian features and bowl-cut black hair, unusually low in rank for an XO post. "We have family back there. I have a husband, a little girl who needs me. Look, I'm not even supposed to be here. I was only filling in for a few weeks after Commander Sulu turned down the job! I'm supposed to join my family at Norkan after the Typhon Expanse survey."

"You *were* supposed to join them," Lucsly replied. "As you've been informed, ma'am, your husband and daughter lost their lives in the Norkan Massacre of 2307. The Department is very sorry for your loss."

"'The Department is sorry,'" Whitcomb scoffed. "Empty boilerplate. You can't understand, you're just a bureaucratic drone trying to keep your paperwork in order!"

Lucsly threw Dulmur an uncomfortable look. Normally it was Dulmur's job to do the handholding. Today he couldn't find it in himself. At least Whitcomb had *had* a daughter. She may have only known the girl for three years, but that girl's life had lasted another twenty-eight beyond that. A brief run, but at least the Whitcombs had known the joy of starting a family.

"There's more, Marion. I want kids. You say you want them too, I used to think you did, but I can't handle any more excuses. Time is finite, Mare. You should know that more than anyone. And I can't live the rest of my life just marking time with you, waiting for you to keep your promises. I need a real family, not a hypothetical one."

How could he explain to her? How could he stand to risk bringing a child into existence when that existence could be negated by circumstances beyond his control? How could he stand not knowing if the child he held in his arms today was the same child he'd had the week before? Sure, the Department had recently begun using phase discriminators to shield its records from temporal alteration, but those records didn't contain everything.

"Now, now, Parvana." Next to Whitcomb, the *Bozeman*'s captain, Morgan Bateson, put a hand on her arm to calm her down. "These gentlemen are only doing their job." He shook his bearded head gravely. "You know Starfleet regulations on the matter. We can't go back."

"Even to prevent a disaster?" Whitcomb cried. "It's easy for you to spout regulations, Captain. You didn't have any close family, didn't lose anyone to the Romulans."

"That's right!" cried the tactical officer, an Andorian ensign named Shelithan ch'Riin. "I lost all three of my bondmates in a Klingon attack just four years after we were trapped! And while it happened, I was just sitting through the same tiresome duty shift I'd sat through five thousand times already! I should've been there!"

"A lot of people have lost their lives in the past ninety years," spoke up Lieutenant Commander Claudia Alisov, the chief engineer, a fortyish woman whose cherubic features were framed by a mass of curly red-brown hair. Her tone was soft, sympathetic, yet firm. "We can't save every one of them. It's history now."

"But does it have to be?" The question came from the science officer, Lieutenant Lloyd Boen, a ruddy-faced human with a gray monk's fringe and goatee. "We don't know for sure that changing the past will erase this future. We could just branch off a new timeline."

"That's right, we can't know," Lucsly said. "That's why we can't take the chance."

"But if we have any chance at all of saving our families," Whitcomb urged, "how can you expect us to sit back and do nothing? How can we not do everything in our power to bring them back?"

Bateson tried to rein Whitcomb in again, but Dulmur was no longer listening. *How can I not do everything in my power?*

"Quit?" Lucsly cried as he followed Dulmur down the station corridor. "You can't quit!"

"Watch me," Dulmur fired back. "This job has ruined my life, and what do I have to show for it? I get to tell other people their lives are ruined too!"

"And what about all the lives you've protected? The lives you've saved?"

"For how long? Huh? What's the point if anything I accomplish can get wiped out of history the next time some tourist falls through a subspace rabbit hole?"

"There'll be just as much risk of that if you quit. More, even."

"But at least I won't have to face it every day! I can forget it, pretend along with everyone else that I actually have a solid footing in reality. I can focus on having a family, maybe even get Meg back if I beg hard enough. I can concentrate on being happy in the time I have instead of obsessing over the latest quantum anomaly or historical inconsistency."

"No, you can't," Lucsly told him. "You're too good an agent to give it up. You're as dedicated as any agent I've ever worked with, because you know you can make a difference."

Dulmur whirled and got right up in the taller man's face. "I'm not 'dedicated,' Lucsly! I'm obsessed! I've lost track of everything else that mattered in life. And you know why? Because of *you*! Because you infected me with your, your autistic obsession with time and order and control. You go around trying to force the whole universe to fit into your nice, neat, clockwork life, and I let you make me into one of the gears! You made me a robot like you, *partner,* and it cost me the one thing I love! Well, no more! I'm through!"

He began to storm away, but Lucsly grabbed his arm and spun him back around. Dulmur was startled by the man's implacable strength. "If you really cared more about family than about the work, you wouldn't have let the work push your family life aside in the first place. You let that happen because you know that what we do matters. This is a job that has to be done, and you're one of the very few people who can do it really well. You can't just walk away from that, Dulmur."

On some level, Dulmur was aware how exceptional it was for Lucsly to praise anyone. But he was too angry to let it register. "That's all that matters to you, isn't it? The work. You're a machine, Lucsly. Even a Vulcan has more passion than you. You, you're a walking grandfather clock. How is that a substitute for a wife who loves me, for children I can take care of?"

He pulled his arm free. "You don't need me, Lucsly. You don't need anyone. You can preserve history all by yourself. I'm through."

He stormed away, and this time Lucsly didn't stop him. He didn't plead. He didn't appeal to their friendship. How could he? Did he even know the meaning of the word? All he said, when Dulmur was nearly out of earshot, was:

"You'll be back."

DTI Headquarters, Greenwich
Prickle-Prickle, The Aftermath 37, 3534 YOLD
(A Monday)
20:16 UTC
"I thought I was finally starting to get used to them being gone," Parvana Whitcomb said, sitting stiffly erect on the comfortable couch in the Temporal Displacement Division's counseling office. "And then this happens." She shook her head. "He was my baby brother. Now, to see him as this wizened old man, wasting away . . . his mind

gone . . ." Her fists clenched in her lap. "It isn't fair! It's only been two months! I only just got back, we barely reconnect and then he dies! He should've had more time! We both should!"

Clare Raymond did her best to project calming sympathy, even though it was hard for her to relate to the lieutenant's anger. In her time, for Jamshid Whitcomb to make it to a hundred and ten would have been a remarkable accomplishment, but his older—well, formerly older—sister saw it as too short a life. But Clare suspected that Whitcomb would see it as hollow if she suggested looking at it from her point of view. However full her brother's life may have been, she'd been cheated out of most of it.

So instead Clare tried to relate it to her own experience. "I know how hard it is to watch a loved one fade away like that. My grandmother . . . she lingered in a hospice for weeks. There's this awful tension, the waiting . . . wanting her to finally be at peace, knowing that she's already gone and wanting to get the dying over with so you can start grieving properly, yet being terrified to answer every time the phone rings . . ."

Whitcomb nodded. "It's like being frozen in time all over again." She was quiet for a time. "You know, we all had this horrible feeling of déjà vu. Somehow we knew that everything we did, we'd done a million times before." She smirked. "That Doctor T'Viss of yours figured out why that happened . . . time was looping back on itself through an extra dimension, our worldlines overlapping themselves, the quantum information getting overwritten each time . . . but with enough spillover that we retained a trace of memory. Sometimes we even heard voices, our own voices echoing from earlier loops. Or the sensors picked up ghost images that shouldn't have been there. But somehow we just didn't bother to do anything about them. Didn't dig into them and solve the puzzle like the *Enterprise* crew did.

"I think we tried to, somewhere in the first few thousand cycles. We must have wondered, investigated, tried to break free of the loop. But we didn't have the technology they did, couldn't crack the mystery. So I think eventually we just gave up. We subconsciously remembered an endless string of failures and just became resigned to it. We went through the motions, the same dialogue and actions cycle after cycle, even though we knew it all by heart."

Clare didn't know what to say. The whole idea of it was mind-numbing to her. She'd never gotten into the sci-fi shows back in her own day; she remembered the boys in school with their lunchboxes displaying pictures from *Lost in Space* and *Batman* and *The Invaders,* but *Bewitched* had been more her speed. She'd had kind of a crush on Lee Majors in her teens, but that was about it. The kind of superscience Whitcomb was talking about was as good as one of Endora's magic spells to her.

Before she could formulate a response, though, the lieutenant spoke again. "Maybe we're still too much in the habit of accepting things as they are. Letting opportunities to escape our situation pass us by."

It took Clare a moment to figure out this was something that should worry her. "Um, escape? What . . . uh, what exactly do you mean by that?"

"Boen's been researching the physics, you know," Whitcomb said. "They say we can't go back without risking the collapse of this timeline, but if Doctor Naadri's ideas are right, maybe we can. The way we came into the future was strictly one-way. If we found another way back, we wouldn't be following the same Feynman curve; there'd be no direct entanglement. We could, we could make a one-way trip to a time, say, six months after we were trapped in the Expanse. We'd just branch off into a timeline of our own without endangering this one. It could *work*!" she insisted, leaning forward, straining as if to leap out of the chair. "But the damn bureaucracy won't even give us a fair hearing. They're too hidebound to take a chance. And Captain Bateson, he's too fixated on setting a good *example* to help us *adjust*—he won't even listen."

Clare struggled to find something to say. She was still new at this; she wasn't even sure why Whitcomb had asked to switch therapy assignments and start meeting with her instead of a more experienced TDD counselor. But she tried to make the best of it. "Look, I understand how you feel, Parvana. It's been . . . rough for me to adjust to being in this time. To have to accept that my husband and my little boys have been . . . dead for centuries, that everyone I ever knew is gone and forgotten. There have been times when I'd give anything for a chance to go back. But—"

"Then you do understand," Whitcomb said. "Clare, you're the only one here who could. That's why I came to you." The lieutenant's dark eyes probed hers. "This is in the strictest confidence, right?"

"Of, of course."

"Some of us have been talking, Clare. People who feel the same way I do, that it's time to stop being complacent and do something to solve our problem. And it would go a lot smoother if we had the . . . understanding of a like-minded person within the DTI. Someone who might be in a position to get us certain information or access.

Someone who could benefit from the same opportunity we're looking for. Do you understand what I'm saying, Clare?"

The idea was just starting to sink in. Whitcomb was talking about going back in time, back to her life—and she was offering to help Clare do the same. For four years, Clare had assumed that was impossible. There'd been no weird time effects involved in bringing her to this era; she'd been preserved the same way as a chicken breast in her freezer back home in Secaucus. Clare Raymond, the Cryonic Woman. Since she'd come to work at DTI, she'd learned that there were ways for people to move through time, but it all seemed so remote and bizarre, too far beyond her comprehension for her to consider that it might be accessible to her.

But now, Parvana Whitcomb was offering her something miraculous—the chance to see her Donald and Tommy and Eddie again, to go home to her friends and family, her house, her neighborhood. To subscribe to all her magazines again and catch up on her soaps, so many of which had been lost to the ravages of time. Could it be?

If it were possible, there'd be so much she'd be giving up—Thomas and Louise and Mary and Darrell, the wondrous machines and health care of the twenty-fourth century, the clean air and water, the cities where a woman could go anywhere unescorted and never be afraid. Now that she considered the possibility seriously for the first time, America in the nineteen-nineties seemed like a Third World country by contrast.

But it was home. It was where her family was. How could she not want to live there?

"I don't know how I could help you," Clare said. "I'm

new here myself, and I'm only a counselor. I mean, I had to go through all sorts of security checks and grillings and sign the Official Secrets Act or whatever they call it now just to get this job, but I don't have any kind of access to . . . anything that would get you where you want to go."

"Still, you can find things out for us," Whitcomb said. "Maybe provide a distraction at a key moment. Maybe," she stressed when she saw Clare was balking. "I don't want to put any pressure on you, Clare. I'm offering this because I think you deserve the same chance we do. Whether you participate actively or not is entirely your choice. You leave the details to us." She smiled ominously. "The Federation today . . . they call this a high-security operation, but they've gotten so complacent. Oh, they've had their border skirmishes here and there, the Cardassians, the Tzenkethi, but they were totally flatfooted when those Borg came and they're still struggling to recover. Now, us, we lived under the constant threat of attack by the Klingons, the Romulans, the Tholians . . . spies and saboteurs everywhere . . ." She pursed her lips. "Let's just say ch'Riin and a couple of others have some skills that should take these modern softies by surprise. When the time is right."

"And . . . and when will that be?"

Whitcomb rose. "Not yet. But an opportunity is bound to come. Take your time deciding whether you're willing to take it." She ambled over to the door. "Thanks for the session, Counselor. I feel much better now."

The doors slid shut behind Whitcomb, leaving Clare alone with her thoughts. *What do I do?* If a patient confessed the intent to commit a crime, was a therapist's obligation to respect the confidence or to break it and warn the authorities? She wasn't sure. And either way, she wasn't sure if she wanted to stop the conspirators. Whitcomb seemed so positive it would be safe. Even if she didn't go with them, how could she deprive them of the chance to regain the lives they'd lost?

For that matter, how could she deprive herself?

Pungenday, Chaos 3, 3535 YOLD (A Friday)
18:09 UTC

Gariff Lucsly was running late.

This intolerable situation was the consequence of the pressure the Department was under lately. It wasn't just the usual New Year rush, in which the Department was inundated by walk-ins making crackpot claims that nonetheless had to be heard and evaluated lest there was some genuine intelligence buried in the chaff. (Many claims this time around were prompted by the fact that both the current stardate year, 46000, and the current Gregorian year, 2369, were divisible by the number 23, which allegedly had some arcane numerological significance.) The monitoring station was now up and running at the temporal distortion in the Typhon Expanse—a multidimensional temporal field similar to the Manheim Effect but having no evident connection to the professor's 2364 experiments—but still had calibrations to run and warning buoys to erect, and the Department's physicists were still coordinating with Starfleet's and the Secretary of Transportation's cartographers to determine safe routes through the area. T'Viss was away on Tandar Prime attending a symposium on multidimensional time. Agent Chall and her new partner Faunt were engaged in a delicate negotiation with Agent Revad of the Romulan TAG, attempting to persuade him to share information about a rumored deathbed claim by a Romulan scientist named Telek R'Mor, deceased approximately one year, three months, that he had received transmissions in 2351 from a Federation starship two decades uptime. The transmissions had reportedly been destroyed by individuals whose description suggested operatives of the Temporal Integrity Commission, but attempts to signal that uptime agency for verification had, predictably, gotten no response.

The rest of the department had been busy with cleanup after the recent Devidian incident, in which the *Enterprise* had discovered that the extraphasic aliens were preying on the biological energy of plague victims in 1893 San Francisco. Some agents had to debrief the workers who'd found the time-displaced head of the *Enterprise*'s android operations officer in the caverns beneath the city, swearing them to secrecy. Others had needed to interrogate the *Enterprise* crew to ensure that history had not been altered. If anything, the incident seemed to have generated a self-consistent causal loop, a so-called "predestination paradox" involving the *Enterprise*'s extremely long-lived El-Aurian bartender, Guinan: since Captain Picard of the *Enterprise* had saved her life in 1893, she had worked in recent years to nudge him in the direction of becoming captain of the *Enterprise* to ensure her own past. It was the kind of temporal impurity that made Lucsly very uncomfortable; in his view, there was one true, correct timeline, the most probable quantum state of the universe as it would exist without temporal intervention, and the idea that time travelers had helped shape his reality made him very uneasy. True, quantum physics said that retrocausation was an allowed phenomenon, and that spontaneous loops could even be part of that natural, most probable state. But the sheer nonlinearity of it stuck in Lucsly's craw.

Meanwhile, the DTI historians were kept busy investigating the *Enterprise* crew's reports of encountering Samuel Langhorne Clemens, aka Mark Twain, in San Francisco at a time when history recorded he was traveling in Europe. It could not be a temporal alteration created by the Devidians, or else recorded history would reflect the change. But it wouldn't be the first time the TIC, the Aegis, or some other temporal agency had covered up an anachronistic event by altering contemporary records—or memories. Clemens had actually been brought briefly into the present, allegedly by accident (though Lucsly blamed Starfleet recklessness), and reportedly had come away with a renewed sense of optimism about the future. Yet history showed that Clemens's life post-1893 was marked by increasing cynicism and depression. The Department's analysts were locked in fierce debate on this issue. Had his memories of the twenty-fourth century been erased, leaving only despair? Or had his glimpses of a better future only made his present seem more bleak and hopeless by contrast, as he struggled with bankruptcy, career difficulties, social injustice, and deaths in his family? Some of the researchers argued that his increasing commitment to equal rights, anti-imperialism, anti-vivisectionism, and other activist causes may have been a manifestation of his exposure to Federation values, while others insisted that gave too little credit to the innate values of the man himself, whose writings had been condemning racism and social foibles long before his anachronistic encounter. A definitive answer was probably unattainable, but the work had to be done nonetheless.

Beyond that, the Department had been gearing up to investigate the Devidian system to confirm that there were no more temporal-displacement chambers like the cavern the *Enterprise* had destroyed. But Director Sornek had just been contacted by Cyral Nine, a Cardassian agent of the Aegis, who advised them to leave well enough alone. It seemed that, despite their predatory ways, the Devidians took great care to preserve the timeline, only preying on those who were about to die anyway, and thus the various agencies that enforced the Temporal Accords considered them a lesser evil, tolerating their actions lest they be driven to more drastic and disruptive measures. Or so Sornek had read between the lines, much to his distaste. The elderly Vulcan would no doubt be relieved to take his retirement next month—another situation that had the Department in an uproar as the process of choosing his successor and adjusting to the transition got under way. Lucsly was hoping that Assistant Director Andos would get the job; over the years, she had proven herself more than capable.

On top of everything else, Lucsly no longer had a partner to share the workload. Even though this had been the case for three months, two weeks, and three days, Lucsly was still adjusting to that absence, and thus had found himself in the unfamiliar and unnerving position of having too much work to fit into his time budget. He was sure he would adjust eventually, but under the current circumstances, events weren't stabilizing enough to let him devise a satisfactory schedule.

So it was that Lucsly arrived at headquarters fully seventeen minutes late for a high-level meeting on the current Aegis-Devidian situation. He left the transporter suite at a brisk pace, hoping to make up a half-minute or so. He was thus not pleased when he was intercepted by a blond woman whom he recognized as Clare Raymond, one of the cryonic refugees restored to life on Stardate 41986. "Agent Lucsly, is it? I need to talk to you, sir."

He strode past without slowing. "I'm sorry, I don't have time."

"It's really urgent," she called, jogging after him. He stiffened as she touched his arm, bringing him to a stop. "Please. I've been wrestling with this for weeks and now it's happening and I had to make my choice and I'm still not sure this is the right one, but I just couldn't, I couldn't bring myself to do this and still be a good example for my kids—"

"Wait. Slow down," Lucsly said. "Or no, don't. Tell me, as quickly as you can without losing clarity, what the problem is."

Raymond spelled it out far more slowly than Lucsly hoped; she could use extensive training in the efficient presentation of information. But once it became clear what she was discussing, Lucsly set aside his concern about being late for a meeting. "I was afraid of something like this," he said. "The *Bozeman* has just been taken to the Kuiper Belt for a shakedown to test its refits. Captain Bateson was unavailable due to a mild illness. Lieutenant Whitcomb took command for the duration."

"I know. They've been waiting for their shot, and with this now, and with you all so busy—"

"Time is of the essence, Ms. Raymond. What do you know of their specific plans?"

"They've been talking about something called the Vault, in a place called Eris. I didn't even know there was an Eris, I thought it ended with Pluto."

Eris. The remote dwarf planet where the Department stored confiscated temporal technologies. And a Starfleet ship of the line, newly refitted with modern weapons and systems, was on its way to raid it right now.

"Thank you for your honesty, Ms. Raymond," Lucsly said.

"Is there anything more I can do to help? I feel so guilty about—"

"You need to go to the Director and tell him what you've told me," Lucsly said. "And tell him that I'm on it."

"On it?" But Lucsly was already turning back toward the transporters. "You're going out there? By yourself?"

Her question made him think, though he didn't slow down. Being partnerless was enough of a hassle as it was. Now, he needed assistance more than ever. And there was only one person he trusted to have his back.

If only he could be persuaded to come.

Paris, European Alliance, Earth
18:14 UTC
Megumi crossed her arms sternly as Dulmur arrived outside the restaurant. "You're on time," she said. "Perfectly, precisely on time."

"I know," he replied, kissing her cheek in apology. "I'm working on it."

She smiled. "One day at a time. Or . . . maybe that's not the best way to put it."

"Either way, honey, I am completely off the clock." It had taken three months, two—no, three months *or so*, but he'd finally convinced Meg to start seeing him again. The same dogged streak that had kept him so monomaniacally fixated on time for the past four years had served him well once he'd redirected it, and he was close to convincing her that from now on, his only obsessions would be her and the family they would start together.

But then his comm signaled. "Aw, nuts."

"Want me to go in and get a table?"

"No, I'll just—" He was about to reject the call when he happened to glimpse at the screen. The signal was on a Department channel, with Lucsly's code. It was flashing Priority One.

Meg was looking over his shoulder now. "Oh, no."

Dulmur's hand tightened around the padd in anger. "No. Forget it. I'm not taking it." He hit the reject button and slipped the padd back in his pocket. "I'm done with that life, Meg. I swear it."

She studied him. "I want to believe that, Mare. You know I do."

But then the padd signaled again. Dulmur winced as he saw the realization in her eyes: he'd left the padd on. She knew Dulmur was not a man to do things by half-measures. If he'd really been determined to stay with her no matter what, he would've shut it off. Hell, he wouldn't have even brought it.

He saw the evening, his wife, his future slipping away from him in that moment. "Meg, I swear, I'll throw the padd away, I'll—"

She put her hand on his. Behind the tears was understanding. "He's left you alone for three months. He's respected your wishes. If he's calling now, it must be urgent."

Her words forgave him, but didn't change the fact that if he took that call, he would lose her forever. "Forget it. They have other people to handle that stuff."

"And still he called *you*."

He gazed into her gorgeous eyes, knowing that this was one of those moments where the probabilities were evenly balanced and history split in two. *No,* he thought. *I won't accept that.* He couldn't tolerate going back to DTI and knowing that another half of himself was living happily with Meg. Nor could he tolerate making a life with Meg and knowing in the back of his mind that half of him had rejected that same commitment. Whatever choice he made, it had to be wholehearted, certain, something that couldn't be changed by the flip of a coin, the flip of an electron's spin in a cortical neuron. It had to be the only choice Marion Dulmur could possibly make at this moment in his life.

His partner needed him.

But which partner?

Dwarf planet 136199 Eris
10.7 billion kilometers from Sol
23:38 UTC

Lucsly had commandeered one of Starfleet's fastest in-system courier ships to get to Eris in time. The couriers were bare-bones vessels, capable of high warp factors at the expense of extremely short range, for times when it was necessary to make interplanetary journeys faster than impulse speeds would allow. Due to the hazards of in-system warp travel, they were mostly reserved for emergencies, although their precise calibration to the gravitational parameters of their home system ameliorated the risks, at least to the couriers themselves.

Even so, the Department had chosen to site its top-secret containment facility on Eris for a reason, and not just because a worldlet named for the goddess of discord was poetically fitting. The massive dwarf planet, one of the first to be discovered, was nonetheless one of the most remote large bodies in the Sol System due to its wide, highly inclined orbit. Ever since the DTI had begun storing confiscated time technologies there in 2291, the pale gray planetoid had been moving farther and farther from the Sun and civilization, and now followed its own lonely path some seven light-hours south of the ecliptic plane. In short, it was a long trip.

On arrival, sensors confirmed the *Bozeman*'s presence in orbit. At Lucsly's instruction, the courier had slipped out of warp behind Dysnomia, using Eris's sole moon to shield it from detection by the *Soyuz*-class anachronism. Attempts to hail the Eridian Vault's guardians on a secure channel proved fruitless; apparently Whitcomb's people had neutralized them. Lucsly automatically began formulating a report in his head on how to improve Vault security, hoping that his final report would include testimony from the Vault personnel rather than their postmortems.

The lieutenant in command of the courier offered to bring his small crew down to support Lucsly, but the agent declined; the Vault's contents were far beyond their clearance level, and Lucsly didn't trust anyone without DTI training near some of the sensitive items stored there. The timeline was at enough risk with just the *Bozeman* mutineers down there. Also, the Vault was buried deep within the planetoid's icy mantle; the more who beamed down, the more powerful the transporter beam and the greater the risk of detection.

But that meant Lucsly was alone against a team of highly motivated Starfleet officers trained in a more violent era of history. So be it. He'd resigned himself to the fact as soon as Dulmur had failed to reply to his priority message. He'd had no time to wait for his erstwhile partner to make his choice, so if Dulmur wasn't going to join him on the courier, that meant Dulmur would be left behind, plain and simple. Lucsly would have to do this on his own.

Once he materialized, Lucsly waited and listened, but there was no indication that his transport had been detected. The containment fields that secured the temporal apparatus within the Vault would tend to obscure the transporter signal, at least from a tricorder scan. That was an issue Lucsly would have to address in his report, though at the moment it was an asset.

Lucsly made his way gingerly past the rows of containment bays where the smaller temporal artifacts were stored. Reaching the end of a tier, he peeked around the corner and spotted the intruders: all *Bozeman* personnel, though now attired in modern two-color Starfleet gear. Parvana Whitcomb led them, accompanied by Shelithan ch'Riin, Lloyd Boen, and three enlisted personnel in security gold. Apparently Whitcomb followed the twenty-third-century tradition of a commanding officer leading her own away teams, given that Captain Bateson was still back on Earth. (According to his medical officer, his mild bout of Cygnian flu had been induced deliberately, no doubt to take him out of play so Whitcomb could make her move.)

The mutineers were standing around a security panel. Boen did something that caused sparks to fly, and the containment fields went down throughout the section. That meant their tricorders would pick up Lucsly's biosigns now. He had no choice but to try to take them off guard.

"Freeze, DTI!" he cried, stepping out into the corridor with his phaser drawn: "Weapons down, hands above your heads, now!"

They didn't take his advice. And ch'Riin and his guards were faster draws than Lucsly. He ducked for cover as the phaser bolts flew, taking refuge behind a large, blue boxlike artifact which emitted a low trilling hum. He could only hope the phaser energies wouldn't activate it somehow. "Listen to me!" he called. "You have to stop what you're doing! The risk to the timeline is too great!"

"Lucsly!" Whitcomb cried. "Of course it's you."

"You're wrong, Lucsly," Boen cried. "We know what we're doing. It'll be strictly one-way travel, no risk to your precious timeline."

"You don't know that! You're guessing, and if your guess is wrong, you'll eradicate countless lives!"

"And bring countless others into existence!" Whitcomb fired back. "Who's to say they have any less right to exist?"

Lucsly rolled his eyes. *Every single time. They say that every single time.*

"I've found what we want," Boen said. "Bay K44, the Ky'rha Artifacts. Two are functional. They just need the power packs restored, and those are in Bay K42."

"Let's go. Zane, Cohen, Siemaszko, you keep Lucsly covered."

"You've just doomed us all," Lucsly called. "Using the Ky'rha Artifacts won't be a one-way transfer. They create a quantum entanglement with the past! A two-way exchange of information! That's how they lock onto a time and place! You use those, you guarantee this timeline ends!"

A pause.

"What if he's right?" Boen said.

"He's lying," Whitcomb snapped.

"No, what he's saying makes sense."

"If the theory is right. There's no proof yet."

"But we're basing this whole thing on that theory. What if—"

"Listen to me!" Whitcomb hissed. "Either way, we get back home and live the lives we were supposed to. Either way, we get to save the people we love. And we'll never know whether this timeline survived or not anyway. It won't make any difference."

"To us, maybe, but what about them?"

"It's too late to back out now, Lloyd! In this timeline, we're all guilty of treason. It's either spend the rest of your life in prison or get a new life back home."

"You help me, Boen," Lucsly called, "and it'll be taken into account in your trial!"

But Whitcomb had offered the greater enticement. "Come on," he heard Boen say. "They're this way."

Lucsly had to make his move. He leapt out firing, his aim a best guess from the positions of the voices. One of the guards fell stunned and Boen took a grazing blow to the leg, crumpling him. But fire from the four others' phasers chased Lucsly and forced him to duck behind an ornate ancient time carriage, using the large disk at its rear as a shield. The device started to heat alarmingly under the phaser barrage, and Lucsly hoped it was merely a sign of an imminent fatal explosion rather than an imminent time jump.

"Hey, you!" came a new voice from the end of the corridor—an impossibly familiar voice. The two remaining guards shifted their fire toward the figure, forcing him to leap out of sight before Lucsly could get a clear look.

But then a phaser beam picked off the guards from the other end of the corridor. "No, over here!" came the same voice as before, though no one could move that fast. Lucsly leapt from cover, aiming at Whitcomb, but she broke and ran, abandoning Boen.

Lucsly stared as his rescuer jogged over into view. "Hey, partner," Dulmur said. "Miss me?"

He shook himself. "Your timing is impeccable," he said, the highest praise he knew. "But . . . who's with you?"

Dulmur smirked. "Nobody. You and I are the only ones here."

Lucsly looked back toward the other end of the corridor. He knew there were devices in here that could send a person into the recent past. "Dulmur, if you've broken regulations—"

"You want to talk regulations or you want to save reality as we know it? Come on, she's got a headstart."

Lucsly paused to look at Boen, but the science officer merely lay there with his head lowered, resigned to his fate. The agent took off after his partner and soon caught up. "How did you even get here?"

"Called in a few favors," Dulmur said. "Made the trip inside a Starfleet Class-eight probe." He twisted his neck, working out a kink. "Makes warp nine, but I'd have more room in a coffin."

They found Whitcomb at Bay K42. She'd already donned one of the Ky'rha Artifacts, a silvery headdress and gauntlet connected by a metallic half-sleeve that draped over the left arm and shoulder, and had just finished attaching the power pack to its gauntlet. It was too large for her frame, but the fit was irrelevant. She worked the controls with her left hand, the changing readouts visible on the translucent visor, as she aimed the phaser with her right. "It's set to kill!" she cried.

But Lucsly didn't even slow down. "You think that'll stop me?" After all, Dulmur could take her out while she was killing Lucsly. That was the advantage of having a partner.

At the critical second, though, Whitcomb hesitated. Lucsly didn't. She went down, stunned hard. Her hand spasmed on the Artifact's controls. Lights began to glow on the gauntlet. *Oh, no. She could end up anywhere.*

He raised the level on his phaser, reluctantly making the choice to vaporize Whitcomb and the Artifact rather than jeopardize history. He raised the emitter, ready to fire.

But Dulmur darted forward and threw himself atop Whitcomb. A second later, they were both gone, with nothing to herald their passage but a quiet *whop* as air rushed in to fill the space they'd left. "Dulmur!" Lucsly looked around frantically, watching for signs of reality fading around him, though he knew it wouldn't work that way.

But then he felt a tap on his shoulder. He whirled to find Dulmur standing there, holding the Ky'rha Artifact. "You called?"

Lucsly stared. "Where's Whitcomb?"

Dulmur gestured with his head, leading Lucsly around a corner. There he found Whitcomb, Boen, and the other mutineers all secured, their wrists bound. "We got lucky. I guess the Artifact defaults to the nearest habitable place and time if there's no firm destination set, and out here that means this place. We jumped back about eight minutes. So when my earlier self got here four minutes ago, I met myself and worked out that little diversion you saw. I held back till you and . . . I were out of the way, then came in and tied up these guys. The rest, you know."

Lucsly glared at him. "I should put you on report, mister! You deliberately interacted with your past self! Why?"

"Because I already knew I would. What, you wouldn't want me to change history, would you?"

Dulmur had him there. Lucsly shook his head. Obviously the man's time away from the Department had eroded his respect for regulations. Still, however questionable his means, Lucsly couldn't argue with his ends. "Dulmur . . ."

"What?"

"I couldn't have done it without you."

Dulmur grinned. "What a coincidence. I couldn't have done it without me either."

Lucsly stared him down. "You're making jokes. About time. You know I hate that."

"Yeah." The younger agent sighed. "I hate that too. Call it a defense mechanism."

There was a long pause. "Megumi?" Lucsly asked.

A longer pause. "That was another life," Dulmur said. "This is who I am now."

"I'm sorry."

"It's okay. Maybe I can't have a wife, a family . . . but I've got a partner. Maybe . . . in its way . . . that's something just as . . ."

"You're not about to say something sentimental about me, are you?"

Dulmur's eyes widened innocently. "Me? No. No way."

"Good."

"Perish the thought."

"Because I hate that."

"Never crossed my mind."

"Just so we understand that."

Dulmur chuckled and clapped his fellow agent on the shoulder. "I missed you too, partner."

PRESENT TIME
STARDATE 58923.8 TO 59046.6

XI

Château Thelian, Loire Valley, European Alliance
04:56 UTC

As Laarin Andos walked down the long corridor separating the presidential residence's transporter suite from its living chambers, she was tempted to ask her escort, security agent Steven Wexler, for information on why President Bacco had summoned her at this hour of the morning. But she could easily read from the man's body language that he was as much in the dark as she was, a state he found puzzling and upsetting given his high status in the president's security hierarchy. Andos knew that humans were generally more tolerant of breaches in accepted hierarchical protocols than Rhaandarites were, but that was a matter of degree; where professional pride and status were at stake, humans could be even more inflexible than her own people, who had multiple tiers of backup protocols to adapt to any conceivable situation. *No, that's unfair to him,* Andos reflected after a moment's more observation. Wexler's frustration was motivated more by a fear that he would be unable to protect the president adequately if not fully informed.

What Andos could not tell at this point was whether his reaction was predicated on a real threat. That was something the president had insisted she would only reveal to Andos in private. Andos was hardly a stranger to discussing classified temporal security matters with the Federation president, but almost invariably it was conducted in the presidential office in the Palais de la Concorde or in the situation room at Starfleet Headquarters, with other key administration or military personnel present, or at least, in Bacco's case, with her inseparable chief of staff, Esperanza Piñiero. And the regular monthly briefing was only a week uptime. A middle-of-the-night command to come alone to the president's sleeping quarters was highly anomalous.

When they reached said quarters, the female Pandrilite guard stationed outside them signaled on the intercom. *"Is Andos here yet?"* came the president's gruff voice.

"She's just arrived, Madam President."

"Well, what the hell is she waiting for, the Pioneers to win the pennant? Bring her in!" Oddly, the voice seemed to originate at a greater distance from the intercom pickup, yet Andos had heard no sounds of body movement. *Curious,* she thought, placing a hand in her pocket.

The Pandrilite didn't notice any anomaly, though. "Yes, ma'am. Director, please go on in."

When Andos entered through the wood-paneled (but tritanium-cored) doors, she found the president's bedchamber dimly lit. A figure moved forward, lean and white-haired. As Andos's eyes adjusted, she was able to see the wizened but lively face of President Nanietta Bacco. The leader of the United Federation of Planets was attired in fuzzy slippers and a nightshirt emblazoned with the legend PIKE CITY PIONEERS and the number 14. "Laarin, hi. Sorry to get you out of bed this time of night. It's much more fun to get Esperanza out of bed this time of night, but this is a situation I can only come to you with."

"Think nothing of it, Madam President. As those in my profession are aware, time is a relative concept."

"Tell me about it." It was President Bacco's voice— but it came from the 'fresher at Andos's right. The director turned to see another Nanietta Bacco standing in the doorway, this time dressed in one of her usual dark suits. Standing next to her was a lanky, brown-haired human with a haughty expression on his thin face. He wore a black uniform somewhat resembling modern Starfleet attire, but with the right shoulder quilted in dark blue. His insignia was a horizontal version of the Starfleet arrowhead in gold combined with a silver diamond shape, and the three rank pins on his collar were chevron-shaped.

Andos nodded at them both. "Madam President," she said. "And Commander Ducane. Greetings."

"Director," Ducane said.

The nightshirt-clad Bacco stared at her. "You know this clown?"

"Yes, Madam President. Juel Ducane is an officer of Starfleet approximately five centuries from now. He is attached to the Temporal Integrity Commission and is responsible for monitoring events in our generation." Andos's gaze shifted between the two Presidents Bacco. "Although I imagine at least one of you has already been introduced."

"Once or twice," the suited Bacco said.

"Mister Ducane, I trust there was some urgent reason for duplicating our president?" Andos asked. "And are we dealing with a temporal reversal or an alternate present?" She kept the terminology simple for Bacco's benefit.

"Believe me, Director Andos, I wouldn't have doubled President Bacco back on her own timestream without a very good reason. You know the TIC takes the integrity of the timeline very seriously."

"Oh, really?" Nightshirt Bacco said. "I never would've guessed, what with you putting it in your name and all."

"My, you got up on the wrong side of the bed this morning," Suit Bacco told her.

"Look who's talking. You got up on the wrong side of reality."

"Madams President," Andos interposed, "if someone could explain, please?"

Ducane seemed reluctant to speak, the usual reticence of uptime agents to reveal information to downtime listeners. But Nightshirt Bacco had no problem filling the gap. "Well, from what I've been told, I'm apparently due to be assassinated in a few hours."

"*Was* due to be assassinated," Suit Bacco hastened to interpose.

"It can't be a 'was,' it hasn't happened yet."

"It has for him," Suit Bacco said, tilting her head toward Ducane. "Apparently, the first time the moving finger wrote, I got written out of the story with extreme prejudice. But somehow, don't ask me to explain the physics, this guy knew his own past had been changed and came back to fix it."

Andos caught the significance of her words. "Then I take it the assassin is not of contemporary origin?"

"That's right," Ducane said grudgingly. "But rest assured, the situation has been resolved."

"Took a few tries, though," Suit Bacco said. "Mister Ducane here apparently failed to save my life at least once on his own—so I apparently got killed twice, which I'm not sure if I should be proud of or creeped out by."

"I failed to anticipate the trap the assassin had set," Ducane said, sheepish under the president's dual glare.

"So he decided to recruit me from just before my death and take me back to earlier so I could help him prevent the trap from getting set up in the first place."

"Unfortunately," Ducane said, "that merely spooked the assassin and led him to jump back several hours to this time frame, intending to murder the President in her sleep. We only just arrived in time to save her."

"I tell you, I thought I was dreaming," said Nightshirt Bacco—or perhaps Downtime Bacco was a more dignified and precise designation. "I'm kinda still hoping I am."

"We've got him tied up in the 'fresher," the suited Uptime Bacco added. Andos strode over to peer inside. There on the floor, unconscious and securely bound, was a bipedal being with a wide domed head, pronounced brow ridges, a triangular muzzle, batlike nostrils, narrow pointed ears, and scaly, wrinkled skin. Andos recognized him as a Shirna, a fairly remote, independent civilization occasionally encountered in the Bajor and Kalandra Sectors. "Ducane wanted us to leave right away, but neither of me was about to let him until we talked to you. What with some of the briefings I've gotten from you lately, I had a feeling this was something you needed to know about."

"I appreciate being notified of the incident," Andos said. She turned to Ducane. "Commander, recruiting contemporary individuals to rescue themselves is a rare tactic for you, apparently one only used in exceptional circumstances. I'm curious why you found it necessary to recruit and temporally duplicate the President herself."

The TIC officer fidgeted. "President Bacco was the only one with the necessary security clearances to get where I needed her to go."

"Bull," said Uptime Bacco. "With your time transporters, you can get wherever you want without setting off security."

"And don't think I'm not going to talk to the Director about that later on," added Downtime Bacco. But Andos's attention was on the Shirna captive. Something wasn't quite right about his body language, yet without more familiarity with his species, it was difficult to determine specifics.

"All right," Ducane admitted with a faint blush. "I admit, the opportunity to work alongside one of history's great Federation presidents was irresistible."

"Oh, please," both Baccos said in harmony.

"Don't sell yourself short, Madam President. You've already helped shape my history by your actions in defense of the Federation. Organizing the unprecedented alliance against the Borg invasion . . ." Andos moved closer. The Shirna was growing increasingly smug, as if pleased to have fooled Ducane into complacency.

"Which accomplished absolutely nothing against the Borg," the downtime incarnation of the President said, "and only led to the formation of the Typhon Pact. Yeah, that went real well." Yet there was an air of tension to the assassin as well, as if readying himself . . .

"Don't underestimate the value of your accomplishment, ma'am."

"Everyone out," Andos cried. "He has a bomb!" She was only guessing about the mechanism of his suicide attack, but it seemed the safest assumption.

The director moved to interpose herself before the presidents and hurry them out of the room. But Ducane calmly pointed a small device at the captive and activated it. Andos felt a split second of heat, saw the room brighten . . . but then it faded. She turned to see the assassin's body completing its reconstitution and then freezing in place.

"Don't worry, he's in stasis," Ducane said. "And we want him alive for questioning. Good catch, Director. But as you can see, there was no cause for panic." Andos declined to dignify his condescension with a response.

"Damn," Uptime Bacco said, gathering herself. "He wouldn't go to those lengths for something I already did."

"Good point," her hours-younger self added. "Is there something else important I'm supposed to be doing soon?"

"I've already revealed too much," Ducane said. "I'd rather not have to resequence your memory engrams, Madam President, before I reintegrate the two of you."

"Reintegrate?" Downtime Bacco asked.

"It's a way of combining two temporal copies of an individual back into one," Ducane explained with casual condescension. "It's not a technique you'd understand in your time."

"Simple enough," Andos said. "Two temporal copies of an individual are a coherent, noncontiguous superposition: the same particles in two different quantum position states. One uses a transporter beam, which is a quantum-level process, to beam one copy onto the same coordinates as the other, allowing them to collapse back into a single quantum state, a single individual." At Ducane's shocked stare, Andos explained, "The procedure was pioneered by Spock of Vulcan during the Black Star slingshot incident of 2267 and 1969. Since the events were classified and there were vanishingly few opportunities to employ the technique further, I'm not surprised you were unaware of its earliest use, Commander."

After a moment, Ducane nodded, poorly concealing his annoyance at being shown up by a member of the DTI—even one who'd just saved his life. "Thank you, Director. We'll have to update our historical records accordingly. But we really should be getting on with the reintegration so I can leave you in peace."

"Don't think you can conceal your intentions from me, Commander," Andos told him. "As soon as you leave here, you will beam yourself back in time and prevent the sequence of events which led to this conversation ever occurring. I wouldn't recommend you attempt it," she added, drawing her padd from her pocket. "Our every word since I entered here has been recorded and uploaded to the DTI's phase-shielded servers. Erase these events and we will find out and investigate."

"Why are you resisting this?" Ducane demanded. "You should understand the importance of eliminating all timeline discrepancies as much as I do."

"I also understand the danger of micromanaging the timeline. Repeatedly jumping back and forth over the same swath of history, creating alternate after alternate in the hope that they will ultimately cancel one another out . . . creating such a complex temporal manifold runs the risk of damaging subspace."

Ducane's jaw worked angrily. "We know what we're doing far better than the . . . the primitives of your century."

Downtime Bacco fixed him with her pale gaze. "Do

you know why Wang Chunxi was able to score three hom-
ers against Faith Martinez in the '81 Series?"

Everyone stared blankly except her older self, who
sighed and said, "Because sometimes experience leads
to overconfidence. You get complacent, lose sight of the
basics that a rookie remembers to pay attention to." She
threw a glance at the time-suspended Shirna, underlining
her point. "Experience doesn't always make you smarter.
Sometimes it just makes you *think* you know everything."

Ducane clearly wanted to protest, but was too cowed
by the prospect of arguing with one of his historical
idols, in duplicate, no less. "Very well. I'll leave you
all—both—with your memories of this event. If any two
people in this time can be trusted with keeping secrets,
it's the two of you."

"What will you do to the assassin?" Andos asked him.

"Don't worry, we'll neutralize the bomb before we
release him. He'll live to get a fair trial."

"Before or after he commits the crime?"

Ducane turned to glare at her. "You're exceptionally
well-versed in our procedures. I should've known Captain
Janeway couldn't be trusted to obey the Temporal Prime
Directive."

"After what they witnessed during their sojourn
aboard the timeship *Relativity,* both Kathryn Janeway
and Seven of Nine deemed it prudent to warn the highest
echelons of Starfleet Command and the DTI of what they
had witnessed."

Both Baccos stared at her, then at Ducane. "Warn?"
Downtime Bacco asked. "I know I've been briefed on
this, but it's the middle of the night and I could use a
reminder."

"I'd advise against that, Madam President," Ducane said.

"I understand why you would," Andos told him. "Madam President, the first time the *U.S.S. Voyager* encountered a member of the TIC, Captain Braxton, he had come back to preemptively destroy them in the belief that they would cause a temporal explosion that would destroy Earth in his century. It was ultimately determined that *Voyager* was blameless and Braxton's own actions had precipitated the sequence of events that caused the explosion.

"Two years, six months later, *Voyager* time, Seven of Nine was recruited by Braxton and Mister Ducane, then a lieutenant, to capture a saboteur from uptime who attempted to destroy *Voyager* in the past and then present. It turned out to be an older incarnation of Braxton who had fallen prey to temporal psychosis, a neurological disorder caused by excessive use of quantum-tunneling–based time travel within a short period of subjective time."

Uptime Bacco stared at him. "You didn't tell me this *before* you took me gallivanting all over the timeline?"

"Let her finish," Downtime Bacco said.

"According to Seven's account—corroborated by Janeway, who was later recruited to complete the mission—Mister Ducane then arrested the younger version of Braxton for the crime that he had not yet committed—and indeed was ultimately prevented from committing in the first place. Yet Ducane made it clear that there would be a trial nonetheless."

Downtime Bacco stared at Ducane in horror. "You prosecuted a man for a crime that never actually happened?"

"It *had* happened in one branch of the timestream,"

Ducane countered. "It could have happened again if we hadn't dealt with Braxton."

"*Could* have?" echoed Uptime Bacco. "So basically you TIC guys see nothing wrong with punishing people for things you kinda sorta guess they might do in the future. Even *executing* an entire starship crew with extreme prejudice—"

"—without even confirming their guilt first!" her other self finished. "And you have the gall to wear that uniform? To call yourself a defender of the Federation? What has happened to the union in your time?"

"Please, Madam President, you have to understand," Ducane argued, still more condescending than pleading. "As this morning's events must drive home, there are many factions and individuals out there who are actively trying to subvert the integrity of history. We're fighting a war literally without end, without even a beginning. If we must sometimes go to extremes to protect reality itself against such an existential threat, then so be it. There's no point trying to defend the principles of a simpler, more innocent time if you fail to defend your very existence in the process."

Downtime Bacco shook her head. "Do you have any idea how many times people have told me I had to treat the Federation's values as optional in order to protect it? That's what my predecessor believed, and it led to a culture of moral compromise that almost brought down the Federation."

"It wasn't betraying our values that saved us," her counterpart went on, "but sticking by them. If you're so hell-bent on protecting your existence, maybe you oughta try giving everyone else less reason to be afraid of *letting* you exist. That's worked pretty well for us 'primitives' who founded your civilization in the first place."

Ducane stared at the Baccos for a long moment, his expression showing grudging respect. "I won't argue with you further, ma'am, because I'm not allowed to explain my reasons in detail. I'll just say I understand why history remembers you the way it does." He glanced back at the time-suspended assassin in the 'fresher. "Who knows? He may actually have been right about you. If anyone could persuade so many . . ."

He shook his head. "I've got to stop running my mouth off. Madams President, if you'll both stand together, I'll have you reintegrated. With both sets of memories intact." Andos was impressed, though she wouldn't give Ducane the satisfaction of seeing it on her face. Spock's makeshift version of the technique had, to all indications, left only the earlier set of memories. Clearly the TIC had greatly refined the procedure in the ensuing centuries.

"Damn," the younger Bacco said, moving alongside her suited counterpart. "With two of me, maybe I'd finally have enough time to get some real work done."

"You kidding?" her double replied. "Now that I see me from the outside, I understand why Esperanza gets so sick of my yammering. We'd drive each other crazy."

"Good point. I'd be positively beside myself."

The uptime Bacco winced and turned to Ducane. "I've changed my mind. Can we let him kill her after all?"

DTI Headquarters, Greenwich
11:03 UTC
"With this latest incident," Director Andos said to the assembled DTI agents in HQ's situation room, "it has become clear that the present is under attack."

Agent Shelan looked around her, gauging the reactions of the other assembled agents. Every field agent currently in Sol System had been assembled for this meeting: Lucsly, Dulmur, Stijen Yol, Stewart Peart, Ranjea, even the novice Garcia, whose provisional pairing with Ranjea for the Axis of Time mission three months back seemed to have stuck. Assistant Director Sonaj of the San Francisco office was in attendance as well, along with Doctor T'Viss, Head of Research Virum Kalnota, and Senior Historian Loom Aleek-Om, an elderly Aurelian who had seen nearly two hundred of his species' annual mating flights. All were somber in the wake of the news about the attack on President Bacco, but some, like Shelan herself, were already catching on that it may have only been a harbinger of things to come.

Andos went on. "September: an attempt on the life of Professor Vard or one of his graduate students, committed by unknown future individuals, deterred by a Federation Temporal Agent. At the same time, a possible attack on Doctor Naadri, perhaps connected with the Vard attack, perhaps instigated by the twenty-eighth-century Sponsor of the Suliban Cabal. October: a sabotage attempt within the Typhon Pact, apparently intended to spark a war with the Federation, possibly instigated by the same Sponsor. Now, just over six weeks later, an assassination attempt against our own president by a future member of the Shirna race—briefly successful but corrected by an officer of the Temporal Integrity Commission. Additionally, there's the impending incident which will send Lieutenant Dina Elfiki back in time to early October, an incident which remains known only to the lieutenant but does not seem to be pleasant.

"The pattern is clear. At least two uptime factions engaging in acts of violence against the present, directly or by proxy. At least two signatory agencies of the Temporal Accords countering their efforts. And all of it concentrating upon a brief span of linear time. Gentlebeings, we must conclude that we are witnessing the opening of a new front in the Temporal Cold War."

A chill went through Shelan, as much of excitement as dread. She knew, better than most here, what the cost of the Temporal Cold War could be on the eras where it concentrated. And yet, if the Cabal's Sponsor was directing a new offensive against the present, it meant that Shelan might have an opportunity to confront him at last, far earlier in her career than she ever anticipated. If she were careful enough, if she were good enough, maybe she could even find a way to bring him to account for his crimes.

Once the murmuring died down, AD Sonaj said, "Perhaps we should review what we know of the factions in the Temporal Cold War, their methods, and their objectives."

"Agreed," Andos said. "Unfortunately, there is little we do know for certain."

They began with the Shirna, the most recent threat. Little was known beyond the fact that, three centuries hence, they would be in an ongoing temporal war with the Vorgons, one in which both sides were apparently willing to engage in extreme measures to alter one another's pasts. Clearly neither species abided by the Temporal Accords, so it stood to reason they were in conflict with the Accordist nations of the future as well. Studying the Shirna of the present day could reveal nothing, for that species had never yet encountered the Vorgons (at least, not contemporary Vorgons) and as yet had no advanced temporal technologies.

And yet there was no known involvement of the Shirna or Vorgons in the primary known front of the Cold War, the period from 2144 to 2154. "Many assume," Aleek-Om said in a slow voice as thin and reedy as his unclothed, gold-feathered body, "that the motive of any temporal interventionists operating in that era . . . particularly given their frequent entanglements with Jonathan Archer and the first *Starship Enterprise* . . . must have been to undermine the formation of the Federation. But that notion does not hold up under scrutiny. The Suliban Cabal spent a decade at war with Tandar Prime . . . attempted to foment a civil war in the Klingon Empire . . . and clashed with the Tholians from time to time . . . but rarely targeted *Enterprise* directly and never targeted a founding world of the Federation. More than once, the Cabal actually aided Captain Archer. In September 2151, they averted sabotage that would have destroyed *Enterprise* . . . and in March 2153, the Cabal's Sponsor personally communicated with Archer to warn him of the temporal intervention behind the Xindi attack on Earth. If anything, it appears the Sponsor was concerned with *preserving* the events leading to the formation of the Federation."

"But what about their attack on Paraagan II in February 2152?" Shelan interposed. "That was done specifically to discredit humanity and bring Archer's mission to a premature end."

"Yes," Aleek-Om said, "the Cabal did attempt to frame *Enterprise* for the destruction of that colony. But they did not destroy *Enterprise* . . . even though they easily could have. And when Temporal Agent Daniels prevented Archer from being taken aboard a Cabal vessel, the effect on future history was devastating . . . suggesting that Archer—and the future Federation, *cher-wit!*—would have survived had he indeed fallen into Cabal hands. So it seems the attempt to discredit *Enterprise* was in response to Archer's previous interference in the Cabal's activities. They only acted against him to remove an obstacle to whatever their actual goals were . . . and otherwise took care to cause no major disruption to the Federation's seminal history."

"But wouldn't discrediting Archer have prevented the birth of the Federation?" Garcia asked, showing no hesitation about speaking up in a room full of far more experienced agents. Shelan smiled. *I knew she had potential.*

"Not necessarily," Lucsly replied. "Archer's importance to history could've been exaggerated."

"Or perhaps he would have filled the same eventual role through other means," offered Kalnota, a round-faced Zakdorn with gray-brown hair and understated jowls. "The Xindi attack and the Earth-Romulan War would likely have brought him back onto the interstellar stage, where his role in building alliances among the founders could've been similar. So the Sponsor may have deemed the risk to history to be minimal."

"But worth taking," Shelan replied, "to get Archer to stop meddling in his real goals. Which means whatever he was after must've been important."

"Do, er, do we have any idea what those goals were?" asked Stewart Peart, a lanky, tousle-haired Englishman who'd been an agent for five years and still seemed like a perpetually flustered rookie—yet was one of the few human agents to last even that long in the job.

"No," Andos said. "We know they targeted the Tanda-rans, the Klingons, and to a lesser extent the Tholians, but the common thread is unknown."

"There's another target, ma'am." Everyone turned to look at Shelan, and she realized how it must have sounded—the Suliban in the room suddenly making a bold declarative statement about a hidden objective of the Suliban Cabal. Suddenly she wished she had her Cabal ancestor's camouflage ability so she could vanish into the woodwork. "I mean, maybe there is," she went on more quietly. "Think about it. Given that the Cabal's Sponsor wanted to discredit Archer, to get him out of the way . . . why choose Paraagan II as the place and time to do it? Why wait until then, nearly six months after their second encounter? There were other, earlier incidents that could've been sabotaged to make Archer look bad. Their rescue of the Klingon ship at the start of October '51, say, or their visit to the P'Jem monastery two weeks later, or their attack on the Tandaran internment camp in December. For that matter, why not go back and strike at Archer even earlier, before *Enterprise*'s launch, before he'd interfered in Cabal affairs at all?"

Dulmur was nodding now. "You're saying maybe it wasn't just about Archer. That maybe destroying the Para-agan colony was the real goal, and pinning it on Archer was just a bonus."

"It would explain a lot."

"Not really," Lucsly told her. "It wouldn't explain *why* the Sponsor would want to destroy Paraagan II, or what his faction's ultimate purpose was."

"Or why he'd be so concerned with protecting the Federation's history," Ranjea added.

"Yeah," Garcia put in, "isn't he the bad guy?"

"Maybe in the future, the Federation *is* the 'bad guy,'" suggested Stijen Yol. The red-haired Trill straightened in his chair and said, "The Sponsor's from the same era as the early Temporal Integrity Commission. And we know they're capable of some highly unethical acts. It's possible that, at least in some future branches, the Federation loses its way, becomes corrupt. Maybe the Sponsor *is* Federation. Maybe he went after the Klingons because they were an enemy of the Federation for so long. Maybe the Tandarans would've been a threat if the Cabal hadn't spent a decade wearing them down."

"Okay, that's a disturbing thought," Garcia said. "But I don't buy it. If this Future Guy was so concerned about protecting the UFP—"

Dulmur stared at her. "'Future Guy'?"

Garcia flushed. "Yeah, let's just pretend I didn't call him that. The point is, if he was so concerned about the UFP, I don't think he would've risked messing with Archer at all."

"Then where does that leave us?" T'Viss demanded. "If you wish to reject one hypothesis, you must have a better one to offer in its place."

Garcia winced at her former teacher's chastisement and pondered the question. "Well, the Tandarans look like an obvious link. The attack on Vard was on Tandar Prime, and Elfiki was found on a Tandaran colony."

"Paraagan," Ranjea said thoughtfully. "Doctor Naadri is Paraagan."

"Did she have ancestors on Paraagan II?" Lucsly asked.

"Illogical," T'Viss interposed. "The attack on Paraagan II was successful. There were no survivors. Had the intent been to kill Naadri's ancestors and prevent her birth, it would have succeeded. However, to my frequent annoyance, that has not been the case."

A grim chuckle went through the situation room. When it died down, Virum Kalnota said, "And what about the Cabal's attack on the Klingons? They aren't exactly known for producing great temporal physicists."

"There is Korath," Peart interposed.

"Korath's a crackpot," Lucsly countered, while T'Viss merely sniffed in contempt. "Lots of big ideas, nothing to show for them. He's shifted almost entirely to weapons development."

"And starting a whole civil war just to prevent one man's birth?" Dulmur added. "Textbook overkill. The risk of unforeseen consequences to the timeline—"

"Is about the same as a war between us and the Typhon Pact," Yol replied, "or the death of President Bacco."

Andos shook her head. "It's an interesting thought, but it's too tenuous. There are other noted temporal researchers from many cultures. As for Doctor Vard, we can't even be certain he was the target, rather than one of his non-Tandaran students. Besides, if temporal physicists today are the target, why strike at their ancestors twenty-three decades ago? Why not a more recent intervention?

"We need more facts, people. Anything that might suggest a pattern. Kalnota, have your researchers pore over the history of the twenty-one forties and fifties for any useful clues. Lucsly, reach out to your uptime contacts, press them for whatever information you can."

"You know they won't tell us anything, ma'am."

"If they'll tell anyone, Gariff, they'll tell you." Lucsly nodded.

"Shelan," Andos went on, drawing the young agent's full attention, "talk with Lieutenant Elfiki, see if she has any knowledge that will help us. Maybe if we've figured out this much on our own, she won't see it as contamination to nudge us the rest of the way."

"Yes, ma'am."

"The rest of you, reach out to your contacts in other governments' time agencies. I'll do the same at the administrative level. Whatever's coming, it's clearly not limited to the Federation. We need to get all of known space on the alert if need be."

"Um, excuse me, ma'am," Garcia asked, her hand raised. "Stupid question, but . . . we already know the Temporal Agents and the TIC are on this. They know what's going on and they can actually time travel to stop it. To put it bluntly, is there any point in trying to handle this ourselves beyond professional pride?"

"Isn't that reason enough?" Yol challenged.

Andos held up a hand, quieting him. "No, it's a fair question. We do this, Agent Garcia, for the same reasons we exist as an agency in the first place. Because time is vast and needs the vigilance of every eye that can be brought to bear. Because the priorities of the future may differ from those of the present, and someone needs to speak and act on behalf of our generation.

"And because, at the very least, we deserve to know what our uptime partners in the Temporal Accords are doing in the name of our defense. We deserve to have a say in it, to ensure that their methods to defend us do not go against the very things we stand for. They must be held answerable to their ancestors. Their technology to traverse and alter time may give them power over us . . . but our knowledge and our choices for the future give us power over them.

"So go. Gain that knowledge. Give us a choice. So that this time, we will not be pawns, but will be partners in our own defense.

"This is our time, gentlebeings," Andos finished. "And we will not let it be wasted."

XII

DTI Headquarters, Greenwich
14:16 UTC

Clare found Dina Elfiki in the holosuite portion of her "guest quarters," an amenity installed to keep her from going stir-crazy during her confinement here. But instead of simulating some lush outdoor vista, the striking lieutenant stood in a bare holosuite, holding a control padd and perusing a hovering three-dimensional crossword grid whose size and complexity staggered Clare just to look at. "Oh, good," Dina said, spotting her. "I'm rusty on history . . . who was the commander of the first manned Saturn expedition? Shaun Geoffrey blank, eleven letters, third is an R, ninth is an H."

"Sorry, that's after my time."

"Well, I'll get it on the crosses. Let's see . . . 'Carreon baggage'? Eight letters . . . Arhh, do they mean the amphibians from Carreon or the humanoids from Carrea? Which one is pronounced that way again?"

Clare had no idea what Dina was talking about, but it wasn't what she'd come to discuss anyway. "So . . . you had a talk with Shelan yesterday, I hear."

Dina threw her a look, then turned back to the puzzle. "And now you're here to try to convince me to tell you what I wouldn't tell her."

According to Shelan, the talk hadn't gone well. Clare wished she could have been there, but she'd been out for the past week, attending a family friend's wedding on Denobula. With three husbands and three brides, the ceremony alone had taken over a day. The old Clare would've been scandalized, but it had really been very beautiful. "I'm just . . . confused," she said. "I thought you *wanted* to tell someone. I thought it was just temporal regulations that were holding you back. It seems that if anything warrants bending the regulations . . ."

"'Man on the beam'? Oh, come on!" she said, working her padd to enter ERICKSON. "Try making it a little challenging!"

Clare stepped in front of her and said, "Eight-letter word: the act of making excuses to av—not talk about something!"

Dina glared at her for a bit, then softened. "Avoidance. That's nine letters, dear."

"Whatever. Do I have your attention?"

The lieutenant's big dark eyes held on hers for a long moment. Then she sighed and said, "Do you know what day it is?"

Clare tried not to laugh. "Is this a trick question?"

"It's Saturday. Stardate 58926. Three days ago, the *Enterprise* was caught in a territorial dispute between an Acamarian refugee convoy and a renegade Betelgeusian argosy. The refugees tried to settle on a planet the 'Geusians claimed as a hunting preserve. Captain Picard tried to negotiate a compromise, said there was plenty of land to go around, but the 'Geusians' pride, their need to win, wouldn't let them back down, and the Acamarians were almost as prickly.

"So shots were fired. The captain put the ship right in between them, of course. It bought Jasminder—that's our security chief—time to devise one of her brilliant strategies and neutralize all their weapons with no loss of life on either side." She winced. "But they weren't showing the same restraint. We lost shields on deck seven aft and five people were killed. Two of them were geophysicists who worked for me. Adrienne Markham and Metta Tharys. They were supposed to be off-shift, but they were rerunning an analysis I'd yelled at them for not getting right the first time." After a tense moment, she whirled and threw the control padd across the room.

"I'm sorry," Clare said after a time. "But you couldn't have known . . ."

"Not then!" Dina cried. "But I knew now. I've had six weeks to warn them, to warn myself. But I couldn't. My duty wouldn't let me. Those big guards posted outside my door wouldn't let me. The analysts monitoring my every keystroke wouldn't let me. For six weeks, I've known I had to just sit back and do nothing and let those people die." She took in a shuddering breath. "And I was able to live with it because I convinced myself that it was out of my hands. That there was nothing I could do about it. I convinced myself that, that all of this was just a replay of something that had already happened, something fixed in the past. That sharing what I know wouldn't make any difference anyway.

"But now—" She barked a laugh. "*Now* your agents come and tell me that it's okay to share it. That maybe I can help prevent something really bad happening. As if it's okay to bend the rules when enough is at stake. Well, what about Markham and Metta? What about their families?

What could possibly be bigger stakes from their point of view?"

"So . . . you're keeping quiet to punish the Department for not letting you help them?"

Dina stared, looking shocked. "No! I . . . I don't know. I just . . . I mean . . . if all my reasons for not saving them, if everything I convinced myself of before, is no longer applicable, then letting them die again was all for nothing. I have to believe, I have to tell myself, that keeping future knowledge to myself is the right thing to do, no matter the consequences. That's the only way I can live with myself."

Clare was silent for a time, not knowing what to say. That was all right; often her job was simply to be a sounding board, to let her patients work things out for themselves. She remained silent as Dina gathered herself, then walked over to retrieve the puzzle control padd. The lieutenant entered a few more words silently. Clare understood that it wasn't frivolous; it was a distraction, and maybe a way to help her feel some sense of control over an orderly domain.

"You know," she finally said, "I'm anything but an expert on theories of time. But it seems to me that . . . when you kept quiet before, that was about preserving the real history, the way it was supposed to go, for better or worse. But what the Department's asking could help them stop someone from *changing* the way history's supposed to go. I think that's why they're willing to make an exception."

"Oh, here's an easy one. 'Therapeutic plant from Earth,' four letters."

Clare chuckled. The easy crosswords in the back of

TV Guide had been more her speed, but even she knew this one. "Aloe."

"Some things never change, huh?" She entered the letters and let out a breath. "They *think* history might be changed if I don't help them. But it's all guesswork. There's just as much chance I could change it if I do. I could prevent some future faction from doing whatever they're trying to do, but in the process I could . . . step on a butterfly. Cause some other monumental change just by accident.

"No—I figure if tampering with the past is that great a risk, then the last thing we should do is try to compound it with more tampering." She studied the grid again. "I will do everything I can to help—when the time is right. But I'm not going to cheat by helping you peek ahead at the answers." She gave a small scoff. "Not that I have many answers anyway."

Clare shrugged. "You've got more than I do." She came over to peer over Dina's shoulder at the padd. "'Gorkon's gun'? Huh?"

"*HIch.*"

"I don't get it."

Norym District, Nivoch
Middle Season, Day 106, 743 UE (A Wednesday)
19:37 UTC

Lucsly and Dulmur found Cyral Nine in a bar in the seediest part of Norym District. They attracted a fair share of suspicious stares from the clientele; Nivoch was a neutral world that had been caught in the middle during the Dominion War, so its inhabitants—all settlers of various species, for the most intelligent indigenous form was a tree-dwelling rodent—tended to mistrust Federation nationals and Cardassians alike. Which made it an odd place for a Cardassian like Cyral to situate herself.

Cyral was at the bar, being unsuccessfully propositioned by a Chandir, his cranial trunk curling suggestively forward over his shoulder. The two DTI agents flanked him, peering at him sternly, until he got the hint and slinked away, his trunk falling flaccid down his back. The agents moved in on either side of Cyral, who took in their visages with bleary eyes. "Lucsly! Dlummer! As always, coming to the rescue of the downtrodden. Bartender! Two more over here!"

"We're on duty," Lucsly told her.

"Who said they were for you?"

"Aww, Cyral," Dulmur moaned, shaking his head at the sight of her. "What happened to you?" The first time he'd met the Aegis agent—back in '70 when she and they had both been attempting to disperse a Turtledove anomaly in the Hugora Nebula before the Obsidian Order could locate it and use it for time travel—she had been so disciplined and self-assured, with an ineffable wisdom and an air of precision that rivaled Lucsly's. Sure, she could be a bit of a stiff, not the most socially gifted Cardassian around, but that was only to be expected when one's ancestors had been abducted by a powerful, mysterious ancient race and bred and trained for dozens of generations to become physically and mentally superior operatives working clandestinely to guide unstable civilizations through their most dangerous times.

But nothing of that enhanced heredity showed in Cyral's bearing now. "What didn't?"

"I understand you quit the Aegis," Lucsly said.

"No. I was fired." She examined the first of her two new drinks for a moment. "Well, I anticipated being fired. I left of my own vol-volition to save them the trouble." She punctuated it by emptying the glass and slamming it down on the bar. "I mean, naturally they were going to fire me, what did you think? Look around! Look at the ruin Cardassia has become! I worked . . . I worked for thirty years to nudge them in the right direction. Protected dissidents from discovery by the Order. Saved copies of Hebitian writings for future generations. The civilian coup? The Detapa Council wresting power away from the Central Command? My work," she said proudly, then downed her other drink. "Even if nobody knew it. Bartender! Again!"

"Cyral," Dulmur began.

"Was it my fault I couldn't see the Dominion coming? I couldn't help it if they infiltrated the Klingons and tricked them into invading us! And that Dukat, ohh, that Dukat. I should've had him killed long before he sold us out, but the Aegis, in their infinite wisdom, frown on such tactics."

"But they know the future, right?" Dulmur asked. The Aegis was unusual among the Temporal Accords' signatories; rather than arising in the future, they had existed for countless millennia and generally operated in linear time. But the mysterious, secretive race that headed the organization—suspected of being shapeshifters themselves, like a more benevolent version of the Dominion's Founders—possessed an advanced facility for intertemporal travel and communication, which they used to coordinate their efforts in multiple eras—efforts which often included thwarting attempts by anti-Accordist time travelers to meddle in history. Of all the factions in the Temporal Cold War, the Aegis was the only one that could be considered indigenous to almost every era involved in the conflict—although they tended to operate more by stealth and espionage than open confrontation. "Couldn't they have warned you, helped you head it off?"

"Ohh, no, no, no. They're big believers in letting history unfold the 'right' way. Just like you, Luckle . . . Lucsly. True, they encourage us to nudge things in a positive direction, to ease pain and suffering where we can, but if a disaster or a war is part of the history that was 'supposed' to happen . . ." Cyral shook her subtly graying head and downed another drink. "No. We stop meddlers from tampering with history. We're not just out for general do-gooding like those damn androids."

The reference went over Dulmur's head, but he let it go, more puzzled by the rest of what she said. "What about Gary Seven? Supervisor 194? Twentieth-century Earth wasn't exactly on the front lines of the Temporal Cold War."

Cyral scoffed. "Wasn't it? Think about it. All that advanced technology suddenly showing up ahead of the curve? Cryogenics, impulse drives, artificial intelligences?"

"Reverse-engineered from the Ferengi shuttle that landed in Roswell, New Mexico, in July 1947," Lucsly said.

"Hah! Do you really believe a mere kemocite explosion could spontaneously generate a survivable time warp? They were pawns. A deliberate act of contamination." She had a point; after the time-displaced *Quark's Treasure* had retraced its Feynman curve to 2372, the DTI's scientists had thoroughly questioned the three Ferengi and one changeling who had been aboard the shuttle and had gone over it with a fine-tooth comb (after shelling out an extravagant amount of latinum to the owner in order to "rent" it), but had never been able to re-create the circumstances that had generated the time warp. Still, Dulmur was unsure how much credence to give to the claims of this degenerate wreck who had once been someone he respected.

"Not to mention the eugenics! Come on, you two. A secret band of geneticists comes out of nowhere with technology generations beyond the state of the art and creates a whole race of Augments less than a generation after your people discovered the double helix? How could you not see a familiar hand in that? Seriously, you call yourselves investigators?"

Dulmur exchanged a startled look with Lucsly, who asked, "Are you saying the Eugenics Wars were orchestrated by the same twenty-eighth-century faction that sponsored the Suliban Cabal?"

"Know the artist by his tools," Cyral told them.

"Do you have proof of this?" Dulmur demanded.

"Maybe I do. But my throat's getting a little parched . . ."

"I think you've had enough, Cyral—"

But Lucsly raised his hand and ordered another two drinks for her. Dulmur glared at him, but it just rolled off of Lucsly when he was like this. "If it was the Cabal's Sponsor," the older agent asked, "what motive did he have to interfere with pre-warp Earth?"

"Who knows? Maybe it was simply to keep Supervisor 194 occupied. Such things happen in the Cold War . . . effect preceding cause, becoming its own cause and effect . . . or effecting the causal . . . It's a loop," she ended up saying. "Two sides look into history, each sees the other acting somewhere in the past, so they both decide they have to go stop the other, and there's no way to say which caused what. Or whom. Or why." She inhaled another round. "Damn, war is stupid."

"Is there anything more you can tell us, Cyral?" Lucsly pressed while she still retained some consciousness. "Anything about the Sponsor's motives? Why tamper in those places and times? Why start again now? What's his goal?"

"And what's going on now, or in the near future," Dulmur added, "that would draw in not only him, but other factions as well?"

"*I don't know!* Damn it, you two, don't you understand? I'm not higher echelon! I'm only level nine! I was born sixty-seven years ago. I've lived in this century all my life. I've never been uptime, never seen what happens. And they've never told me more than I needed to know."

She picked up her last drink, examined it, then screamed and hurled it across the room, just barely missing the Chandir Lothario and making him squeal like a child and duck for cover, spoiling his chances with the Boslic woman he'd been hitting on. "*They never told me!* They knew what was going to happen to my home and they let it happen! Forced me to let it happen! Damn them! You think I would stay with them after they did that to me?" She sank back onto her stool. "Those bastards . . . they raised me, taught me everything, shepherded me through every mission, and all the time . . ."

She broke down sobbing, and Dulmur took her in his arms uneasily. "It's so beautiful there . . . the crystal spires . . . the silver trees against the orange sky . . . those vast, extraordinary beings with their great eyes . . . do you remember Vuri? That beautiful laphound . . . he was always by my side . . . and all the time he knew . . . but I miss him so much . . ."

Dulmur comforted her as best he could, irked that Lucsly was hanging on her every rambling word in hopes of divining some deep secrets about the Aegis or the Cold War. But soon her reminiscences degenerated into mumbling too incoherent for the translators to parse. Lucsly paid Cyral's hefty bar tab and the two agents made sure she got safely to the run-down hotel that was her only home.

"I wish we could do more for her," Dulmur said as they left.

"I wish she could've told us more," Lucsly replied.

"Well, if she was right about the Augments, if the Sponsor caused the Eugenics Wars, it rules out the idea of him being pro-Federation."

"Does it?" Lucsly asked. "The Eugenics Wars are part of the tapestry of events that led to the Federation. Without the technological advancements they drove, would Cochrane have made his warp flight when he did?"

"That's a reach."

"Or maybe the Sponsor felt an augmented humanity could achieve more, sooner. Make for an even stronger Federation."

"We're just guessing."

"We're hypothesizing," Lucsly countered. "When have we ever had more than guesswork about the motives of uptime factions?"

Dulmur held his partner's gaze. "When have we ever needed solid facts more?"

Garcia Residence, Ealing, London
Late Season, Day 11, 743 UE (A Sunday)
18:52 UTC
When Ranjea signaled at Teresa's door, she answered in an informal yet enticing ensemble, creatively baring large portions of her skin in a way that was fashionable in her home time but somewhat daring in the current, postwar era. "Hey, boss. What's up?"

Since it was a typically chilly January here in Britain, Ranjea surmised that Teresa's date would involve either beaming to a more temperate climate or simply staying indoors. Either way, he regretted having to deprive her of the experience. Once she'd shown him in and secured the door behind her, he said, "I'm afraid you and Stewart will have to cancel your date. There's trouble at the Axis of Time."

Teresa's eyes widened. "Did Lirahn finally make a move?"

"Hard to say. All we know is that none of the ships that have gone in, either Vomnin or Starfleet, are coming out anymore."

"I'll get changed."

Teresa's apartment was small—apparently she felt no need for more—and she made no effort to close her bedroom door or otherwise hide herself from his view as she shed her lightweight garments. Yet nothing in her body language suggested another attempt at seduction, beyond a playful thrill of flirtation as its own end—which he accepted in the spirit intended, coming to stand in the doorway as a casual spectator. After all, it was nothing she hadn't let him see before, so apparently she saw no reason to hide it now—an unusually mature attitude for a human. "Lovely outfit," he teased.

"Thanks." She threw him a quick grin, but then so-bered and began donning her undergarments. "Is *Titan* still there? Anyone we know trapped inside?"

"No, *Titan* went on its way once the *Asimov* arrived."

"*Asimov*? Appropriate name." Naturally, they had both read *The End of Eternity,* and Ranjea had to agree. Perhaps whoever had assigned the ship had recognized its suitability.

"It's a scout ship, *Nova*-class like the *Everett*. They've lost two shuttles, one already inside before the problem arose, one sent in to try to retrieve it."

"Oh, don't tell me," Teresa said as she pulled on her trousers. "We have to go inside too. Risk getting trapped with everyone else."

He picked up her suit jacket and held it out for her. "Hopefully it won't come to that. But if duty requires . . ."

"Yeah, yeah." She slipped her arms into the sleeves, smiling up at him. "Don't worry about me, boss. Leaving my life behind forever? Hell, I can do that blindfolded."

He felt the shudder of fear run through her body. Sensing her need, he wrapped his arms around her from behind. He chose not to take her hands and offer her empathic comfort; if overdone, that could create a depen-dence in her. Instead he shared his love through a simple hug, which she soon relaxed into. "Thank you," she whis-pered when it was done.

She reached for her hairbrush, but Ranjea placed his hand on hers and took the implement from her, leading her to her seat before the mirror. Grooming was an im-portant bonding ritual for species with hair, an act of both sensuality and comfort, and Ranjea had studied the prac-tice. He took satisfaction in the way Teresa relaxed as he brushed her shoulder-length yet luxurious black hair. "If we do not see home again, there will be joy in discovering our new life," he said. "Still, I will not let you lose this home if I can help it."

She met his eyes in the mirror, smiling tenderly. "I know you won't, boss." Her eyes widened. "Oh! Stewart! I'd better tell him the date's off."

Ranjea was sure Agent Peart would take it in stride as an occupational hazard of the job. Like many organizations doing highly classified work, the Department encouraged dating among coworkers, in order to keep the secrets contained without forcing the agents to lie to their partners or maintain barriers of secrecy. He waited as Teresa went into the other room—apparently this *was* something she preferred some semblance of privacy for—and let Peart know that duty had overridden their plans for the evening. She said nothing about the prospect of a more permanent separation, though, keeping it light and casual. He studied her as she came back in; she did not seem unduly stressed at the prospect of losing Peart forever. "Are things well between you and Stewart?"

"Oh, fine," she said. She saw the look in his eyes, got his message, and shrugged. "Okay, he's adorable, and he's satisfying on a purely recreational level, but he's, well, kind of flighty. And beneath the feckless charm there's this British reserve that makes it hard to open up to him." She smiled. "Like I can to you."

"Still, it's good that you've found physical companionship."

"Oh, yes. Physical companionship is a very good thing, as a rule." She winked. "Not that I have to tell you that."

They went back out into the main room. Teresa went

to retrieve her padd from its charging platform and took a moment to update her status. "So do you think whatever's happening with the Axis is connected to the TCW?"

"Hard to say. That's one thing we'll have to find out." The Department's investigation into the prospect of a new Temporal Cold War front had somewhat fizzled due to a lack of incidents and leads. At this point, six weeks after the attempt on President Bacco's life, things were settling back into a sense of routine, albeit with a heightened level of tension and alertness which Ranjea found bracing.

"I'd be surprised if it's a coincidence. It seems like every major power's had some kind of temporal incursion lately. And the Vomnin are the biggest power in the Gum Nebula."

"True," Ranjea said. "Which reminds me, there's more news on the Carnelian situation. The Temporal Oversight Administration has confirmed that there are a number of discrepancies between their shielded records and their current history. A number of individuals in the records no longer exist, including at least two noted temporal researchers and a long-term planning director."

Teresa shuddered. "Damn. So we're living in an altered timeline now? We're different people?"

"Not really. There are no detectable changes in our own records. The Regnancy's very far away and has infrequent contact with us, so there's no real impact. Yes, by now we've merged with our duplicates in the parallel timeline, but there was no difference between the two versions of ourselves, so by all quantum-physical and philosophical definitions, we and the Federation, and all our immediate neighbors, are the same entities we were before."

"Weird," Teresa said. "It doesn't feel right, you know. Being part of two timelines at once."

"Ahh, but remember T'Viss's lectures on quantum Darwinism. What we think of as a linear history is more of a blur of alternatives that average out to a single timeline. More a fuzzy piece of yarn than a monofilament."

"Yeah, but that's on a microscopic scale, over in nano-seconds."

"Usually, but sometimes a pair of competing states can be quasi-stable for seconds, hours, or even longer before one wins out. That's how parallel timelines can happen at all—a duality exists long enough for a different choice to be made in one branch and produce a permanent, large-scale divergence.

"But such divergences don't affect the entire universe simultaneously, but rather spread out from their point of origin at the speed of interaction. Which, in a universe containing tachyon fields and subspace entanglements, is quite fast even on a galactic scale. So from our perspective, it may seem the entire universe splits at once."

"But the split is really local," Garcia interpreted. "So . . . part of the universe can be in two or more parallel timelines at once while another part just carries on unchanged."

"More or less. There would've been some subtle quantum variations—"

"Don't. I don't want to think about that. If you say I have an excuse to think of myself as the same continuous person after this, then I'll take it. Don't ruin it for me."

Ranjea clasped her shoulder, helping her relax again. She put her hand on his briefly, then headed for the door.

Once in the corridor, she continued the conversation softly. "More temporal scientists. You think somebody's targeting civilizations that become temporal powers in the future? Trying to unmake their enemies?"

"Quite possible."

"Do the Carnelians have any plans to go back and fix things?" While the Regnancy of the Carnelian Throne was generally not much more advanced than the Federation, the DTI was fairly confident that they did possess time-travel technology in a form more reliable than slingshot maneuvers and unpredictable ancient artifacts.

Ranjea shook his head. "Apparently the Chief Overseer of the TOA has children in this timeline that didn't exist in the other. Since there's been no catastrophic change to their civilization, only the loss or alteration of certain individuals, she's deemed it an acceptable divergence."

"And what if she'd lost kids she'd had before?"

"We cannot know or judge that, Teresa."

Ranjea felt her tension growing as they neared the neighborhood transporter station. "What troubles you, my friend?"

"It's just . . . I hate leaving the Federation when I know it's in trouble. When I might be able to help. What if we get trapped in the Axis and there's some big temporal attack we could've helped with?"

"That's another thing we cannot know. All we can do is accept where life sends us."

"Yeah, well, it's not that easy for me."

He took her hand, and she instantly relaxed somewhat. "You've succeeded in mastering far more intense frustrations," he reminded her. They shared a conspiratorial smile. "This is no different. Simply let go of craving for what you cannot have, and instead focus on finding the joy in what you can have. Remember how it thrilled you to explore the Axis, to study the life of eras amazingly far removed from our own? Now you can do that again."

"Yeah . . . maybe for the rest of my life."

"Would that be so bad?"

"No," she said. "As long as I had my partner by my side."

"That you will always have."

"But what about you?" she asked, those vast eyes gazing up at him in sympathy. "If you could never be with another Deltan . . . how would you cope?"

The thought filled him with pain, which he embraced and made a part of himself like every other sensation. "I will always carry the memories of my home and loved ones with me," he said. "If I am separated forever from home, then my loved ones will live on in me, and I in them."

As the transporter whisked them away to the *Capitoline*, Ranjea prepared himself for the prospect of separation by immersing himself in his memories of home. From Delta to the DTI to the Axis . . . it was all one continuum. His experiences at home had led him here, and from here to wherever he would go. And so home would always be a part of him.

DOWNTIME
STARDATE 49572.0 TO 50912.6

XIII

Ilia Memorial Space Center, Yongam Island, Dhei-Lta (Delta IV)
08:52 UTC

Delta IV was not what Agent George Faunt had expected.

He'd made the standard run of hedonistic planets in his youth, more than once, and had a good basis for comparison. The Risians' beliefs were built on generosity, so they were happy to cater to the whims of outsiders. The Argelians lived for pleasure, a reaction to the brutal puritanism of the prior civilization that had almost destroyed their world, and didn't care whom they shared it with. And the Selkies of Pacifica—the younger, amphibious ones charged with raising their young—envied the freedom from responsibility of their fully aquatic elders and were thus prone to indulge themselves with outsiders who didn't understand or care about the perceived impropriety of it. On all three planets, the younger Faunt had thus had no difficulty finding opportunities to . . . witness and participate in the local customs in the interest of expanding his cultural horizons.

As for Delta, of course, he'd known that participation was out of the question. But Faunt had expected the sights and sounds of the place, the activities of its inhabitants, to be similarly stimulating. Instead, what he saw around him was a populace as serene and dignified as the Vulcans, though without the emotional restraint. Certainly the men and women around him were all unusually attractive by human standards. Certainly they were attired in loose, wrapped garments that left much of their smooth bronze limbs and chests bare in the warm local weather. Certainly their lack of any body hair save eyebrows and lashes gave the impression of an even greater degree of nudity. And certainly—oh, very certainly—the wash of Deltan phero-mones in the air made Faunt's pulse race despite the inhibi-tor injection he'd received before planetfall. But he had not beamed down into the middle of a citywide orgy. What he saw around him was peace, dignity, serenity. The various Deltans interacted in a much more tactile way than humans generally did, showing no concept of personal space and touching each other warmly even for casual interactions; but it was relaxed and unselfconscious, like the comfortable closeness of a couple who'd been married for fifty years.

"Agent George Faunt?"

The mustachioed human turned to see a tall, dark-complexioned Deltan male wearing a kaftan in solid red with gold piping and insignia. "Yes."

"I am Meyo Ranjea of Planetary Security. Welcome to Dhei."

Faunt reminded himself he'd have to get used to hearing that. The early space boomers in their low-warp ships, far re-moved from any central authority to enforce regularity of no-menclature, had loved cataloguing the systems they visited or charted with faux-Bayer designations consisting of random Greek letters like Alpha Omicron or Epsilon Gamma or the like. So when the *ECS Horizon* had made first contact with a foundered starship in 2141 and been told by its beautiful, hairless occupants that their homeworld was Dhei of the star Lta—"Dhei-Lta"—they had entered it in their charts in the predictable way, and it had stuck.

"Thank you," Faunt said. "You're the investigating officer for the . . . incident?" The Deltans may not have been crowding as close to him and the other offworlders as they did to each other, but there were still many people in easy earshot.

Yet Ranjea evinced no such concern for secrecy. "Yes. I was in charge of security for the time perceptor. Its theft was my failing, its recovery my responsibility."

Faunt cleared his throat. "Perhaps we should discuss this more privately."

Ranjea smiled as if Faunt were a child that had just said something adorably absurd. "Agent Faunt, the time perceptor was on display in the Yongam Museum, freely accessible to researchers and—availability permitting—inquisitive patrons. There is no need for secrecy."

Faunt reminded himself that the Deltans had been an advanced, starfaring civilization thousands of years ago before their culture had "outgrown" their expansionism and turned their attention inward to mental and spiritual development. They had retained spaceflight capability at a limited level, and their renewed contact with humans and others over the past 231 years had led them to improve on it since then, creating the impression that their starfaring capability was a recent innovation. But their technology from thousands of years in the past had been more formidable, and had even included the invention of a technology that used quantum wormholes to view events in the past. The perceptor had been abandoned

along with most spacefaring and weapons technology
during the birth pangs of the modern Unity Era, nearly
forty-five standard centuries ago. But eight years ago, a
working perceptor had been discovered in a ruin and
brought to the museum.

"All right," Faunt said. "Then could we at least go to
the scene of the crime?"

"Certainly," Ranjea said, casually placing a hand on his
back to guide him through the crowd as if they were dear
friends. "I hope you don't mind walking."

"Can't we beam there? Or take an aircar?"

"And waste a fine afternoon like this?" Ranjea asked,
gesturing at the warm glow of V2292 Ophiuchi, which
hung in the deep blue sky, larger yet dimmer and subtly
oranger than the sun of Faunt's native Earth.

"Mister Ranjea, time may be of the essence here."

"Time is always of the essence. Which is why every
moment of it must be cherished. And it's just Ranjea,
please."

As they headed through the streets, Faunt couldn't
help but admire the lush architecture, the intricate clothing, the complex aromas that wafted from eateries, the
delightful music that pervaded the air. The Deltans' reputation for embracing all forms of sensory and emotional
stimulation was evidently well-earned. But their greater
reputation seemed underrepresented.

Embarrassingly, Ranjea saw right through him.
"You're wondering where the public displays of sexuality are," the security officer said. "Most offworlders do.
Don't worry, they do occur, but not in regions where
offworlders congregate. Would you make love in front of
your children?"

Faunt glared. "Just because we aren't constantly pre-occupied with sex doesn't mean we're immature about it."

Ranjea looked surprised. "But you are preoccupied with it. Or so it appears to us. To the Dhei'ten, sexuality is merely one of the many facets of existence that we cel-ebrate. Yet it seems to be the only facet of our culture that offworlders take any interest in."

Faunt grew more subdued at his words. "And that's why you think we're immature about it?"

Compassion filled Ranjea's eyes. "We find it sad that humans and others go through so much anxiety and dis-tress over something that for us is so simple and joyful. You dwell on it, mythologize it, and so you raise such high expectations about it that it terrifies you." His hair-less brows rose in apology. "Perhaps 'immature' is a harsh way of putting that. What I should say instead is that we believe it is a difficulty you have the potential to outgrow." He smiled. "You are a people of great spiritual potential, and sometimes we grow impatient waiting for you to achieve it."

Faunt wasn't exactly mollified, but at least he was no longer sure whether to be insulted or flattered. He de-cided it was best to drop the subject. "Well, that's the fu-ture. Right now, I'm more concerned with the past. Both recent and otherwise."

"Indeed," Ranjea replied, effortlessly adapting to the shift in subject. "It's this way."

Yongam Museum
09:57 UTC

Identifying the culprits in the theft was not a problem. The Deltans had little need for security cameras, but some patrons of the museum had been making a sensory record of the time perceptor exhibit when it had been raided, and Ranjea allowed Faunt to view it. Although "view" was not the correct word, for it was a full sensory immersion experience, complete with the emotions experienced by the patron making the recording. It unnerved Faunt to experience fear and anger that were not his own—particularly when he felt them being embraced and mastered so effortlessly in ways he couldn't understand.

But he reminded himself to concentrate on the attackers themselves. They were blocky, hirsute, gravelly-skinned humanoids dressed from neck to toe in red body armor—almost a diametric opposite to the Deltans in appearance, as well as in politics, for they were clearly soldiers of the Carreon. Hailing from a system only a few parsecs from Lta, the Carreon had entered space in the 2150s using low-warp technology purchased from human space-boomer traders, and had soon begun clashing with the Deltans for possession of worlds that the elder civilization still held a nominal claim on after thousands of years. A treaty had maintained a tenuous peace for two centuries, but the Carreon nurtured a resentment of the Deltans that often threatened to erupt into violence.

Now, apparently, it had. The raiders had entered the city as tourists, using concealed, unpowered weapons to pass spaceport security. They must have charged the weapons at the hotel they'd checked into; its utility logs showed a commensurate power demand in their quarters. Their raid on the perceptor display had been quick, efficient, and brutal, costing the life of one curator and leaving one guard injured, another in critical condition. A security field had been automatically raised, but the Carreon had used a pattern enhancer to allow their orbiting ship to lock on and beam them away with the time perceptor.

"An inconceivable act," Ranjea said when Faunt had completed reviewing the record. "To bring such pain and loss, for a mere historical curiosity? Why? What do they hope to gain from it?"

"How does it work?" Faunt asked. "Not the technical stuff, just . . . what exactly does it let you do?"

"It allows us to experience events in the past."

"How far in the past?"

"We have been able to probe back tens of thousands of years."

"But more recently too?"

Ranjea shrugged. "As little as a generation or two."

"And where? Just in the same location?"

"No; the perceptor can show any location on Dhei or in its orbit; anywhere within, oh, roughly half a million kilometers of its location."

"Hm." Faunt frowned. "Any time in the past, this location would've been the middle of empty space."

"The perceptor uses the quantum ansible effect to entangle with itself in the past. Its position in the past is the origin point for the quantum wormholes it generates."

Faunt nodded. The ansible effect was a nonlocal phenomenon, independent of distance, allowing instantaneous communication between quantum-entangled objects. It often showed up in time-travel situations, such as the incident nearly six months ago where the chief of operations of Deep Space 9 had been repeatedly displaced five hours uptime by a unique interaction with a Romulan singularity core, probably in combination with the exotic energies of the Bajoran wormhole. Luckily his self-entanglement had created a subspace link that caused him to materialize in proximity to his future self each time, otherwise he would have teleported into the vacuum left behind once the station had moved five hours ahead in its orbit. When he'd debriefed the DS9 personnel about the incident, Faunt had so much trouble keeping the overlapping causality loops straight that he almost found himself wishing the man *had* just popped into vacuum and made the whole scenario that much simpler.

"And what information do you get from these wormholes?"

"Whatever we wish. Bandwidth permitting, we can experience past events with full sensory resolution."

"Like from that recording you just showed me? You experience an event through someone else's senses?"

"Yes." Ranjea's gaze grew distant, enthralled by the thought. "The opportunity to live history as it happened . . . to feel the great loves and adventures and triumphs and sorrows of our forebears . . . it gives us a more intimate connection with who we were, binds us closer, present and past."

"Hm." Faunt gave a sardonic chuckle. "'The Dead Past.'"

"Excuse me?"

"It's the name of a story by a Terran author named Asimov. Speculative fiction from centuries ago. He imagined a device a lot like your perceptor, something that could view any moment in history. There was a later book, *The Light of Other Days,* that was also about a very similar device, right down to the quantum wormholes. And they both pointed out something very important about how such a device could be used."

"And what was that?"

"The past isn't just a generation ago or a millennium ago, Ranjea. What about a week ago? An hour ago? A second ago?" At Ranjea's startled look, he went on. "We think of the past as something separate from the present. But when you hear my voice, you're hearing sound waves that were emitted a few milliseconds in the past. When you look at me, you're seeing photons that reflected off my face a few nanoseconds in the past. There's really no such thing as the present; there's just the most immediate slice of the past."

Ranjea grinned. "What a delightful observation!"

"No, actually it's a pretty terrifying one. Focus, Ranjea. Is there any reason your perceptor couldn't be set to a time that recent?"

"I'm not certain, but based on what I've learned of the device to date, I don't think there's any lower limit on the timespan. It gets easier the closer into the past you look." He shook his head. "But why would anyone do that? If we wish to share an experience with people in the present, all we have to do is ask them."

"Don't you see the enormous potential for voyeurism?"

Ranjea looked puzzled. "Voyeurism. I've heard of that practice among offworlders, but it's not something we engage in here. Why settle for merely witnessing an act of joy when you can participate?"

The corner of Faunt's mouth quirked. "I guess I should've figured that. With no concept of privacy, there's no illicit thrill from invading it. But that's among Deltans. How would a Carreon see it?"

"By the One," Ranjea breathed. "You're right, George. They have a history of engaging in espionage against us."

He chuckled. "They profess to find our open ways repellent. Yet rather than avoid an experience they find displeasing, they pursue it all the more fervently to give themselves more grounds for condemning us."

Faunt hadn't invited Ranjea to use his given name, but he was surprised it had taken the Deltan this long. "And now they have a way to spy on you anywhere and anytime they want. They can invade the most secure levels of your military and government, know all your secrets in real time, so long as they keep the perceptor within half a million kilometers."

"Possibly farther," Ranjea said. "The range of the wormholes is proportional to the power applied. Connecting an external power source could extend the range."

"On the other hand," Faunt mused, "you're not a people who have a lot of secrets."

"From each other, no," Ranjea said. "But there is information our defense forces must conceal to preserve security. Not to mention technological secrets we keep to maintain the advantage that keeps them from abrogating the treaty. With unlimited access, they could undermine us in many ways."

"Then we have to find out where they went," Faunt said. "It can't be far, if they intend to gain current intelligence. Somewhere within the system."

"Their ship was able to cloak its drive trail by diving near Lta during a stellar flare." Faunt nodded. The "V" in V2292 Ophiuchi meant variable; its luminosity didn't change enough to affect the climate of Dhei, but it had an unusually active chromosphere and gave off frequent X-ray flares, which were safely absorbed by the planet's robust ozone layer. "They could be anywhere."

"We need to find out if they said anything, dropped any hints about where they were going."

"You saw the sense record yourself. It revealed nothing definite."

"That's because the guy recording it was cowering behind a statue. We need to talk to the surviving guard."

"That may not be possible, George. She does not have long to live."

Faunt stepped closer and held the taller man's gaze. "Then time is really of the essence."

Eternal Love Hospice
11:09 UTC
The human DTI agent was surprised by the nature of the facility Ranjea took him to. "A hospice? With your medical knowhow, couldn't you do more to save her?"

"Prolong her life, perhaps," Ranjea told him. "But at the cost of ongoing discomfort. Better a short, comfortable life than a longer, unpleasant one."

George Faunt frowned. "I thought you Deltans reveled in every sensation equally."

"We do accept whatever experience life gives us," Ranjea explained, "and try to find fulfillment and meaning in it. And yes, there are those among us who enjoy pain, fear, aggression . . . but in controlled, safe contexts, and only with others who share the same fetishes willingly. To inflict suffering on one who is lost and helpless . . ." He shook his head sternly. "That we will not do."

The hospice facility was designed to maximize comfort for those near the end of their lives, with gentle lights, warm colors and textures on the walls, soothing music and scents wafting through the air, and most importantly, companionship—not only a large staff of dedicated care-givers to provide comfort to clients and loved ones alike, but abundant open space to accommodate each client's circle of loved ones for the final sharing.

And yet the room containing the dying museum guard, Riroa Nadamé, was oddly empty. Besides the care-givers who always remained close at hand, Ranjea saw only four people attending the dying one, and they seemed wistful and distressed, huddling together and caressing one another for comfort yet keeping a subtle distance from the guard herself.

Ranjea came up to the group, gently placing his hands on the shoulders of the nearest two, and introduced him-self. It took them little prompting to explain; they were eager for someone to commiserate with. "Riroa never let anyone become truly close," said Nijen, a young, dark-complexioned woman in a blue floral-patterned kimono. "We were her regular lovers, but she never let it go deeper than everyday intimacy. That was fine; it was what she de-sired, and we all had deeper bonds with other partners."

The other woman in the foursome, an older, fuller-figured Dhei'ten named Kelia, clasped Nijen's hand tightly. "But now, Riroa's body is failing. If she doesn't open herself fully to us now, she will be lost forever."

Sensing Faunt's puzzlement, Ranjea left the women and their companions to embrace one another and stepped back to explain to the human. "We believe each of us lives on through the love we share with others. When we bond, the barriers between us vanish; we become one another, and something of us remains in one another after our bodies part. But if Riroa has never shared herself fully with anyone, and does not do so now, then very little of her essence will survive." He shook his head. "If such . . . isolation is her wish, of course we must respect it, but it is difficult to understand."

Faunt peered at Riroa, thinking. "When you do this joining . . . is it just sensations and emotions, or is there knowledge passed on too?"

"Not detailed knowledge, but understanding, yes. Experiential awareness, inner certainties."

The human puzzled over that for a moment, then let it go. "So if, say, she had some secret about who and what she was, that could come through?"

Now Ranjea was puzzled. "In a true sharing, the kind needed to preserve the essence at death, it could not fail to be known."

Faunt cleared his throat and spoke tentatively. "This final sharing . . . is it something you could ask to be a part of?"

"Anyone could. The more Dhei'ten who share in the essence, the more it endures. But why would you think my presence would make a difference? Riroa never knew me."

"I'd rather not tell you that until I'm sure. But if my hunch is right, then she has a reason for not opening up to her, uh, friends here—but if you let her know what's at stake, let her know we're looking for the perceptor, I think she'll open up to you for the same reason."

His reticence was foreign to Ranjea, but there was something very enticing about it, about the challenge of solving a mystery. It was why Ranjea had gone into security in the first place. "Very well," he said, smiling. "At the very least, if I can help preserve her essence, it will be worth it for that."

He went back to Riroa's friends and made the offer,

which they all accepted readily, glad to expand the dismay-ingly small sharing circle. "I regret that you cannot join us as well, George," Ranjea told him, "but the level of inti-macy here is as deep as in lovemaking, if not deeper. You would lose yourself."

"I get it."

"You may witness as a spectator if you wish. However, you may find aspects of it . . . challenging to your taboos," Ranjea went on as he and the others began to disrobe.

"Oh. Got it. I'll . . . wait outside. How long will this take?"

"As long as needed. Perhaps hours. You may wish to wait at your hotel."

"No, I'll . . . keep myself occupied," he said as he departed.

Ranjea finished disrobing and moved to join the oth-ers, saddened that Faunt's inhibitions made him unable to witness such a beautiful ceremony. The baring of the flesh was necessary to maximize the neural contact between the participants, to allow the connection to become as deep and profound as possible. There was a sexual element to the bond, inevitably in something so immersive of the entire being, but it was not mere self-gratification or pruri-ence—not necrophilia, as Faunt might imagine.

The five Dhei'ten came together through touch, open-ing their minds and hearts to one another, offering the same openness to Riroa. *Become us. Live on with us, so you may release your failing flesh.* Yet they met resistance. Of-fering love and unity was not enough. Something stood in the way—a sense of purpose, of duty. An obligation that compelled this tragic isolation.

Ranjea met it with his own sense of purpose. He

concentrated on the theft of the perceptor, on his responsibility for its retrieval, on his self-identity as a protector. It resonated with the desires that held Riroa back, and Ranjea understood her. *Become me,* he pleaded to the part of her that clung to its secrets. *Release your burden to me, so I may fulfill your purpose.*

There was willingness, but reluctance—now on his behalf rather than her own. The perception was not verbal, but if it had been, Riroa might have said, *Take care before you accept this burden, for you will never be free of it. It will change you forever.*

Ranjea could not resist a challenge like that. He was content in his life, in his loves, but to become something new, plumb uncharted mysteries? He welcomed it gladly.

Riroa did not need to convey gratitude. She did so by lowering her barriers at last, allowing herself finally to connect fully and without restraint—a release she had always craved, though duty and training had prohibited it. Now she shared her innermost self with him—and with Nijen, Kelia, Rodda, and Avel as well. Yet with the sharing came a deep understanding of the need to control this knowledge. The other four released it, let it pass through them and leave only an abstract trace of essence. They allowed Ranjea to take the full weight of it into himself, though they each gave him something of themselves along with it, a font of gratitude, love, and strength to help him bear the responsibility.

With her duty finally discharged, Riroa let go at last. Ranjea and the others—for indeed, there was no distinction now—experienced her death, knew her dissolution as a separate entity, and grieved it with all their being. They had preserved her essence, true, but the unique synergy of mind and flesh that had been hers was lost, and would never gain further experiences, conceive its own unique thoughts, create beauty through its touch and scent and voice and motion. This was death among Dhei'ten, the harmony of loss and perpetuation, grief and joy—two facets of the same experience just as mind and body were.

With Riroa gone in the flesh, the remaining five members of the bond came together and loved each other as one, sharing their grief and need. Before, none of them had truly known Riroa deeply, but now they knew and loved her as profoundly as anyone could, for now she was a part of them. And yet by the same token, they had given part of themselves to her before her passing. They had all died a little today. And so they needed one another to replenish their life. To give each other the experience of life, through sensation, through passion, through unity.

When they finally came out of it, they found that the hospice staff had removed the body (for postmortem, under the circumstances, rather than the usual dissolution and reunion with the soil) and left food and drink to replenish the partners and washbasins for their cleansing. The fivesome partook of the offerings and made idle conversation and loveplay, for the ordinariness of life went on even in the face of the profundity of death. Finally, cleansed and refreshed on multiple levels, Ranjea donned his uniform and went to collect George Faunt.

"Did you, uh, learn anything?" the human asked, still tragically uneasy at these events.

"I learned much, my friend. But what is relevant to you is that, as I think you must have suspected, Riroa was not native to our time. She was sent by some future agency—I have no name or specifics, just the general awareness—to guard the time perceptor. She kept herself aloof because of this secret."

Faunt snorted. "Aloof. Right. Only four lovers."

"Yes, and very casual ones at that. Quite a sacrifice, but she believed it was worth it."

"And what do *you* think about that?"

"I don't have to think, George. I know, as deeply as she did. Her mission is mine now: to protect the perceptor from abuse. To protect time from those who would violate its natural flow. And if I must leave my home and my loves—even if I must take the Oath of Celibacy and leave Dhei—then I must."

The human stared for a long moment. "Wow. I, um . . . okay. But did you get any actual information from her along with that . . . new mission? Anything to lead us to the perceptor?"

"Nothing I consciously know that I know. But I feel I *understand* the perceptor now. As we investigate, if we find something meaningful, I know I will recognize it."

"Doesn't sound like you got much for all that effort," Faunt said.

Ranjea clasped his shoulder. "I got more than I could possibly explain, George. And I thank you for leading me to it."

U.S.S. *Bozeman* NCC-1941
Day 45, Inner Eye, 6470 AR (A Tuesday)
01:34 UTC

"We're closing on the source of the quantum fluctuations, Captain," reported Ensign Heather Petersen from the *Bozeman*'s science station.

"Good," Morgan Bateson replied. "Sound Red Alert."

Next to him, his first officer, Commander Claudia Alisov, opened the shipwide channel and ordered, "Red Alert, Red Alert! All hands to battle stations! Tactical, shields up, phasers to ready status."

From his perch near the back of the bridge, George Faunt observed the battle preparations with satisfaction. After that initial glitch with the mutineers, the remaining members of Bateson's crew had become reliable allies. The *Bozeman* and her crew had been attached to the DTI for missions requiring Starfleet support, nominally due to their experience with temporal phenomena. Many of them had initially resented the assignment, seeing it (not without reason) as a way for the Department to keep a close eye on them to preclude another mutiny; but over the past three years and change, they'd more than proven themselves worthy and the initially tense relationship had become more comfortable, though not exactly close. Agents like Lucsly and Dulmur had little patience with Starfleet and their recklessness, but Faunt appreciated their discipline and courage. Sometimes the ramifications of this job scared the willies out of him, and though one could rarely solve a temporal conundrum with a ship-mounted phaser bank, he took a certain irrational comfort in believing that maybe you could.

Next to him, Ranjea watched the goings-on a bit more warily. "I guess there aren't a lot of soldiers on a planet of empaths," Faunt said.

"As a rule, no," the unfairly tall and good-looking Deltan replied. "But there are some who have a . . . fetish for aggression and conflict, and they are able to find a constructive release for it in our defense force."

Faunt stared. "You send people who get off on

violence to man your fleet? No wonder things are so tense between you and Carrea."

Ranjea shrugged. "If the Carreon find fulfillment in conflict with us, who are we to deny them?"

"Indeed," Captain Bateson said from his command chair. "And if they're inclined to pick a fight with Starfleet too, well, we're willing to oblige. The old girl's been eager to show she's not as obsolete as they say."

Alisov chuckled. "Well, not once we had her upgraded with state-of-the-art weapons, engines, shields . . ."

"Hush, Claudia. You take the poetry out of everything." The bearded captain turned to face aft. "Ensign Petersen. Any new fluctuation readings?"

The newly minted ensign, less than two months out of the Academy but already distinguished by her work in applied temporal physics, shook her strawberry-blond head. "No, sir, not for over an hour. Officer Ranjea, could you, uh, consult with me?"

The pretty, young ensign's request wasn't just motivated by the lust she tried and failed to keep out of her voice. It had been Ranjea, using the insights he'd gained from the mind of the deceased temporal operative Riroa, who had devised a method of scanning for the time perceptor, once he'd taken a few hours to study Faunt's temporal tricorder and adapt its scan protocols to register a particular type of quantum fluctuation—effectively a sort of effervescence in the quantum foam, spillover from the perceptor as it was supercharged beyond its normal operating parameters—which should let them track the Carreon spies. Given the potential military nature of the crisis, Faunt had already had the *Bozeman* on standby, so it was a quick matter to call them in.

Although they'd never have been able to get the old *Soyuz*-class ship's sensor array adapted to Ranjea's (or Riroa's) methods in time if not for Petersen's skills. Her own field experience with the ansible effect had led her to suggest a refinement that increased the sensitivity of the scan. Faunt was convinced she was putting on her A game in hopes of impressing Ranjea, but at least that was better than becoming flustered and useless around him as Faunt's adolescent cousin always did around her Deltan neighbor.

But even working together, Petersen and Ranjea were unable to detect any further quantum effervescence from the ice dwarf they now approached, one of hundreds in the Lta system's cometary belt. Soon, the tactical officer, Lieutenant Joaquin Perez, offered the beginnings of an explanation why. "Captain, I'm picking up debris. And residual radiation consistent with a battle."

Before long, they found the Carreon ship, its hull torn open by vicious fire. "Is this the work of your aggression fetishists, Mister Ranjea?" Bateson asked.

"No," Ranjea said, hushed. "Whatever their sources of excitement, they are trained to act with restraint. This . . . this is an act of passion, to be sure, but of crude, primal passion. Violence without control. They left not a single compartment pressurized."

"The weapon signature isn't Deltan," Perez confirmed. "It's . . . nothing in our database comes close."

"Let me see," Faunt said. At Bateson's nod, Perez allowed Faunt to download the beam signature into his temporal tricorder, which held classified files on the signatures of weapons that hadn't been invented yet. Faunt was hoping to get no result, but he wasn't so lucky. "Aw, hell.

Whoever attacked them wasn't from the twenty-fourth century. More like the twenty-ninth."

Ranjea tensed, taking on an air of urgency that somehow didn't seem to be entirely his own. "Are there bodies in the wreckage? DNA traces, at least?"

"Too much radiation to be sure," Petersen said.

"Launch a short-range probe," Bateson commanded, and Petersen obliged. The small, maneuverable probe soon entered the Carreon wreck through one of the gashes in its hull, and before long came upon a scene of carnage in the hold. Four Carreon bodies floated there, along with one other—a bat-featured humanoid with parchment-yellow skin.

Ranjea tensed. "I don't know why, but I feel very frightened by this sight."

Faunt thought he recognized the species. He soon confirmed it through the tricorder's records. "You should be. They're called Na'kuhl. Once, they tried—will try—to launch a blitzkrieg through history so they could rewrite time at their whim. At least, there was some side branch of time where that happened; the alterations were negated, our main timeline preserved. That fanatical branch of the Na'kuhl probably no longer exists, seeing as how time is still stable at all. But it looks like this group of Na'kuhl is still pretty militant about its time travel."

"Look at the layout of the scene," Ranjea said. "Something was there, in the middle of the room, connected to those power feeds. The Carreon were surrounding it, defending it. They lost, and now it's gone. Not destroyed in the battle; this is the most intact part of the ship. It was taken."

Faunt stared. "The perceptor?"

"No question. These Na'kuhl have it." He turned to Petersen. "Heather, could you scan for chroniton residue, please?"

The ensign leapt to oblige, somehow managing to do it without ever averting her eyes from Ranjea. Faunt came over to check the results. They were easy for him to interpret. "They've gone. They took it and went back uptime."

Next to him, Ranjea closed his eyes and murmured at a volume only Faunt could hear. "I'm sorry, Riroa. I've failed."

04:58 UTC

As the *Bozeman* entered orbit of Delta IV—of Dhei—Faunt walked with Ranjea toward the transporter room. "I suppose your involvement in this affair is over," Ranjea said. "The perceptor is gone, the Na'kuhl are gone. In a way," he said without rancor, "I imagine the loss of the perceptor makes matters simpler for the DTI."

"Not necessarily," Faunt said. "It depends on what the Na'kuhl plan to use it for."

"Probably to gain some strategic advantage in their Temporal Cold War."

Faunt frowned. "I didn't know you knew about that. Riroa's memories?"

"No," Ranjea said. "Ensign Petersen seems to become uncontrollably loquacious in my company."

"I'll have to have a talk with her about that." They fell silent as a pair of enlisted crew passed them in the corridor. Once the pair was out of earshot, Faunt asked, "So what happens now on your end?"

"Difficult to say, in the short term. On the one hand,

the threat of Carreon espionage is ended. On the other hand . . ." His fists clenched. "I failed in my responsibility. A priceless historical treasure, a tool that let us commune with our past in a profound way, is gone and no doubt being perverted to serve violent ends. More, I failed in my obligation to Riroa."

"Hey. You did everything you could. That's what it's like, taking on time travelers. They usually have a big advantage over you. Winning isn't something you learn to expect. If, at the end of the day, you've done everything you could reasonably be expected to do, that should be enough."

"Is it?"

"Hell, no," Faunt said. "I'm gonna have nightmares about this. Those Na'kuhl are scary bastards, and the thought that they could be watching my every move from the future . . ." He shuddered. *I really have to work on not letting the job get to me so much. Be a rock, like Lucsly.*

"Would it help if you had another hand pitching in at your department?"

"What do you mean?"

Ranjea tilted his head. "I may have failed to complete Riroa's mission, but she is still a part of me. I feel her need to preserve the organic flow of time. And for myself, I feel a need to make amends for my inadequate performance. Besides . . . I do not think I have a future in planetary security."

"You think they'd fire you over this?"

"No. They would try to understand my failure and work with me to avoid a repetition. But it would feel like . . . standing still, when I have an opportunity to move forward. These events have changed me, George, and I do not think I should pretend to be the man I was."

Faunt considered it. He wanted to give Ranjea the usual spiel about how tough it was to pass the hurdles and get into the Department. But Ranjea was smart and perceptive, he had experience as a detective, he had an emotional stability Faunt envied, and just maybe he had an extra edge thanks to the late (or not-yet-born) Riroa. Given how narrowly Faunt himself had squeaked through, he was the last man who should be questioning Ranjea's ability to pull it off.

Besides, Lucsly would probably hate the guy. That was reason enough to recommend him right there.

XIV

DTI Branch Office
Sadvis, Aldebaran III
13:36 UTC

Lucsly monitored Agent Ranjea's interview technique with grudging approval. The novice Deltan agent, just four months, twenty-five days past graduation, handled himself with considerable aplomb when faced with the anomalies that fell under DTI's purview, though his manner was somewhat more touchy-feely than Lucsly was comfortable with. If nothing else, Ranjea had an undeniable passion for the work, and that was something a DTI agent needed to remain stable. Agent Chall had lost her passion for the work after the Akorem Laan incident five months, fourteen days ago, dismayed by the power of the Bajoran wormhole's occupants to modify the timeline in a way that preserved memories of both old and new versions, threading the formerly disappeared Bajoran poet Akorem back into history without bringing about the quantum collapse of the original timeline state. Chall was now back home on Bolarus IX, a career of nine years, seven months of distinguished service cut short by a single crisis of faith. Lucsly found it incomprehensible that anyone could give up the defense of the default history so easily. For him, the best therapy had always been the work itself. He could cope with the insanity so long as he felt he was taking action to hold it at bay.

Luckily, Ranjea was proving an excellent, even superior replacement for Chall. Much of that was probably due to the intuitive knowledge he'd absorbed from the temporal operative Riroa, but any advantage was welcome where Lucsly was concerned. And it was no slight to Ranjea's own abilities. He still needed to interpret those anachronistic intuitions on his own, to study temporal theory and DTI procedures and technology in order to decipher them. At first, Lucsly had been concerned that the infusion of Riroa's knowledge might lead to anachronistic advances in DTI technology, jeopardizing the proper flow of the future, but it seemed Ranjea's insights were limited by the knowledge he had available to filter them through. So it made him a quick study, able to master new theories and techniques quite easily, but not a prophet or an innovator before his time.

Lucsly imagined, though, that Ranjea's skill at interviews came from his own police training. Right now, that skill was proving quite useful. Handling one Professor Vard was difficult enough without having to deal with a second one.

"So you're not our *Professor Vard?"* Ranjea asked the duplicate of the Tandaran scientist, who sat in an interview room on the other side of the Aldebaran Branch Office while Lucsly and Dulmur rode herd on the original Vard here in the research lab. Or rather, Dulmur kept an eye on Vard-1 while Lucsly monitored the interview with the other on the lab viewer.

"That's what I've been trying to tell you!" said Vard-2, distinguished from the original by his less flamboyant clothing and the lack of dye in his graying hair. *"The device*

*you confiscated from me is not a time machine. It is a device
for crossing the barriers between orthogonal histories!"*

"So you're from an alternate dimension? A parallel
timeline?"

"Exactly! You see, three years ago, in my reality, a
Starfleet officer named Worf encountered a quantum fissure
that caused him to begin leaping across timelines, switching
places with his parallel counterparts. His experience
confirmed the existence of over two hundred and eighty
thousand parallel timelines at the very least."

"Yes. The Worf of our timeline reported an equivalent
occurrence."

"I'm sure the same befell all two hundred and eighty
thousand of him." Lucsly remembered the report of the
alleged incident on Stardate 47391. According to Worf,
by sealing the fissure he had reset time to before his encounter. Beyond a faint, ambiguous quantum flux echo
in the *Enterprise* officer's body, clothing, and shuttlecraft,
there had been no proof of the incident beyond Worf's
own word—and the Klingon had nearly torn Agent Yol's
symbiont out of his pouch when the latter had questioned
whether that was enough. So there had been little follow-
up of the incident—at least in this quantum history.

"In any case," Vard-2 went on, "by analyzing his quantum flux readings and his description of the quantum fissure,
I was able to perfect a mechanism for traversing parallel
histories at will—although without displacing one's parallel
self in the process. You see . . ."

The mechanism the alternate Vard went on to describe
was intriguing, potentially far more useful than the multidimensional transporter device that inhabitants of one documented alternate history had employed to make incursions

upon starbase Deep Space 9 on Stardates 48724.8 and
49725.5, a device replicating the accidental crossover that
James Kirk—always Kirk—had made to that same history on
Stardate 3645. That device had simply been a relay creating
a Weinberg-Polchinski entanglement between transporter
mechanisms in the two timelines, and could only be targeted upon a previously identified alternate realm. Vard-2's
innovation was self-contained and free of those limitations.

"Well, Doc?" Dulmur asked Vard-1 after a time. "Can
it do what he says?"

"Hmm, very possibly, very possibly, Agent Dummer."

"Dulmur."

Vard-1 showed no sign of hearing the correction.
"I certainly wouldn't put it past a genius of my—er,
our caliber to pull off such a feat. I'd need to study it in
considerably more detail to be sure . . . but, then again, we
have the word of an unimpeachable source."

"Don't be so sure," Lucsly said. "He's from a different
history, a different life. We don't know enough about his
reality to know what kind of man he is."

"True, true. For one thing, the man clearly has no idea
how to dress!"

"So what was your goal in developing this device?" Ranjea
was asking on the monitor.

"I had a vision," Vard-2 replied. *"We know that only a
finite number of timelines exist, but if nearly three hundred
thousand branches can surround the life of one individual,
one starship, imagine how many must exist overall!"*

*"But many of those alternative branches Worf described
were only infinitesimally different. Most likely they were
artificially prolonged by the quantum fissure and would have
collapsed into a smaller number."*

"Yes, yes, but still, there could easily be millions of parallels within the history of our respective species, say. Consider it, Agent, ah, Ranjea. Why risk traveling forward or backward in time to create a desired state of affairs, thus jeopardizing the continued existence of entire quantum realities, when you could just travel sideways *in time and find a naturally occurring reality that already conforms to your needs? Everyone could inhabit the universe of their dreams without having to jeopardize anyone else's existence! Once I realized that possibility, I could no longer stand to work for my Tandaran Empire's Temporal Warfare Division. I resigned in order to invent the track-jumper. Err, that's what I call it, because—"*

"Yes, I understand." Ranjea asked the question that had immediately occurred to Lucsly. *"But what about the version of yourself who already lives in that ideal timeline? What if he doesn't wish to cede that life to you?"*

"Ahh, yes, well, there are still some conceptual faults to be worked out," Vard-2 conceded. *"But I am willing to work with your Federation to perfect the technology. I would be glad to share it with every timeline I can reach, and begin a new era of interdimensional travel and trade."*

Dulmur was at Lucsly's shoulder now. "What do you think?" he asked.

"A way to give people an alternative to time travel? Put an end to existential threats to the timeline?" Lucsly replied. "It's an enticing thought. But I have to wonder: why'd he come to share it with us instead of his own people? I don't think he's telling the whole story."

"And you just know it'd create a whole rash of new problems," Dulmur said. "Like, what if everybody decided to migrate to the best timelines? Things would get awfully crowded in some of them. People would multiply like . . . like tribbles."

Lucsly threw him a look. "Tribbles again? You're still wishing you'd gone back to the *Enterprise* with Sisko, aren't you?"

"Hey, I never said I wanted to go back there."

"Come on. 'Probably would've done the same thing myself'? You'd have tried to shake James T. Kirk's hand?"

"There wasn't any handshake. Sisko just said a few words to him."

"But still. *Kirk*." Lucsly may have shuddered at how close the Klingon spy known as Arne Darvin, who had used the Bajoran Orb of Time to send the *Defiant* back in time to Stardate 4523, had come to retroassassinating James T. Kirk with an exploding tribble and altering all subsequent history . . . but he could certainly understand the man's choice of target.

Dulmur shrugged. "Well, if you think about it, the Department wouldn't exist without him."

"You can't encourage people like that. The Deep Space 9 staff's becoming almost as bad as Kirk already."

"They're near a wormhole. Anomalies are bound to crop up."

"All the more reason not to encourage recklessness."

Vard-1 cleared his throat loudly. "Ah, would you two like to be alone?"

He subsided under their joint glare, but the point was made. After a moment of silence, Dulmur spoke in a more subdued tone. "Is this about the promotion?"

Lucsly turned back to the monitor. "*Possible* promotion." Dulmur had recently been offered the assistant directorship of this very branch office.

"Let's face it, Lucsly, I'm not getting any younger. I'll be forty-five in thirty-nine days. I know you'd never consider giving up field work . . ."

"The field is where I can do the most good."

"But we can't do it without support. If I take the AD gig, I'll still be fighting the good fight."

"From the sidelines."

"I've been doing this for eight years, partner. Racing all over creation to keep it in one piece. I've done my bit. I deserve to slow down. Maybe even get a second chance at starting a family."

"You tried that. It didn't work."

"That was when I thought it was a choice between my family and my job. If I did my job in one place, and found someone patient enough with it, maybe someone from inside, then it wouldn't have to be a choice."

"You're dreaming. Our job takes total commitment. How many married agents do you know?"

Dulmur sighed, his patience at the familiar argument exhausted. "It's the damn time loop all over again." After a few moments listening to Vard-2's running commentary, Dulmur said, "You'd find a new partner, you know."

"I don't want a new partner. It took me two years, six months, twenty-four days to break *you* in."

Dulmur laughed, but the moment passed quickly. "Change happens, Lucsly. You can't fight it forever."

"Then what's the point of doing what we do?"

Before Dulmur could formulate an answer, the comm signaled. The branch office's outgoing AD, Farimah Hamidi, appeared on a secondary monitor. *"A starship has just materialized in space, approaching Aldebaran III. Not a warp incursion, no signs of cloaking technology. But it does have a quantum signature matching that of our recent visitor, and we're reading particle traces like those emitted by his device."*

"Oh no," said Vard-2. *"They've found me."*

"Who has found you, Professor?" Ranjea asked, keeping his tone calm and soothing.

"I'm afraid I haven't been entirely honest with you, Agent. Oh, I hoped I'd have more time before they found me, time to develop a defense . . ."

"Who are they?"

"The Temporal Warfare Division, of course!" Vard-2 said. *"My former employers. You see, they . . . fear my device. If it became known on Tandar—my Tandar—then it would obviate the need for temporal alterations, and the TWD would no longer have an unlimited budget and carte blanche to do as they wished. They stole my invention, duplicated it, but only to ensure that I was prevented from publicizing it."*

"Oh, my," Vard-1 said, studying the sensor readings of the intruder ship. "They appear to have formidable temporal armaments. Chroniton-based torpedoes . . . they could shift out of temporal phase and penetrate our shields effortlessly."

"They can do far worse than that," Vard-2 said. *"Any move you make to block them, they'll simply jump back several moments and avoid it. Oh, I was a fool to bring this down on you . . . please, you must return my device to me and let me lead them away to another quantum history! My only hope is to stay ahead of them, find someone who can defend me."*

Lucsly turned to Hamidi on the monitor. "Director, we can't just let this technology get out of our control."

"We don't have a choice, Lucsly. They just incapacitated

the Cyrus *with a single torpedo. Right through their shields, just as Vard said. We're not the Eridian Vault here, we don't have the defenses to hold them off. So you two, get that device back to the other Vard and get him out of this timeline with all possible haste. That's an order."*

The agents and Vard-1 were already on the run with the track-jumper. "Professor," Lucsly asked, "did you get detailed enough scans to replicate the technology?"

"I barely had time to scratch the surface," the Tandaran said. "And it's not my field anyway. I'm sure I could pull it off given a few years, but I have more important and much more interesting research of my own to do. Honestly, the man has no more taste in physics than he has in clothing. You could give it to someone else, like that upstart Naadri, but it would take them at least a decade."

Lucsly sighed. Dulmur was probably right; it would turn out to be just one more source of trouble rather than an end to it. Best to get rid of it and maintain the status quo, such as it was.

Not that the status quo is likely to remain for long anyway, he thought, throwing a look at the back of Dulmur's head. But if his partner really wanted to take the promotion, Lucsly had to confess there was little he could do about it. Change came whether he wanted it or not.

But I really hate breaking in new partners. . . .

McKinley Station, Earth Orbit
Mehr 16 1752 AP (A Sunday)
18:29 UTC
"You should be receiving our report in about six weeks," Dulmur said as he showed Captain Jean-Luc Picard to the door of McKinley Station's conference room.

"Six weeks?" Picard echoed in his clipped European tones. "That seems a bit excessive."

"You gave us an awful lot of material to review, Captain." He softened a bit. "But it's just paperwork. No one's denying the service you and your crew have done for history. And as for some of their actions in 2063 Montana . . . well, who wouldn't want to share a drink with Zefram Cochrane?"

The captain, who had grown increasingly irritated at the intense examination Dulmur and Lucsly had subjected him to for the past four hours, forty-three minutes, was mollified somewhat by Dulmur's words. "Who indeed," he said with grudging politeness. "But if you'll excuse me, I must return to my ship."

"Of course. We'll be in touch."

Once Picard had gone and the door slid shut, Dulmur sagged against the wall and let out a groan. "Shit. We are so screwed."

"Mm-hm," Lucsly replied. Picard no doubt thought the story was concluded; the crew of the *Enterprise* had successfully compensated for the Borg's efforts to destroy Zefram Cochrane and his prototype warp ship, prevent first contact with the Vulcans, and erase the Federation from history. Indeed, some of his crew had even ended up taking the place of Cochrane's copilots and flight crew, becoming an integral part of the history that had shaped them, although that fact had been kept out of the history books thanks to Cochrane's discretion (and probably a little judicious editing of history by the contemporary Aegis operative). For them, the mission was complete, the day was saved, and they could move on to the next adventure in classic Starfleet fashion.

But Dulmur and Lucsly had to look at the big picture, and that picture had suddenly become much more frightening. That was why Dulmur had delayed taking his AD post at Aldebaran in order to conduct this one last debriefing with his longtime partner. Picard's report had changed everything. "The Borg. The Borg have time travel. How can we fight that?"

Lucsly frowned, lost in thought. "I'm not sure we have to," he finally said.

"What do you mean?"

"Think about it. What are the odds that the Borg just happened to acquire time travel recently after existing for thousands of years? If they had it at all, the odds are that they would've had it and used it a long time ago. Our timeline wouldn't even exist; the whole galaxy would've been retroactively assimilated. It just doesn't make sense."

"Hm. You're right."

"There's more. The whole thing seems out of character for the Borg. Dealing with an enemy by going back in time to a key moment in their history, sabotaging it, and creating an alternate history in which they never existed? That's too convoluted to be a Borg strategy. Too creative. They don't think laterally. They just plod forward methodically, absorbing everything in their path. If something destroys one of their drones, they just send two more. If something destroys one of their cubes, they just send two more. They keep pushing until they overwhelm by sheer persistence."

Dulmur conceded the point. If anyone understood that kind of plodding, straightforward mentality, it was Lucsly. The Borg wouldn't do a thing like this as a rule. But the alternative Lucsly was leading toward was at least as frightening. "Are you saying someone gave the Borg a time machine and sicced them on Earth?"

"It's the most logical explanation."

"But why?"

"Same reason the Suliban Cabal's Sponsor used them. Protective camouflage."

Dulmur nodded. If the Accordist factions knew who was behind an attack on history, they could act to prevent or correct it. Acting clandestinely was the safest option. "So you think this was a move in the Temporal Cold War? But who'd be crazy enough to give a time machine to the goddamn Borg? The Na'kuhl?"

"They strike openly. Proudly. They wouldn't hide it. Maybe Counter Strike." It was possible; that rogue offshoot of the Aegis was as fond of clandestine operations as their more benevolent counterparts. "Or some wild-card player. A temporal power trying to make their name by erasing the UFP."

"Or it could just be an isolated incident. Maybe the Borg only recently assimilated a time machine for the first time. It's not impossible."

"And they never assimilated one before? In thousands of worlds for thousands of years?" Lucsly shook his head. "It's a safe bet the Accordists work overtime to keep temporal technology out of Borg hands. If something slipped through the net, it probably means someone ran interference to make sure the Borg got a chance to use it."

Dulmur sighed and moved to sit down opposite his longtime partner. He could read the anxiety in Lucsly's face, even though—or perhaps because—he'd never seen that precise look before. "You're thinking there's a new front opening up in the Cold War."

"First the Deltan time perceptor incident, then this happening a year, two months, and a week later? And don't forget the Tox Uthat incident in '66."

"That's nearly a six-year gap."

"Not a huge interval from a perspective centuries uptime."

Dulmur thought it over for a long while. "Well. There's no proof. Three future incursions in seven years—one only speculative."

"Still . . ."

"Still . . . if there's even a chance you're right . . ." He spent another long moment in thought. "We have to be on our guard, partner. More than ever. If something's gonna happen, we need to be out where we can do the most good."

Lucsly studied him, his expression guarded. "'We'?"

A heavy sigh. "Yeah. If we need to be at our full strength, then there's no sense breaking up the team. We do work pretty well together."

"Mm," was all Lucsly said. A moment later: "What about Aldebaran?"

"Aah, I never liked shellmouths anyway. Present company excepted." Lucsly gave him the mildly annoyed look that was the closest thing in his repertoire to a show of appreciation for a joke. "And who'm I kidding, I'd probably go stir-crazy stuck in an office all day." He'd felt himself confined by his lack of career advancement, but now that he thought about his prospects in the face of a potential major threat, he realized he would feel far more powerless behind a desk by himself than he would in the field alongside his partner.

Lucsly offered only companionable silence in response, but it was enough. It had always been enough.

PRESENT TIME
STARDATE 59061.4 TO 59087.2

XV

Fourth Day of Xan'lahr, Year of Kahless 1008,
Klingon Imperial Calendar
A Saturday

Vulcan Science Council Research Station 1
40 Eridani System
10:53 UTC
Agent Shelan wondered if it would really hurt diplomatic
relations with the Klingon Empire all that much if she
tossed Korath, Son of Monak, into an antimatter reactor.
Surely if anyone would recognize homicide as a valid response to intolerable annoyance, it would be the Klingons.
Then again, by Klingon standards, the physicist's relentless, graceless come-ons would probably be considered
endearing.

Korath was one of a number of participants in a scientific exchange program recently organized by the Bacco
Administration. The Federation had spent nearly the past
year working to strengthen ties with those states who had
allied with it during the Borg invasion—including the
Klingon Empire, the Imperial Romulan State, the Ferengi
Alliance, the Cardassian Union, and the Talarian Repub-
lic—and President Bacco wished to dispel the Typhon
Pact's allegations that her intent was to create a military
bloc. And so, with the first anniversary of the Borg's final
defeat less than a month away, this exchange was one
of several programs under way to promote the cultural,

scientific, and humanitarian benefits of a strengthened alliance. Most of the other governments had sent some of their top scientists to tour the Federation's leading research facilities, while some of the Federation's greatest minds were doing the same in neighboring nations. The Klingon Science Institute had included Korath as one of its envoys, perhaps to get him out of their hair for a while. Shelan had been assigned to keep an eye on him and the other researchers with temporal credentials in the group, such as Ronarek, a former member of the Imperial Romulan Institute of Research who had defected when the IRS was dissolved late last year, and Nart, a Ferengi physicist whose work was reportedly underwritten by Lant, a Ferengi businessman who had used an ancient Ludugian temporal transporter to make a killing in the investment market in 2376 (and earlier) and was believed to be trying to replicate his time-travel feats after the Starfleet Corps of Engineers had destroyed the device.

If anything, Shelan would have expected Nart to be the one to spend most of his time plying her with degrading come-ons. But she supposed that, as a Suliban, she should know better than to buy into stereotypes. Nart was actually rather adorable, a shy, soft-spoken Ferengi whose desire for acquisition was directed entirely toward knowledge. Though he worked for Lant, he seemed interested only in the pure research and not its illicit applications. His demeanor was absently yet consistently polite, always listening with sincere attention to anyone who spoke to him and never seeming to care—or perhaps even notice— whether the speaker was male or female.

Korath, on the other hand, was aggressively aware of Shelan's femaleness. In theory, she might not have minded so much; the tall, still-youthful warrior-scientist was not bad-looking if one's tastes ran that way, and he had a rich, operatically trained baritone that was rather pleasant, particularly since his delivery tended to be less bombastic than that of many Klingon nobles. But he was an ambitious, greedy sort, and the way he looked at Shelan was that of a spoiled child eyeing a desired toy. Rather than trying to woo her, he treated her as something he was entitled to possess, and it angered him when she rebuffed his advances. It had been a delicate balance to assert her unavailability without scuttling her mission to protect him.

Moreover, though he was undeniably a genius, his scientific curiosity and effort were geared exclusively toward weaponry and warfare, with little regard for ethics. Now, for instance, the scientists were being lectured by Dr. T'Pan, the noted subspace morphologist, on the Science Council's latest discovery, a new form of exotic matter with the ability to amplify gravity and mass, potentially offering a new, more efficient means of creating artificial gravity. "Unfortunately," T'Pan told the assembled group, "the reaction, once triggered, propagates exponentially. As yet, we know of no means to limit or control the gravitational increase. We cannot even safely experiment with the substance aboard this station."

"But it is neutral until triggered by a sufficient energy infusion, correct?" Korath asked. "So it could be handled safely prior to use."

"With adequate containment, yes. But until we can harness the effect sufficiently to allow for constructive use—"

"Who said anything about constructive uses?" Korath countered, grinning. "What you have here, if it performs as you claim, could be a devastating weapon. I would like to see a demonstration immediately."

"That is out of the question," T'Pan insisted.

"I stand ready to offer a generous trade—"

"It is *not* for sale. Even if it existed in more than trace quantities, which it does not as yet, we would not make it available for military use."

Korath growled in his throat. "Then naturally you will publish your work so that we may attempt to replicate it for ourselves."

T'Pan exchanged a look with Secretary of Technology Forzrat, the Androssi female who served as the visiting scientists' host. Forzrat stepped forward and said, "That's a matter that can be explored in the future. If we succeed in establishing a stronger alliance, a process for scientific and technological exchange will be a major part of it—along with a set of mutually agreed-upon ethical safeguards as well."

Korath looked frustrated, but now his own supervisor from the KSI was staring him into silence. Shelan suppressed a grin.

The rest of the tour was about as boring as one would expect from a group of Vulcans lecturing about arcane science to other scientists. There wasn't even any actual temporal research going on here for Shelan to be professionally concerned about. *This is ridiculous,* she thought more than once in the ensuing hours. *Somewhen out there, the Cabal's Sponsor and others like him are planning attacks, maybe even undermining the course of history right now. And I'm stuck babysitting an amoral fool who's only ever dabbled in temporal physics. I didn't join the DTI to stand on the sidelines! There's a war on and I need to be fighting it!*

It was a relief when Shelan was able to return to her quarters for the night, after brushing off one more attempt by Korath to invite himself in with her. After running a quick tricorder sweep to ensure he hadn't planted any microcameras, Shelan thankfully undressed and stepped into the sonic shower.

Only to find herself in a far more humid environment. Far bigger, too. She looked around wildly. She was in a grotto of volcanic stone, enclosed on all sides by high outcroppings. She stood on a narrow shore around a bubbling hot spring. The gravity was noticeably lighter than the Vulcan-normal level aboard the research station. She was somewhere very far from where she was supposed to be. And she was completely naked.

"Don't be alarmed," came a voice. Shelan spun to see an exotic-looking woman soaking in the bubbling pool. Her bare skin was bronze with a tinge of green and her dark hair was pinned up over intricately scalloped ears. "You seemed tense . . . I thought you might like a relaxing place to have a conversation."

Shelan did relax just a bit. Her hostess had chosen to make herself just as vulnerable as Shelan, if not more so, so the intent was not to intimidate. Besides, she recognized the woman from Dulmur's descriptions. "You're Jena Noi," she said. "Federation Temporal Agency, thirty-first century."

"Good. No need for introductions."

"Where am I?"

"Nowhere you'd know. Beyond your current borders. But it'll become a major vacation spot in about forty years."

Shelan's heart raced. "*When* am I?"

"Don't worry, I didn't bring you through time," Noi said. "I know your employers frown on that. Well, no more than an hour or so. And I'll be returning you to the exact moment you left. No one will know you were gone, even if you decide to linger here awhile. Which I would really recommend. It's wonderful."

Shelan sighed. "Why not?" she said, and gingerly lowered herself into the pool, not too close to Noi. "I have to say, you've taken the concept of a secret talk in the shower to new heights." She settled in and took a shuddering breath. It really did feel quite refreshing. "So who are we keeping it secret from?"

"Everyone," Noi said. "Do you have any idea how hard it is to keep a secret centuries after the fact?"

Shelan deliberated. "Sometimes it's easy. Knowledge is forgotten all the time. Records are lost, miscopied, or never made at all. Historians interpret and distort the history they study."

"And time travelers can go back and fill in the gaps in that knowledge."

"If they know where to look."

Noi smiled. "Good. I knew I was right to call on you. Whatever your agency's technological limitations, you train good people."

"A hot bath, sweet talk . . . you must really want something big from me."

Noi frowned. "Why the mistrust? We're on the same side."

"When it suits you," Shelan said. "But if you've studied me—and I assume you did so rather thoroughly before contacting me—then you know I have an interest in . . . twenty-second-century history."

Noi pursed her lips. "It came up."

"I've read up on your . . . associate Mister Daniels, or so he called himself. Some of the claims he made to Jonathan Archer were rather . . . extravagant. Really—schoolchildren building temporal communicators at their desks? Any civilization that reckless would've wiped itself out of history by the lunch period. He also claimed time travel hadn't been perfected yet in the Cabal Sponsor's time, when we know the Federation has it at least two centuries earlier."

Noi gave a long-suffering chuckle. "Ahh, Daniels . . . well, you know we couldn't reveal too much about the future to Captain Archer. Daniels had his own . . . idiosyncratic way of keeping secrets. His point of view was that he had to tell Archer *something*."

"And what's your point of view, Agent Noi?"

The uptime operative stood and came closer to Shelan, lowering herself back into the water next to the Suliban agent. "That we're all in this fight together, Shelan. I know we rarely treat your department as equals, but it's not from lack of respect. You were the ones who started it all. The first step that led to us. That's why it's so important to protect you." She sighed. "And that's why I don't make this request of you lightly."

Shelan let her shoulders sink into the hot water's embrace. "Oh, here it comes. Why me? Don't you usually go to Lucsly?"

"This mission is one uniquely suited for your heritage and abilities."

There was only one thing that could mean. "My Cabal genes are dormant, recessive. I don't have any special abilities beyond endurance and flexibility. Which I doubt would be of much use to you—unless there's an additional reason you've brought me here naked," she added with a smirk.

Noi smiled. "You underrate yourself. Aside from the courage and dedication of a DTI field agent, you have great potential that only needs to be unlocked. I can help you access it."

Shelan straightened, searching Noi's lambent eyes. "And in return?"

"I won't lie to you, Shelan. What I'm asking of you is probably the riskiest mission any DTI agent has ever undertaken. But it's also, without question, the most important."

Shelan studied her a bit longer, then gave an insouciant chuckle. "Why go to all this trouble? You should've just told me that in the first place. Now tell me more. . . ."

Axis of Time
Early Warp Age, Anthropocene Epoch
As before, all attempts to crack the problem with the Axis of Time from the outside proved futile, forcing Ranjea and Garcia to penetrate the pocket universe once again in hopes of finding an internal solution. This time, however, the occupants of the shuttle *Cincinnatus*—including Commander Heather Petersen, temporarily reassigned from the *Everett*—went in with full awareness that unless they found a solution, they might never come back out, at least not in their own era.

Progress had been made since the agents' original visit. Upon their arrival within the Axis timespace, they found a small station of Vomnin design occupying the local interface zone. They were promptly hailed and invited to dock—with a sense of urgency, Ranjea thought. Once they docked and disembarked aboard the station, they found Subdirector Sikran loping forward in haste to meet them. "Thank the Ancients you're here!" the stout Vomnin representative cried. "Please tell me you've come to offer us a way out!"

His words confirmed that the simplest assumption had been correct: the occupants of the Axis were simply trapped within it. In the days that the crews of Bezorek station and the *U.S.S. Asimov* had spent trying in vain to communicate with the Axis interior, hypotheses had been formulated ranging from the death of everyone within the Axis to the abduction of new arrivals for unknown purposes. "I'm afraid not," Ranjea replied. "We're here to investigate the problem."

Sikran sagged. "Then you are trapped here along with everyone else."

"Everyone?" Garcia said. "So it's not just our interface that's affected?"

"No. The entire Axis has been cut off from the outside universe. Or rather, ships may still enter, but leaving is impossible. Any attempt to depart through the interface zones brings you right back to your starting point, just like in the rest of the Axis."

"And the occupants don't know why?" Heather Petersen asked. "It's not something that's happened before?"

"Oh, they have their suspicions," Sikran replied. "You'll have to speak to them about that."

"So they shall," came a new voice. The agents and Petersen spun to see a contingent of Axis security which had suddenly arrived. The leader was a powerfully built, red-scaled reptilian with a golden head crest, a compact forward-leaning body, and a heavy, counterbalancing tail. Ranjea recognized him as a Talich, a member species of the same Colloquium of Progress to which Councillor Oydia belonged.

The burly Talich strode forward to confront the new-comers. "The Council has questions for you. You will attend."

"Gladly," Ranjea said. "We have questions of our own."

Axis Hub Station
Middle Calabrian Age, Lower Pleistocene

"You claim you had nothing to do with this?" Councillor Damyz demanded. The elderly Yeshel spoke slowly, but his usual gentle manner had been replaced with suspicion.

"Some of our own people were trapped here along with you," Ranjea reminded them.

"So they claimed," said Councillor Temarel, raising an upswept brow in a very Vulcanoid gesture. "Perhaps Starfleet is even blameless. But you made it clear that your civilian government opposes trade through the Axis. Per haps you took preemptive action."

"Councillor, my government also opposes forcible intervention in the affairs of others. This is not our doing."

Councillor Oydia came up to him and stared, her huge violet eyes holding his gaze. Ranjea sensed a release of pheromones drawing him into an empathic rapport, an induced merging like a more one-sided version of the Deltan opening of the self. He responded to it in kind, taking Oydia's silver-furred hands in his and opening himself empathically. Soon she was as transfixed as she had intended him to be. But he promptly released her from it. She gasped and took a moment to gather herself. A smile snuck out and was quickly masked. "I, ah, I believe he tells the truth," the councillor told her fellows.

Lirahn, who had been quiet until now, stepped forward. "Of course he does," the statuesque Selakar said, stroking Ranjea's cheek. "Despite the efforts of Shiiem's cronies to blame outsiders, we all know that this sabotage was committed from within. Rather than allow the democratic process to dictate trade policy, the conservative faction has chosen to take drastic action to enforce their denial of free trade."

"Absurd!" Temarel cried. "We would not take such extreme measures."

"Who but the Zcham are advanced enough to manipulate the nature of the timespace itself?"

Councillor Shiiem had also held back, letting his ally Temarel have her rein, but now he spoke in cool, controlled tones. "The Selakar, for one," he replied. "The knowledge in your era was great enough."

"But what would we have to gain?" Lirahn demanded. "Our advocacy of free trade is no secret. We, and those we hoped to benefit, are the greatest casualties. Whereas preventing any cross-temporal trade, any threat to your precious timestream, is clearly in your interests."

"Now, wait there, Lirahn," Damyz said. "Let's be fair. After all, some of the people in here . . . well, they may have things they were meant to do that they haven't done yet. If they're trapped here, well, then it could change history, not, ah, not preserve it."

Shiiem and Temarel looked surprised, yet gratified, at the elder statesman's support. "He is correct," the Zcham councillor said. "This sabotage is in no one's interest. It threatens all of us, and its cause must be found."

"You're certain it's not a natural phenomenon?" Petersen asked.

"That much we do know. There is only one way this change could have been brought about." Shiiem moved closer and adopted a lecturing tone. "By traveling to the far downtime end of the Axis, you return to the moment of its creation, even while remaining in its internal present. The nature of that duality is such that, by altering the conditions of its creation, you alter the nature of its spatiotemporal metric—as though it had been created in that form all along. Essentially you reset the Axis to its starting point. But that past is also its present, so the redefined conditions are only perceived from the internal moment of the change forward."

Garcia put her hands to her temples. "Oh, hell, I thought I'd outgrown the headaches."

"You know this was done?" Ranjea said.

"We know," Temarel replied, "because the change *has* happened, and could not have happened any other way. But we do not know who was responsible. Travel within the Axis is not closely monitored—only travel to and from it."

Damyz let out a heavy sigh, wrinkling his snout. "Nor can we comprehend why. An action like this . . . tampering with the very, ah, genesis of the Axis itself . . . why, it risked destabilizing the entire realm. Had the perpetrators erred, everything we have built here could have been eradicated. These, ah, these terrorists, yes, are a threat to us all, regardless of our differences of policy. We must set aside political recriminations and seek these criminals together."

If Lirahn was upset to see Damyz thinking for himself instead of backing her political play, she didn't show it.

Instead, she adapted smoothly, circling Ranjea and brushing her hand across his shoulders. "I have a suggestion. Our new visitors are professional investigators. Discovering the perpetrators of temporal crimes is exactly what they're trained for. Who better to track down the ones responsible for this?" There was no question in Ranjea's mind that Lirahn's outrage at being trapped was sincere. It radiated from her quite strongly, her raw emotion confirming what logic already made clear: that her own agenda was undermined by this lockdown.

Shiiem nodded. "I agree. An investigation by outsiders would defer questions of objectivity. Are you amenable, Agents, Commander?"

"We will gladly assist, Councillors," Ranjea replied.

"Yeah," Garcia said. "We're as eager to get home as the rest of you are."

"Wonderful," Lirahn said, beaming. "For once, all of us in the Council are on the same side. May it set a precedent for days to come."

DTI Headquarters, Greenwich
15 Xan'lahr YK 1008 (A Monday)
19:04 UTC

Director Andos was as somber as Dulmur had ever seen her as she looked around the situation room at the assembled staff, including himself, Lucsly, Yol, Sonaj, and T'Viss along with Kalnota and several of his researchers. "Mister Felbog of our research department has made an alarming discovery this morning," she told them. "I will allow him to report it himself."

The young Choblik approached the podium timidly, egged on by a nod from his supervisor Kalnota. To

Dulmur, he looked uncannily like a deer cowering under a predator's gaze. "Ah . . . thank you, Director. Well . . . I was . . . conducting a routine search of the shielded records when I came upon . . . the following mission report, transmitted to the Aldebaran branch office from a DTI-issue padd yesterday evening."

He pressed a contact and a female voice played over the speaker. *"Mission report, Agent Shelan, Stardate 59084.352. The exchange group has completed its survey of the Coridan Engineering Institute without incident, and we are now en route to Tesnia. Korath, Nart, Ronarek, and the other scientists are all doing well. No threats have manifested, and I have their protection well in hand. Korath has predictably expressed an interest in the weapons potential of the Tesnians' microsingularity research, but . . ."*

"Shelan?" T'Viss interrupted. "I thought Agent T'Lem was assigned to the scientific exchange group. Who is this Shelan?"

Felbog halted the playback and spoke reluctantly. "According to the shielded records . . . Shelan is a Suliban female who has been a DTI agent since Stardate 56518—two years, six months, and twenty-three days ago."

The room erupted into murmurs. "This has got to be some kind of forgery," Dulmur said, looking to Lucsly for reassurance.

But his partner offered none, his expression stony. "You know how secure the shielded records are."

"I have consulted the records going back three years," Felbog said. "They contain numerous, regular reports by Agent Shelan, along with a complete record of her application, background check, training, and certification as a DTI field agent." He projected an image of this Shelan in the holodisplay. Dulmur did not recognize the Suliban woman, but her pleasant face conveyed warm confidence, her eyes great determination. "However, beyond the shielded records, we can find no evidence for the existence of a Shelan. Her listed parents and siblings exist, members of the Suliban community on Niburon IV, but that world's records show no evidence that a Shelan was ever born to them."

After an awkward moment, he went on. "As for Agent T'Lem, the shielded records list her as a researcher only. Agent T'Lem's training took place in the summer of 2379, the same term as this Shelan. The records show them as classmates, with Shelan outcompeting T'Lem in many measures of performance."

"History's been changed," Lucsly grated, putting it into words so it could no longer be denied. "Someone targeted a DTI agent and wiped her from history."

"Do we know she was the target?" Stijen Yol asked. "What about the rest of us? The rest of the galaxy? What else has been changed?"

"My researchers have been investigating that all morning," Virum Kalnota told the Trill agent. "We have found essentially no discrepancies in the historical record beyond those pertaining to the life of this Shelan and the DTI career of Agent T'Lem. Even the ripple-effect discrepancies you would expect if a single person were never born are absent. As far as we can determine, every significant act accomplished by Agent Shelan in the unaltered timeline was performed here as well, either by Agent T'Lem or some other individual, or else through unexplained chance circumstances."

"Probability," Lucsly muttered, a mantra to himself. "The universe tends toward the most probable configuration."

"Even that is not an adequate explanation," T'Viss said into the ensuing silence after reviewing Kalnota's data at high speed. "The level of convergence here is astonishing. What we have here is a surgical excision of a single individual from history, done with such care and precision as to have minimal impact on any other factors."

"Minimal impact?" Dulmur cried. "Try telling that to her family, her friends!"

T'Viss raised a brow at his emotional outburts. "That would be pointless, for they no longer recall that this woman even existed."

"That's the point!" Dulmur cried. "My God . . . somebody's exterminated one of our own, and they didn't even leave us our memories. We can't even grieve properly. Who was she? How did we feel about her?" He shook his head. "They didn't just kill her. They killed all that too."

Hesitantly, after a long moment, Felbog said, "We . . . we have her reports. In the shielded records. Those can tell us . . . help us to remember her."

"That just makes it worse," Lucsly said. "Whoever did this has to belong to some uptime faction. Someone with the resources to pull off such a thing. That means they must know we have shielded records. They must have known we'd find out that Shelan had existed. And they didn't care. They wanted us to know what they'd done."

"So it wasn't about Shelan herself," Dulmur realized. "It wasn't the fact of her existence they were trying to hide. It must've been something she knew. Something she found out about the Temporal Cold War, or something she was about to do. They wanted to stop her before she made some important difference."

"Then why not just kill her?" Yol asked through

clenched teeth. "Why not at least leave us our memories of her? Why erase her all the way back to her birth?"

"Sheer vindictiveness," Dulmur said. "Whoever did this . . . it wasn't just a pragmatic move. It was personal."

"But against Shelan," Kalnota asked, "or against us?"

"We're going to find that out," Andos told them all. "From here on, this agency's overriding priority is to discover what happened to Agent Shelan . . . and to discover whether we can reverse it."

Heavy silence filled the room as the impact of her words sank in. Actively changing the past, for whatever reason, was normally off-limits, a task for only the most extreme circumstances. If Andos was openly endorsing such a tactic . . .

Not that Dulmur had any objection. He gazed up again at the image of Shelan, a relic of a vanished history. He wanted to know her. He wanted to remember knowing her, serving alongside her. "Felbog. Is there anything in her last transmissions that gives any sort of clue? Any evidence why she was targeted?"

"Nothing," the Choblik said. "Just the routine mission reports from the exchange tour. There was one more transmission in the shielded records, received on Shelan's frequency at oh-two-oh-four this morning. But it's just static."

"Play it," Lucsly said.

"We've analyzed it, sir, and there's—"

"Play it."

With a shrug of his cervine head, Felbog complied. There was a burst of sound, nothing resembling speech, just a high whine that quickly modulated out into pure white noise before breaking off. Two seconds of static that sounded almost like a dying scream.

The room was silent for a time after that.

"Are we . . ." The tentative words came from Rani Mohindra, the pretty researcher that Faunt had held hostage nearly eleven months ago. "Does this mean we aren't the same people anymore? If we're from an altered timeline . . ."

"As I said," T'Viss told her, "the variations are inconsequential. Our own individual wave equations are virtually unaltered. As with the Carnelian incident, we can effectively regard ourselves as the same individuals we were before, with only certain discrepancies of memory."

"Excuse me," Felbog asked. "What about Lieutenant Elfiki? Shelan's reports show that she was the one who met Elfiki on Pyrellia and brought her here. Yet the conventional records show that Agent T'Lem performed that task."

"Your point?" Andos asked.

"If two separate timeline branches were created—one where Shelan was born and joined the Department, one where neither occurred—and those two branches have now converged into one . . . and if Lieutenant Elfiki comes from a point in the future of that single, converged timeline . . . then would she not have gone back to only one branch? If she was sent back into the Shelan timeline, should she not be absent from ours . . . the one we remember?"

T'Viss contemplated the question for all of a second and a half. "As stated, the degree of orthogonality between the two histories is extremely low. The quantum resonance is great enough that they could be considered only slight variations on the same history, adjacent within the solution space of the universal wavefunction. Thus, the lieutenant could have undergone an analogous quantum superposition of her own wavefunction and thereby participated in both histories.

"Alternatively, the possibility exists that no altered history was generated prior to this date. It could be that some advanced technological means was used to reconfigure the local wavefunction. An interference pattern could have been generated which canceled out certain harmonics within the wavefunction, leaving the impression that they had never been present."

"If I may interpret," Andos said, "you're proposing that instead of going back in time to prevent Shelan's birth, someone may have merely altered the state of the present continuum to erase every trace of Shelan and her actions."

"Perhaps. The universe would proceed from that point as though she had never existed. But it is functionally no different from a scenario in which two parallel histories converge and the quantum information of one is deleted in favor of the other. In this case, the similarity between the two histories is so great that either scenario could be applicable."

"Either way," Dulmur said, "what matters is that Shelan *did* exist. The timeline where she lived was there, it was real, for as long as she was in it. That's true whether it merged with a parallel one or just got rewritten. Her life happened. It mattered. And we owe it to her to bring whoever did this to justice—even if we have to throw open the Vault and chase them down through history ourselves."

"Dulmur." Andos's voice was sharp, cutting him off. She was alert, attentive, as if listening to something only she could hear. "I want to see you and Lucsly in my office right away. The rest of you . . . proceed with your investigations. Dismissed."

Dulmur threw Lucsly a confused look, getting only a shrug in return. The two agents followed Andos to her office, but she would say nothing until they reached it. Dulmur strode inside the empty office behind Andos, and Lucsly closed the door behind them.

And then Dulmur saw Jena Noi standing there, though he could've sworn the room was empty a second before. He hated that. Yet clearly she'd been the one to summon Andos, for the director was unsurprised to see her. "Agent Noi. I take it you're aware of the temporal attack on the Department."

"Yes, I am," Noi said, her melodic voice softer than usual. Her manner was subdued, solemn. "I'm terribly sorry for your loss."

"Sorry?" Lucsly spoke up before Dulmur could. "That's all you can say? Time has been altered! You have the power to fix it! Why aren't you doing it?"

Dulmur saw her jaw tense, but she gave no other outward sign. "I understand how you feel, Lucsly. But I'm telling you to stay out of it. Shelan was a casualty of something she should never have been involved in. I can't let the rest of you get dragged in as well."

"Why?" Dulmur challenged. "Because we're just the local cops? Because we're too small and helpless to make a difference? They took out one of our own, Noi! We have a right to hunt them down!"

"Just because we don't travel in time, that doesn't make us useless," Lucsly told her. "It anchors us. Gives us a perspective you lack."

"This isn't about doubting your competence, Gariff.

On the contrary. I'm here because I believe you *can* uncover the truth. And because you need to understand that some truths must remain hidden."

She turned to Dulmur. "Believe me, I sympathize with your anger. What was done to Shelan was . . . pure evil. But this is bigger than individuals and their pain. It's even bigger than Shelan's life."

"You can't just shut us down!"

"Yes, she can," Lucsly said, though to damn rather than defend. "You know she can. She's shut us down before. Bullied us when it suited her purpose."

"When it served the future," Noi said. "You know that."

"Yes, I know." Lucsly strode forward to loom over her, closer than he was usually comfortable getting with another being. She gazed up at him, unintimidated, and suddenly Dulmur found the tableau very familiar. "I know it all too well."

DOWNTIME
STARDATE 55049.0 TO 55089.5

XVI

U.S.S. Voyager NCC-74656
21:42 UTC

"Now let me get this straight," Lucsly said as he and Dulmur sat across from Captain Kathryn Janeway in her ready room. "An older version of yourself came back from twenty-six years in the future, instructing you to use anachronistic technology to violate the Temporal Prime Directive . . . and you went along with it. Even though you knew it was a crime against law and nature, you played havoc with the natural flow of history in order to get your crew home sixteen years ahead of schedule."

"No," Janeway said, her voice and manner stony. "That was what Admiral Janeway wanted. If it had been for that alone, I would have refused. But we had an opportunity to use the intelligence and technology she brought us to strike a crippling blow against the Borg and save billions."

"Or condemn them," Lucsly said. "You don't know what consequences may have been set in motion by your actions. Drag the timeline off its natural, most probable path and the ramifications are incalculable."

"I can't base my decisions on abstract possible futures, Agent Lucsly," the captain fired back. She was a dainty, delicate-featured woman, but her personality was that of a bulldog. "My responsibility is to defend against threats to my crew, the Federation, and sentient life in the here and now. The Borg are the greatest menace this galaxy has ever known, and I for one wouldn't want to live in a future where they remained strong. We had a once-in-a-lifetime opportunity to deal the Collective a crippling blow, one that might even neutralize them as a threat indefinitely. I took that opportunity, and I will stand by that decision no matter the consequences."

Janeway's self-righteousness disgusted Lucsly. The woman's contempt for the timeline was monumental. The logs *Voyager* had sent home from the Delta Quadrant over the years, as it had gradually found ways to restore contact with the Federation, were a litany of temporal violations that staggered the imagination. Next to *Voyager*, the crews of *Enterprise* and Deep Space 9 seemed downright responsible. Picard's crew had been relatively free of temporal citations since the Cochrane incident, aside from that time a former protégé of Picard's had used his powers as a fledgling member of the advanced Traveler race to try to wipe the Maquis rebels from history for what he thought was the greater good (an incident that only Lucsly remembered once he'd argued the foolish young godling into restoring the correct timeline). And Sisko's people had actually proven themselves remarkably conscientious toward the timestream in incidents like the causal loop at Gaia on Stardate 50814 and the crisis involving the Red Orbs of Jalbador on Stardate 51889—though there had been the noted exception of Major Kira Nerys's unconscionably reckless use of the Bajoran Orb of Time to investigate a personal matter on Stardate 51814. Lucsly had sought to prosecute the major, but the Bajoran government had declared it a protected religious observance, and Sisko had refused to penalize his first officer, nominally on Prime Directive grounds.

But Janeway's crew must hold some sort of record for temporal disruption. They'd been in the Delta Quadrant less than a week before experiencing their first temporal paradox within the event horizon of a type-4 quantum singularity, and it had only escalated from there. Perhaps it was only to be expected that the end of *Voyager*'s tenure in the Delta Quadrant would be heralded by the most egregious temporal crime ever committed by a Starfleet officer.

"Very noble, Captain," Dulmur was saying, drawing Lucsly's thoughts back to the present. "But it would ring more true if you hadn't also used that opportunity to do what your future self wanted in the first place and bring *Voyager* home ahead of schedule."

Janeway gave a careless shrug. "If we were already creating a new history anyway, why not take full advantage of the possibilities? And after all my crew has endured over the past seven years . . . all the good they've done for the galaxy whether anyone recognized it or not . . . they deserved something in return for their sacrifices. They've been through more than should be asked of any crew."

"So instead you sacrifice the rest of history to serve the comfort of a few dozen people," Lucsly ground out. "You've spent so many years in isolation that you've forgotten there's a bigger universe out there."

"Are you even listening to me, Mister Lucsly?"

"Captain," Dulmur said, "it's not the first time you've taken advantage of intelligence from the future to alter the destiny of your crew. On Stardate 48618, you halted an attack by a future version of your Ocampa crewperson

Kes and then used the information you gained to prevent its repetition."

"How is it wrong to prevent someone from going back in time?"

"On Stardate 50312, you allowed your Emergency Medical Hologram to keep a mobile holo-emitter based on twenty-ninth-century technology, rather than confiscating and destroying that technology."

"The Doctor needed that mobility to be able to do his job at peak efficiency. I couldn't risk having my ship's only medical officer trapped in sickbay indefinitely."

"And didn't you think about the consequences to Federation technological progress once you got back?"

"Frequently. But I studied the device. Whatever century it came from, its operating principles weren't too far ahead of the current state of the art. I expected that by the time we got home, probably decades in the future, the technology would already have caught up."

"So now that you're home after only seven years," Lucsly interposed, "do you intend to confiscate the technology?"

Janeway shook her head. "The Doctor has earned his right to mobility many times over, and I consider him a personal friend. If Starfleet or the DTI wants to shackle him again, that's on their heads, but I won't be a part of it."

"Let's move on," Lucsly said. "Stardate 50834. Another temporal incident involving Kes. A future accident involving a biotemporal chamber causes her consciousness to regress through her life, with the process finally halted on that date. Kes provides you with information about the future events she witnessed, and you permit her to do so."

"There was little she could tell us," Janeway said. "Her

experience of the future was fragmentary, and every time she leapt back, it seemed she altered it anyway. By the time she reached our present, her original timeline was probably already lost."

"So suddenly you *can* base your ethical decisions on abstract possible futures."

Janeway spoke coldly. "I based my decisions on the best information available to me in the present, regardless of its provenance. As far as I'm concerned, the future isn't predetermined. It's a consequence of our choices, our free will."

"And you made the deliberate choice to act on Kes's future intelligence. When you encountered the Krenim on Stardate 51252, you chose to avoid their territory rather than seeking passage."

"And thus spared my crew from what Kes described as a year of hell, yes," Janeway said. "But the timeline had already begun to unfold differently on its own, for reasons having nothing to do with what Kes told me. In her timeline, Seven of Nine had not joined our crew, and obviously Kes had never evolved to a higher level and left us. And from what she described, the Krenim attacked without warning, without mercy. In our encounter, they contacted us first and gave us the option to withdraw." Janeway shook her head. "Maybe allowing events to unfold a second time caused random variations to occur. But that was out of my hands."

"Just like the quantum slipstream incident of Stardate 54125?" Dulmur asked. "You seem to make a habit of getting saved by future versions of your crewmates."

"What am I supposed to do? Ignore them? Let my crew die when I have the means to save them?"

Lucsly said nothing aloud, but privately he thought, *It would've made things a lot easier for all of us if you had.*

DTI Branch Office, San Francisco
Virgo 21, mY 408 (A Thursday)
19:56 UTC

"We've got her," Lucsly told Assistant Director Gelim Kreinns as he stepped down off the transporter pad, Dulmur by his side. "Janeway is unrepentant, and the evidence against her is overwhelming. I'm going to put her away for so long that she'll wish she'd spent those thirty-three years in the Delta Quadrant like nature intended."

"And that's only if we don't get clearance to go back and fix it ourselves," Dulmur added as the three of them left the transporter suite and headed down the corridor toward the AD's office. Lucsly had been reluctant to bring that possibility up. It was an extreme measure, an option of last resort. And it was usually the province of uptime agencies like the TIC or FTA anyway. But if they hadn't already corrected the timeline, Lucsly thought, maybe it was because they couldn't. Maybe the altered history they now occupied led to a future so drastically changed that the Federation never developed time travel. In which case the only resort might be to dig into the Vault and find some artifact that would let them do the job themselves.

And if, for whatever reason, they were stuck with living out their lives in this violated timeline, at least Lucsly would see to it that Janeway paid for her obscene crime against reality. It was the least he could do.

Kreinns shook his balding head, his pronounced jowls jiggling. "You know Starfleet refuses to prosecute," the stout Zakdorn said.

"I know," Lucsly replied.

"You know the government's going to resist."

"I know."

"We're still hurting from the Dominion War, even after two years. They'll say the people need something they can celebrate."

"I know."

"And the woman may have ended the Borg threat for the foreseeable future, Lucsly! Nobody's going to want to prosecute her after that!"

"I know!" Lucsly moved his taller frame in front of Kreinns, halting him. "I know all the excuses, Director! But if we don't uphold the laws of the Federation, we damn the Federation. And if we don't fight to preserve the correct, natural flow of time, then all that's left is chaos. I'm nailing Janeway's ass to the wall and I don't care if I have to go through you, Andos, and President Zife himself to do it!"

Dulmur tapped his knuckles against Lucsly's arm, looking over his shoulder. "Uhh, partner . . ."

Lucsly turned to see Director Andos standing in the door of the AD's office that had formerly been hers. "Agent Lucsly. Agent Dulmur. Would you join me, please?" she asked. Her manner was reserved, contained, but overpowering in its authority. Kreinns nodded at her and moved away, and Lucsly and Dulmur silently filed into the office.

Only it wasn't the office. Lucsly whirled around, recognizing the cavernous space surrounding him from his multiple visits here, most recently to secure the last of the ancient time portals excavated on the Bajoran colony world Golana over the past three years. He, Dulmur, and Andos were in the Eridian Vault.

Lucsly knew of only one technology that could

produce such a seamless transition. "Noi!" he called. "What's this about?"

"Calm down, Lucsly." Jena Noi's dulcet tones echoed through the Vault more softly than his own. He turned to face her, and saw she was not alone. She was accompanied by a lanky Starfleet officer in a twenty-ninth-century uniform and a Cardassian male in bland, neatly tailored civilian attire.

Andos stepped between them. "Agents Lucsly and Dulmur," she said, "you know Agent Jena Noi of the Federation Temporal Agency. This is Commander Juel Ducane of the Starfleet Temporal Integrity Commission, and Rodal Eight, Aegis Supervisor 341."

"And this is Meneth," Rodal added, stroking the dark green furred Simperian civet draped comfortably over his shoulders.

Dulmur frowned. "What happened to Cyral Nine?"

"My predecessor's career choices are not relevant here," Rodal said. "We are here to discuss the matter of Captain Kathryn Janeway."

Lucsly brightened, filled with relief. "Finally. I was wondering what was taking you so long to step in and fix things. What do you need us to do?"

"Nothing," Ducane said. "Do absolutely nothing."

"What?" He was taken aback. "You go to all this trouble, the three of you together, just to give us the standard line about letting you handle it?"

"There is nothing to be handled, Agent Lucsly," the Aegis supervisor said. "For any of us."

Lucsly was stunned, speechless. After a moment, Dulmur filled the gap. "Are you serious? A timeline disruption of this magnitude and you want to leave it the way it is?"

"That's exactly what we want," Ducane replied. "Do

nothing to restore the timeline to its original state. Do nothing to punish Kathryn Janeway or her crew for their actions."

"What?" Lucsly gaped. "What's going on here? You're the people who tried to destroy *Voyager* when you thought it would destroy the Earth!"

"An act of desperation," Ducane told him, his manner apologetic, approachable. "And one that many of us fought against. Captain Braxton was always prone to extreme measures."

"You wanted *Voyager* left alone," Dulmur realized. "All this time? That's why you didn't confiscate the mobile emitter, didn't fix the disruptions caused by the Ocampa girl? Why? What possible reason could you have for letting such a menace to the timeline have free rein?"

"It's necessary," Jena Noi said. "Just accept that the way things are now is the way they need to be."

Meneth growled. "Agent Noi," Rodal said sternly.

"Jena," Ducane cautioned.

Lucsly looked back and forth among them, realizing what she was implying. "We're in your timeline now. The one that leads to all of you." Noi lowered her gaze, confirming it. "You're doing this to protect your own existence! It's not about the integrity of the timestream to you, it's just about covering your own asses!"

Noi took a step forward, looking up at him pleadingly. "It's so much bigger than that, Gariff."

"Jena, don't say any more."

"I know, Ducane!" She sighed and turned her gaze back to Lucsly. "Believe me, you'll understand in time. Just be patient. Let things unfold the way they must."

She reached for him, but he pulled back in disgust. For all their clashes over jurisdiction and methods, Lucsly had respected Jena Noi for the work she did, the important role she played in keeping the natural flow of time safe from artificial disruption. What she was asking of him now betrayed everything he stood for, everything he'd thought she stood for. "Janeway has to be punished," he told her. "Even if, for some sick reason, we have to leave this corruption of history uncorrected, we need to send a message to others. You let her get away with this and you set a precedent that could tear reality apart."

"It's not as bad as you think, Gariff. Really. And as for Janeway . . . in the long run, it won't make much difference. For now, though, she has her role to play."

"You've said enough, Agent Noi," Ducane said, growing more stern.

"I don't answer to you!" she snapped. But she subsided and stepped back nonetheless.

Looking satisfied, Ducane went on. "Bottom line, Agents, we don't have to explain anything to you. We tell you to do nothing, and you do nothing. That's all there is to it. Defy our orders, and there are consequences you don't want to become aware of." The face that had seemed so boyish and amiable at first was now revealing a very nasty streak underneath.

Lucsly stared at the uptime agents, seething. Then he turned to Andos. "And you're going along with this?"

"They are all absolutely certain that this is necessary, Agent Lucsly," the Rhaandarite said. "And I have no authority to defy them, or to permit you to do so. I'm sorry, Gariff, but this investigation is hereby closed."

Lucsly held her eyes for a long moment, refusing to look at the uptime agents or even at his own partner. "Fine," he finally said, drawing his temporal tricorder and his secure padd from his pockets and tossing them at Andos's feet. "If this department doesn't protect the timeline anymore, then I have no place here. I resign, effective immediately."

Dulmur gaped, taking Lucsly's arm. "Whoa, hold on, man! Think about this first!"

Lucsly shook off his grip. "It's done." He held Dulmur's eyes for a moment, offering a silent apology, but he was too furious to risk staying around him right now, for fear of what he might say to destroy his only real friendship.

Instead he turned his back on all of them and stepped away. "Now somebody get me out of here. I'm no longer authorized to be in the Vault."

He kept walking down the dark, cold corridor until he found himself in the hallway of his own apartment building. *Noi,* he thought. He reached for the contact on his apartment door and let it slide open.

Inside, he beheld his haven of order—everything perfectly in its place, nothing in excess of requirements save his precious clocks, antique timepieces from across the galaxy, replicas built or originals restored by his own hands. His shrine to the regular, linear perfection of time.

It was all a lie now. Meaningless.

He turned and ran from his apartment, hearing the door close behind him. If he'd stayed another moment, he would've smashed it all apart.

Robinson Township
Tharsis, Mars
Kanya 6, mY 408 (A Thursday)
16:12 UTC
Dulmur finally found Lucsly in one of the seediest dives on Mars, a bar in one of the old underground lava tube

settlements on the flank of Arsia Mons. He almost didn't recognize his partner (he refused to prefix an "ex-"), for Lucsly was actually scruffy and unshaven, a condition Dulmur had never seen him in nor even imagined him capable of.

After maneuvering around a Draylaxian pleasure provider who insisted on displaying her triplicate wares to him, he took a seat on the barstool beside Lucsly. The older man (Dulmur had never noticed until now how gray his hair was becoming) didn't look up from his drink, but said, "Took you long enough to find me. Thirteen days, twe-twenty hours . . . umm . . . nine minutes."

"Ten minutes, pal," Dulmur said gently. "Maybe you've had too much to drink."

"It took you a minute to cross the room."

Dulmur laughed, reassured. Lucsly was still Lucsly, even drunk. Dulmur ordered a shot of bourbon just to be sociable, but he barely sipped it. "Look at you, partner. This isn't you."

"Why should it be? My reality's gone. I don't exist anymore." He shook his head. "A lifetime spent fighting to protect the original timeline . . . fighting cold warriors and Starfleet idiots and bureaucrats who didn't know a parallel history from a hole in their head . . . heads . . . and for what? For nothing, that's what!"

"Lucsly . . ."

"The whole time!" he cried, whirling to face Dulmur, giving him a snootful of foul breath. "They knew the whole time. Noi and Ducane and the rest . . . they were laughing at us."

"They weren't laughing at us," Dulmur said when he was done coughing.

"They told us they were with us. Fighting to keep history pure. And all along, they were working to make sure it got cor . . . twi . . . bent off course right when they needed it. They tricked us!"

Dulmur spoke carefully. "You know . . . it's not like our timeline was ever completely pure to begin with. We knew Agent Daniels's original history didn't include the destruction of Paraagan II or the Xindi attack. We knew the role *Quark's Treasure* played in advancing Earth's spaceflight technology. We knew Ambassador Spock would never have grown up if he hadn't gone back through the Guardian and saved himself as a child. It's never been a completely pure history."

Lucsly winced and put a hand to his forehead. "You're not helping."

"I'm just telling you what we already knew, pal."

"I know. I know." He sighed. "At least before . . . at least I could believe those things were out of our hands. That they were accidents or retrocausal loops, or enemy action that caught the Accordists off guard. At least I thought they were trying to keep things on track as much as possible." He took a look at his drink, then downed it. He coughed a few times. "At least . . . at worst, I could convince myself those things were all in the past, that going forward we were all trying to keep history from changing any more."

"From their point of view, that's what they're doing now," Dulmur said.

Lucsly laughed. "'Now.' What the hell does that word mean anyway? Everything's now to somebody. How does it go? The distinction between past, present, and future is persis . . . no, that's not it . . ."

He trailed off and ordered another drink. For a moment, Dulmur thought he'd forgotten what they were discussing, but then Lucsly said, "But this . . . a Federation citizen committing such an ugly, selfish . . . ugly crime against history . . . and our own people letting her get away with it . . . intervening to make sure she got rewarded for it . . . that's just *petty*."

"Jena said they had a good reason. Their hands are tied by history as much as ours are. We don't get to pick and choose which parts of the past we like. It's our past, and we protect it. Can you really blame her—any of them—for doing the same?"

A heavy sigh. "I guess not." Lucsly stared at his drink for a while, but didn't do anything else with it. "How can I go back, Dulmur? How can I keep doing it if I don't know whether any of it really accomplishes anything?"

"First off," Dulmur told him, "you stop overreacting." Lucsly stared, but Dulmur went on. "You know how I got into this business in the first place? I lost a case. I lost a case, I lost a job, and I thought it was the end of the world. And that brought me to the Department, and I'm grateful for that. But in order to do my job at the Department, I had to learn that you just can't win 'em all. Sometimes the problems are out of your hands. Sometimes all you can do is watch from the sidelines while starship captains muddle through history and try to tidy up the loose ends afterward. Sometimes you have to plead with foreign governments and hope they'll see reason. Sometimes you have to step back and let the Accordists handle things and hope to hell they know what they're doing. And sometimes," he finished, "sometimes, my friend, you just have to take one on the chin."

Lucsly gulped down his drink. "Damn. That sounds like a really lousy job. How do you cope?"

Dulmur smiled. "By remembering what my partner taught me from day one. That we're not heroes. We're not here to save the universe. We're government employees. Our boss gives us a job, and we do the job we're given to the best of our ability, and at the end of the day, if we finish that particular thing and get all the paperwork in order, then we've done everything that's expected of us. You don't drive yourself crazy wondering what it all means, you don't dwell on how your actions will affect the future hundreds of years from now. That's not your department. You just focus on the job in front of you. And if you lose a case, then you file your report, you take your lumps, and you move on to the next file on your desk."

Lucsly thought it over for a long time. "And that's enough? Just being cogs in the machine?"

"Gears in the clock, man. They don't need to know where the hands are pointing, they just need to keep on turning."

Lucsly's eyes grew unfocused, wistful, like he was imagining himself somewhere else. Somewhere peaceful and simple.

Then he looked down at himself in disgust. "Let's get out of here. I need a shave. And a shower. And my suit."

Dulmur happily led him toward the door. "Right this way, partner."

"And I'm three hundred thirty-four hours late to water my fern."

"Welcome back, Lucsly."

PRESENT TIME
STARDATE 59087.2 TO 59155.0

XVII

DTI Headquarters, Greenwich
19:16 UTC

"Come on, Lucsly," Jena Noi said. "Surely by now you understand why we had to let Admiral Janeway's actions go uncorrected. If the past and future Janeways hadn't destroyed the Borg transwarp hub, the Borg wouldn't have been provoked to invade the Federation when they did, and the Caeliar would never have transformed them." She took in their reactions. "I know what you're thinking. Sixty billion dead to preserve our future. But the alternative was death or a worse fate for quintillions more. In virtually every known branch of the future where the Borg threat isn't ended in this century, they become too big to defeat. They assimilate the entire galaxy by 2600 at the latest."

"So every uptime temporal agency," Andos interpreted, "occupies a timeline where the Borg have been eradicated."

"Exactly. If Admiral Janeway hadn't violated the Temporal Prime Directive, whatever her motivations, the entire galaxy would've been lost."

"Why not just go back and prevent the time loop that created the Borg in the first place?" Dulmur asked.

Noi fidgeted. "That produced its own benefits too. You both know how it works. Sometimes a tragic event in history is necessary for the greater good of the future."

"Or maybe it's just that the Caeliar won't let you tamper with those events," Lucsly said. Noi glared at him, but said nothing. "Tell me I'm wrong," the DTI agent insisted.

"I can't tell you anything!" she shouted. Lucsly was taken aback; he'd never seen her lose her cool like that. "You think I want to do this, to shut you down after what they did to Shelan? After you've been violated like this?" She shook her head, eyes glistening. "I know you think I don't respect the DTI, but we're all partners in the Accords. This hurts me too, Gariff. More than you can know." She looked away.

Andos's Rhaandarite perceptions missed nothing. "You know exactly who crased Shelan and why," she accused. "And yet you do nothing to restore her."

"I don't know *why*," Noi said. "Not why it had to be this way. It was so needless."

"Yet you feel culpable for it. You had a hand in it."

At Andos's words, Dulmur charged forward and slammed Noi against the wall. "You? Tell me what you did, dammit!"

"Dulmur, you'd better let me go, you know I'm a lot stronger than I look."

"Tell me!"

"Dulmur!" At Lucsly's shout, his fellow agent froze, then relaxed a moment later, resigned. Lucsly stepped forward and laid a hand on his shoulder, pulling him back, but Dulmur swept his arm around, brushing him off and moving away under his own power.

After a tense moment, Noi looked at Andos. "The fact that I let my guard down enough to let you read that much should tell you how deeply this affects me. But that's all I can give you. That and the promise that if there is anything I can do to bring Shelan back, I will do it. I consider it my personal responsibility."

"That's not good enough," Lucsly said. "To you she's just a pawn on the chessboard of history. This century is *our* home. *Our* jurisdiction. And Shelan was one of ours. You don't have the right to take this from us."

"I don't have the choice to do anything but. The best way to serve *both* our common goals is to keep certain things from ever being found out."

She caught her breath fractionally, hoping they hadn't noticed it, but Andos had. "'Ever'? You're not just talking about something you won't tell us, but about something *you* don't know. Something you don't want to know."

"But you know about Shelan," Dulmur growled. "This is something bigger, isn't it? Whatever these attacks are building up to, it's something massive. Something so big it's got half the factions in the Temporal Cold War up in arms. And you expect us to believe you don't *know* what it's all about?"

Noi gave a wistful smile. "Think about it, Dulmur. What's the best way to keep a secret safe from time travelers?"

"Keep it out of the history books," Lucsly answered. He stared. "Is that what all this is? Are all these random attacks an effort to flush out some secret? Or—" The other possibility was horrific to contemplate. "Are you all just guessing? Striking at random and hoping you hit the right target? What stakes could be so great as to justify such psychotic recklessness with history?"

But Noi had firmed up her self-control and gave him no more. "Trust us, Lucsly. All the full Accordists are working nonstop to protect history. You know that."

"You failed in the Carnelian Regnancy."

"We minimized the impact."

"You failed with Shelan," Dulmur reminded her.

"And I'll fix that mistake if I can," she said. "But wars have casualties. She's far from the first. Just be grateful they limited it to her instead of wiping you all out!"

The agents stood firm, and Noi gave a sad laugh as her golden eyes roved across them. "You aren't going to be talked out of this, are you? I should've known. How could I have thought for a moment that Lucsly and Dulmur could ever be convinced to back down?" She shook her head. "You have no idea how much you two are respected by every time agent who's ever worked with you. It's why we're willing to trust you with any information about the future at all. But if there was ever a time when the secrets had to be kept, this is it."

"Even if it keeps us from heading off a time war in our backyard?" Dulmur challenged. "Even if it costs us more of our own?"

Noi sighed. "If there's anything you can do to help, I will let you know. You deserve that much. But for now, you have to respect the temporal chain of command." She straightened. "By the authority vested in me by the Temporal Accords, Fourth Revision, I hereby order you to halt all investigations into incidents suspected of relating to the Temporal Cold War, until further notice." After a moment, she stepped forward and looked up into Lucsly's eyes. "I'm sorry, Gariff. You're off the case."

"The order is acknowledged and understood," Director Andos said, her tone utterly formal and precise.

"Thank you," Noi said.

A moment later, the DTI agents and director were alone in the room. Silence reigned for a long moment. "Gentlemen," Andos said at length, "you're dismissed."

The two agents left the room together. "You know," Dulmur said, "there's no record of that meeting."

"No, there isn't."

"It's like she never talked to us at all."

"Officially, she didn't."

"So officially, we're still under orders to investigate."

"Mm-hm." Technically, that wasn't so; there was certainly a record uptime, and there were procedures in place under the Accords for penalizing agents who defied the temporal chain of command. But from a linear point of view (the kind Lucsly was most comfortable with), any such records and procedures wouldn't exist for generations yet. And Lucsly had good reasons for favoring that point of view, reasons he'd read in Jena Noi's face. "Someone screwed up. Shelan's gone because someone uptime made a mistake."

"So who are they to tell us they know best?" Dulmur said.

"Who indeed. Let's go."

Vomnin Confederacy Outpost, Axis of Time
Early Warp Age, Anthropocene
Subdirector Vennor Sikran glared at Ranjea and Garcia as they sat across from him at a low Vomnin table, flanking

him. "Why am I the first person you interrogate in this investigation?"

"The principle of proximity," Ranjea said. "Something must have recently changed to precipitate this rash action to blockade the Axis. The greatest recent change in the status quo is the beginning of contact with the Vomnin Confederacy. So it's reasonable to investigate whether you may have done anything—however inadvertently—to trigger such an extreme reaction."

"Neither I nor the Confederacy could possibly benefit from this," Sikran said.

"We're not suggesting you did this," Garcia said. "You're absolutely right—what's happened here is damned inconvenient for you and Lirahn. It blows all your plans right out of the sky."

"That's exactly right," Sikran insisted.

"So maybe that was the whole idea." She leaned forward. "Maybe whatever it was you and Lirahn were trying to do spooked someone so much that they were willing to sabotage the entire Axis to stop it."

Sikran puffed out his cheeks, a Vomnin gesture of confusion. "I can't imagine why."

"What were you trying to get from her?" she pressed, getting more aggressive. Ranjea allowed her to continue; she made a more convincing "bad cop" than he did. "What ancient technology did she have to offer you that was so dangerous to the timeline?"

"Nothing!" Sikran insisted. "You have it all wrong! I was the provider of the artifacts, not the purchaser!"

Garcia broke off, trading a puzzled look with Ranjea. The Deltan agent turned back to Sikran. "Lirahn was seeking to obtain artifacts from you?"

"From the Confederacy, yes." Sikran spread his hands. "It was nothing like you suggest. Nothing dangerous. She was fascinated by our archaeological findings," he said proudly. "Particularly those from her own era. She was able to direct us to new places to search for artifacts, the ruins of Selakar and other contemporary civilizations. In exchange, she wished to obtain selected pieces for her own collection."

"Wait, wait," Garcia said. "She told you where to find half-million-year-old ruins from her own civilization, and bought them from you?"

"Selected pieces, yes. As compensation for her information."

"Didn't you find that a little strange? I mean, she *lived* in the time these artifacts were made. If she wanted them, why not just stay in her own time and get them when they were new?"

The Vomnin tilted his broad head. "Lirahn is a refugee. I assume she no longer had access to her native technology in her own era."

"Then why come so far forward? Why not pick the next era after her own and get them when they were only a few thousand years old, not half a million?"

Sikran laughed. "Young lady, surely you are aware that the value of antiquities appreciates with age."

"And depreciates with condition," Ranjea said. "After so much time, what could be left that was functional?"

"The Selakar built extremely well. True, we found nothing in a functional state, but we could certainly learn much by reverse engineering. We have never encountered such formidable psionic technology."

"So if nothing's left that works," Garcia pressed, "what does she get out of it?"

The Vomnin spread his hands again. "Some collectors have eccentric tastes."

"It didn't really matter to you what her motives were, did it?" Ranjea asked. "She was providing you with the means to locate potentially valuable relics of a highly advanced civilization, and thus augment Vomnin technology—or your own career, or both. So you didn't stop to question what her true purpose might be."

"It's not my place to pry."

"Well, it is ours," Garcia said. "So why don't you tell us exactly what you gave her?"

Sikran called up the items on his padd and showed it to them. "Just fragments of devices, mostly, as you can see."

Ranjea studied them: seemingly simple, decorative constructs of organic crystal, but the Vomnin's analysis showed complex biocircuitry within them. He pointed out one in particular, a lenticular blue crystal about half a meter wide and a hand's width in thickness. "This device seems almost intact."

Sikran looked it over. "Yes. A remarkably strong carbon-based quasicrystal, almost indestructible."

"And your analysis suggests it has psionic properties."

The subdirector nodded. "Possibly, yes. Much technology of that era was psionically based. However, it's useless without its power core, and no such artifact exists."

"Can a substitute be made?"

Sikran shook his head. "The design is unique, an organically grown crystal matrix we have no means to replicate. The instrument is useless."

Ranjea and Garcia exchanged a look. "Maybe

someone else doesn't know that," Garcia said. "Or
doesn't believe it."

"A psionic device," Ranjea said. "Potentially very powerful. Potentially able to augment the psionic powers of a
Selakar?"

Sikran looked nervous. "It could serve as an amplifier
of some kind. But perhaps just for communication?"

"Perhaps. But we know the Selakar have considerable
coercive powers."

Garcia's eyes widened. "Powers that they use to enslave the Siri. And the Siri are gifted engineers."

Ranjea rose to his feet, Garcia right behind him.
"Gifted enough to alter the initial conditions of Axis
timespace?"

She grinned. "Let's go ask them."

DTI Headquarters, Greenwich
Day 19, K'ri'lior, 1148 AS (A Saturday)
09:06 UTC
Considerable consternation reigned at Greenwich when
Agent T'Lem confirmed that Korath, Ronarek, and Nart,
each of whom had quietly excused himself from the scientific exchange tour to pursue a separate errand over the past
week, had all failed to arrive at their reputed destinations
despite records and images to the contrary, records that
had proved to be cunning forgeries. Two weeks of delicate probing since Agent Shelan's erasure from history—
hopefully delicate enough to evade notice by the uptime
agencies—had produced nothing but frustration, and
now this. The possibility that Shelan had been erased to
leave the temporal researchers vulnerable lingered in every
agent's mind.

Yet the consternation became even greater when T'Lem tracked the three physicists down—because of where they were headed. *"I made contact with the Ferengi who arranged their transport—and their cover stories,"* the young Vulcan agent reported over the holomonitor in the situation room, with Andos and multiple agents looking on. *"He proved amenable to pecuniary persuasion, and informed me that their destination was the Rakon system."*

Lucsly and Dulmur exchanged a look. "Tandar Prime," Dulmur said.

"Vard," Lucsly replied.

Attempts to contact Professor Vard revealed that he had recently gone on sabbatical at an undisclosed location, and was incommunicado until further notice. "That can't be coincidence," Dulmur said.

Lucsly turned to Virum Kalnota. "Have your people check the whereabouts of every prominent temporal physicist."

"Right," the Zakdorn said, running for the door. He almost ran into T'Viss on her way in. "There's one, at least," he muttered.

Before long, the researchers turned up one more conspicuous absence. "Doctor Naadri was last seen on a transport to Kantare," Felbog reported. "Fellow passengers recall her presence, but she did not log in at the spaceport on Kantare and has not been seen since."

"Kantare," Agent Yol echoed. "That's in the Tandaran Sector."

"What do you want to bet she's headed for the same place as the others?" Dulmur said.

"Some secret gathering of temporal physicists?" Andos asked.

"Hm," T'Viss said. "They would invite Naadri and Korath but not me? This *must* be Vard's doing. Only he would make such irrational selections."

"Vard is Tandaran," Lucsly said. "Korath is Klingon. Naadri is Paraagan."

"The races targeted by the Suliban Cabal," Dulmur added. "Is this why the Sponsor targeted them all? To prevent this?"

"Why strike so far back?" Yol asked.

"And what about Nart and Ronarek?" Felbog asked. "We know the Typhon Pact was targeted by Romulan Augments believed to be working for the Cabal's Sponsor, but we're aware of no hostilities against the Imperial Romulan State. And we have no evidence that the Ferengi have ever been targeted by the Cabal."

Aleek-Om, the historian, cleared his throat with a chirping noise. "The Ferengi civilization underwent a period of massive upheaval and an extended economic depression . . . beginning in the late twenty-one fifties CE. It impaired their ability to function as a spacegoing power . . . for over a century thereafter. It is conceivable that Cabal agents could have surreptitiously engineered this crisis . . . without the Ferengi ever discovering the true cause."

"We have to get to Tandar Prime," Lucsly said. "Whatever's going on, we need to find out."

Andos nodded. "I'll instruct the *Everett* to stand ready for you and Dulmur. Yol, you may be needed as well."

The agents didn't waste time responding; they just nodded and headed out for the transporter suite.

Along the way, they were met by Clare Raymond. "Dulmur, Lucsly!" she cried, jogging to catch up.

"Not now, Ms. Raymond," Lucsly said. "Time is pressing."

"Time's just the issue," she said, putting herself in their path. "Dina Elfiki contacted me, she said it's urgent. She said to tell you, 'It's happening now.'"

Lucsly turned to Yol. "Go ahead. Brief Captain Alisov." The older Trill nodded and ran on while Lucsly and Dulmur followed Clare downstairs to their guest's quarters.

Elfiki was waiting just inside the door, her sleek body taut with energy. She had a duffel bag slung over her shoulder. "I need to get to the Rakon system," she said. "I need to be there within nineteen hours."

"That's when you get flung back?" Dulmur said.

"I just need to be there."

Lucsly frowned. "Lieutenant, if you have any intention of preventing yourself from being displaced in time . . ."

"Then I would've warned myself when I first got back," she insisted. "I can't undo what's happened, but I'll be damned if you don't let me pick up right where I left off. I have a better chance of making a difference if I'm able to experience the situation from two points of view—and with the benefit of the four extra months of knowledge I've been able to gain."

"Ms. Elfiki, your sentiment is appreciated, but we can't run the risk of anyone seeing you or identifying you until after your younger self has left this timeframe. Once that moment's occurred, you'll be free to—"

"Haven't you noticed what I'm wearing?!" Elfiki interrupted. Looking down, Lucsly realized her outfit, a nondescript civilian garment, was supplemented by an elaborate belt with controls on its buckle. She worked a switch—and shimmered. Once the shimmer was gone,

Dina Elfiki had been replaced by a matronly Bolian woman in the same outfit but a simpler belt. "Portable holographic camouflage," she said in a subtly altered voice. "Just a surface illusion, but as long as I don't get too physical with anyone, nobody will know it's me."

Dulmur laughed. "Well, what do you know. The guy was right after all."

"What?" Lucsly asked.

"Nothing. Long story. Where'd you get that thing?"

She stared at him impatiently. "A holosuite makes a pretty good design and replication facility if you tweak it a bit. You thought I was just going to play games all this time?"

Lucsly gave Elfiki's disguise one more once-over. The eyes and mouth were still recognizable as hers, but they were unlikely to meet anyone who knew Elfiki well enough to tell. "Come on," he said, and he and Dulmur headed out the door. After a second, he paused and looked back at Elfiki. "That means you."

"Oh! Right." The lieutenant seemed almost shocked at being let out of her confinement of sixteen weeks and six days, even though it was at her own insistence. But after a moment, she burst from the room and soon outpaced the agents down the corridor. "Come on, what are we waiting for?"

Lucsly noticed his partner taking an inordinate interest in the sight of Elfiki running away from them. "Damn," Dulmur muttered. "That's one thing she should've disguised better. It's pretty memorable."

Lucsly rolled his eyes. "You're one-point-eight-two times her age."

Dulmur smirked. "Chronological or biological?"

U.S.S. *Everett*, Entering Rakon Star System
20:01 UTC

Even before the *Everett* reached Tandar Prime, it was evident that something was up. "Some kind of subspace interference is affecting sensors," announced the disguised Elfiki, sitting in at the bridge science station. Mercifully, Captain Alisov had worked alongside the DTI long enough not to question why a "civilian" was doing a Starfleet officer's job. "I recommend we proceed with caution into the system."

"Acknowledged," Claudia Alisov said. "Helm, stay above the ecliptic plane for now. Let's minimize the risk of micrometeorite impacts." The last was no doubt added for Lucsly and Dulmur's benefit. "Engage lidar sweeps as backup, increase power to navigational deflectors." The helmswoman acknowledged. "Communications?" Alisov asked.

Ensign Preston at ops replied, "Long-range is iffy, but I'm still getting the local nav beacons five by four." Dulmur knew that one: full volume, not quite full clarity.

"Science, source of the interference?"

Elfiki answered the captain, but her gaze was on the agents. "I'm picking up a chroniton signature," she said. "As yet unable to localize its source."

"Agents?" Alisov said. "Should we continue attempts to contact Professor Vard, or do you want to track down the source of that interference?"

Lucsly and Dulmur exchanged a look with each other and Agent Yol. "The interference," Dulmur said, passing their wordless consensus on to Alisov. "If it isn't Vard and the others, it's probably somebody coming after them."

At reduced speed, it took them hours to narrow in on the source of interference. It didn't seem to be moving, except at normal orbital velocity, which Dulmur chose to take as a good sign; at least it wasn't a Na'kuhl or Vorgon timeship charging in for the kill. But the frown on Lucsly's face—a subtly deeper frown than usual—reminded him that there were nastier things it could be.

Finally, as they closed in on Rakon's innermost Jovian planet as the likely source of the interference, they received a hail. "It's from an interplanetary shuttle, forty-three million kilometers off the port bow," the ops ensign reported.

"On screen," said Alisov.

A young Kantare woman, humanoid with mottling along her temples, appeared on the screen. *"Attention Starfleet vessel. Please break off your approach."*

Dulmur stepped forward, recognizing the woman as one of Vard's graduate students, a survivor of the bombing incident in September. "I know you. You're—"

"Yes, I am," she said. *"But I'd rather not have it stated over an open channel. I know who you're looking for. But if you keep calling attention to them, all could be lost. Please, just go. And please erase all records of this conversation."*

"We can't do that," Lucsly said. "You and . . . the people you're with could be in grave danger. We need to speak to them."

The Kantare sighed. *"He said you'd be stubborn. Very well. Agents Lucsly and Dulmur, you alone may beam over to this shuttle. Matters will be arranged from there."*

Elfiki rose from her seat, catching Dulmur's eye urgently. "Us and one other person," Dulmur said. "A DTI scientist." He gestured her forward into view.

"I was told it had to be just the two of you. Why do you need this person?"

"Hey, you guys get to make arbitrary demands, so do we," Dulmur told her. "Or would you like us to keep scanning and sending out hails for Professor V—"

"All right! All right. But only you three."

The agents traded a nod, then turned to Yol. The Trill agent shrugged, deferring to the inevitable. Just as well; at least one of them should stay up here to ride herd on the Starfleet types. Alisov had certainly earned their trust, first as XO of the *Bozeman,* then as captain of its successor vessel once Morgan Bateson had moved on to command the *Atlas,* but she was still more Starfleet than DTI. "Acknowledged," Lucsly said. "Stand by to receive us."

The screen went dark. As the agents and Elfiki headed for the lift, Alisov rose and asked, predictably, "You sure about this? I'd feel more comfortable if there were a Starfleet presence along."

Elfiki fidgeted a bit. "Don't worry, Captain," Dulmur said. "You'll be with us in spirit."

Undisclosed Moon of Rakon IV
Day 20, K'ri'lior, 1148 AS (A Sunday)
00:18 UTC
The shuttle didn't take them directly to their destination. Rather, the Kantare pilot explained that they would be beamed from the shuttle through a series of transporter relays to a secret location. Vard was being downright fanatical about security.

And it was Vard's party; the flamboyantly attired Tandaran physicist was there to greet the agents and their guest when they materialized, a scowl upon his heavily lined face. "Lucsly, Dombler, what's the meaning of this? I specifically requested just the two of you!"

"You're in no position to give the DTI orders, Professor," Lucsly told him. "Organizing a secret gathering of temporal physicists? Attempting to evade the lawful oversight of the Federation Science Council? You have a lot to answer for."

"My designs, Agent Lucsly, are purely defensive, I assure you," Vard insisted. "Come with me. Come, I'll show you."

The trio followed Vard out into the main chamber of the facility, where a number of others were gathered. "Agents Lucsly and Dumble of the DTI, I believe you know Doctor Naadri of the Paraagan Science Council. These are Korath, Son of Mokan—"

"Monak!" the lanky Klingon boomed.

"—Doctor Ronarek, late of the Imperial Romulan Institute of Research . . ." The Romulan scientist nodded wordlessly. ". . . And Doctor Nark of the Commercial Science Institute of Ferenginar."

"Nart. A pleasure," the Ferengi said with no trace of duplicity. "Are you going to introduce your charming companion?"

Dulmur looked over at Elfiki, who'd been trying to stay in the background. "Uhh, this is Metta," he said, giving the name Elfiki had used aboard the *Everett*. "She's one of our scientists."

Naadri looked her over skeptically. "One of T'Viss's protégés, hm? Good—maybe we can free you from her hidebound thinking."

"Exactly what is going on here, Vard?" Dulmur demanded.

"Well you might ask," Vard replied. "I don't know if it's come to your attention, but there have been a number of troubling incursions from the future over the past several months, most notably the assassination attempt against myself."

"We've noticed," Lucsly said.

"Yes, but what have you *done* about it? What the Department always does—you react. You wait for trouble to strike and then you *investigate* it. Which basically just means you interview the survivors and make sure there's a report filed about it somewhere."

"Whereas we," Korath declaimed, "have chosen to take action! To ready ourselves for the enemy before they strike!"

"It's only prudent to prepare oneself for danger before it comes," Ronarek said. "That's why Professor Vard arranged this gathering—to brainstorm possible defenses against these enemies from the future."

"More than that," Vard added with a chuckle. "Whoever's behind these attacks is no doubt trying to prevent me—err, us—from achieving some great breakthrough. It is my hope that by gathering the most innovative and unconventional minds in the field of temporal physics, we may stumble upon the very achievement our enemies hope to prevent! Who knows—the very time-travel technology they employ may be invented right here at this conference."

Before Dulmur could ask why they'd try to prevent the creation of their own means of time travel, Lucsly spoke. "Our theory is that these attacks are intended to prevent the occurrence of a particular event involving Tandarans, Paraagans, Klingons, and possibly Ferengi and

Romulans," he added pointedly. "All of you are in grave danger just being here."

"Nonsense," Vard said. "Nonsense! You fail to appreciate the Tandaran expertise in temporal security!"

"The chroniton field?" Dulmur asked. "That's you, right?"

"That's one of mine," Naadri said, tapping her inhumanly high forehead. "It should be sufficient to disrupt any temporal incursions."

Lucsly shook his head. "That won't stop someone from going back to before the field was erected. Planting a bomb, a trap, anything."

"Let them," Korath said. "I welcome the chance to face my enemies directly."

"Even if you face them in tiny pieces?" Dulmur asked.

Vard laughed. "You worry yourselves unduly, my friends. The future will never find out about this meeting! Even if history should record in general terms that it occurred, they will never be able to find exactly when or where. You see, we Tandarans have been aware for centuries of the need to maintain security against enemies from the future—enemies who can read our histories, unearth our artifacts, study our declassified files."

Lucsly frowned. "Centuries? Wait—you knew that the Suliban Cabal had backing from the future?"

"Of course we did!" Vard crowed. "But you see, we kept that fact out of the history books! We went to great lengths to ensure that the information was not kept in any records, and limited to only a very few trustworthy minds. Oh, there were some early oversights. A couple of our personnel let the knowledge slip to your Jonathan Archer, in their overzealous attempts to ply him for information about the Cabal. But later on, our diplomats met secretly with Archer and Earth officials and persuaded them to redact their records, to conceal the fact of our awareness."

"But why?" Dulmur asked.

"Well, isn't it obvious? Whoever the Cabal's backers were—will be—they must have targeted the Tandarans in the past because they are aware of our modern expertise in temporal physics. Their aim must have been to undermine our civilization before we could achieve that level of temporal knowledge." He grinned. "But if they knew we were aware of the true motives behind the Suliban Cabal's attacks, they would realize the truth: that it was those attacks that *inspired* our ongoing research into temporal physics in the first place!"

Dulmur's eyes widened. "So they don't realize that by attacking you, they're causing the very thing they were trying to prevent!"

"Exactly! The strategic logic of the time loop. If they knew their attempts to prevent our temporal research had backfired, they would go back and prevent their own agents from attacking us in the past, thereby leaving us vulnerable in the future. So our best defense is to make it a self-fulfilling, or rather self-negating, prophecy. Secretly turn the foe's actions to your advantage, so that they cause your desired history in the very effort to nullify it!"

Lucsly was skeptical. "You're making an awfully big assumption. What if the Cabal wasn't attacking Tandar to prevent your future temporal research?"

"Oh, it's no assumption, Lucsly. We were given guidance by a temporal agent from the distant future. He informed us, err, elliptically, of our great destiny in the field of temporal physics." Vard spread his arms to take in their surroundings. "A destiny which we, today, may well be about to fulfill!"

"You're taking too great a risk, Professor!" Dulmur cried. "We were able to track Naadri's chroniton field. It's causing systemwide subspace interference."

"By its very nature," Naadri said, "the field is impossible to localize to its source."

Dulmur saw "Metta" start to say something, then fall silent. While Lucsly went on debating with Vard, Dulmur moved over to the holographically disguised Elfiki and asked, "What is it? You know something."

"You'll find out soon enough," she said.

"If it's important—"

"Just wait for it," she said. "And be ready."

02:58 UTC

Once it became clear that there was no talking Vard, Korath, or Naadri out of their participation in this conference (and that Nart was too agreeable by nature to go against the consensus), there was nothing the agents could do but take Elfiki's advice and wait—and listen while the physicists went about their discussions. Naadri talked with Vard about using Paul Manheim's research into nonlinear quantum physics and multidimensional cosmology to create an "Everett-Wheeler radio" for communication with parallel timelines, while Vard offered insights from his brief study of his alternate self's timeline-jumping apparatus eight years, seven months, and four weeks before. Meanwhile, Naadri brushed off Korath's attempts to speak to her about the weapons applications of her theoretical negative entropy or "anti-time" phenomenon. Once Korath had given up on that, he plied Nart for information about the Ferengi's unsuccessful attempts to develop a chroniton-based transporter. Korath engaged him in a discussion about the functional similarities between transporter emitters and deflector arrays and began to speculate about the possibilities of something he dubbed the "chrono-deflector."

After a while, Dulmur just tuned it out. These abstract theoretical discussions wouldn't lead to anything disastrous in the next few hours, and Lucsly would let him know if he thought they came up with anything threatening enough to the future that the Cabal's Sponsor or other anti-Accordist factions might be motivated to attack.

What drew his attention at last was when one of Vard's grad students came running into the main hall. "Professor!" the young Benzite cried. "There's a starship in orbit of the moon! A big one!"

"What? Impossible!" Vard exclaimed. "Whose is it?"

"I think it's Starfleet. I can't be sure, the static is so bad."

"Nonsense," said Naadri. "My chroniton field shouldn't generate that much interference!"

"Incompetent child," Vard muttered. "Let me see this for myself."

Dulmur and Lucsly followed Vard and the others to the sensor room. Indeed, the levels of interference had become severe, but it was clear enough that a large starship of Starfleet configuration was indeed orbiting the moon. "Your ship?" Nart asked.

Lucsly shook his head. "Too big." He pointed. "They're trying to hail us."

"No response!" Vard said. "We can't let anyone know we're here!"

"If they didn't already know we were here," Dulmur said, "they wouldn't be hailing us."

Suddenly, the transporter pad lit up. "They're trying to send someone down!" the Benzite said.

Dulmur's eyes widened. "Will they be able to get through all this interference?"

"With our transporter acting as a focus and amplifier, yes," Vard said. "Ohh, this is not how I wrote it on my to-do list!"

Three figures shimmered into being on the transporter pad, resolving as Starfleet officers, two human women and a massive Klingon male that Dulmur recognized. The Klingon stepped forward, taking them in. "You are DTI?"

"That's right," Dulmur said. "Agent Dulmur."

His partner stepped forward. "Lucsly. DTI. You're Commander Worf of the *Enterprise*."

"That is correct." He gestured toward his teammates. "This is Lieutenant Jasminder Choudhury, chief of security." The tall, elegant Indian woman nodded in greeting. "And our science officer, Lieutenant Dina Elfiki."

The two agents traded a look. *Here we go,* Dulmur thought. He'd wondered why "Metta" had declined to enter the room with them. As for this earlier Elfiki, she noticed the agents' reaction to the sight of her, but didn't seem to find it strange. She was undoubtedly used to men's stares.

Vard didn't even seem to notice her, however. "What are you doing here?" he demanded. "How did you find this place?"

Worf loomed over him. "The question is, what are *you* doing here? Are you responsible for the temporal disruptions?"

"What temporal disruptions?"

"All we've done is generate a simple chroniton field," Naadri said.

"Then you claim to know nothing of the escalating series of temporal anomalies that have manifested throughout the sector over the past eight hours?"

"The field blocks long-range communications," Dulmur said.

"What kind of anomalies?" Lucsly asked.

"There are reports of events repeating themselves," Choudhury said, "much like the Manheim Event of 2364. We've personally experienced future echoes—glimpses of our own future actions. One Kreetassan ship was nearly torn apart by a severe time dilation differential it passed through."

"The incidents are becoming more frequent by the hour," Worf said. "And they center on this star system."

"As soon as we arrived here," Elfiki said, "we detected spacetime ripples emanating from this moon. Your facility is radiating time distortions that just keep getting more intense."

"That doesn't make any sense," Naadri insisted. "There's nothing being done here that could generate such effects."

"Not yet," Lucsly said.

A moment later, Vard caught on. "He said the

incidents are increasing over time. Like . . . negative echoes of something that is *about* to happen!"

"Something that resonates both forward and backward in time," Korath added.

"What could do something like that?" Worf asked.

Vard gazed at the DTI agents, his tone more subdued than Dulmur had ever heard it. "Something . . . very powerful. And very dangerous. We need to get to the lab."

The group hurried out of the sensor suite and down the corridor. But when they passed through the doorway to the physics lab, they found themselves back in the sensor suite, watching themselves hurry out the door. Dulmur spun to see only a solid wall behind him. He recognized the way his brain glossed over the experiential discontinuity of the transition. "A Manheim loop," he said. "The effects are happening here now."

The others traded uncertain looks. "Shall we try again?" Choudhury suggested.

"We cannot stay here," Worf replied. "Perhaps if we try a different route."

They headed out more carefully this time, with Vard leading them on a more roundabout path through the compound's corridors. But as they neared an intersection, Dulmur heard an unfamiliar sound from the connecting corridor. Worf and Choudhury tensed, exchanging a look that confirmed Dulmur's suspicion: it was some kind of weapons fire.

The connecting corridor lit up with energy bolts. Dulmur heard screams, and the footsteps of a running figure. Oddly familiar footsteps.

The figure turned the corner and skidded to a halt. It was Agent Marion Dulmur. "Whatever you do," the other Dulmur cried to the group, "don't go down that corridor!"

Then a beam struck him and he screamed as his body disintegrated into hot vapor.

Dulmur and the others wasted no time heading the other way.

Colloquium of Progress Outpost, Axis of Time
Late Tarantian Age, Upper Pleistocene Epoch
Questioning soon revealed that a number of Siri—notably
one matching the description of Vikei, Garcia's guide and
resistance contact from before—had been sighted down
near the creation point of the Axis, way back in the Lower
Pliocene, not long before the lockdown occurred. But
they had evidently scattered along the Axis in the time
since. Tracking them down required some good old-
fashioned legwork, questioning denizens of the Axis for
information on their whereabouts, while Heather Petersen
conferred with the Axis science teams to try to devise solutions to the blockade. The agents had to be careful with
their questions; the Axis denizens were largely angry and
panicked about being trapped here, and if the Siri were
blamed for the crisis, there could be mass violence against
the lot of them.

Finally, Councillor Oydia got a tip from one of her
fellow Caratu that Vikei had been spotted aboard the
outpost of their Colloquium. Ranjea and Garcia made
their way promptly, accompanied by the red-scaled Talich
security chief, Alenar.

After getting a lead from one of the locals—a massive
alien called a D'drauk'k, reminding Garcia of a six-limbed
spider-ape with sabertooth tusks—the young agent stared

behind her at the very distinctive being. "Only eighteen thousand years between us," she said to Ranjea as they trailed the Talich officer through the outpost's corridors, "and we know nothing about these guys. What happened to them?"

"We are far from Federation territory," Ranjea reminded her. "We never knew the Vomnin existed until less than two years ago."

"Still," she said. "Councillor Temarel's from not much further in *our* future, and she's never heard of the Federation—even though she's got to be descended from Vulcans or Romulans or both." Her brow furrowed. "Is what we're fighting for really that ephemeral? Does it really make so little difference in the long run?"

"Time travel can give a skewed sense of perspective," Ranjea said. "What we do matters to us. To our friends, our neighbors, our families, our children. How is that less meaningful than its impact on those tens of millennia removed from us?"

She smiled, taking his hand. "You have a point." Then her smile faded as she noted the tension in his grip. The prospect of being trapped here, cut off from Delta, must be constantly on his mind, though he did his best to manage it. She squeezed his hand more firmly, wordlessly reminding him that she'd always be there for him. She was an expert on being cut off from one's own time, after all. She sensed his gratitude in return.

Ahead of them, Alenar halted and made a hissing noise, studying his hand scanner. "I think I've spotted our Siri."

The scanner led them into the outpost's maintenance tunnels, forcing Alenar and Ranjea to hunker down, though they both moved with impressive grace and stealth despite their confinement. Garcia's smaller size and extensive tunnel-crawling experience made it easier for her.

Soon they came out into a dimly lit chamber to behold a familiar blue-and-brown carapace. Vikei's eyestalks were focused in all directions, so there was no possibility of sneaking up; he scuttled for cover as soon as he saw them. But once Alenar could stretch his powerful legs again, he dashed forward with startling speed for his bulk and overtook the Siri, whirling so the smaller creature slammed into his heavy, outstretched tail. Vikei fell back, dazed, and soon found himself surrounded. Garcia was concerned that the crustacean might use his sharp pincers as weapons, but Vikei instead fell passive.

"Please," the Siri said. "You must not take me in. If I am questioned by Lirahn, all will be lost."

"Why did you sabotage the Axis, Vikei?" Garcia asked. "To trap Lirahn?"

"Yes." He spoke urgently. "I understand the consequences for the others, but we were forced to take desperate action."

"The device Lirahn acquired from the Vomnin," Ranjea said. "What was it?"

Vikei looked around nervously. Perhaps sensing that the diminutive Siri was no longer a threat, Alenar drifted back, giving him more space. Vikei sidled a bit closer to the agents. "I have told you that the Selakar have great power to insinuate their will into the minds of others."

Garcia nodded. "Mm-hm."

"But it takes time, and can only work on so many beings at once. As a race, the Selakar ruled hundreds of worlds, but individually they are limited. It made them vulnerable in the Great Psionic War."

"That was why they were defeated?" Ranjea asked.

"Ultimately, yes," Vikei said. "But only by the narrowest margin.

"As their enemies eroded their power, stole worlds from them by the dozen, the Selakar initiated a project to develop an ultimate weapon—a psionic amplifier that would augment their mind-control abilities thousands of times over, allowing them to instill permanent, absolute obedience in any mind with a single thought. They intended to use these weapons to enslave their enemies, or if their enemies' minds proved too strong to enslave, to turn their own servant races against them. And once the war was over, their foes destroyed, the Selakar would make enough of the amplifiers to let them rule the entire galaxy."

"So what stopped them?" Garcia asked.

"The Siri did," Vikei replied with pride. "We have always had more ability to resist the Selakar's will than we let on. But we played along to preserve our cover, clandestinely helping their enemies when we could. My people were trusted enough to assist in the creation of the prototype amplifiers. Recognizing the magnitude of the threat, the Siri who worked on the project informed the empire of Arret of its existence and helped Arretian agents stage a raid to capture the prototypes. Many lives were lost. The Siri agents were exposed, their whole genetic lines exterminated to eliminate the 'flaw' of resistance. They knew this would be the consequence, but they accepted it for the greater good of all life. And it was worth it, for the amplifiers were taken, their designers killed."

"But the amplifiers were not destroyed," Ranjea said. "I imagine the opposition hoped to employ them for their own ends?"

"Those who tried were driven mad. It was tailored exclusively for Selakar. So one of the protoypes was destroyed. The release of psionic energy from its destruction killed half a planet and wiped the minds of the rest.

"After seeing their destructive potential, the Arretians chose to keep the remaining two prototypes as weapons of last resort against their enemies. They were stripped of their power cores and buried deep beneath the crust of two Arretian colony worlds, in impenetrable bunkers. The Selakar tried for decades to recover them, but every attempt to penetrate their defenses failed. There was no way to retrieve them short of cracking open the planets, and while the Selakar would have happily done that, it would have risked destroying the amplifiers.

"Soon thereafter, the Arretians shattered the Selakar's power once and for all, and they were hunted down across the galaxy. As far as I know, only Lirahn and her cronies survived by finding the Axis."

Garcia threw her partner a look. "Where she found she could reach the distant future, hundreds of thousands of years after her time. After the Arretians had fallen." She recognized the name as an alternative designation for the progenitor race that scholars tended to call Sargonians, after their last surviving leader.

Ranjea nodded. "And enough time for even the most robustly built vault or bunker to fall prey to erosion. To decay enough for the Vomnin to penetrate it."

"Yes," Vikei confirmed. "Mercifully they only found one, but it is enough." Garcia wondered if the other had played a role in the final destruction of the Arretians. "With it, her will alone could enslave entire planets."

"Wait, wait," Garcia said. "If she's got the amplifier now, why aren't we already her brain puppets?"

"It lacked a power source," Ranjea recalled.

"Yes," said Vikei. "The amplifiers were new, but their power cores were fairly standard. Yet the cores would not be able to survive half a million years. A few thousand at best."

Garcia shook her head. "It's always the battery that goes first."

The Siri leaned toward them urgently. "This is why we had to close off the Axis. If she returned to our own time, she could recover a suitable power core and activate the amplifier. She would become a virtual goddess, impossible to resist."

The agents paused to take in Vikei's story. Finally, Ranjea said, "Vikei, no one can deny the validity of your cause, or your dedication and courage in fighting for freedom. But we cannot support your methods. By closing off the Axis, you've deprived everyone here of *their* freedom. Thousands of people, many of whom may have important roles to play in the history of their eras."

"I regret that," Vikei said. "But the sacrifice is small compared to what the galaxy would lose if Lirahn were set free. The Axis must be her prison, even if all of you must be trapped as her wardens."

"There's gotta be another way, Vikei," Garcia said. "We can take the weapon from her, lock her up."

"No. Even without it, she can still bend anyone near her to her will. I have tried to murder her in her sleep, but just being near her, I find myself unable to contemplate harming her. It is only at a distance that I can disobey her. Her defenses are too strong.

"That is why you must let me go. If I am taken in, she . will find me and force me to take her to the device."

"The device you used to rejigger the Axis?" Garcia asked. "You still have it?"

Vikei turned all six eyestalks away. "I will say no more. The less you three know, the better." His stalks froze, then darted around the chamber. "Three . . . there were three of you!"

Garcia and Ranjea looked around. Alenar's burly red frame was nowhere to be seen. "Get me out of here!" Vikei cried. "He's gone to tell Lirahn!"

The agents didn't question further. If the Talich had snuck away rather than openly reporting, he must not have been reporting to the Council. Unless it was someone on the Council who was firmly, secretly, in Lirahn's clutches, as Shiiem suspected Oydia of being. "Let's go," Ranjea said.

But they didn't get far before they were confronted by Alenar and two other armed guards—with Lirahn backing them up, clad in a stylish but functional green jumpsuit. The agents drew their phasers. Garcia's weapon hand trembled; she hated the thing, she didn't want to use it, certainly not on someone as charming and lovely as Lirahn . . .

Okay, she oversold that one, Garcia thought, regaining her focus and bringing the weapon to bear. She couldn't bring herself to point it directly at Lirahn, but the reluctance didn't extend to the guards.

Ranjea tapped her shoulder. "This way." They retreated with Vikei scuttling behind them, keeping their phasers on the guards. Garcia felt a reluctance to move, a mental pressure to stay where she was, but it wasn't strong enough to stop her. *That's why she needs the guards. Her power's subtle, insinuating. It takes time.*

But the three guards were totally under her power. "Go," Lirahn said, and the three of them charged forward into the line of fire. Two of them fell stunned, one from each of the agents' beams, but Alenar dodged, circled, and spun, his heavy tail taking Garcia in the side and sending her flying into Ranjea, knocking him over. In agony, she dropped her phaser, and a kick from the Talich disarmed Ranjea as well.

Vikei was scuttling for the exit, but Lirahn strode forward, her eyes wide and gleaming. The Siri's retreat slowed to a crawl. "No!" he cried, but it was feeble, strained. "No . . . no . . ."

"No, of course not," Lirahn said. "You don't want to keep any secrets from me. You know how I cherish our openness. And you know how much I miss the stars of home. You wouldn't want to keep me from them, would you?"

"Nnnoo . . ."

"Good little one. Now tell me where the device is and how to use it." Her hands went to the sides of the Siri's upper carapace, where its brain must be.

Garcia wanted to scream at Lirahn to stop, but she seemed to be too busy screaming in pain. She was pretty sure Alenar had broken her arm. But a moment later, she felt a sense of euphoric detachment overcome her. The pain was still there, but it didn't seem to matter. It was just in her body, and she was beyond her body, inhabiting the whole room. She realized Ranjea was clutching her hands, easing her pain in the Deltan way.

"There," Lirahn said after a time. "That's a good Siri. You won't defy me again, will you?"

"No, mistress," said Vikei. "Do you need my help undoing what I've done?"

"No. I've taken everything I need from your mind.

You just sleep now. Sleep as long as you want. No need to ever wake up again." Vikei clattered to the floor. From her detached place, Garcia found it sad.

"Lirahn." It was Ranjea. He was no longer holding her hands, but had stood and was walking slowly toward the Selakar. Garcia started to become more aware of her body again, though she was still too euphoric to care about the pain. And she was *very* aware of Ranjea's body. Distantly, she noticed Alenar starting to move forward to block Ranjea and Lirahn waving him off. But mainly she noticed Ranjea and how very enthralling he looked from this angle, below and to the rear. And she noticed that Lirahn's eyes were just as fixed on him as hers were.

"Lirahn," he said, his voice low and sultry, making her skin tingle. "There's no need for us to be at odds. Why don't you come with me? We'll go somewhere nice and private."

Pheromones, she realized. *He's pulling out all the stops, seducing her.* She was grateful—though not without regret—that Ranjea was moving away from her, the potency of his allure diminishing slightly with distance. She just hoped it was hitting Lirahn commensurately harder.

"Ohhh, you dear man," Lirahn purred. Her hands went around his neck, stroking his smooth head and strong shoulders. "I'd be happy to take you with me when I reclaim my empire. You'd be a charming novelty—literally."

"Your empire is gone, Lirahn. A relic of history. Why live in the past? Let go of it. Use that great potential to build something new."

She chuckled. "You wish to stop me from altering your history. But my dear . . . how do you know what that history is? You've forgotten so much. You never even heard of the Selakar, though we ruled an arm of the galaxy for millennia." She smiled. "So how do you know the restoration of the Selakar Empire under Lirahn the Magnificent isn't already a part of your forgotten prehistory? You could be changing the past if you *don't* let me go."

Ranjea froze. After a moment, Garcia began to think more clearly, realizing his seductive efforts were weakening. She saw uncertainty in his eyes.

Lirahn laughed. "Got you," she said. She gave Ranjea a deep kiss, then sauntered away with a girlish giggle. Ranjea started to move forward, but Alenar and the other, now-recovered guards interposed themselves, holding them at bay. As they retreated, Lirahn's giggle intensified, moving dangerously toward "evil cackle" territory. *Well, maybe that wasn't a cliché yet in her time*, Garcia thought through the returning pain.

Ranjea closed his eyes for a moment, gathering himself. Then he hurried over to Garcia's side. "Come on, we need to get you medical help."

"No," she said. "Make sure Vikei's all right."

"That's next on the list," he reminded her. She remembered her training: see to your own teammates first, since they can't help others if they aren't intact themselves.

They checked Vikei, finding him alive but deeply comatose. "Could she be right?" Garcia asked. "Do we have to let her go to save history? Let her turn billions into her absolute slaves?"

Ranjea met her eyes. But he had no answer for her.

Vomnin Confederacy Outpost, Axis of Time
Early Warp Age, Anthropocene

With transporters not being an option, the wounded had to go to the nearest suitable medical facility by shuttle.

The Colloquium-era outpost was suspect due to Lirahn's influence, so Ranjea chose the Vomnin outpost where the Starfleet shuttles were docked. Luckily for Garcia, one of the stranded *Asimov* personnel was a medic, so she didn't have to chance getting her arm patched up by someone who'd never treated a human before. While the medic worked, Garcia studied the historical database in her temporal tricorder, correlating it with the Axis's own records from periods following Lirahn's. Nearby, Ranjea sat with Vikei, trying to connect with his mind enough to coax him back to consciousness. Subdirector Sikran hovered nearby, trying to look important.

Eventually, Ranjea came over to her. "How are you feeling?"

"What? Oh, that. Good as new. How's Vikei?"

"Resting normally now. He'll awaken when he's ready."

She sighed. "Great."

"Found anything?"

"Nothing useful," she said, shaking her head. "Yeah, there's evidence of great swaths of the galaxy being dominated by powerful empires half a million years ago. We already knew about some of them—Sargon's people, the Talosians, Ma-aira Thenn . . . but there's no way to know for sure if one of the other empires was Lirahn's."

"No indication that one empire arose from the ashes of the others?"

"Sure, more than once. Vikei talked about a Great Psionic War, but the one he knows is probably just one of several over a couple of millennia. But was it the final one? Hard to say."

"Hm." Ranjea pondered it silently.

"So what's the procedure in a case like this, boss? How do we decide what to do when we don't know which action will change history?"

"Normal procedure is to err on the side of inaction. The fewer entities who intervene in the past, the less risk of disrupting it. If history *is* changed, then hopefully the DTI in that new timeline will discover the change in its shielded files and be able to do something about it."

"If there *is* a DTI. I don't know about Delta, but half a million years ago was kind of an important time for hominid life on Earth. If Lirahn did change things, with the kind of power that amplifier would give her, I wouldn't be too sure our own past would go unaffected."

"That's a good point." He pondered. "It could be argued that, since all times are simultaneous within the Axis, whatever Lirahn would do upon leaving it hasn't happened yet. From our perspective, it's still the future. So whatever we choose to do would be part of the original, natural course of history rather than a retroactive alteration."

Garcia thought it over. "If Lirahn does reopen the Axis," she said solemnly, "maybe we find a way to re-blockade our part of it. Keep anyone from returning to our own time. Then the two timelines won't be entangled and the original won't collapse. Whatever Lirahn does, at worst it'd just create a stable parallel history."

"Good thought," Ranjea said, "but it won't work. There's already been two-way exchange between the Axis and our time. The entanglement already exists."

"Damn it!"

"You needn't worry about it," Sikran said, having just received a report on his wrist-mounted padd. "Council security has blockaded the downtime end of the Axis. There's no way Lirahn can get past them."

"Don't bet on it," Garcia said. "She's got a lot of friends on the Council."

"Not anymore. Oydia has been discredited and Damyz has renounced Lirahn. Shiiem's side is making the choices now. And I've sent our own ships to join in the blockade," he added. "Along with numerous others, true, but the Vomnin are . . . highly motivated to stop her." On his broad face, anger vied with embarrassment over how he'd allowed Lirahn to use him.

His padd pinged with an update. "They've spotted her! Here, hold on." A keystroke on his padd sent the sensor feed to the medical bay's wall screen. The occupants watched as a small, ornate ship, which the display called out in Vomnin script as Lirahn's, drew toward the vast, universe-straddling construct of the hub station. While there were broad gaps in its lattice to allow even large ships to pass through, those gaps were all occupied by ships of various configurations, including several Vomnin craft. Lirahn's shuttle veered away, trying to find an opening, but none presented itself. She opened fire on the blockading ships, knocking two of them out of formation, though fortunately it was a short limp to a safe dock for both pilots. And more ships simply flew in to take their place. Then someone in the blockade signaled the others, instructing them in how to expand and link their shields. Soon there was an impenetrable barrier facing Lirahn. She flew laterally across the pocket spacetime, searching for a weak spot, but all she did was repeatedly cross back over her own path. After firing a few more futile shots, Lirahn turned and flew back in the uptime direction.

"Yes! We beat her!" Sikran crowed.

"But she's not slowing down," Garcia said, noting that she was thrusting uptime even faster. The image feed switched to follow her; a few ships tried to apprehend her as she flew near, a few stations tried to use their low-powered docking tractors, but she simply veered laterally and spiraled around them, taking advantage of the closed but borderless geometry of the Axis's lateral dimensions. In essence, she had infinite space to either side but was still following essentially a straight-line path uptime. "There aren't enough ships up here to catch her! Everyone's clustered at the hub!"

"What does it matter?" Sikran said. "She can't get to the downtime terminus, so she can't reopen the Axis. We can apprehend her at our leisure."

"No!" The cry came from Vikei, now awake and agitated. "You must stop her! You cannot let her reach the terminus!"

Garcia ran to his side. "It's all right, Vikei. The only terminus she's heading for is the uptime one, where the supernova destroys it a million and a half years from now. She can't change the Axis's beginning from its ending."

"You don't understand. *All* external times are simultaneous within the Axis. Its creation, its destruction—they are the same moment relative to an internal observer. So there is no preferred direction of causality here. Time is completely symmetrical. As far as the fabric of Axis timespace is concerned, its destruction is functionally interchangeable with its creation!"

Ranjea's jaw dropped. "You mean Lirahn could use your device to modify the timespace parameters from either terminus?"

"Exactly!"

Garcia gazed up at her partner. "Boss, we're close enough to intercept her. Should we even try?"

"You must!" Vikei said.

Garcia winced. "Look . . . I sympathize about your people and all, but we don't know . . ."

"The threat is more immediate than that. The two termini are symmetrical in effect, but not in energy. The supernova that destroys the Axis is vastly more powerful than the forces that created it. But our device is calibrated for the energy levels at the creation point."

"So what happens," Ranjea asked, "if that device taps into the energies at the destruction point?"

"Its effects would be greatly amplified. The dimensional interface at the uptime terminus was delicately balanced by the Axis's creators to allow in just enough of the supernova's energies to provide a power source for its occupants. If Lirahn taps into that energy and uses the device to increase the permeability of the interface, it could create a feedback loop. A runaway release of energy."

Garcia swallowed. "You mean . . . a nuclear blowtorch, clear down the Axis. Vaporizing everyone."

"Worse," Vikei said. "The supernova's energies would blow open the interspatial portals, spreading them out across parsecs. Every neighboring world in every era the Axis connects to would be engulfed in lethal radiation pouring out of subspace."

Ranjea straightened. "No choice," he said. "We *have* to stop her now."

Garcia stood and put her hand on her phaser. "Can't say I'm unhappy about that."

XIX

Third Moon of Rakon IV
Exact Time Undefinable

Albert Einstein once reportedly said that "Time is what keeps everything from happening at once." Unfortunately, that was no longer true in Professor Vard's lunar facility. Something had turned the timeline into a multidimensional knot. Past, present, and future had become interchangeable, completely nonlinear. Lucsly deeply hated that. It left him feeling adrift, unsure of himself.

Dulmur, conversely, was toughing it out surprisingly well, considering he'd seen himself vaporized mere subjective minutes before. He didn't even flinch when the agents and the *Enterprise* away team turned a corner to find themselves in a darkened, chilled corridor, too cold to be in the same time frame as the one they'd just left. Indeed, Lucsly looked back to see that while the corridor they'd just left was still there—for quantum entanglement kept them anchored to the facility as it moved through space—it was now just as dark and lifeless. The scientists, who'd been right behind them, had disappeared.

"Lieutenant," Commander Worf said as soon as he noticed. Lucsly wondered which lieutenant he was speaking

to, but somehow the security chief, Choudhury, understood his intent and raised her tricorder.

"This way," she said, conveying urgency without
losing her serene manner. The DTI agents ran after the
Starfleet team, catching up with them at a closed door
that Worf pulled open with pure muscle. A charnel stench
assaulted them, and they entered the room, a lab of some
sort, to find the bodies of Vard and the other physicists, all
dead and terribly burned.

"Oh, no," said Elfiki—the one with the *Enterprise*
team, for the disguised one was nowhere to be seen. "Did
we jump forward? Are these . . ."

Dulmur checked his temporal tricorder. "We're in the
future, all right. About ten hours."

"Then it can't be the people we just left," Choudhury
said. "These bodies have been dead at least a day."

"An alternate timeline?" Worf asked, prompting Lucsly
to remember the commander's prior experience with the
concept.

"Mm-hm," Dulmur said, continuing his scan. "The
quantum signature's subtly different."

"Look here," Choudhury said, indicating a Romulan corpse. "I thought this was Doctor Ronarek . . . but
it's someone else." She ran her tricorder over the body.
"Odd . . . this Romulan had genetic augmentations."

Lucsly stared. "Let me see." They synched tricorders,
transferring the data. Lucsly checked the readings against a
particular pattern of augmentation that DTI tricorders were
routinely programmed to recognize. The readout confirmed it,
and Lucsly nodded at Dulmur to confirm what they both suspected: that the augmentations in this Romulan showed many
of the same genetic signatures as those of the Suliban Cabal.

"That explains the who," Dulmur said.

"Mm-hm. And the how. Ronarek isn't here."

"So he must be a ringer. Impostor?"

"Or a deep-cover spy." With time travel, you could easily enough create an authentic, decades-long cover for a sleeper operative.

Worf looked irritated—well, more than usual. "A spy for whom? The Typhon Pact?"

"It's a long story," Dulmur said. "Suffice to say, we've gotta get back to our own scientists before Ronarek turns on them."

"I'm reading a temporal fluctuation through that door," Elfiki said, pointing to the far end of the lab. "No way to tell where it leads."

"But we cannot stay here," the Klingon said. "Proceed with caution."

They moved through in a tight formation, maintaining physical contact to ensure no one was left behind. Lucsly brought up the rear, gingerly holding on to the material of Dulmur's sleeve. Once they were through, they found themselves back in a warm, lighted corridor. Lucsly tried in vain to detect the actual process of transition, but his confused brain insisted on perceiving the doorway itself as the interface between time frames. He hated how *contrived* that felt.

The sounds of a firefight echoed down the corridor. Typically, perversely, the Starfleeters ran *toward* it, leaving the agents little choice but to follow. Soon they spotted Vard, Naadri, Korath, Nart, and all three grad students crouching behind an overturned storage cabinet. Beyond, a two-way firefight raged, but Lucsly had to keep his head low and couldn't make out the combatants. "There you are!" Vard hissed. "Where have you been for the past twenty minutes?"

Obviously more time had passed for the scientists than for the others, but there was no time to explain that now. "We have to warn you," Dulmur said. "Doctor Ronarek is—"

"We know," Korath interrupted. "The traitor smuggled in a team of assassins in some kind of dimensional pocket."

"Like the Shanial Cabochons, or the containment device for the Koa homeworld," Naadri added. "It let him *carry* them in, hidden in a clothing decoration!"

"So much for your precious chroniton field," Korath sneered.

"The field should have disrupted its dimensional metric," Naadri countered. "Whatever exotics it uses to counter stress-energy divergence must be incredibly robust."

"Can we deal with that later?" Dulmur asked. "If we're all here, who's shooting back at them?"

"Tricorder," Choudhury said to Worf. He handed his over. She interfaced it with hers, then tossed it carefully over the storage cabinet. It landed almost perfectly, its visual sensors sending an image of the battle to Choudhury's tricorder.

Lucsly saw the Romulan Augments in the distance, led by Ronarek. Or perhaps "led" was not the word. The gray-haired physicist/spy was speaking to a blurry humanoid figure projected in miniature above a handheld holocommunicator. The echoing words the figure spoke were unclear from this distance, but it was clear that Ronarek was following his orders. Lucsly stared intently, realizing who the humanoid figure must be. This was the twenty-eighth-century Sponsor of both the Suliban Cabal and the Romulan Augments. The being who had exploited innocent species, fomented wars, and destroyed entire colonies in the past in pursuit of his nebulous goals.

This was the being who had violated the DTI by wiping one of its own from existence. And he was almost within reach. If only there were a way to get to that communicator. Lucsly had some questions he was determined to ask.

But the battle was raging too fiercely for that. The Romulans were using all their augmentations in the fight, climbing on the walls and ceiling as they dodged blue energy beams, camouflaging themselves in an attempt to elude detection. Some were hit nonetheless, becoming visible again, but Lucsly saw their wounds healing as he watched. The beams were fired by three orange-skinned humanoids with heads like terra cotta pots, dressed in dark, layered clothing. "Vorgons!" he cried.

"Any idea why they're protecting you?" Dulmur asked Vard.

"Obviously they recognize my, er, our importance to the future!"

"But this isn't their fight," Lucsly said. "All they care about is their war with the Shirna."

"Are these the same aliens that tried to steal the Tox Uthat from Captain Picard?" Worf asked.

"Same species," Dulmur said, studying the tricorder feed. "Not the same individuals."

Worf frowned. "How would you know that?"

"Long story."

Three tricorders beeped: the agents' and Elfiki's. "New anomaly behind us," the young science officer said.

They turned to see a corridor that looked little different from the one they were in, though their readings showed, as Elfiki reported, "It's about two days ago."

But this corridor wasn't empty. A pair of helmeted Shirna crouched with their backs to them, firing on someone who was sheltering behind the next corner down. As their opponent ducked out briefly to return fire, Lucsly's eyes widened in recognition. "Noi!"

At his improvident outburst, the two Shirna turned, startled. They exchanged a look, and one turned to fire on the (to him) new arrivals while the other held Noi pinned down. But Choudhury's phaser made quick work of the first one, and the second broke and ran down a side passage. ·

"I had him," Worf said.

"Not your job anymore, sir," the elegant security chief replied. Dulmur glanced back and forth between them and chuckled, discerning something Lucsly hadn't.

"Lucsly? Dulmur?" Jena Noi jogged down the corridor to meet them, then looked around. "Oh. You're uptime. Look, you need to know, Ronarek is—"

"Fallen," Korath announced. "The Vorgons felled him as he tried to slither above them. Excellent weapons they have. I must study them."

"Okay," Noi said, "now we have to get away from the Vorgons."

"What?" Naadri asked. "But they saved us!"

"They want you alive for interrogation. We can't let that happen." She met Lucsly's eyes. "Lucsly, if ever I needed you to trust me . . ."

He decided quickly. "All right. But we need some explanations."

"As much as I can," she promised. "Now come on!"

They fled down the corridor, turned a corner, then found themselves back in the same corridor where they'd started, watching themselves retreat to the end and turn a corner. Behind them, the Vorgons were closer; a blue beam struck Nart, and Worf deftly flung the stunned Ferengi over his shoulder, barely breaking stride. "You bring honor to your house," Korath told his fellow Klingon, evidently their version of a thank-you.

Worf looked back at him. "The two of you are close?"

Korath scoffed. "He owes me money."

"What's going on, Noi?" Lucsly asked as they ran. "What's causing this . . . this . . ."

"Manheim manifold," Naadri supplied. "A topologically complex knot in all three dimensions of time. Time within our local frame has become not just a line, but a volume, and our worldlines are following an erratic, recurring path through it!" She sounded like a giddy schoolgirl. She was living out her wildest theories.

"Only in here, so far," Noi added. "Though the effect could spread much farther if I don't get back to my local time frame."

As they passed a darkened lab, Lucsly glimpsed the holographically disguised Elfiki working on something within. Catching Lucsly's eye, she placed a finger to "Metta's" blue lips and pulled back into shadow. Throwing a glance at the younger, uniformed Elfiki ahead of him, Lucsly realized that (assuming a consistent worldline, which perhaps was no longer a safe bet) the older Elfiki must already know where she had been and was consciously avoiding herself, while getting ready for . . . something. Lucsly found himself wishing he could ask the older Elfiki for insight on what lay ahead, but he cursed himself for his weakness. Her actions were totally proper under regulations, and he could only admire her discipline.

"Why back there?" Dulmur was asking. "You still haven't told us what's causing this."

A door opened, and beyond it was a hellish vista of smoking, red-hot wreckage. A gust of air almost blew Noi and Dulmur through the door, but Worf caught Noi, who caught Dulmur in turn. There must have been an atmosphere leak on the other side, though thankfully not a total vacuum or they would've all been blown through instantly. The pressure was already equalizing, making Lucsly's ears pop, but substantial heat was radiating through the door. The party fell back and the door slid shut again.

"That was part of it," Noi said once she'd caught her breath. "You just saw what the Na'kuhl intended to do to this conference. I guess that's a time track where they succeeded."

"The Na'kuhl?" Dulmur asked. "Holy crap, how many of you people are here?"

"That's an interesting question," came another, familiar voice. Lucsly turned to see Commander Juel Ducane approaching from down the corridor—his usual dapper self in his blue-and-black twenty-ninth-century uniform, but more sheepish than usual. Behind him came the even more dapper figure of Rodal Eight, the Cardassian Aegis supervisor, with his Simperian civet Meneth trotting alongside . . . and behind him came *another* Juel Ducane, this one looking more ragged and clutching a wounded right arm.

At the sight of the two Ducanes, Noi rolled her eyes. "Oh, no. I should've known."

"Well, we couldn't wait around for you to get in on this," Ducane-1, the healthy one, said. The two time agents glowered at each other.

Choudhury came forward to tend to Ducane-2's wounds. "Let me help you with that. What kind of weapon was it?"

"Modulating plasma pulse," he said.

"Na'kuhl technology," Noi said. She cocked her head toward the door. "Were you trying to stop that?"

"Actually, I was on my way to save these scientists from a band of Romulan Augments sent by our friend from the twenty-eighth century. The Na'kuhl came out of nowhere to attack me, I don't know why."

"I guess that was my fault," Ducane-1 said. "I'm from a time track where I *did* confront the Augments. They ambushed me, and the TIC beamed me away just before they killed me. Apparently the Augments had been tipped off when an even earlier version of me went back to two days ago to stop the Na'kuhl from planting a bomb."

"Which he succeeded in doing with our help," Rodal said, leaning over to stroke Meneth's elongated, green-furred head. "But not until the Na'kuhl had warned their agents in the past, alerting them to lie in wait for Mister Ducane." The lean Cardassian turned to the injured Ducane-2. "You are the result of that."

Noi shook her head. "You arrogant TIC fools, thinking you can keep micromanaging a single segment of time until you get it right. You've just compounded the problem!"

"Hey, we didn't start this!" Ducane-1 shouted back. "In case you haven't noticed, it's a feeding frenzy in here. We're just one of the temporal technologies interfering with each other—including yours," he finished pointedly.

His wounded counterpart spoke up. "And this chroniton field pervading the place doesn't help any."

Naadri straightened. "I was trying to *prevent* exactly this from occurring!"

"Well, it sure worked out, didn't it?"

"Gentlebeings!" Rodal's tone was civil yet firm. "We have greater concerns right now. In this chaos, with timelines overlapping and being rewritten like mad, our respective futures are in jeopardy." Meneth made a caterwauling noise. "Meneth is right. We have to put a quantum lock around this facility immediately!"

"That's taken care of," came Ducane's voice—but it was not one of the two already present. The group turned to see a third Ducane, unwounded but stained with ash and blood.

Noi rolled her eyes. "Oh, great. Your even earlier version, I presume."

Ducane-3 started at the sound of her voice, then gazed at her earnestly. "Please, you have to come with me," he said. "She's dying."

Noi froze, reading his face. Then she ran toward him, the others following. "Where?"

"When," Ducane-3 replied. "Earlier time zone, fifty-three hours ago." He held up his tricorder. "Everyone gather close."

Lucsly hated the idea of voluntary time travel, but it was better than chancing the random, shifting fluctuations of local spacetime. Besides, it was no further back than they'd already been. A quick shimmer and they were then. Ducane-3 looked around, cursing, and checked his tricorder, leading them down the hall.

"What's a quantum lock?" Lucsly asked Rodal as they ran.

"Come, Lucsly, you should be able to deduce that. A given state of a quantum superposition wins out over its rivals as it entangles with the broader universe, its influence resonating outward."

Lucsly understood. "But so long as a system remains isolated, the superposition can last indefinitely."

"As long as the lock is in place, the rest of the galaxy, present and future, is safe from the timeline duplications and alterations occurring within."

"That's good," Dulmur said. Meneth gave a wary hiss, and the look on Rodal's face echoed his familiar demon's reaction. "Isn't it?"

"That depends on which reality has finally won out at the end of this mess, when the lock comes down and we re-entangle with the rest of the universe," Rodal said. "If we do not save the physicists, and all the rest who should not die here and now, the futures known to Noi, Ducane, and perhaps all the Accordist powers are in jeopardy."

Up ahead was a dainty, bleeding figure in the striated black of a Federation Temporal Agent. Jena Noi gasped as she recognized herself in such dire straits.

Ducane-1 smirked. "So we're not the only ones looping back on ourselves."

"Shut up, Ducane!" Noi ran to her own side. "What happened? Can you speak?"

The second Noi gasped, but nothing coherent came out. Ducane-3 knelt by her. "She saved me," he said. "When the Na'kuhl attacked. She helped me escape . . . we put up the quantum lock together, but then they found us . . . shot her . . ." He trailed off.

Choudhury knelt by the wounded Noi and scanned her. She looked up sadly at the healthy Noi, shaking her head. "There's nothing I can do."

"That's okay," the healthy Noi said. She clasped her other self's hand. "It'll be okay in a moment."

Her fingers worked against the seams of her uniform around her waist. There were no visible controls in the shimmering fabric, but after a moment, both Nois were engulfed in a transporter-like glow . . . and when it faded, there was only one Jena Noi there.

All three Ducanes gaped. "You have auto-integration?" Ducane-1 said.

Dulmur laughed. "So how does it feel to be kept in the dark by the folks uptime?" He was glared at in triplicate.

Noi was blinking, looking disoriented, but soon took a deep breath and relaxed. "Okay, I'm up to speed now. I—she—the me who almost died fought the Shirna too, but didn't intersect with the future. Instead I crossed over into a parallel track where I found Ducane here," she said, pointing to the bloodied one, Ducane-3.

"Enough!" Worf cried. "Every time someone here explains something, it only confuses the situation further! You," he said to Noi. "Can you merge Commander Ducane as well?"

She shook her head. "Until we can get him home, we're stuck with three of him."

"And we can't risk returning me home," Ducane-2 said, "until we're sure the future's safe."

"You!" came a new, multitonal voice. *Now what?* Lucsly thought. A Vorgon stood at the end of the corridor, unarmed, her mittlike hands spread wide.

"Temporal agents! We need your assistance!"

"Excuse me?" Ducane-1 asked.

"*Our* assistance?" Ducane-3 added.

"We all wish to get out of here alive. The Na'kuhl and the Shirna are working together—they have a temporal disruptor and they're willing to use it."

The uptime agents stared at each other in shock. "Show us," Noi said.

"What's a temporal disruptor do?" Dulmur asked her as they headed off after the Vorgon.

"It fragments spacetime," Noi replied. "Tears apart everything within its field of effect."

Dulmur harrumphed. "Why not just use a bomb?"

"Some things can survive bombs. But attack the underlying fabric of spacetime and even neutronium's vulnerable. Besides," she added grimly, "to the victims, it feels like it takes an age to die. It's a particularly vicious terrorist weapon, banned by every temporal convention. Even the anti-Accordists tend to avoid them."

"But the Na'kuhl are vicious enough?" Lucsly asked.

"They are," Ducane-1 said. "But they just used a conventional bomb here. And I thought we'd long since managed to eliminate the Shirna factions extreme enough to use teedees."

Noi glared at him. "I guess you missed a time track."

"Or perhaps," Rodal suggested, "these Na'kuhl are a later iteration, escalating after the failure of their bomb."

"Does it matter?" Worf demanded. "We must stop them!"

The Vorgon had rejoined her two colleagues, both male. "Will they help us?" the taller one said.

"Yes," the female replied, then turned to the group.

"Come, we will surround them. The scientists must remain here."

"The others, perhaps," Korath boomed. "But I am a warrior first!"

"That's why the others need you to protect them," Choudhury told him. "Under these circumstances, nowhere is safe."

Korath brightened at those words. "Very well. I will lie in wait for whatever comes."

"All right," Ducane-1 said, striding forward. "But this had better not be another trap."

A rift in reality opened up in front of him and he fell through it. Beyond was a dark mass of yellowish clouds, and the whiff of sulfur came through as Ducane-1 fell out of sight, his scream choking off.

The others jerked back from the rift, but it closed on its own. Elfiki stared at her tricorder, dazed, holding it like a lifeline. "That was . . . a Class-N atmosphere. There's no planet like that in this system."

Ducane-3 studied his own tricorder. "It's a subspace fracture. An after-effect of the temporal disruptor."

"You mean a before-effect," Noi said. "Retrocausal echoes of an event that hasn't happened yet."

"Like the ones that drew us here in the first place," Elfiki said.

"And tipped off everyone in the future about this 'secret' conference," Noi added.

Worf frowned. "But are they not the ones whose intervention caused the distortions?"

"They were," Rodal said. "They just didn't know it yet."

"The disruptor will interact with the other temporal

fields," Ducane-3 went on, "warping spacetime severely enough to create rifts bracketing the detonation time. Don't know why the quantum lock isn't stopping them . . . we must have shifted back to before it was activated."

"Please," the Vorgon leader said, ruffling her respiratory folds in distress. "We must stop the disruptor before the effects get any worse."

"But if we're already seeing its consequences," Choudhury asked, "does that mean we fail to stop it?"

"In these conditions," Noi told her, "we can both fail and succeed. What matters is that we succeed *last*."

The Vorgons, Rodal, and Meneth went one way while the other time agents and the Starfleet team went another. As they stealthily moved into position around the target area, Lucsly moved up to Noi and Ducane-2. "This is what it's all been about, hasn't it? All the recent attacks, everything the Cabal's Sponsor did in the twenty-one forties and fifties. It was all done to try to prevent this conference, either by targeting the participants directly or disrupting history enough to ensure it never happened."

"That's why we have to stay focused on keeping these scientists alive," Noi replied.

"But what are they going to do that's so important to the future?"

"You know we can't tell you that, Lucsly," Ducane-2 said.

"Even now?"

"Especially now. Some things have to remain unknown."

"I don't know, Juel," Noi said. "If this *is* the event we all suspect it is, maybe the secret's already blown."

"Under the circumstances, you'd better damn well hope it isn't."

Ahead of them, Worf held up a fist, signaling that they should stop. Lucsly checked his tricorder—the source of the time distortion was just ahead, as were a number of anachronistic biosigns. Worf gestured to the agents to stay behind while he advanced slowly.

But then a series of subspace fractures began to open around them. Lucsly almost fell through into a fierce thunderstorm on a raging sea, but Noi grabbed onto his arms, her surprising strength pulling him away from it. They clutched one another until it closed, and then Lucsly pulled away, clearing his throat and brushing down his suit. Noi smiled and winked at him.

The next rift opened onto the surface of an icy planetoid lit by the dim light of a distant red dwarf. Air was sucked through, but this time everyone was a safe distance away, and it soon closed. Elfiki was again studying her tricorder. "That was Wolf 1246. Seven light-years from here. Why are they always connecting to planet surfaces? Something about the gravitational potential . . . or quantum resonance of physically similar bodies?"

Just be glad they do, Lieutenant, Lucsly thought, having a strong feeling he knew what was coming next. He stepped gingerly away from Elfiki, touching Dulmur's shoulder. He sensed his fellow agent tensing, ready to move, to say something. But at Lucsly's glare, he relaxed.

As Elfiki took a step forward, another fracture opened up beside her. Startled, she jerked away and fell back, but the rift expanded and swallowed her up. Lucsly saw her tumble onto the bright, arid surface of Pyrellia's dayside on the other end. *The circle is complete,* he thought.

But not quite. Other fractures were opening up all around the party. One almost took Noi, but Ducane-2 threw her aside and was taken himself to who knew where.

"Somebody do something," Ducane-3 cried as the rifts surrounded them. "I'm running out of lives here!"

Suddenly, a new sound pervaded the chamber, a low drone that set Lucsly's teeth on edge, and a wash of warm energy followed. The rifts began to close, normality restoring itself.

"That sounds like an entrance cue if ever I heard one," said Dina Elfiki, still in civilian attire but no longer disguised as a Bolian. She carried a largish, hand-held device, just the right size to fit in the duffel bag she'd brought with her from Greenwich. It was the source of the droning hum.

"Lieutenant!" Worf said, staring in shock. Then he gathered himself. "You are out of uniform."

"I apologize, sir. It's a long story." She glanced at the DTI agents. "Four months long." Her face lit up in a smile of profound relief. "But it's over now."

XX

Third Moon of Rakon IV
Nowish

With the subspace fractures healed locally by Elfiki's field device, the next step was to take down the Na'kuhl and Shirna before they set off the temporal disruptor. But as the team carefully advanced, they saw that the battle had already been joined—not only by the Vorgons, but by *themselves*. Well, mostly. The duplicate group, battling amid a field of subspace fractures, included one Ducane and the civilian-outfitted Elfiki but not her younger counterpart. However, that group's Choudhury and Lucsly were missing, and Dulmur saw himself lying crumpled and motionless on the ground, and the duplicate Noi was struck and vaporized as he watched. One Vorgon took out a Shirna sniper, allowing a furious duplicate Worf to fire a blast that struck the temporal disruptor and caused it to blow up in the Na'kuhl's pale, batlike faces. A ripple of distortion swept out from the detonation site, and then the battle was joined again, the same group but with the other Dulmur still standing, the other Choudhury firing on the Shirna until a rift opened up and engulfed her in an outpouring of superheated gases from some Jovian's inner atmosphere, leaving little recognizable behind. Dulmur retched and turned away, and was comforted when the real Choudhury—it helped to think of her that way, though the other was no less real—took his arm and led him away after the rest of the team.

Once they had reunited with the physicists, making sure they were all safe within the stabilizing field, Noi threw a look at the surviving Ducane. "I guess you aren't out of duplicates after all."

"Hey, that wasn't the TIC's doing. I've already reached my limit. That must've been a spontaneous quantum divergence."

"Fully intercausal?" Noi shook her head. "Ohh, the spacetime breakdown is getting worse. Even without the disruptor being activated, we're still in serious danger of quantum collapse."

"We should go back," Ducane said. "Take the scientists somewhere safe, plant a stasis device here before the other combatants arrive. Trap them all in temporal limbo."

Noi stared. "Are you crazy?"

"Look, we have to accept that keeping this conference unaltered is a loss! The important thing is to keep the scientists alive!"

"Agreed, but not that way! You go back earlier and they'll just go back earlier to get ahead of you, and so on! That's how we got into this mess in the first place!"

Ducane sneered. "You civilians. You've gotten soft and timid. I can't believe my Federation degenerates into the likes of you."

"We're *careful*," she fired back. "We aren't fascists who think we can force reality and people's identities into the shape we want!"

"We get the job done!"

"You just make things worse! Why do you think they dissoved the TIC and put civilians in charge of temporal enforcement?"

"Noi, remember your protocols," Rodal cautioned.

"Ohh, that's a future I hope to avert one way or another," Ducane fired back.

"And you, Ducane!" Rodal said. "Remember, she is your chronological superior!"

"Who are you to talk about superiors?" the human commander snarled. "You can't make a move without clearing it with your shapechanging masters. Who don't even have the courage to show themselves." Meneth extended her claws and snarled. "That's right, kitty, keep up the act. It's all you're good for. Remember, the Federation isn't under your jurisdiction anymore!"

"Perhaps we were premature in making that decision!" Rodal shot back.

"HEY!"

Everyone turned to look at Dulmur, who took a deep breath or two before going on in a more normal, but still angry, tone. "Listen to yourselves. *You're* supposed to be partners in the Accords? No wonder this situation's such a mess."

"He's right," Lucsly said, coming up beside him. "We're all equally in danger here. Continuing the fighting won't do any good for anyone."

"The Vorgons had the right idea," Dulmur went on. "What we need is a cease-fire. We need to get everyone, and I mean *everyone,* sitting down together to work out a truce before we all go out in a puff of quantum smoke."

The time agents exchanged a series of sullen, chastened looks. Rodal's civet made a small mewling sound.

"Meneth's right," Noi said, surprising Dulmur. "It's the only way . . . but it can only work if we can find a neutral mediator. Someone everyone can trust to be objective."

"Someone nobody would consider a threat," Ducane added.

"Someone," Rodal finished, "who's well known for having no agenda save the integrity of time itself."

Dulmur grinned when he realized that all the time agents, himself included, were looking at Gariff Lucsly. He grinned wider when his partner took it entirely in stride, as if he'd been expecting it all along. "Fine," Lucsly said. "But if Dulmur and I are to mediate a settlement . . ."

"Why him too?" Ducane challenged.

Lucsly stared at him. "Because he's my partner." Dulmur smiled, but Lucsly gave no response to it. He didn't need to.

Ducane saw that no one else questioned Lucsly's terms, so he subsided. Lucsly went on: "If we're to negotiate a settlement, then the need-to-know clause comes into effect. We'll need to be briefed on just what it is all the factions are fighting over. Why this event is so important to the future."

Noi exchanged a look with the others. "Agreed," she said. "But only the two of you." She looked around, taking in the *Enterprise* team and the physicists. "I can't allow anyone else to know. I'm sorry, Doctors, Commander Worf, but you all understand the Temporal Prime Directive."

"Agreed," Worf said, looking unhappy but stoically accepting. "Just find a way to end this."

Noi was quickly able to replicate Elfiki's stabilizing effect using the circuitry integrated into her jumpsuit's intricate fabric, allowing her to lead the DTI agents away into a separate group. Ducane was able to do the same with his temporal tricorder and Rodal with his stylus-shaped servo device, so they and Meneth went off to make the cease-fire offer to the anti-Accord factions. Soon, Dulmur and Lucsly were alone with Jena Noi, and she began to talk.

"By now you know this is a focal point of the Temporal Cold War," she said, "though this is one of the points where it's become hotter. What you don't know is why we fight a *cold* war—why we engage each other through proxies in the past rather than attacking each other directly."

Lucsly and Dulmur traded a look. Dulmur had never thought about it, but Noi's words made the answer self-evident. "You have some kind of defense against temporal incursion," Dulmur said.

"One that hasn't been invented yet," Lucsly added. "So you're free to strike in the past, before it existed, but not in your own respective centuries."

Noi nodded. "Exactly."

"Is this the place where it gets invented?" Dulmur asked.

Lucsly shook his head, peering at Noi. "No . . . you're just guessing it might be. Best way to keep a secret from time travelers—keep it out of the history books."

"That's right," the exotic Temporal Agent said. "Sometime in the twenty-fifth century, someone invents what we call the temporal defense grid. It's a network of detector satellites tuned to register the subspace, quantum, and other signatures of every known type of temporal incursion. Upon detection, a subspace pulse or other appropriate countermeasure is focused on the point of the incursion—an advanced wave focused back in time to the moment it begins, to correct for the detection and processing lag. It collapses the temporal connection before it forms and bounces the time traveler back to the point of origin. Any place within its field of influence is protected against invasion from other times, other dimensions."

"And you don't know who invented it," Dulmur said.

She shook her head. "The temporal security behind the operation was staggering, far better than what Vard attempted here. The grid went online in every major power in the Alpha and Beta Quadrants at once—the Federation and its Khitomer Accords partners, the Typhon Pact . . . or whatever it evolves into," she added with a wink, "the First Federation, the Sheliak Corporate, the Vomnin Confederacy, the Carnelian Regnancy, some you've never heard of. It must've taken decades to develop and deploy in secret. And once it was active, they didn't even tell anyone at first. It took a while for the civilizations to figure out they were protected. So we don't even know exactly when the grid went up, except by trial and error, finding the latest point we can travel to. And even that's not definitive, because once the main network was in place, other powers copied it, and by twenty-five hundred it had spread to most of the known galaxy. The grid allows communication between times—phase-shielded to protect against timeline collapse—and you can arrange for clearance through it for consensual time travel. But any uninvited incursion to any point after the late twenty-fifth century is blocked.

"But even though we know how to control the grid, we don't know where it came from. The systems are a mix of many species' technologies, some of which are probably red herrings. The developers not only worked in secrecy

and wiped all records of their work, they planted extensive false leads in the historical record, so that whatever
evidence they couldn't destroy was lost in the noise. We
think they must have even wiped their own memories after
it was done, because nobody ever boasted or let anything
slip about it afterward." She shook her head. "We have the
power to go back to any place and time we want, but it's a
big galaxy and a lot of decades to cover. We can't find out
who built the grid if we don't know where to look."

Lucsly shook his head. "So all the anti-Accordists had
to work with was conjecture. Best guesses. Historians'
theories and reconstructions."

"Exactly. Some of the leading theories focus on the
Carnelians, a civilization as advanced as your own, more
than capable of pulling it off. But since the changes in
their history didn't unmake the defense grid, their role
must not have been the pivotal one. The Sheliak have
been under attack too, but they'd never deign to tell you,
and their own temporal agency is . . . highly efficient,
so they've escaped significant change. And the Typhon
Pact . . . well, you can try getting those stories out of
Revad if we get out of here alive.

"As for the Vomnin, they're more scavengers than
innovators. The First Federation is cautious enough
and advanced enough, but too timid and isolationist to
mastermind such a thing. So the bulk of the remaining
theories focus on the Federation and its allies. On the
temporal physicists of this generation, who made pivotal
breakthroughs in our civilization's understanding of time.
The Shirna went after President Bacco because many believe that only she would've had the boldness, the vision,
and the deviousness to mastermind something like this.

But many have focused more on the physicists, people like Vard, Korath, and Naadri. The timing is right—depending on how long it took to organize the project, they could have been its initiators, or maybe the mentors of those who were."

"But what's the point?" Lucsly challenged. "Even if they create a new timeline where the defense grid doesn't exist, they must know better than to think they can erase the timelines where it does. It's one thing to try to erase the past—you can collapse the timeline, end its existence once and for all. But even if they create an alternate past or present for themselves, the fact that you're here proves that your timeline, defense grid and all, still survives centuries beyond them. So how can they threaten the existence of that future?"

Noi shook her head. "It's so much more complicated than that, Gariff. I guess it's our own fault, constantly crossing into each other's eras and timestreams to wage our cold war, play our games. We've entangled our histories together so intimately, bound them in such a Gordian knot of multidimensional time, that there's no way we can coexist separately anymore. For all I know, my thirty-first century is part of a Manheim loop with no future. It could all reset to an earlier point and play out differently. I've been to my own future, seen possibilities where my Federation survives, but the Cold War rages there too, and it's just as entangled, just as vulnerable, as the rest.

"All I know is that eventually, hundreds or thousands of years from my time, only one history will survive after all the others involved in the war have collapsed into it. We're all fighting to make sure that that final history will be as close to our own realities as possible. Trying to turn each other's timestreams into close parallels of our own, trying to duplicate and reinforce our own histories, because a larger sheaf of closely related histories will have more collective probability and will win out in the eventual merger." She went on with growing intensity. "If we'd just left well enough alone, then maybe we could all have created our own separate, parallel streams and coexisted indefinitely. But in fighting to promote our own preferred histories at each other's expense, we've trapped ourselves in a situation where only one can survive. We all should know better, but the whole thing was already happening before we were even born, and so we had no choice but to play our part in the self-fulfilling prophecy."

Dulmur and Lucsly looked at each other, processing these revelations. Noi took the time to catch her breath. "God, I hate this war," she muttered. "You two are lucky to have been out of it until now."

Lucsly furrowed his brow, realizing *why* they'd been out of it until now. "The Borg. You said before, every future faction is from a timeline where the Borg threat has been ended."

Noi nodded. "Nobody could risk attacking the Federation prior to February 2381. We all depended on that sequence of events that would eliminate the Borg from the galaxy. So everyone, even the anti-Accordists, had to focus their attacks either now, after the Borg had been absorbed by the Caeliar, or before the UFP was founded in 2161."

"Not everyone," Lucsly said. "The Vorgons on Risa in '66. You told them they were taking an irrational risk striking when they did, interfering in the life of Jean-Luc Picard."

"Now you know why I was so angry at them."

"And the Na'kuhl stealing the Delta time perceptor in '72."

"They always were reckless," she said. "They took the perceptor in hopes it would give them an edge in finding where the defense grid was invented. Oh, the tales I could tell you about our struggles to get it back from them. That was my first death."

Dulmur tried to avoid thinking about that one. "Were they the ones who gave the Borg a time machine and sicced them on Zefram Cochrane?"

"That was the Sphere Builders," she said.

The DTI agents nodded. "You mean the transdimensional species that engaged in the large-scale reconstruction of the spacetime of the Delphic Expanse as a prelude to its colonization," Lucsly said, "and pitted the Xindi against Earth in an attempt to prevent the formation of the Federation that would otherwise defeat their invasion in the mid–twenty-sixth century?"

"Mm-hm," Noi confirmed. "Well, the Borg attack was their third try. They figured if Cochrane never invented warp drive, Jonathan Archer could never have been a threat to their plans. And they didn't care if the Borg survived or not, since Borg drones couldn't survive the altered physics of the realm the Sphere Builders were trying to create." She winced. "We let that one get past us, I'm afraid. Luckily the laws of probability arranged for Picard's *Enterprise* to be in the right place and time. And we put the Builders in their place afterward."

"And that's why the Cabal's Sponsor warned Archer about the Xindi," Dulmur said.

"Exactly. He didn't want to risk losing the Federation, not until after the Borg were gone."

"Though now that they are, he didn't mind sending his Romulan Augments to try to start a war with the Typhon Pact."

"You've got it."

"But his tactics in the past were just as reckless," Lucsly said. "Besieging the Tandarans for a decade to prevent their temporal research? Starting a Klingon civil war just to prevent Korath's birth in a later century?"

"The Sponsor can model alternative possibilities precisely in order to predict the effects of his actions," Noi said. "Our own simulations suggest that the civil war would've had little long-term effect on Klingon history—they were killing each other off so constantly and having so many political upheavals at the time that its impact would've soon been lost in the noise—but it would've led to the extermination of the houses that led the rebellion, including Korath's ancestral house."

"And the destruction of Paraagan II?" Dulmur asked. "Naadri's ancestors can't have been from there, or they would've been killed."

"They were from there," Noi said. "But once my . . . fellow Temporal Agent whom you know as Daniels became aware of the alteration to history, he went back earlier and arranged for Naadri's great-great-great-grandparents to win a contest whose prize was an off-world cruise. They weren't there when the colony was destroyed."

"Why didn't he put the original history back the way it was? Save all the Paraagan colonists?"

Noi sighed. "We did what we could. You can't win every battle, no matter how much the idiots in the TIC wanted to think you could. Trying to fix every hitch in reality is a losing proposition, especially when an enemy's matching you move for move. It leads to messes like this one."

Dulmur stepped closer, forcing Noi to look up at him. "And Agent Shelan? Was she just another 'hitch in reality' you've washed your hands of?"

Noi's bright golden eyes met his squarely, and to his surprise, there were tears in them. "You don't even remember her. I do. I knew her. I liked her. And I talked her into the mission that ended her life, and I have to live with that. So don't you get self-righteous with me, Dulmur."

"What happened?" Lucsly said. "And don't say we don't need to know."

"There's no reason to hide it anymore," Noi said. "I knew Ronarek was an agent of the Sponsor. A shapeshifting impostor who'd killed the real Doctor Ronarek so he could infiltrate Vard's conference and kill the physicists. But nobody but an Augment, one with the right genes, could get past the security on his ship. When I tried it, I was caught in a time dilation field, captured, almost killed before my people yanked me back."

"But Shelan had a Cabal ancestor," Dulmur said. "She had the right genes."

Noi nodded. "In a dormant form. But with her permission, and a few days of thirty-first-century gene therapy, I was able to activate them. I gave Shelan her full Augment powers, including the ability to shapeshift and pass as a Romulan. Her genetic signature let her get past the security on Ronarek's ship and penetrate to his temporal communications chamber."

"Why? What did you send her to do?"

"The Sponsor is smart," Noi said. "He doesn't travel

in time, doesn't even show himself openly to his Augments. So his identity remains a mystery. We know he's from roughly the middle of the twenty-eighth century, but we don't know the year, his species, his location, even what his ultimate goal is. We have suspects, but he's spread plenty of false clues through history, and nothing solid has panned out. We only know him by his Augments in various centuries and species. Giving anachronistic genetic enhancements to his proxies is a favorite tactic."

"Including Khan's Augments?" Lucsly asked. "Did he really give genetic technology to Project Chrysalis?"

"That's what the Aegis suspects, but Gary Seven could never prove it. Even under servo hypnosis, the surviving scientists insisted they'd made the breakthroughs themselves. We think the Sponsor must have given them memory blocks as an extra security precaution, since he was treading so close to Aegis operations, but we can't be certain."

"Shelan," Dulmur reminded her. "What was her mission? To backtrack the Sponsor's temporal signal? Let you lock onto his origin point?"

"That's right," Noi said. "She was the only one who could've done it. The only Accord-certified temporal operative in history with enough undiluted Cabal genes to penetrate their security. Once she understood that . . ." She blinked away tears. "God, I wish I could integrate you with your earlier selves, let you remember that woman. She was so dedicated, so driven to bring down the being who'd brought such suffering to her people. The look in her eyes when I sent her in . . . it was like she was fulfilling her purpose, her whole reason for existing. She wanted nothing more than to expose the Sponsor and help us bring him to justice once and for all."

When Noi fell silent for several moments, Lucsly spoke more gently than Dulmur had ever heard him. "What happened to her?"

"I was on comms with her the whole time—an ansible beacon, untraceable. We were monitoring her every move, ready to pull her out if things got hot. Ready to get the information the instant she sent it so our forces could move in on the Sponsor." She closed her eyes. "She reached the chamber, she ran the tricorder protocols we gave her . . . she was just starting to send us the information we needed . . . and then it all went to quantum static." She sniffled. "That must've been the exact moment when the Sponsor sent an agent back into Shelan's past to do . . . whatever they did."

"That was when the timelines merged?" Lucsly prompted.

"Yes. Shelan, her tricorder, every trace of her life, they just quantum-tunneled out of existence. Forgotten. Except by me, because I'm shielded." She ran a hand over her jumpsuit—or was it her own body she was indicating? "Phase discriminators built right in."

After a moment, Lucsly asked, "Can you bring her back?"

Noi shook her head slowly, solemnly. "If I knew who the Sponsor was, if I could get my hands on the bastard, maybe I could make him tell me what he'd done so I could fix it. But without the information Shelan was stopped from sending, it's hopeless." She took them both in with her soulful eyes. "I'm so sorry. I'm sorry for everything we put you through in our stupid, selfish battles."

After a pause, Lucsly spoke. "I saw him. Ronarek had a holocommunicator projecting an image of the Sponsor. If we could get that device . . ."

Noi had perked up when he started to speak, but now showed disappointment. "What size communicator?"

"Handheld. A miniature image."

She shook her head. "Just a relay. It wouldn't have the temporal circuitry we'd need to trace his signal. All we could do is watch him taunt us and gloat," she finished through clenched teeth.

Lucsly surprised Dulmur again. He stepped forward and placed a hand on Noi's shoulder, actually initiating physical contact without seeming uncomfortable. "You'll have other chances in your subjective future," he said. "Provided we end *this* battle so we can all go home safely."

"Right," she said, smiling up at him and placing her delicate hand atop his. "Thanks, Gariff. Don't ever change."

"I don't plan to."

She chuckled, then straightened and gathered herself. "Now let's go see how the others are doing."

Noi moved off, and Dulmur peered at his partner. "Is there something you want to tell me about you and Jena?"

Lucsly was as stony as ever as he moved off. "You don't need to know."

Dulmur thought about it. "No," he muttered to himself, "come to think of it, I probably don't *want* to know."

Vard tried to insist on being allowed to attend the talks, saying that as the parties being fought over, the physicists had a right to representation. But Lucsly and Dulmur put their feet down, and Worf and Choudhury were more than willing to keep Vard contained. As for Elfiki, she was happy to stay out of the talks. "I'm curious, of course . . . but I've had my fill of having to keep quiet about the future. From now on, no more spoilers." She was needed where she was anyway; even if all the respective leaders joined the talks, the factions were still fighting, some in alternate or anachronistic time frames which made coordination difficult. The scientists were still in danger from the combat as well as the threat to local spacetime. They would need all three *Enterprise* officers to protect them.

It took surprisingly little time to bring all of the anti-Accord factions to the table. The female Vorgon, who had been far enough away to avoid the time loop that had trapped her male partners, had consented willingly. Ojav, as she introduced herself, was distraught at the loss of the males, who apparently had been her mates. "All I want is to end this," she said. "No more fighting." As for the Shirna, most of their leaders had been caught in the time-looped explosion, effectively irretrievable, leaving command to a junior officer who said his highest priority was the safety of his troops.

Rodal had managed to bring the Na'kuhl leaders to the table, though he demurred and said that Meneth deserved the credit. The black-uniformed, bat-faced aliens were staring at the Simperian civet with a look that could be either respect or fear, but Meneth was content to curl up in the middle of the table and wash herself.

Finally, Ducane brought the Romulan Augments aboard, in the person of the impostor Ronarek himself, who was not as dead as Korath had claimed; apparently he too had been temporally duplicated. "I'm willing to listen," the gray-haired Augment spy said, offering no name beyond his false one. "But I and my troops will do as my Sponsor commands."

Dulmur leaned forward. "Then by all means, bring the Sponsor in on this. We're all looking forward to meeting him face-to-face."

Ronarek—for that name would have to do—sneered at him. "You are not worthy to look upon our benefactor's visage. Nor to waste his time with diplomatic sophistry."

"If he's your benefactor, then he'll want you to get out of this alive, right?" Dulmur asked. "And if that's going to happen, then everyone at this table has to have the power to make decisions and make them stick. I think he'll want to be in on this."

The Augment sneered. "Very well."

He placed his holocommunicator on the table and activated it. The vague humanoid figure appeared and looked around as Meneth roused herself and padded over to sniff at it. *"Greetings,"* he said in a reverberating baritone, needing no explanation from Ronarek; clearly he'd been anticipating this or monitoring it all along, and the impostor's objections had been mere bluster. *"What a rare opportunity to confer with so many of my rivals in one place."*

"Welcome to these negotiations," Lucsly said in a carefully neutral voice. "How shall we address you?"

The featureless head turned to regard him. *"'Sir' will do."*

Dulmur wanted to scream at him, to curse him for damning Shelan to nonexistence, stealing his memories so he couldn't even mourn her. He felt violated just looking at the blurry figure. But he sensed Lucsly's gaze upon him, glanced aside to see his partner sitting there as cool and businesslike as ever. It reminded Dulmur of what they were all about: getting the job done, regardless of personal drama or philosophical angst. He was a stiff in a suit, a nobody with an unglamorous role to play. That was why they were the only ones who could negotiate a settlement: because, when you stripped away the Accordists' sweet talk, ultimately none of these time travelers took the DTI seriously enough to perceive them as a threat. Normally that rankled, but right now it was an advantage. So he schooled himself to calm, following Lucsly's lead.

But he promised himself that, someday, there would be a reckoning with the Sponsor.

"I know you all have different reasons for fighting in this cold war," Lucsly said once everyone was seated. "But that's not what we're here to deal with. We don't have to solve any of the big issues. All we need to do is agree to walk away from this fight. Put an end to the battles, deactivate our various temporal technologies so the local spacetime can return to normal." He looked around at the group. "If we don't, then that spacetime collapses and we all cease to exist on a quantum level. So this should be an easy decision to make. All we should have to talk about is how to coordinate our cease-fire and withdrawal. Agreed?"

"I agree," said Ojav. She turned to the Shirna leader, Drash. "There is no point in continuing this conflict."

The goblin-featured Drash nodded gravely. "I agree. We have both lost too much."

"*If I may interpose,*" said the miniature Sponsor. "*The Vorgons are known for their deceitful tactics. How can you be certain they won't snatch the physicists away the moment you turn your backs?*"

Drash's pointed ears twitched. "He has a point."

"We won't allow it," Jena Noi said. "You have our word."

"And why," the Sponsor asked, *"should the Shirna trust the word of the FTA?"*

"He's right," Drash said. "You have persisted in denying us the means to defend ourselves against the Vorgons' attacks on our past!"

"Our attacks on *your* past?" Ojav protested.

"Quite right," put in the Na'kuhl leader, Ghretch, his pale batlike visage glaring at the Accordists. "The enforcement of the Temporal Accords is an exercise in oppression—the temporal defense grid a tool of tyranny. All races deserve the freedom to employ temporal technology as they see fit."

"Indeed," intoned the Sponsor. *"Why should we settle for a resolution that preserves the status quo, defense grid and all? That only serves the Accordists."*

"Because we don't know that's what we'll get," Rodal pointed out. "At this point, it is impossible to tell whether your attempts to disrupt this conference have already undermined the development of the grid or perhaps even accelerated its development. None of us knows if the future will be better or worse if we step away. It's an equal gamble for all of us."

It went on like that for a while. As simple as it should have been just to pack up their toys and walk away, the various factions had too much history, too much baggage which the Sponsor seemed happy to stir up. Lucsly and Dulmur had to probe for common ground, bases for consensus. As the Sponsor systematically scuttled their efforts, they were forced to find ways to balance the factions against each other, to ensure that both sides would have mechanisms in place to enforce a cease-fire. If anything, the Sponsor's disruptive efforts worked in the Accordists' favor, since the expanded checks and balances the agents negotiated to ensure the various factions would agree to leave the events of this day alone in their respective futures would probably help deter other temporal attacks on the present-day Federation and its allies.

Still, as the Accordists, the Vorgons, the Shirna, and even the Na'kuhl came more and more into agreement on a protocol that would allow them to stand down their forces and walk away safely, the Romulan Augments remained the only holdout, due to the Sponsor's relentless refusal to cooperate. Since none of the other parties knew who, where, or when he was, none of them could exert any leverage over him the way they could over one another.

"You must end this soon," Worf insisted over the DTI agents' communicators fifty-one minutes into the negotiations. *"The Augment forces are continuing to advance! No one else is attacking the scientists anymore, but all are under attack from the Augments."*

"What is wrong with you?" Dulmur demanded, leaning over the blurry hologram on the table. "You know what's at stake here. It's not just our lives and your troops' lives. If the spacetime in here collapses, the quantum lock could go with it, and then whatever version of the timeline is left will spread out into the universe. You don't know what reality that's gonna be. You could be dooming your own timeline to collapse."

"I have the utmost confidence in Agent Noi's quantum lock," the Sponsor said mockingly. *"I'm quite sure it will last longer than the integrity of the spacetime within."*

"That's what you're counting on, isn't it?" Lucsly realized. "You *want* the local spacetime to collapse. That way, the physicists die. The future goes on without them, without their work. You get what you want."

"You're crazy!" Commander Ducane cried. "You don't know if destroying this conference will prevent the defense grid from being built!"

"Maybe not. But I do know that in all our respective histories, Korath invents the chrono-deflector in the first decade of the twenty-four hundreds. The first practical, replicable time-travel mechanism invented among the Khitomer Allies." Dulmur was surprised. That gun-happy blowhard was the one who'd make the breakthrough? You never could tell. *"Without him, and without the theoretical advances made by Naadri, Nart, and several of Professor Vard's protégés, the development of temporal technology among the future Accordist powers will be set back by decades, perhaps centuries."* Just as well Vard wasn't here; he would be crushed to learn he wasn't the target after all. *"Enough time for other, less . . . inhibited civilizations to achieve their own temporal breakthroughs."*

Jena Noi's eyes were wide. "So with or without the defense grid, your side gains the edge over the Accordists. Maybe the Temporal Accords never happen at all."

"Now, you understand," the Sponsor said. *"Either way, I win."*

Dulmur turned to Ronarek. "Do you hear that? This just became a suicide mission for you guys. Your vaunted 'benefactor' is tossing you on the trash heap. Are you gonna stand for that?"

Ronarek met his gaze proudly. "We owe everything we are to the benefactor. Our lives are his to do with as he wishes."

"Your heirs shall be rewarded for your loyalty, my

servant," the Sponsor said. *"History will remember your sacrifice."*

Ronarek stood. "I think these negotiations are over."

"You're insane!" Noi shouted at the hologram. "Forcing that kind of collapse *inside* a quantum lock is like setting a fire in a pressure chamber! You'll intensify the destruction. The damage to subspace will tear apart this system, cause chaos across the whole sector! Billions will die!"

The blurred figure shrugged. *"The Borg killed over sixty billion not far from there, just over a year earlier. In the grand sweep of history, a few billion more deaths, a slightly larger volume of devastation, will make little difference."* Though the hologram's face was featureless, Dulmur was certain he was smiling. *"My Augments will be remembered. But the lot of you, I fear, will be no more than a footnote."*

XXI

Axis of Time Power Station
c. 1,409 Millennia After Present

Garcia had never regretted the absence of transporters so much. Though it was only about a 1,500-kilometer flight from the Vomnin outpost to the uptime terminus, a journey of mere minutes, it felt like an eternity. Lirahn had a head start on them, in more ways than one, and Garcia had no idea if they would reach her before she activated the Siri device and allowed the supernova's energies to pour freely into the Axis and beyond.

The Starfleet teams from both *Asimov* and *Capitoline* had come with them to provide muscle, and it proved necessary. Lirahn's enthralled forces met them in the power station's hangar as soon as their shuttles landed, and a phaser battle was joined. It was Garcia's first real firefight, and she could barely keep track of what was happening in all the noise and blinding light and confusion. But she stayed close to Ranjea, and soon she realized that the Starfleet team had given them a path to the exit. "Come on!" shouted a lavender-haired Catullan guard whose name Garcia didn't know. She followed him and Ranjea into the corridors, their tricorders leading them toward the power core. Before they got there, two more guards pinned them down with particle fire. The Catullan stunned one of them, but the other fired a beam that grazed his hip, felling him. Ranjea took that guard down a second later.

Ranjea ran toward the security crewman, but the Catullan waved him off. "I'll manage! Stop her before we all burn!"

So it was up to the two of them to confront Lirahn and save the Axis. Garcia tried not to think about it. This wasn't supposed to be a DTI job! They were investigators, not fighters! But the job, she reminded herself, was whatever it needed to be to protect the timeline.

Luckily, they weren't immolated in supernova fire before they reached Lirahn. But she already had the Siri device, a jury-rigged array of crystals, opti-cable, and what looked like bioneural circuitry packs, hooked into the power core, a massive construct like a vault door with a glowing hemisphere in the center. Ranjea pulled out his phaser, Garcia following. "Lirahn!" the Deltan called. "Step away from the device."

She turned to them and smiled. "Come now. You don't want me to do that, do you? Not when I'm so close. You wouldn't want me to be disappointed."

Garcia felt her aim wavering. She didn't want to shoot, didn't want to stop Lirahn. She strove to remember that was an illusion the Selakar was placing in her mind.

Ranjea managed to hold his focus better. "Lirahn, listen. That device isn't calibrated to handle the energies you're tapping into. It could tear open the interfaces. The supernova would be unleashed to destroy all life within the Axis and for parsecs around all its interfaces."

"Oh, dear boy, I appreciate your concern, but do you really think I'm not aware of that? I've calculated how long the process will take. My ship should be fast enough to make it back to my era in time and warp away from the danger zone."

"And what about everyone else?" Garcia demanded. "They'll die!"

Lirahn shrugged. "If they're too slow, that's their own fault."

"And what if they try to stop you?" Ranjea asked. "Their ships are closing in. We were here first, but they won't be far behind. They could slow you down until it's too late."

"This is my chance to regain real power," Lirahn told him. "It's worth the risk for that."

Ranjea took a step forward. "For power?" he asked in a gentle voice. "Or to avoid living with the loss of everything you knew, everything you had? Believe me, Lirahn, I understand that pain. Teresa and I, we both understand that sense of loss. We understand the desire to fill it with something."

"He's right," Garcia said, following his lead. "It can be overwhelming. You'd do anything to satisfy that craving."

He threw her a look: *Let me do the talking.* She nodded, understanding instantly. "But don't you understand, Lirahn?" Ranjea asked. "If your life is ruled by desire, by the pursuit of what you do not have, then it will only lead to frustration . . . for, no matter how much you have, you will always want more." As he spoke, moving subtly closer and drawing Lirahn's attention away from her, Garcia began to creep around behind the Selakar. "Desire is a trap, Lirahn. The path to fulfillment is to let go of desire and craving, to learn to find the joy in what life gives you."

Lirahn's smile widened. "But that's exactly what I'm doing, my dear. I know I can't have it all. My time in the

Axis has shown me that. I can never have an empire that lasts forever. I can never have my name heralded and wor- -shipped down through the ages. I know that, no matter what I do, eventually it will all be forgotten, eroded away over the span of cosmic time. So I've learned to accept the limits on what I can have. I don't care if I rewrite your precious history or not. I don't care if my rule reshapes the galaxy or even outlasts my own lifetime." She spread her hands insouciantly. "All I want is to enjoy the rewards of ultimate power over a few paltry billions for the few hundred years I have left. Can't you allow me that small indulgence?"

"And what about all the billions you'll kill along the way?"

"What about them? From where we stand—quite literally," she added with a wry smile, gesturing around them—"they've all been dead for ages anyway."

Garcia felt a surge of anger at the Selakar's cal-lousness. Perhaps what made her angriest was that she understood it. How was it any different from her own detachment at unearthing relics of civilizations lost in ancient cataclysms, or thrilling at the excavation of a well-preserved corpse? Could she really blame someone from Temarel's time or Shiiem's for failing to shed a tear over her own death, or the deaths of sixty-three billion people in the Borg invasion?

She realized that Lirahn was looking over her shoul-der now, directly at Garcia, and wearing a less pleasant smile than before. "You poor dear," she purred. "You're so right." *What does any of it matter in the cosmic scale, dear? We're all just relics and fossils waiting to happen. Soon enough, nobody will remember our names, nobody will know or care what we did. None of it will ever make a difference. So what's the point? Why even try?*

She lost track of where Lirahn's thoughts ended and hers began. *I'm already a relic. I should've died sixteen years ago, a million years ago. I should've died on the* Verity. *I should've let them kill me. Those sixty-three billion people . . . all dead because I believed it made a difference how a few petty decades unfolded. I should've taken my punishment for that.*

No! she thought, fighting it. *We need to learn from pain. Not erase its lessons.*

But the other voice within her was implacable. *But what if you learn that some pain is too much to endure?* Her phaser hand lifted, turned inward, toward her own head.

"No! Teresa!" Ranjea rushed to her, grabbed her arm before she could bring the nozzle to bear, but she resisted, and he didn't dare risk greater force. "Fight it, Teresa. Don't let her take you."

"Ooh," Lirahn said, leering at their embrace. "That's unexpected. The little primitive is more than just a plaything to you. You cherish her." She chuckled. "For all your platitudes, you crave her. And the way her body reacts to you . . . oh, this will be *much* more entertaining."

Lirahn concentrated on Ranjea, and a moment later, his scent became stronger, overpowering, filling Garcia with instant arousal and need. Dropping the phaser, she clutched his body closer, felt his heat, knew he was as aroused as she was. "No . . ." he gasped, trying but failing to keep his hands from roving over her body. "You mustn't . . . you don't know what this will do to her . . ."

"To *her*? Dear Ranjea, what about the things all this deprivation has been doing to you? You shouldn't have to be alone anymore. And neither should she. Think of how you've been hurting her all this time, cheating her out of what she needed most." Lirahn's hand stroked his smooth, nude scalp. "But it's all right now. I give you permission. Share what you both deserve."

His lips engulfed hers, and it was like no kiss they'd ever shared. This time it was a Deltan kiss, the opening of a connection that went far beyond the physical. She felt his arousal, his pleasure, and he felt hers, and it fed back through them both, amplifying every touch, every motion. Having fabric between their bodies became intolerable, agonizing to two halves striving to become a whole. Their hands moved swiftly, surely, to divest one another of the lifeless encumbrance. They moved as one, feeling each other's every response, every need. In moments the clothing was gone, and all that remained was flesh exploring flesh. Her sense of self had migrated beyond her head, inhabiting her lips, her hands, her breasts, her loins, every part of herself. She could feel it starting to move beyond even that, spreading to encompass both their bodies at once. While she retained some lingering sense of separateness, her touch eagerly explored every inch of the body that would soon join her in oneness, delighting in its smoothness, its firmness, fascinated by the intimate discovery of the ways in which Deltan anatomy was just different enough from human to be compelling while still oh so compatible.

And at the same time, she felt *him*, his feelings, his hopes, his connection to the things he valued. Such a fear of isolation, making her loneliness seem trivial in comparison. And such a deep attachment to her, a depth of affection he had longed to express. Now it could finally be his. They would be one forevermore, and he would never be alone again. And she would never be herself again. She would be lost forever in the joy of their unity, all her guilt and doubt forgotten. Lirahn was right; it was a better way to go.

Lirahn! she thought, and she became more aware of herself for a moment. There was something important they needed to do, something Lirahn was doing . . . but then he touched her *just* where she needed to be touched the most, *just* the way that would give her the most ecstasy, and she was lost in sensation again.

Until she heard Lirahn's laughter. "Oh, this *is* much better! Very athletic, both of you. I didn't think the girl had it in her. Ohh, if I had time, I'd join you. Well, maybe I'll take you with me."

If I had time . . .

Time . . .

Garcia opened her eyes. Or at least, her free-floating consciousness, centered somewhere between her fourth and sixth chakras, became aware that her eyes had opened. She instructed her head to turn toward Lirahn. The chocolate-brown Selakar woman with her green-gold scalp and dark green jumpsuit was working on the strange blue-and-silver-and-black device connected below the large white hemisphere, which was getting brighter, oh so blindingly bright, intensifying every color in the room. They were all so pretty to look at. So dazzling and colorful and satisfying.

Except for those two piles of gray cloth lying crumpled near her head. Those were so dull. So ordinary. There was no joy in them, only . . .

Duty.

Dedication.

Responsibility.

Time.

"DTI," she gasped. "Ranjea . . . we're DTI. We have . . . a job to do."

Later. She couldn't tell whether he spoke it or thought it. *We're so close now. Almost united.*

She wanted that so badly. But the light was still getting brighter. And she'd gotten used to being isolated—with a lot of help from her best friend. "We *are* united. We're partners. We . . ." She searched her feelings, her memories of their months together. So much love, so much understanding . . . but not through flesh and passion. Through kind mentoring and guidance . . . through sharing the load, no matter how terrifying or tedious the responsibility . . . through the obligation they both felt to make amends to time itself for their failures. A burden that was lightened because they bore it together.

"Riroa," she told him. "Think of Riroa. You loved her. She lives on in you." And in turn, she thought of the billions whose loss she had to live with, whose sacrifice she struggled to give meaning through her work.

The passion they shared was still strong, their connection all but total. Yet now responsibility and duty echoed through that connection as well as love. Each of their returning resolves reinforced the other's just as their passion had before. They didn't break the bond so much as redirect it.

What followed was still physical, still intensely stimulating. They used their bodies as they had been trained, lunging at Lirahn. Taken by surprise, no doubt unused to defending herself physically, the statuesque Selakar nonetheless had the size and reach to hold her own at first, knocking them back and drawing a weapon. The light behind her still brightened, the room growing hotter by the second. "Idiots! Let me go or we're all doomed!"

But the partners still felt one another's bodies even though they were separated, and they still moved as one. When she feinted, he moved in to disarm. When he overbalanced the foe, she struck low to bring her down. When she pinned Lirahn's legs, he struck with precision at her neck and chest, generating just enough overpressure within her circulatory system to render her unconscious.

Still acting as one, Ranjea dashed to the Siri device while Garcia retrieved her phaser and stunned Lirahn to keep her neutralized. Vikei had given them instructions, so it wasn't long before the light began to dim again.

It was still quite hot, though, and Garcia realized she was sweating profusely. Then she realized that she was becoming aware of inhabiting her body again. Her parietal lobe, with its associated sense of the self as a distinct entity, was kicking back in. She no longer felt Ranjea's body as a part of her. Though when she looked at him, her heart still raced and she couldn't look away.

"Ah," Ranjea said, a bit awkwardly. "Her influence seems to be wearing off." She could see him bringing his arousal under control, feel the diminution of his overpowering scent. Still, she was grinning like an idiot at the sight of him, the memory of him.

Holding her gaze, he strode over to his suit and tossed hers over. "Aw, do you have to get dressed?" she asked. "It's awfully hot in here."

"I think it's a good idea," he replied, glancing toward the entryway. Garcia looked over to see that the remaining conscious members of the Starfleet team had finally arrived. All of them male.

"A-huh!" she got out, snatching her suit and hastening to dress. Ranjea cleared his throat and drew the men's attention.

"It's secure now," he told them. "The crisis is passed."

"Good job," said the lieutenant in charge as his men moved to take Lirahn into custody.

"My partner deserves the credit," Ranjea said, smiling at her with great warmth. "Her strength and sense of duty saved the entire Axis, and far more."

She blushed under his praise . . . and looked over his now-clothed body with deep regret. *I never thought I'd feel so disappointed to save a universe.*

XXII

Third Moon of Rakon IV
Eleventh Hour

Conditions were growing worse inside the quantum-locked lunar facility. The quantum stabilizer fields that protected the time agents, physicists, and *Enterprise* officers were weakening, and it was a tossup whether they would break down before reality itself did. Outside the fields, the battles were intensifying as the Romulan Augments did everything they could to worsen the fighting. By now, all the factions had duplicates from different time frames or quantum branches overlapping with each other, so even if some could be persuaded to stand down, there were still others from subjectively earlier times, unaware of the agreements that had been made. It was easy for the Augments to stir them up into attacking one another, using their various temporal devices to try to jump back or forward and outmaneuver each other, to lock each other in temporal stasis, or the like. All of it was making the spacetime metric within the facility ever more unstable, ever closer to collapse.

Worse, a band of Starfleet TIC shock troops from Ducane's timeship, enhanced with cybernetic implants of some sort, had apparently been sent to back Ducane up at some point, in some other time branch. They were engaged in battle with virtually everyone, trying to trap them all in temporal stasis bubbles or just shoot them. When the time agents and *Enterprise* team tried to approach them and warn them of the problem, they came under fire and had to retreat to cover. "Why are they firing at us?" Worf demanded. "Can they not tell we are Starfleet?"

"You're not their Starfleet," Ducane said. "Our stabilizer field gives off a temporal signature. They're reacting to us as a threat."

"Typical," Noi snarled. "Shoot first and try to stitch history together afterwards."

"Can you two play nice for once?" Dulmur demanded. "Ducane, talk to them!"

"I'm not going back out there! Didn't you see? They were with one of me, one of the duplicates that branched off here. As long as they have one of me, the others are an acceptable loss."

Dulmur shook his head, disturbed to see what Starfleet would degenerate into by the twenty-ninth century. He took heart that reforms had evidently set in by Jena Noi's time—or in her timeline. He still wasn't clear on whether she and Ducane came from the same future. Given what Noi had said earlier about the Gordian knot of the Cold War, maybe they weren't clear on that either.

"Let Meneth and me try," Rodal suggested.

"Good idea," Noi said, then threw Ducane a look. "I assume the TIC recognizes Aegis neutrality."

Ducane nodded. "In theory. If their combat conditioning is still in a low enough mode."

The Cardassian Aegis agent exchanged an uneasy look with his familiar, but Meneth made a low noise and headed back toward the TIC forces. Rodal nodded to the other agents before heading off after her. When Dulmur's eyes shifted back, he saw that the civet was no longer there, replaced by a stunning woman with golden skin and dark green hair. She winked at him before vanishing around the corner, Rodal close behind.

Dulmur turned to Noi and Ducane. "Okay, the shapechanging pets. Are they really the aliens running the Aegis? Do you know who they are, where they're from?"

The two uptime agents traded an uneasy look. "Sorry, Dulmur," Noi said. "There are rules we have to follow if we want to keep the Aegis's cooperation."

Soon, Rodal and Meneth (in her civet form again) returned in some haste. "No success. There was a phase shift between us. I don't think they could see or hear us clearly." He grimaced. "The deterioration of spacetime is worsening, and even Meneth can't see a way out of it. I think our best hope at this point is to rely on our successors to find a way to reverse these events, or at least to obtain justice for our deaths."

Worf gave a fatalistic smirk. "I would say it was a good day to die, if I had any idea what day it was."

"What hope is there of getting justice?" Noi demanded. "We still have no idea who the Sponsor is. Damn it! If only Shelan had had a few more seconds!"

Rodal threw her a look. "You mean that the timeline convergence occurred just before she sent you the Sponsor's coordinates?"

"At the exact moment she started to send them."

Meneth mewed. "Yes," Rodal agreed. "A startling coincidence. The kind that crops up with surprising frequency in cases of temporal alteration. Doctor Naadri would say that her negative-probability 'anti-time' force was acting to cancel the excess probabilities by creating a circumstance with the potential to restore the original history."

"Maybe," Noi said. "Or maybe the Sponsor specifically timed it that way to thumb his nose at us."

"Either way, we may have an opportunity," Ducane said. "If Shelan sent her ansible transmission *during* the timeline collapse, there should have been enough quantum uncertainty around that moment that some of the information may have survived."

Noi shook her head. "That was the first thing we tried. There's some information there, but not enough to let us extrapolate the rest."

"Are you sure?"

"Damn it, we're two centuries more advanced than you! It was nothing but noise! This is the best we got!" She worked a hidden control on her sleeve. The burst of static seemed to come from the air around them: a high-pitched squeal that quickly faded out to white noise, albeit with tantalizing hints of a pattern underneath.

"Wait," Lucsly said. "Play that again."

Noi repeated the playback, and this time Dulmur caught what Lucsly had. It sounded familiar, almost . . . like a dying scream.

"When exactly was that sent?"

"In your terms . . . Stardate 59085.1678."

"Two weeks ago Monday," Lucsly interpreted.

"Don't tell me," Dulmur said. "Oh-two-oh-four UTC."

"And twelve seconds."

Noi looked between them. "What is it?"

"I've listened to that same sound approximately a thousand times," Lucsly said, pulling out his tricorder. "The final transmission on Shelan's frequency in our shielded records was transmitted at that exact moment." He played the file. It was the same shriek of static, only less detailed.

"Good girl," Dulmur whispered, almost imagining he could remember training her. At more normal volume, he said, "She must've sent a backup transmission to us, just in case something happened to her. She wanted to make sure a record was preserved."

Lucsly handed his tricorder to Noi. "Can you do anything with the signal?"

The Temporal Agent traded a look with her counterparts from TIC and Aegis. "It's static, but it's different static. Sent through subspace instead of ansible. It would enlarge our sample of the quantum information."

"It's worth a try," Ducane agreed.

As the three of them went to work with their various equipment, Worf turned to Elfiki. "What are they doing? Can they recover information from an erased timeline?"

The science officer shrugged and turned to the DTI duo. Lucsly replied to the Klingon. "The perception that our timestream has a single, unified history is an illusion resulting from the fact that we can't measure all of it. One set of information dominates and is agreed on by all observers, and that's what we call reality. But the rest of the information is there too. Every infinitesimal quantum state that lost the Darwinian competition, every fully realized parallel history that eventually merged into our own, it all remains, a palimpsest in the vacuum fluctuations. But the only way you could recover that information is to measure all the data in the entire universe at once."

"Normally, yes," Ducane replied, looking up from his future version of a temporal tricorder. "But we don't have to reconstruct the entire timeline—just one specific signal from it. We know exactly where and when to look for the lost data . . . we just need to know what to look for."

"And if we can reconstruct that timeline's quantum signature from the fragments of Shelan's signal," Noi added, "it'll be like a cryptographic key, a way to tease the right bits of information out of the quantum noise."

"If the reconstruction is good enough," Rodal said. "And if we can get that information to our respective agencies so they can scan the area from enough different perspectives to reconstruct the information more fully."

"Rrrrrah," Meneth said.

Noi and Ducane exchanged a look, as if reacting to the civet's contribution to the discussion. "Well?" Ducane asked. "Do we risk it?"

"Risk what?" said Dulmur.

"We can communicate with our own times through phase shielding, like the Augments can with the Sponsor. But to do what has to be done, our agencies may have to break that shielding, entangle with the larger universe. It would bind our home timeframes to the outcome of these events, one way or the other. It could change things in unpredictable ways."

"Could," Lucsly echoed. "If we don't stop this, we know the future *will* be changed. For the worse."

"He's right," Noi said. "We have to."

Ducane's tricorder beeped. He read it, looking both gratified and worried. "We have a legible signature," he said.

Noi studied a readout Dulmur could see projected

onto her cornea. "And enough of a signal template. That should do it."

"Then shall we?" Rodal asked.

Noi nodded readily, Ducane more reluctantly. But before they began, Noi turned to the DTI agents. "Lucsly, Dulmur, if this works . . . we all have the DTI to thank."

"We have Shelan to thank," Dulmur said.

"Mm-hm," Lucsly said.

"If it's at all possible, I'll see that you can thank her personally." Trading one more look with Ducane and Rodal, she hit a wrist control and sent the signal. The other two agents did the same.

"Now what?" Worf said after a silent moment.

"We wait," Rodal said.

"For how long?"

Ducane's tricorder beeped. He read it and smiled. "Not long. Time travel, remember? Come on, they're this way."

From the perspective of Juel Ducane's predecessors in the Temporal Integrity Commission of the 2770s, the manhunt for the Sponsor had taken years. The reconstruction of Shelan's signal, sent to them via temporal communication from their uptime counterparts and the timeless Aegis, had given them enough information to identify his time and place of origin, but he'd fled before his TIC contemporaries could arrive there. Subsequent investigation had revealed his identity and affiliations, and the hunt had been on. Over time, his other facilities had been raided and shut down, depriving him of places to retreat to. Eventually he had fled into the past, before the defense grid's erection, but he had been pursued. He had been apprehended after an attempt to intervene in the Earth-Romulan War, on the Romulans' side, had been thwarted with some local assistance. He must have grown truly desperate to have been willing to risk the Federation's existence like that.

But finally he stood before them, in the very conference room where his hologram had mocked them before, hours ago for them, years for him. Now his haughtiness was subdued; he stood with his head bowed, covered in a worn, hooded cloak of twenty-second-century Romulan design. He had been brought in by none other than Agent Daniels himself, who was visibly delighted to have his longtime nemesis in his clutches at last. "His name is Jamran Harnoth," the nondescript human told the assembled agents; the Starfleet crew were back with the scientists, defending them from the ongoing struggle. "He's a founding member of the Order of Omega."

"Of course," Ducane said. "I should've known. They were on our suspect list, but there was never anything actionable."

"Who are they?" Lucsly asked.

Jena Noi answered. "A latter-day eugenics movement, multispecies Augments."

"Of course," Dulmur said, remembering Cyral Nine's words. "Know the artist by his tools."

"But it wasn't enough for them to enhance their genomes; they thought their superiority gave them the right to augment societies as well. To take them over, by politics or by force, and subject them to ruthless social engineering in hopes of 'improving' them. The death and suffering they caused were monumental."

"Survival of the fittest, my dear," Harnoth murmured

from under his hood. "Surmounting challenges is what makes us strong."

"And apparently," Daniels added, "Harnoth here decided it wasn't enough to engineer the future. He wanted to reshape the past as well."

"And why not?" Harnoth raised his head, giving Dulmur a tantalizing glimpse of the face beneath. "History is a chaotic mess, filled with pointless suffering. Why shouldn't the superior mind strive to refine and improve it?"

"Improve it?" Daniels snarled. "One of your experiments in the twenty-fifth century led to a cataclysm that tore the Federation in half and left much of the quadrant impassable to warp travel! It sparked a new Romulan war that lasted for decades! If we hadn't been able to isolate that timeline . . ."

Harnoth shrugged. "What can I say? Using Omega particles seemed poetically appropriate. Matters got out of my control, but the long-term results could have been impressive nonetheless. As I said, improvement comes from surmounting obstacles."

"Is that why you gave genetic augmentation to groups in the past and stirred them up to conflict?" Lucsly asked. "To get a head start on their 'improvement'?"

"Of course!" Harnoth cried, throwing back his hood. "See the results for yourself!"

The Sponsor of the Suliban Cabal and the Romulan Augments was a lanky, lean-faced man with blue-gray eyes, craggy features, and dark hair swept back from a high, pronounced forehead. He had the pointed ears and heavy brow of a Romulan, yet his skin had a subtle mottling that was distinctly Suliban. And between his upswept eyebrows was the characteristic chevron-shaped ridge of a Tandaran.

Harnoth laughed at his reaction. "Why so surprised, Agent? Do you really think my Cabal could have battled the Tandarans for ten years without ever knowing they were aware of my intervention from the future? Did you really believe Tandaran temporal security could be good enough to keep that secret from posterity when Vard couldn't even succeed at keeping this conference a secret? The fools. I *wanted* the Tandarans to know of the threat from the future. I needed it to inspire them to an aggressive pursuit of temporal research —for that research would eventually produce the means for my mastery of time. Just as the augmented genes I gave the Suliban, the Romulans, and others planted the seeds from which the Order of Omega would one day grow." He laughed again. "Do you see? All I have done was necessary to secure my own creation! Merely by existing, I have already won! I am my own beginning and ending. I am the Alpha and Omega!"

Dulmur was just about to lunge forward and wipe that grin off his motley face. But to his surprise, Lucsly beat him to it, grabbing Harnoth by the collar and slamming him back against the table. "And what about Agent Shelan?" Lucsly demanded. "How was her eradication necessary to bring you about?"

"It wasn't," Harnoth said. "But defiance must be punished. She tried to use the gifts *I* gave her to strike against me. That could not be tolerated."

"So you had to erase all memory that she'd ever existed?"

"Her existence was a mistake. I corrected it."

Lucsly loomed over Harnoth a moment longer, staring at him. Then he relaxed and stepped back, and Dulmur saw what his partner saw. "You're sweating," Dulmur said.

"Bluster all you want, but you know you're right here in the soup along with the rest of us. You can't just sit back and watch from the shadows anymore. We die, you die. How's that for leverage?"

"Call off your troops," Agent Daniels told his prisoner. "Work with the other factions to stabilize local spacetime. It's the only way your *superior* mind will live on."

Harnoth seethed, but he knew he was beaten. He glared at Daniels. "I'm just glad I got to kill you at least once."

"Didn't take," Daniels said. "Now give the order."

Grudgingly, Harnoth accepted the comlink Daniels handed him. "This is your benefactor," he said to his Romulan troops beyond. "Stand down immediately. I repeat, stand down immediately. We will coordinate with the enemy forces for an orderly withdrawal." He couldn't resist adding, "Any defiance of my orders will be swiftly punished."

"Great management style you've got there, pal," Dulmur said. "Very evolved."

Harnoth bristled. "To think that a being as superior as myself was brought down by primitives like you! You aren't even proper time travelers!"

"Time travel is overrated," said Lucsly. "And more trouble than it's worth."

"It wasn't just the DTI who brought you down," Dulmur said. "It was DTI Agent Shelan." He stepped closer, getting right up in Harnoth's face. "Remember her name."

XXIII

1 Zhēngyuè (Chinese New Year), Year of the
Water Tiger, Cycle 84, Xia Calendar
A Sunday

Vomnin Space Station Bezorek
03:26 UTC
Restoring the Axis of Time to normal had been an easy
matter once Lirahn's influence was broken—in more ways
than one. Vikei had used the Siri device to restore Axis
timespace to its normal configuration, and Lirahn and her
Selakar followers had been promptly exiled from it. The
Siri had been granted their freedom to go wherever they
wished, and while Vikei and many others had opted to
stay within the Axis, perhaps someday to migrate to other
times, more than half the Siri, even while separated from
Lirahn's direct mental influence, had chosen to remain
in her service. "They have been servants for so long they
can imagine nothing else, even now," Vikei had said sadly.
"Still, it would not be a truly free choice if that option
were denied them."

There had been some questions of jurisdiction, but the
Axis Council had decided to remand the Selakar into the
custody (and era) of the Zcham, more than a million and a
third years after their own time. Not only were the Zcham
the only Axis participants advanced and powerful enough
to hold their own against the Selakar, but their time was
farther forward than anyone else's currently in the Axis, so

anything Lirahn might potentially do there would have no effect on any earlier era of history, even if she did escape Zcham control. "Do you really think there's a chance she might get away from you?" Garcia had asked uneasily.

"We will do our best," Shiiem had replied, "but I can make no absolute guarantees." He had stepped closer and given her a conspiratorial smile. "After all," he had finished, giving her a great deal to think about, "we are only human."

Just before the agents left, the Axis Council, now with Vikei sworn in to fill its recent vacancy, had voted to reaffirm their cautious policies for intertemporal trade, and had imposed trade sanctions on the Vomnin Confederacy for the role their reckless enthusiasm for relics had played in bringing about the near-disaster. Once they returned to normal space and time (two subjective days but two objective weeks after they'd left, since the Siri's lockdown device had apparently induced a significant time dilation), Ranjea and the chastened Sikran had spent the next two days negotiating with the Vomnin Bureau for Historical Resource Development, persuading them to pursue a more responsible policy for temporal resource management—and to establish closer ties with the DTI and other temporal agencies in the quadrant so that a more consistent policy for timeline protection could be developed.

With all of that going on, it was a while before Garcia and Ranjea were finally able to sit down in private quarters and talk about what had happened. "Teresa," Ranjea said, clasping her hands, "I have so much to thank you for. You've forced me to reconsider some . . . perhaps rather arrogant assumptions I'd made about Deltans and humans. When it came down to it, you had more mastery of your emotions than I did."

She laughed it off, pulling her hands free and stepping away. "You were under Lirahn's power."

"And you were under mine. It's amazing that you could resist at that point." He paused. "I've been thinking about why that must be. Maybe it's your DTI training to hold on to your sense of identity no matter how much our work calls it into question. Or maybe it's what you said when we were together . . . that we're already bound as partners, so that the bond of lovemaking is just an extension of that."

"Does it matter?" she asked, moving over to look out the window at the shimmering Axis portal. "It's over. I'd rather just move on."

"But that's what I'm saying, Teresa. I'm not sure it has to be." He stepped closer. "It would mean a great deal to me to be able to show my affection for you in the way that is natural and routine for my people. And after what happened . . . I think maybe it would not be as impossible as we've assumed. Not for us." His hands clasped her shoulders. "Teresa . . . maybe if we proceeded carefully . . . if we taught each other . . ."

"Stop," she said, stepping away and turning to face him. "God, Ranjea, there's still so much of me that wants nothing more." She shuddered. "But what Lirahn did to me . . . what she did to *you* . . . it was an assault. After I . . . came down and could process it with a clear head . . . I felt so violated. On your behalf as much as mine, that she turned such a beautiful, giving part of you into a weapon."

He shook his head. "That was her own folly. She hurt me, yes, and she hurt you through me. That places a burden on me too, but the burden is part of her, not me. It doesn't change what my sexuality means to me."

"Well, maybe you can separate the joy of it from the invasion. But I can't." She gazed at him, aware of what this meant to him, how courageous and kind his offer had been. "I'm so sorry, Ranjea. You're a dear friend, and a great partner. But I think it'll be a while before I'm comfortable letting you touch me again."

He gazed at her for a long time, and she let him. Finally he nodded. "All right. All I want is your happiness."

She smiled. "It's okay, boss. We'll be okay."

He blinked quite a few times, then sighed. "Well, it's all right. There's a Deltan medical officer aboard the *Capitoline*. He and I should be able to satisfy each other's physical needs, at least."

"Good, fine. See you tomorrow?"

He smiled, nodded, and let himself out. She stared at the closed door for a time . . . then blinked. "'*He* and I'?" *Maybe touching's off-limits, but I wonder* . . .

"No," she said aloud, shaking her head. "Uh-uh, Teresa. Some things really are best left to the imagination."

Third Moon of Rakon IV
5 Zhēngyuè, Year of the Water Tiger, Cycle 84
(A Thursday)
06:11 UTC
Sometimes Dulmur was surprised by the robustness of the fabric of spacetime. Even after all that had happened in and around Vard's facility over the past several . . . whatever, once the various artificial influences on its spacetime metric were eased off with proper care, it soon settled back down into a normal configuration—or nearly so. "It'll take a while to settle down fully," Jena Noi told the DTI agents. "We'll install some stabilizers to keep

any anomalies from resurfacing. Like a bandage while the spacetime heals."

When things had settled down, there were still a number of temporal or quantum duplicates of several of the facility's occupants, but that was a good thing, in a way. A lot of the people here had died in one or more iterations, but there were enough temporal and quantum spares that the final survival rate was effectively one hundred percent. In fact, that was part of the cease-fire arrangement; the various factions worked together to ensure that at least one copy of everyone was recovered before their respective timestreams were quantum-converged back into the whole. As for the remaining duplicates, Noi and the TIC were already in the process of reintegrating them via transporter. Where the duplicate physicists were concerned, according to Noi, the reintegration would be calibrated so that only the earliest set of memories was preserved, leaving the physicists in the dark about most of what had occurred here. "We don't want them to get any head starts on their future discoveries," she said.

As for the trio from the *Enterprise,* they were allowed to keep their memories, at least those of the versions that had been inside Elfiki's stabilizer field, as thanks for their role in saving the day (and quite a few others), though of course they were sworn to strict secrecy. As for Elfiki herself, she was eager to return to her ship and her crewmates, which from her perspective she hadn't seen in four months. "I keep thinking they'll have given my quarters to someone else," she told Dulmur, "until I remember I only left them a few hours ago. This is going to be strange— being so out of synch with my friends on board."

"Do not worry," Worf told her. "I have some

experience with making such adjustments. Let me know if you need any assistance."

"Thank you, Commander."

"And hey," Dulmur said, "you know Clare is just a subspace call away if you need to talk."

"I know," she said. "You know you all have my gratitude for helping me through this. But I think I'd really rather put this part of my life behind me and start moving forward again."

"We must return to the *Enterprise* soon," Worf told them. "If matters are resolved here, we will be needed elsewhere in the sector. The anomalies are dying down, at roughly the same pace with which they arose before the event, but there will be consequences to deal with."

"That's our department, Mister Worf," Lucsly reminded him. Dulmur nudged him with an elbow. "But . . . we appreciate your assistance." Worf nodded solemnly. Lucsly turned to Elfiki. "And thank you in particular, Lieutenant, for finding a way to make a difference *without* compromising the Temporal Prime Directive." His eyes drifted to take in Commander Ducane, who stood nearby conferring with his cyber-enhanced troops. "I wish all of Starfleet would follow your example."

The *Enterprise* team made their final farewells and departed. Dulmur saw that the uptime forces were beginning to withdraw as well. The Vorgons and Shirna had already left, and Rodal and Meneth had escorted the Na'kuhl off the premises and out of the century. But the TIC troops were still keeping a wary eye on the Romulan Augments, and Noi and Daniels were flanking Jamran Harnoth, keeping a close eye on the elusive Omegan. Trading a look, Lucsly and Dulmur made their way over to the three of them.

"This is unjust, you know," Harnoth was saying as they approached. "The other factions are allowed to withdraw without penalty, but I am to be taken into custody? Why should my Augments continue to obey the cease-fire, then?"

"You negotiated in bad faith and tried to destroy everyone else here," Daniels reminded him. "We all agreed that exempts you and your Augments from the agreement. The Augments will have their enhancements deactivated, and you'll be tried for your crimes."

Harnoth scoffed. "You'll never track down all my Augments. The struggle will continue."

Daniels leaned closer, speaking with deceptive softness. "There is still the matter of jurisdiction, you know. The thirty-first century has first claim on you, since we led the fight against you—and, well, since I'm one of the people you had killed. But you know, the TIC of 2774 makes a compelling case that as your contemporaries, they should have jurisdiction. Now, they're not as bad yet as they are in Mister Ducane's time, but still . . . the things they do to temporal criminals on your level . . ."

Harnoth was trying and failing to conceal his alarm. "Very well," he grated. "I will cooperate in neutralizing my Augments of this century in exchange for being tried in the thirty-first."

Jena Noi stepped around to face him. "You're still up on some pretty damning charges," she said. "It could help ameliorate your sentence if you tell us what you did to erase Shelan from history—and how we can bring her back."

Harnoth chuckled. "There was no one thing," he said. "Do you know how difficult it is to remove one person from history and ensure that nothing else is changed? It took years of planning and dozens of subtle manipulations to accomplish. It was a masterpiece of temporal engineering, the most satisfying work I've ever done." His smile turned cruel. "And all the more satisfying because it was revenge on an ungrateful creation. If that revenge backfired and led to my arrest, then all the more necessity for the revenge itself to stand. It's only fair."

Seething, Noi reached her dainty, strong hands toward his throat. But Lucsly placed a hand on her shoulder. "Let it go," he told her. "Shelan knew the risks of this job. Further meddling with time on her behalf is the last thing she'd want. It would be too great a compromise of the principles she sacrificed her existence to uphold."

Noi lowered her arms and stared at him for a long moment. "I'll never really understand the DTI," she said. "But I guess . . . whether I agree with it or not . . . if it's what she would've wanted, then I owe it to her to respect that."

Lucsly nodded. "Yes, you do."

The uptime agent smiled sadly. "But don't worry. She will be remembered. She may be forgotten in her own time, but future history will know what she did . . . who she was. I'll make sure of that."

"Thank you."

After a respectful shared silence, Dulmur cleared his throat. "It just occurred to me to ask . . . did we win? Are your futures still intact? Does the temporal defense grid still get invented? Was this even the critical point at all?"

Noi traded a knowing smile with Daniels before the senior time agent escorted Harnoth away. "Sorry, Dulmur. You don't need to know any more. All you need to know is that your time is safe now."

"Really?" Lucsly asked. "After all the random attacks in recent months . . . . . ."

"All the ones that affected your territory were attempts to prevent this, and they failed. And the next plausible nexus point for the development of the defense grid is decades from now." She looked at each man in turn, her gaze wistful. "I wouldn't exactly say it's safe for you to retire, but from here on in, the temporal incidents shouldn't be as concentrated as they've been in the past year. This front of the Temporal Cold War has closed."

Dulmur furrowed his brow. "And what about on your end? Now that Harnoth's out of the picture, is the war finally over?"

She grew sadder. "A time war is never truly over. There are always other factions. That's what happens when you fight across time. You inevitably overlap with other people's time wars, and totally unrelated factions end up clashing, like Harnoth and the Sphere Builders, or allying, like us and the Aegis. It all becomes too big a mess to keep track of. And that's not even counting the alternate realities." She sighed. "But if you can stop the cold war from becoming hot, if you can minimize its impact on the natural flow of probability, then that's a win."

She noticed Daniels gesturing at her. "I have to go. I'm six hundred and sixty-eight years early for an appointment." Lucsly glared in annoyance at the time-related humor, and Noi chuckled at his reaction. She pursed her lips. "Ahh, what the hell. Time is finite."

She pulled Lucsly's head down and smothered him with a deep, passionate kiss that went on for a good forty-seven seconds. When she broke away, she was panting, though Lucsly was as cool as ever. Jena seemed satisfied by what she saw in his eyes, though. "See you around the calendar, Gariff." She strolled away with a spring in her step and waved idly over her shoulder. "Bye, Dulmur!"

Dulmur stared at her, then at his partner, then back at her—except, of course, she was no longer there. So he went back to glaring at Lucsly. "Now, that's just totally unfair. Why didn't I get a kiss? What have you got that I don't?"

Was that the tiniest smile on Lucsly's face? "Perfect timing."

XXIV

DTI Headquarters, Greenwich
14:08 UTC

Some information was too sensitive to transmit over subspace . . . and some news was too painful not to deliver in person. So it wasn't until Garcia and Ranjea returned to headquarters, filled with prideful news of their success at the Axis of Time and their strengthening of ties with the Vomnin Confederacy, that they were told what had happened to Agent Shelan.

Andos nodded gravely at the shock and sorrow on their faces. "I suspected this. In a way, I hoped for it. The two of you were outside our time continuum at the moment the histories converged. As a result, you were shielded from the change. Out of all of us, only you still remember Shelan."

At first, Garcia wished she didn't. She envied the others their oblivion, their freedom from the devastation she felt now. But she reminded herself: *Pain needs to be remembered. Learned from. Not erased.* She looked at Ranjea, thought about how he must be dealing with his grief. Letting himself experience it as openly and deeply as any other passion . . . making it part of himself and growing from it. That was what she had always believed was right. What she did this job to uphold.

But it had rarely felt so hard.

Clare Raymond came over and embraced her. "I'll help you through this," she said. Garcia realized that, in a way, she was a temporal displacee all over again now. She was grateful Clare would still be here for her.

She met the others' eyes, seeing the envy in them, the longing to know the Shelan she and Ranjea had known. "I wish I remembered her better," she said. "I barely had time to get to know her. She was a great help during training, but since then, we've been so busy . . ."

Ranjea caught her gaze, keeping a respectful distance as he had since their conversation twelve days before. "I trained her, mentored her, worked with her for three years. But to me, it also feels I barely had a chance. Yet what I do remember is so vivid, so vibrant. Shelan had such passion for the work." The other agents drew in around him, eager to relearn what they had forgotten. "Her desire to defend the timeline arose from a great injustice that was done to her people. And yet she was not vindictive. Her greatest desire was to protect, not avenge. She sought to give comfort where she could, both to her fellow agents and to the civilians whose lives she touched. And I believe she found true joy in the work." His eyes glistened with tears. "The Deltans believe that when we die, we live on as pure love pervading other beings. We may not remember Shelan, but her quantum essence will never be completely gone from the continuum. Her love helped to keep our reality intact, and so it shall always be a part of our lives."

Garcia was crying now too, as were a number of others. She found herself moving toward Ranjea and placing an arm around him. His arm went around her shoulder in turn, and she felt no distress, no arousal, only warmth and safety.

"Tell us more," Felbog asked them. "What was it like to train her?"

"Ahh, well," Ranjea said, "there was this one time I remember fondly. It was back when they flew that replica of the *Enterprise* XCV-330—you know, the prototype warp vessel that used ring-shaped engines like Vulcan craft of the era?—on the quarter-millennial anniversary of its final flight." Felbog nodded. "Well, Shelan was so buried in her studies of the past and future that she was barely living in the present, barely paying any attention to everyday life. So Dulmur decided to teach her a bit of a lesson. We sent her to the site of an alleged temporal anomaly and let her stumble upon the ringship. She was so panicked that a critical piece of Federation history was in jeopardy and it was up to her, a mere trainee, to get the ship back home safely. She tried so hard to follow the protocols, to keep contact to a minimum, but the ringship crew spacewalked over in person, leaving her no choice but to let them come aboard. She was petrified that she might say or do something that would collapse two and a half centuries of history!

"When the 'crew' took off their helmets and she saw it was Dulmur and me, she turned so many colors that I thought her Cabal camouflage powers had activated! She almost threw us back out the lock without our helmets! But once it sank in what we were trying to do, she laughed longer and louder than any of us, and gleefully told all her classmates about it later without sparing herself a single iota of embarrassment." He took a breath and went on more softly. "After that, she never forgot that what we're working to protect, above all, is normal, everyday life. And she never let herself miss out on it again. She made the most of the time she had."

Garcia snuggled closer against her partner, grateful that she could remember Shelan, that she could grieve for her. She and Ranjea would have to remember for all of them.

"Look at that," Dulmur said to his partner as they stood on the outskirts of the group listening to Ranjea's stories.

"What?" Lucsly said.

Dulmur pointed to Teresa Garcia. "Five and a half months ago, she couldn't be in the same room with Ranjea without her warp core going into overload. Now it's like they've been best friends forever. I've never seen a human that comfortable that close to a Delta." He frowned, peering closer. "Hey, you don't think they actually . . . no, that's impossible, it would never . . . could it?"

Lucsly glowered at him. "What matters is that they've meshed well as partners. That's good. We've lost two agents in the past three hundred fifty-three days. It's fortunate we've gained a reliable new one." He turned his gaze back to the two younger agents. "A good partner is hard to find."

Dulmur looked back at him. "Mm-hm."

He pondered the group of his fellow agents for a while, then sighed. "Too bad we can't tell them the whole story of what we did while they were out of the universe."

"You know why we can't."

"I know." They hadn't even told Andos about the temporal defense grid. It was imperative that no one in the twenty-fourth century find out about it, that no record be made, and not just for the usual reasons of temporal security. Andos knew they were keeping something from her—even Lucsly wasn't stony-faced enough to pull one over on a Rhaandarite—but the director understood the need-to-know regulations better than they did.

"We shouldn't even talk to each other about it," Lucsly went on.

"I know."

"We should try to forget we ever heard of it."

"I know, I know." After peering at him a bit longer, Lucsly nodded and let it go.

Dulmur sighed. "Coffee?" he asked after a moment.

"Mm-hm."

As Dulmur went to the replicator, Lucsly returned to his desk and resumed work on his reports. Dulmur shook his head. He understood the need for temporal security as well as anyone, but still, the detective in him yearned for answers. He'd gotten a tantalizing glimpse of the future and he couldn't help wanting to know more, to see how the story turned out. Even after sixteen years and eight months together, he couldn't fully understand how his partner could be so content with his plodding, day-to-day routine when there were so many adventures out there.

But no, he reminded himself—Lucsly was right. Adventure was what happened when people overreached and got themselves and others into trouble. Lucsly's drab, mundane way of life may not have been the sort of thing that changed the world or shaped the future. But it was just the sort of attitude the DTI needed to keep the timeline stable and untroubled. And, Dulmur reminded himself, it was just what he needed to keep him grounded when faced with the craziness of time.

"Don't ever change, Lucsly," he muttered as he pulled his partner's black coffee from the replicator and took it over to his desk.

UPTIME

EPILOGUE

Undisclosed Location
Undisclosed Date

Gariff Lucsly looked around him at the small but eclectic group assembled in the nondescript meeting room: Revad of the Typhon Pact's Chronological Defense Corps (now merged with the Temporal Assessment Group); B'etath of the *poH HubwoQ*, the Klingon Time Defense Authority recently organized by the High Council; Vennor Sikran of the Vomnin BHRD; Mogon, a bovine-featured Gororm representing the Carnelian Regnancy's Temporal Oversight Administration; and, encased within an environmental field, a Sheliak of unpronounceable name who represented the Corporate's temporal security agency. It had taken less time than Lucsly had expected to bring this group together despite the policy differences of their various governments and the flaring of assorted tensions among some of them. But the events of 2382 had reaffirmed the importance of interstellar cooperation on temporal matters. The trickiest part had been arranging the logistics of the meeting in a way that would attract no attention and leave no record.

He felt the absence of Dulmur by his side, but reminded himself of the necessity of it. Some weights simply had to be carried alone. Besides, the responsibilities of an assistant director were demanding enough without burdening him with this.

"All right, Lucsly," Revad said after a moment. "We're all here, as you arranged. You don't know how hard it was for me to pull this off. So are you going to tell us why we're here?"

Lucsly met the Romulan's gaze, then took in the rest of the group. "We're here," he said, "because we're unimportant."

"What?" B'etath cried, rising from her seat. "I did not come here to be insulted!"

"You haven't been," Lucsly said. "Importance is overrated. History always concentrates on the big names. The presidents and emperors who make the laws. The starship captains who make new contacts and discoveries. The generals who win the wars. The physicists who make new breakthroughs.

"And that means that historians tend to overlook the little guys. The bureaucrats. The middle managers. The chair-bound suits doing the drudge work—the real work without which all the emperors and captains and generals would be completely lost."

He looked around at the others, and he knew he had their attention. None of them were glamorous or famous. Their work was quiet, confidential, meticulous, uncelebrated. They worked in offices to minimize the damage from others' adventures.

"All right," Sikran said, "so none of us will ever be immortalized in holoprograms. What's your point?"

"What if you wanted to create something entirely in secret?" Lucsly asked him. "Something massive. Something expansive. But something whose origins would be lost to history, so that no one could ever come back and prevent its creation. Could a president pull that off? Or a starship captain? Or a famous physicist with his own series of popular hololectures? No. They'd draw too much attention. They'd be the first people the historians would look at.

"If you wanted to make it work," he went on, "the entire project, from the initial conception to the final execution, would have to be the province of the little guys. The nondescript suits who could work invisibly behind the scenes." He leaned forward. "The people who handle the paperwork—and know how to lose it."

The other temporal investigators traded looks. They recognized that this was going somewhere. "I imagine you'll tell us what this is all about in time," Revad said.

"Once I'm confident you understand what's at stake."

Mogon tilted her long-faced head uncertainly. "What you're proposing . . . to operate in complete secrecy would introduce many delays. The work would have to be done piecemeal, in small enough increments that no one would notice our absence or our diversion of resources."

"That's right," Lucsly said. "This is the work of decades. Maybe generations. It would require profound focus and unwavering commitment. But our ancestors have achieved such projects in the past. Cathedrals and monuments that took the ancients centuries to build, knowing they wouldn't see the result in their lifetimes. Environmental restoration projects, sacrifices made in the present for the sake of future generations.

"It won't be easy. But it can be done, by the right kind of people." Lucsly looked his fellow temporal security agents in the eyes or optical receptors, one by one.

"People who take a long enough view of time."

ACKNOWLEDGMENTS
AND FURTHER READING

Agents Lucsly and Dulmur, DTI, were introduced in the *Star Trek: Deep Space Nine* episode "Trials and Tribble-ations," which teleplay was written by Ronald D. Moore & René Echevarria, from a story by Ira Steven Behr & Hans Beimler & Robert Hewitt Wolfe. Their scenes total only three minutes and forty-five seconds of screen time, with Dulmur speaking 170 words, Lucsly a mere 99. Yet the performances of actors Jack Blessing (Dulmur) and James W. Jansen (Lucsly) left an indelible impression, creating an enduring fan interest in the two DTI agents, as well as giving me essentially everything I needed to get a handle on who these men were.

A number of earlier authors have portrayed Lucsly, Dulmur (usually with the variant spelling "Dulmer"), and the DTI in assorted works of short fiction. I'm particularly indebted to William Leisner's "Gods, Fate, and Fractals" in *Star Trek: Strange New Worlds II*, which inspired several elements of this book (including the phase-shielded DTI files and the Joe Friday–esque portrayal of Lucsly) and with which this novel is largely consistent. *Star Trek: The Next Generation: Section 31—Rogue* by Andy Mangels and Michael A. Martin established Lucsly and Dulmur's interview of Picard after the events of *Star Trek: First Contact*, as seen in Chapter XIV. As for the other DTI stories out there, my interpretation differs from theirs in a number of respects, but I have borrowed inspiration from several. Dayton Ward's "Almost, But Not Quite," also in *Strange New Worlds II*, established Dulmur as a divorcé and provided the seed for the family-man side of his character, as well as informing the timing and circumstances of the DTI's formation. Kevin Dilmore's "The Road to Edos" in *Star Trek: New Frontier: No Limits* introduced novice agent Stewart Peart and the TDD. And Last Unicorn Games' *All Our Yesterdays: The Time Travel Sourcebook* in their *Star Trek: The Expanded Universe* series provided some useful ideas about the DTI's organization and equipment and the layout of its headquarters (though not its location, for which I'm indebted to Google Maps, Wikipedia, and the websites for the University of Greenwich and the Royal Observatory, plus a UK real-estate site that helped me home in on the exact buildings where HQ should be).

Effectively every *Star Trek* episode and film pertaining to time travel is at least obliquely alluded to herein, but the most heavily featured ones include the *Star Trek: The Next Generation* installments "We'll Always Have Paris" (written by Deborah Dean Davis & Hannah Louise Shearer); "Time Squared" (written by Maurice Hurley; story by Kurt Michael Bensmiller); "Captain's Holiday" (written by Ira Steven Behr); "Cause and Effect" (written by Brannon Braga); and *Star Trek: First Contact* (story by Rick Berman & Ronald D. Moore & Brannon Braga; screenplay by Ronald D. Moore & Brannon Braga); plus the *Star Trek: Voyager* series finale "Endgame" (teleplay by Kenneth Biller & Robert Doherty; story by Rick Berman & Brannon Braga & Kenneth Biller). The Temporal Cold War was established in multiple episodes of *Star*

Trek: Enterprise, including "Broken Bow," "Shockwave," and "The Expanse" (each written by Rick Berman & Brannon Braga); "Cold Front" (written by Stephen Beck & Tim Finch); "Detained" (teleplay by Phyllis Strong & Mike Sussman; story by Rick Berman & Brannon Braga); "Future Tense" (written by Phyllis Strong and Mike Sussman); and "Storm Front" (written by Manny Coto).

Paul Manheim was played by Rod Loomis in TNG: "We'll Always Have Paris"; Clare Raymond (Gracie Harrison) is from "The Neutral Zone" (teleplay by Maurice Hurley; story by Deborah McIntyre & Mona Clee); Morgan Bateson (Kelsey Grammer) is from "Cause and Effect." His bridge crew depicted herein is based on the unknown extras who appeared behind him in that episode. Korath (Vaughn Armstrong) appeared in the alternate future of "Endgame" but was created by René Echevarria & Kenneth Biller for the *Klingon Encounter* ride of the Las Vegas *Star Trek: The Experience* attraction. Then-Lieutenant Ducane (Jay Karnes) and the Temporal Integrity Commission appeared in VGR: "Relativity" (teleplay by Bryan Fuller & Nick Sagan & Michael Taylor; story by Nick Sagan). *Enterprise* gave us Agent Daniels (Matt Winston) and the mysterious "Future Guy" (James Horan). Dr. T'Pan (Joan Stuart Morris) is from TNG: "Suspicions" (written by Joe Menosky & Naren Shankar). Aleek-Om was a bit character in the animated *Star Trek* episode "Yesteryear" (written by D. C. Fontana), though his portrayal here is based largely on Alan Dean Foster's adaptation of that episode in *Star Trek Log One.*

The Borg invasion occurred in the *Star Trek: Destiny* trilogy by David Mack. Dina Elfiki and Jasminder Choudhury were created for *Destiny,* although they debuted in

my TNG novel *Greater Than the Sum*. Heather Petersen
is from DS9: *Invasion: Time's Enemy* by L. A. Graf (which
also introduced Ursula K. LeGuin's ansible concept to the
Trek universe). President Bacco was introduced in TNG:
A Time for War, A Time for Peace and *Articles of the Federation* by Keith R. A. DeCandido. The term "Feynman
curve" comes from the DS9 trilogy *Millennium* by Judith
and Garfield Reeves-Stevens, whose detailed and well-
informed discussions of temporal physics are reasonably
compatible with the model I present here. Discussions
with David A. McIntee helped me keep this novel reasonably consistent with his recent TNG novel *Indistinguish-
able from Magic*; David contributed the concept of the
rarity and difficulty of successful slingshot maneuvers.
My portrayal of Deltan culture is based on behind-the-
scenes story notes reprinted in *The Making of Star Trek:
The Motion Picture* by Susan Sackett and Gene Roddenberry, while the Deltans' conflict with the Carreon was
established in TNG: *Gateways: Doors into Chaos* by Robert
Greenberger. The Clan Ru incident is from *Star Trek: First
Frontier* by Diane Carey and Dr. James I. Kirkland. Turtledove Anomalies are from *Star Trek: Crossroad* by Barbara
Hambly and are presumably a nod to alternate-history
novelist Harry Turtledove. The Null and the Sentry AIs
are from *Star Trek: Titan—Synthesis* by James Swallow.
Lant's temporal manipulation of the Ferengi stock market
is from *Star Trek: Corps of Engineers:* "Buying Time" by
Robert Greenberger.

The name "Aegis" for the secret organization employ-
ing Gary Seven, from the original series' "Assignment:
Earth" (teleplay by Gene Roddenberry and Art Wallace;
story by Art Wallace), and the concept of its participation

in timeline defense were introduced by Howard Weinstein in "The Peacekeeper" in issues 49–50 (June-July 1993) of DC Comics' second monthly *Star Trek* (TOS) comic book, and elaborated on by Greg Cox in *Star Trek: Assignment: Eternity* and the duology *The Eugenics Wars: The Rise and Fall of Khan Noonien Singh*. I've also alluded to elements of John Byrne's recent *Assignment: Earth* miniseries from IDW Comics, although it conflicts in some respects with Cox's version (perhaps representing an alternate timeline).

Inspiration came from classic works of time-travel fiction including Isaac Asimov's *The End of Eternity*, Gregory Benford's *Timescape*, and Stephen Baxter's *The Time Ships* and *Manifold: Time*. Poul Anderson's *The Time Patrol* series provided the idea of alterations to history canceling out over the long term except at critical nexus points. *The Light of Other Days* by Arthur C. Clarke and Stephen Baxter inspired the Deltan time perceptor. Greg Egan's novella "Singleton," available online at http://www.gregegan.net/MISC/SINGLETON/Singleton.html, helped give me general insight into quantum physics and planted the seed for the quantum lock concept herein. Certain ideas pertaining to the ultimate strategy of a time war were inspired by concepts developed by David Mack for his novel *The 4400: Promises Broken*.

Living up to my usual preference for scientific credibility was a particular challenge when dealing with *Star Trek*'s time-travel adventures. To my surprise, though, I was able to find real justifications for most of *Trek*'s temporal weirdness. The root of my physical model in this book (as well as the model followed in the 2009 *Star Trek* feature film) is Hugh Everett's relative state formulation of quantum mechanics, better known as the Many-Worlds Interpretation. "The Everett FAQ" at http://www .hedweb.com/manworld.htm is a thorough, accessible overview of the MWI. Another good, only slightly technical primer is "The Interpretation of Quantum Mechanics: Many Worlds or Many Words?" by Max Tegmark (available online at http://www.arxiv.org/abs/quant-ph/9709032/). These documents provided the critical revelation that parallel histories, once diverged, are not absolutely forbidden from recombining. This was the key to reconciling a plausible MWI-based temporal theory with *Star Trek*'s portrayal of timelines being erased or destroyed by time travel. Physicist David Deutsch's work in quantum information theory influenced my model of quantum entanglement across timelines and the destruction of incompatible information being the key to such "erasure." The "Quantum Decoherence" page at http://www.ipod.org .uk/reality/reality_decoherence.asp also helped me figure out the physics of timeline mergers.

The theory that time has more than one dimension is the work of Itzhak Bars, discussed on Bars's site at http://physics1.usc.edu/~bars/research.html#2T and in Chapter 7 of *Extra Dimensions in Space and Time* by Terning, Bars, and Nekoogar (Springer, 2009), available on Google Books. (This is not to be confused with Stephen Hawking's "imaginary time" dimension, which is merely a mathematical convenience.) Bars's work leads to the conclusion that a third dimension of time would result in negative probabilities, a concept considered physically meaningless. Doctor Naadri's interpretation of negative probability is my own fictionalized twist on the idea, grafted with the concept of "anti-time" from TNG:

"All Good Things . . ." (written by Ronald D. Moore and Brannon Braga). Meanwhile, the role of non-linear quantum mechanics in allowing interaction between timelines (including Naadri's "Everett-Wheeler radio") and other violations of conventional causality is discussed in Baxter's *The Time Ships* and more formally in John Cramer's essay "Quantum Telephones to Other Universes, to Times Past" at http://www.npl.washington.edu/AV/altvw48.html.

Quantum Darwinism is a theory developed by Wojciech H. Zurek et al. to explain how the singular classical world arises from the multivalued quantum world. It gained preliminary experimental support in 2010, and may be the solution to the generations-old mystery embodied in the famous Schrödinger's Cat thought experiment. Zurek's 2005 paper at http://arxiv.org/abs/quant-ph/0505031 is the basis for Lucsly's discussion of quantum palimpsests in Chapter XXII.

For help with the various calendars referenced in the chapter and scene headings, I'm indebted to the Calendar Converter page at http://www.fourmilab.ch/documents/calendar/, as well as Tarek's Universal Converter at http://bennyhills.fortunecity.com/elfman/454/calindex.html, the Darian Date Converter at http://pweb.jps.net/~tgangale//mars/converter/calendar_clock.htm, and the Erisian Date Converter at http://jubal.westnet.com/hyperdiscordia/dateconvert.html. Thanks to Michael A. Martin for providing insight on the Vulcan, Klingon, Romulan, and Andorian dating systems he employed in novels such as *Star Trek: Enterprise—The Romulan War: Beneath the Raptor's Wing* and *Star Trek: Excelsior—Forged in Fire*. The Stardate Calculator page at www.hillschmidt.de/gbr/sternenzeit.htm was also a great help.

I want to give particular thanks to Jaime Costas and John Van Citters for seeing this project as something worth pursuing when even I wasn't convinced it could work.

Most of all, I want to thank my sister Kathleen, her fiancé Larry, and my father's friends Jerry Galvin and Tim Fischer (yes, this time I got his name right in the acknowledgments), as well as the caring staff of the Hospice of Cincinnati, for handling the medical, legal, financial, and other matters surrounding the end of my father's life that I was unable to handle by myself, thus enabling me to complete this very complicated project on deadline (nearly) and with the assurance that my father and his affairs were in the best of care. And thanks to Shirley, Clarence, and Cynthia for keeping me company when I needed it most.

ABOUT THE AUTHOR

CHRISTOPHER L. BENNETT's tenure as a distinct entity within the space-time continuum commenced at 4:13 PM Eastern Daylight Time on a Monday in the Year of the Earth Monkey, Cycle 77, Chinese traditional calendar. Eight-point-nine-eight Venusian years later, he discovered *Star Trek* and fell in love with space, science, and science fiction. After earning bachelor's degrees in physics (on 14 Asmá', 150 BE, Bahá'í calendar) and history (on Misra 23, 1718 AM, Coptic calendar), he went on to author such critically acclaimed novels as *Star Trek: Ex Machina* (January 2005), *Star Trek: Titan— Orion's Hounds* (January 2006), *Star Trek: The Next Generation—The Buried Age* (July 2007), and *Star Trek: Titan—Over a Torrent Sea* (March 2009). He visited alternate timelines in *Places of Exile* in *Myriad Universes: Infinity's Prism* (July 2008) and "Empathy" in *Mirror Universe: Shards and Shadows* (January 2009). Shorter works include *Star Trek: SCE* #29: *Aftermath* (July 2003) and "The Darkness Drops Again" in *Star Trek: Mere Anarchy* (February 2007), as well as short stories in the anniversary anthologies *Constellations* (original series' fortieth), *The Sky's the Limit* (TNG's twentieth), *Prophecy and Change* (DS9's tenth), and *Distant Shores* (VGR's tenth). Beyond *Star Trek*, he has penned the novels *X-Men: Watchers on the Walls* (May 2006) and *Spider-Man: Drowned in Thunder* (January 2008) and had several original short stories published in 2010. More information and annotations can be found at http://home.fuse.net/ChristopherLBennett/, and the author's blog can be found at http://christopherlbennett .wordpress.com/.